THE QUEST FOR FREEDOM

THE QUEST FOR FREEDOM

THE CONQUEST TRILOGY
BOOK ONE

MATTHEW DEVITT

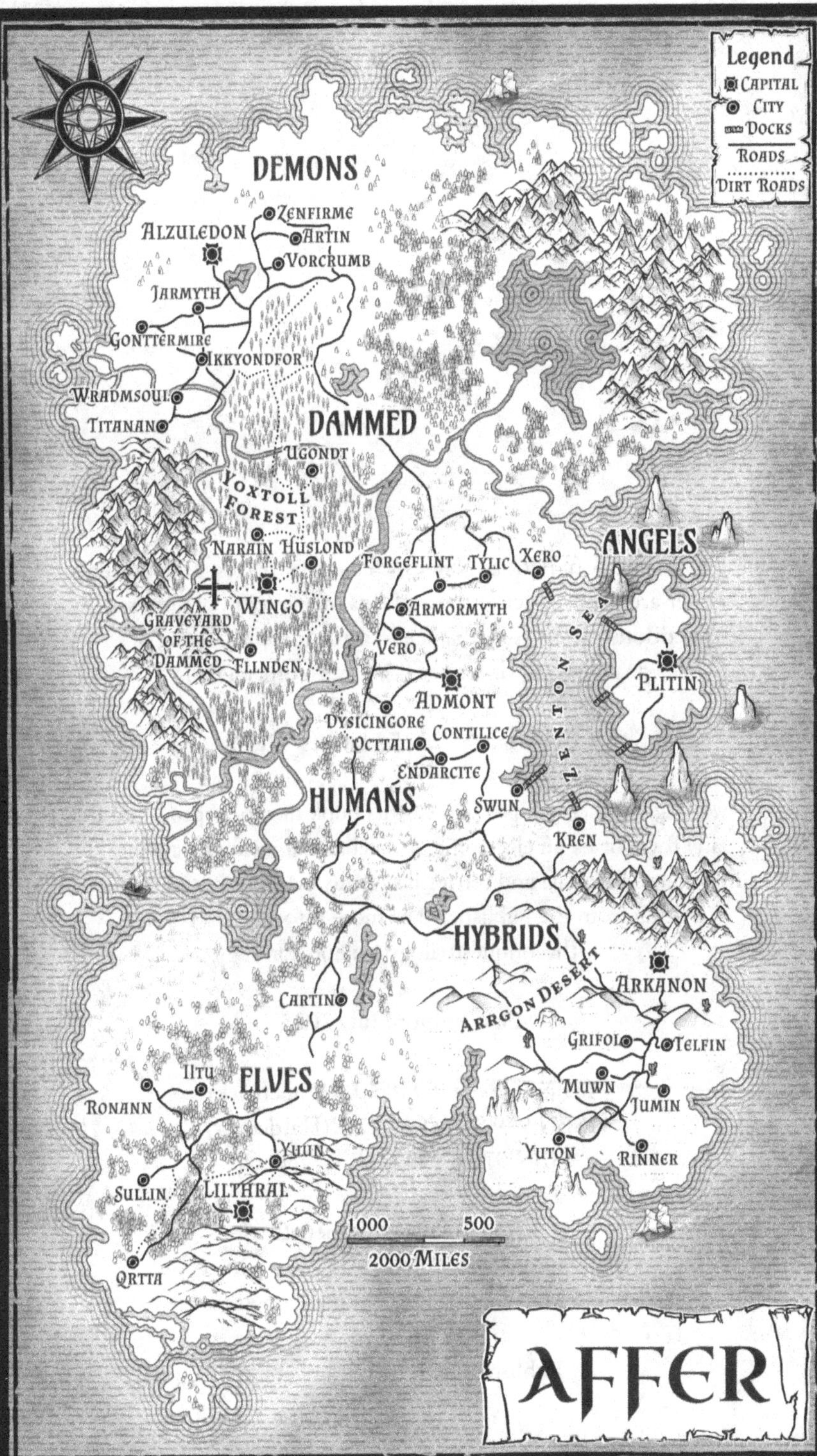
Legend
CAPITAL
CITY
DOCKS
ROADS
DIRT ROADS
DEMONS
ZENFIRME
ARTIN
ALZULEDON
VORCRUMB
JARMYTH
GONTTERMIRE
IKKYONDFOR
WRADMSOUL
DAMMED
TITANAN
UGONDT
YOXTOLL
FOREST
NARAIN HUSLOND
FORGEFLINT
TYLIC
XERO
ANGELS
WINGO
ARMORMYTH
GRAVEYARD
OF THE
DAMMED
VERO
FLLNDEN
ADMONT
PLITIN
DYSICINGORE
CONTILICE
OCTTAIL
ENDARCITE
HUMANS
SWUN
KREN
HYBRIDS
ARKANON
CARTIN
ARRGON DESERT
GRIFOL
TELFIN
ELVES
MUWN
ILTU
JUMIN
RONANN
YUHN
YUTON
RINNER
SULLIN
LILTHRAL
1000
500
2000 MILES
QRTTA
AFFER

First Edition: July 2025

ISBN 979-8-9989388-0-1 (Paperback)
ISBN 979-8-9989388-2-5 (Hardcover)
ISBN 979-8-9989388-1-8 (ebook)

Text Copyright © Matthew Devitt
Illustrations copyright © Alejandro Colucci
Map copyright © Saumya Singh

Published by BOLD Publishing

This book is dedicated to my parents.
Thanks for always being there for me and
raising me to be the man I am today.
Love you both.

PROLOGUE

Four hundred seventy-three years ago, the planet Affer changed forever. Five species: angels, demons, dammed, hybrids, and elves allied against the humans in a battle that was known as the Great War. City after city fell, until only the capital, Admont, was left standing. Despite humanity's power, they were hopelessly outnumbered, and in a single night, Admont was conquered. A three-year war came to an end as the humans were defeated. Hundreds of thousands had been killed, but the ones who survived suffered a worse fate, as they were enslaved.

For years, the five species treated the humans fairly. But as time passed, they became lazy and demanded more. As the humans struggled to keep up, the species began to abuse their power. It became common for slaves to be beaten, sometimes to the point of death, so most of the kingdoms set laws in place to ensure they would have servants for centuries to come. The only ones that didn't were the angels. Humans were treated the worst there, and death was viewed as a gift. Despite that, the angels became the strongest species on Affer. Next were the demons, who were substantially weaker but still feared by every kingdom below them. The dammed were in the middle. They were neither powerful nor weak and were the most peaceful of the five. Fourth were the hybrids, a mighty group that had fallen after the Great War but was now regaining its power. Lastly were the elves, who were the weakest and looked down upon by the other four.

The years passed, turning into decades and centuries, without any change. Eventually, the humans accepted their fate as slaves...all except one. Fletcher Rush, a man born a slave, would become the leader of the most significant uprising the world had ever seen. It didn't matter how far he had to go or if it cost him his soul. Fletcher had dedicated his life to freeing his kind. For eleven years, he trained with the sole purpose of escaping enslavement and bringing Affer to its knees, until the day arrived for him to begin his conquest.

ONE

"You're insane!" Abe said to Fletcher as his friend was about to put his plan into action.

"No one sane is going to change the world," Fletcher said, grinning as he walked over to his anvil.

Fletcher had been preparing for war ever since he had been put to work at the age of ten. For the next eleven years, he trained, pushing himself to the point of exhaustion countless times. While he built his body, he also devised a strategy to escape and reclaim the rights of his species.

There were many days when he passed out or threw up, but he didn't quit. He kept going, even when he wanted to stop. At times, he doubted himself and thought death was the only way he would ever be free, but he stood back up no matter how hard he was knocked down. It took years for him to see results, but eventually, he put on muscle and grew stronger in both body and mind.

He had become so strong that a sixteen-hour workday in the forge didn't faze him. That is, until he was no longer an apprentice and began working on his own. It took him another three years to get used to forging swords and training, but eventually, he became the strongest human in Titanan, the third-largest city in the demon kingdom.

Now, after all those years of preparation, it was finally the moment for Fletcher to make his move, and it began here, in the forge.

"Good luck, Fletcher. If you succeed, make sure to free the rest of us someday," Abe said, turning away from his friend and going back to forging the axe he was working on.

"I don't need luck, Abe. I'm going to succeed with pure skill, and once I build an army strong enough, I'll free everyone here." Fletcher grabbed a pair of tongs and took a sword from the blazing-hot furnace. He set the weapon down on the edge of his anvil, facing Abe's workspace. Letting it teeter, he tossed his tongs onto his workbench. Fletcher watched the sword fall and clatter to the ground next to Abe's feet.

"You idiot!" Abe snapped, provoking a fight with Fletcher exactly as they had discussed.

"I must have set the blade down too close to the edge," Fletcher said, glancing at the sword on the ground. "My bad, Abe."

"My bad?! How incompetent can you be?! You've been a blacksmith for years, and you still suck at it! This is why you can't forge armor by yourself!" Abe grabbed a hammer off his workbench and walked over to Fletcher.

"There's no need to do this! It was a simple mistake!"

"Mistake—" Abe started, but was interrupted by one of the demons walking over to them.

"What's going on here?" the demon asked in an uncaring tone, his dark red eyes glaring at the two in annoyance.

"The blade I was working on fell and hurt Abe."

"Because you're careless! You're the worst blacksmith I've ever taught, and it's not even close!"

"Quit making a big deal out of it and bandage up your leg, then go back to work," the demon said, turning away from the two.

"See, relax," Fletcher said, walking away from Abe. "You're acting like a child."

"YOU—" Abe yelled, stepping toward Fletcher and swinging his hammer at him. The heavy steel slammed into the side of his head, and everything went black.

TWO

Fletcher opened his eyes and immediately closed them, blinded by a bright white light. His head hurt, and he felt a bandage wrapped around it. Opening his eyes again, he let them adjust and then sat up. He saw that he was in the infirmary, which was exactly where he wanted to be. This wasn't the first time he had been sent to the hospital; most of the slaves in Titanan had been there dozens of times. However, Fletcher intended for this to be his last.

So far, everything was going as he had planned, although he wished Abe hadn't hit him so hard.

"You could have held back, Abe," Fletcher muttered to himself, touching the spot where he had been hit.

I can't waste time. I need to get to work, he thought, getting off the hay bed.

At the moment, no demons were in the room, and only a few other humans were present, all of them passed out or asleep. Walking down the aisle between the beds, Fletcher stopped at the only door in the room and put his ear against it. After he didn't hear anything, he slowly twisted the handle and opened it a sliver. Peering out into the hallway, he saw two demon guards keeping watch at the distant end.

Eyeing them both, he realized they wouldn't be going

anywhere. Needing to readjust his approach, he slowly closed the door and turned around.

Fletcher shouted as his light gray eyes met a pair of hazel ones. "You scared the shit out of me, Ji!" he scolded the brown-haired man.

"Sorry. But what are you doing?"

"Today's the day I escape. I accomplished the first step, but now I need to get past those two guards."

"You'll have to get past a lot more than that," Ji said.

"I know. I have everything planned out. At least everything that's in my control."

"Look, you should understand better than anyone how impossible it is to escape. All you ever talk about is freeing our kind and getting revenge."

"I don't care how hard it is or how much the odds are stacked against me. I'd rather die a free man, or perish while trying, than live as a slave."

"I'll help you escape, but I want to come with you."

"Deal," Fletcher said. He didn't know Ji that well, but he wasn't much younger than Fletcher, and both of them were often in the infirmary, so they weren't strangers. Although Fletcher intended to leave alone, he would gladly accept help. "Why would I be opposed to that? I'm going to need allies. I can't do this by myself."

"I don't want to make it too easy to free our kind."

"If you could single-handedly change the tide of battle to the point where taking over Affer would be easy, I would *definitely* want you to escape with me."

"I guess you'll have to wait and witness my unrivaled talent for yourself," Ji said, taking a fighting stance and pretending to swing a sword.

"I'm sure our enemies are already shaking in fear with those sword skills," Fletcher said in a serious tone. The two of them were quiet before they burst out laughing. "Jokes aside, we need to get out of here."

"What's the plan?"

"We wait for the doctor to come, and then I'll kill him."

"Take this," Ji said, reaching into his pocket and handing Fletcher a screwdriver. "It should make killing him easier."

Fletcher looked at the tool before he shoved it into his pocket. "Lie down in a bed and don't move until you give me the signal."

"Me?" Ji faced the other man. "What's the signal?"

"When you're ready, say, 'angel,'" Fletcher said, lying down in bed. "But while we wait, we might as well discuss our next move."

It was nearly two hours later when they heard the doorknob turn. Before the doctor opened the door, Ji began to cough. The demon walked in and scanned the room before his eyes stopped on Ji.

"What's wrong with you? You don't even work in the mines!" the doctor said in an irritated voice. Nonetheless, he came over to Ji and pulled out his stethoscope.

"I'm...not sure," Ji wheezed out, rolling over on his side and curling up into a ball. "I just...know it...hurts."

"You humans are so weak it's repulsive," the doctor said in disgust. "Now sit up so I can check your breathing."

Ji sat up, still doing his fake cough, and the demon placed the stethoscope against his chest. "Your lungs sound fine. What happened?"

"I woke up...and felt dizzy...then I started coughing...and that's when I... I saw an angel."

Fletcher instantly jumped out of bed. The demon turned back, but it was too late.

Ji wrapped his arm around the demon's throat and leaned back, using his body weight to hold him down. Fletcher wasted no time attacking and plunged the screwdriver straight into the demon's ear canal. Black blood spurted out, splattering all over Ji and Fletcher. Pulling the tool out, the demon's body went limp, and Ji let go, shoving him to the side and letting his head hit the concrete floor.

"That takes care of one of them," Ji said, wiping the blood from his face.

"Are you ready for the next part?" Fletcher handed the screwdriver back to Ji.

"I'm waiting on you, slowpoke!" Ji pocketed the tool and ran out the door.

THREE

"**H**ELP, HE'S GONE INSANE! HE KILLED THE DOCTOR, AND HE TRIED TO KILL ME, TOO!" Ji screamed, running at the two guards stationed at the end of the hallway.

"GET BACK HERE, JI!" Fletcher yelled, bolting out of the room, his hands, face, torso, and pants covered in blood.

The two guards looked at each other before eyeing Ji and then turning their attention to Fletcher. Silently agreeing to eliminate the psychotic man, the two demons walked toward Fletcher.

As they passed Ji, he grabbed his screwdriver and stabbed the guard to the right in his left thigh, bringing him to his knee. Before either of the demons had a chance to react, Fletcher sprinted down the hall and drop-kicked the other guard in the abdomen. At the same time, Ji threw a left hook at his foe, breaking his nose. Fletcher came over and followed up with a kick to the demon's head, knocking him down.

Pulling the tool out from the demon's thigh, Ji stabbed the other guard in the ribs, missing the bone and going straight into his liver. Fletcher rammed his elbow into the wound, causing the guard to keel over in pain and drop to the floor. Meanwhile, the other guard had gotten back up and punched Fletcher in the face. As the demon's fist slammed into him,

Fletcher stumbled back but didn't fall. He felt dizzy, and his vision briefly blurred, but with the adrenaline rushing through his veins, he barely noticed. He was sure the only way to stop him now was to kill him.

"Fletcher!" Ji shouted, throwing him the screwdriver.

Fletcher caught the tool and took a step forward, stabbing the demon in the eye. The guard roared out in pain as Fletcher repeatedly stabbed him.

While Fletcher killed one guard, Ji attacked the other. He dashed forward and grabbed the dagger from the demon's belt, but was thrown back by a punch to the stomach. Doubling over, he vomited. Before he could recover, the demon locked him in a chokehold. Ji struggled against the guard's arm, but it was hopeless against the demon's strength. Using his weight, the demon drove Ji to his knees and pressed down, cutting off his air. Ji's arms dropped to his sides, his face turning red as he gasped for breath. Just before he lost consciousness, the pressure vanished, and the demon's arm slackened.

Ji gasped for air as the pounding in his head stopped, and his blood started flowing again. "Took you long enough!"

"Sorry about that. I got carried away."

Ji stood after he had recuperated somewhat and surveyed his surroundings. Right away, he noticed that Fletcher was covered in more blood than before, and the demon he had killed wasn't even recognizable. Fletcher had made over a dozen holes in his face, and a massive puddle of blood had formed around his head. Turning away, he glanced at the other guard and saw that he had a hole in his neck.

Grabbing the sword from the second demon, Fletcher looked at Ji. "Catch," he said, tossing him the weapon.

Instead of catching it, Ji panicked and jumped back. "What's wrong with you?!"

"That's your fault! You should have caught it."

"Screw that! I'm not a blacksmith!" Ji said, bending down to pick up the sword.

"What does that have to do with anything? Do you think we toss weapons to each other?!"

"I don't know, and guess what? I don't want to know. You can keep whatever goes on in that room of terror to yourself."

"Room of terror? Honestly, that's a fitting name," Fletcher chuckled.

"Now I really don't want to know what happens in the forge. But thanks for the save. I would've died there if it wasn't for you."

"We're in this together. Your life is just as important to me as mine. That's what it means to be allies," Fletcher said, walking down the hallway.

"I feel the same," Ji said, falling into step next to Fletcher.

"We need to get to the garage. Currently, we're on the fourth story of the hospital, so we need to get to the basement and take the tunnels to the military post, which connects to the garage. That's the closest building we can get to from the tunnels."

"Then?"

"Patience, Ji. Don't try to climb steps you haven't reached yet; you'll end up falling."

Fletcher reached the end of the hallway and peeked around the corner. Fortunately, no one else was there. Racing down the hall with Ji directly behind him, Fletcher arrived at the stairwell. Reaching for the door handle, he stopped as it started to turn. Getting ready to attack, they came face to face with a six-and-a-half-foot-tall demon. His light gray skin was stretched tight over his huge muscular body, and his black horns were colossal. They could tell he sparred often by the scars littering his body, not to mention the fact that his exoskeleton, which covered his collarbones, sternum, knuckles, and spine, showed considerable damage.

Fletcher acted immediately, stabbing the demon in the stomach and ducking to give Ji a chance to strike. Ji instantly reacted, seizing his chance to wound the guard. He slashed across the demon's throat, missing the kill but damaging his vocal cords and rendering him unable to call for help. Fletcher sliced the demon's legs right under his kneecaps and rammed into him with his shoulder, pushing the demon back a few feet out of the doorway, giving him and Ji more room to fight.

The battle had been one-sided, and the two of them weren't going to let that change. Ji moved to the left of the demon and drove his sword into his hip, twisting the blade when he couldn't go any deeper. The demon tried to let out a scream, but only succeeded in making more blood pour from the wound on his neck. Ji kicked the guard in his right leg with the flat of his foot, then grabbed the sword that was still sticking in the demon's hip, putting his body weight on the weapon. The demon collapsed to his knees and squealed, the agony unbearable even for his kind. Once he was down, Fletcher stuck his sword into the demon's gaping mouth, straight through the roof and into his brain. The demon's pupils slowly faded to black, and his body went limp, falling to the metal floor of the stairwell.

"That's four!" Fletcher said.

"Only about two hundred thousand more to go."

"Keep counting down, Ji, and before you know it, we humans will be back at the top."

The two silently made their way down the stairs, hoping they didn't run into any more guards. Reaching the lowest level, Fletcher stopped and placed his ear against the door.

"Do you hear anything?"

"No, but there are always two guards standing watch at the tunnel entrance. Thankfully, there aren't any guards in the basement. Still, there's no way around the ones at the tunnels, so we'll have to kill them," Fletcher said, removing his ear from the door and grabbing the handle.

Before Fletcher opened it, they heard the door on the level above them open.

"Hey... There's demon blood, and a lot of it. SOUND THE ALARM; WE HAVE A KILLER IN HERE!"

Fletcher glanced at Ji before throwing open the door and rushing through it.

"We need to get into the tunnels as quickly as possible!"

There were three rooms in the basement; two housed medical supplies, while the third connected to the tunnel system that ran beneath the city. The tunnels weren't used frequently in the summer, but in the harsh, cold winter, they were used every day. The winters were bad on the north side of Affer, but Titanan had it the worst. In January, there would be two to three feet of snow on the ground, and temperatures dropped as low as negative sixty degrees. To minimize going outside, every city in the demon kingdom had a tunnel system connecting to each building.

"When we get to the guards, attack right away!" Fletcher said, turning to Ji, who nodded in response.

As they burst through the door, they were surprised to find the guards in the middle of changing shifts.

Four demons stared at them as they rushed in with their swords drawn, eyes filled with killing intent. But neither Fletcher nor Ji stopped their charge, even when they saw four guards instead of the two they were expecting.

The startled demons stood in place, thrown off by the humans running straight at them. But they quickly snapped out of it and drew their swords. Nevertheless, Ji and Fletcher stabbed one demon each before they got their bearings.

Fletcher parried a blow from his left and jabbed the demon in the face. Bringing his arm back, he turned his sword and blocked an attack from the other guard with the flat of his blade. Taking a step to his right, Fletcher narrowly avoided getting stabbed, but the blade still nicked him. Blood ran down his left shoulder, mixing with the black blood of the demons that covered his body. The injury hurt, but Fletcher ignored it. The pain he was experiencing was nothing compared to the pain he had endured to get here. Day after day, he trained and slaved away, making weapons for a species that had brought his kind nothing but misery. That stung far worse than any physical pain he could ever endure.

Fletcher stepped forward, dodging a strike and stabbing the demon in the throat, causing him to stumble backward. He wasn't dead yet, but before Fletcher dealt the finishing blow, he heard a sword whistling toward the back of his head. Fletcher dropped as fast as he possibly could, accidentally letting go of his weapon but avoiding the blow.

Hitting the gravel floor, Fletcher cut his palms on the small rocks. Rolling to the left, he knocked the second guard over. Pinning the guard's wrist with his knee, Fletcher took the screwdriver out of his pocket and stabbed the demon in the heart.

Fletcher yelled, stabbing the guard two more times. He wanted to go on for hours, but stopped when he was sure his enemy was dead and turned his attention back to the other guard, who had wrapped a strand of cloth around his neck to slow the bleeding.

"Come on, you ugly motherfucker! What are you waiting for?!" Fletcher shouted while he picked his sword back up.

The demon sprinted at Fletcher, and instead of swinging his sword at him, he threw it. Fletcher knocked the weapon away, but didn't have a chance to do anything else before the demon tackled him. He felt the air leave his lungs as he hit the ground.

The demon put his hands together, making a large fist, and raised it above his head, aiming to bring it down on Fletcher. Before he could, Fletcher stabbed the demon in the crotch, causing him to scream out in pain. Pulling the tool out, Fletcher stabbed him again. The demon wailed in agony but mustered enough composure to grab Fletcher and shove him away, pulling the screwdriver out afterward.

"That armor you're wearing is great," Fletcher said, walking over and grabbing his sword again. "But here's the thing: I've helped make over a hundred of them. Do you know what that means?" He smirked and glared down at the demon. The guard looked up to see the human standing before him, Fletcher's face twisted into a sick, sadistic smile. "It means I know the weak spots better than you bastards do. See you after death." Fletcher grabbed the demon by his horn and shoved the sword into his face, piercing through his skull.

Pulling his blade out of the demon's head, Fletcher checked on Ji and saw him fighting one-on-one. This guard seemed to be giving him trouble, as he was covered in sweat and breathing heavily, not to mention that he had already been wounded a few times.

I should help him out, Fletcher thought, making his way over to his ally.

FOUR

This demon's the highest rank we've fought, Ji thought, eyeing the guard's armor.

Ji had been panting for most of the fight as he tried to keep up with the demon. He landed a shallow cut across the back of the guard's legs, which allowed him to take care of the other one, but he felt his energy draining away by the second.

Ji knew he wasn't going to win, but he needed to buy enough time until Fletcher took care of his opponents and came to help. There was a small chance that Fletcher wouldn't win, but in that case, Ji was dead no matter what.

He blocked an attack, only for the guard to throw him off and immediately bring his sword down at blinding speed. The weapon cut into Ji's right thigh, going in a quarter-inch. He let out a painful grunt and screamed. The pain was worse than anything he had ever felt, and he had felt a great deal working as a slave for the demons.

Once the blade drove into his leg, Ji was done; his body slowly gave out, and when he blinked, he was on his knees. The guard grabbed him by his hair and said something he wasn't conscious enough to catch. All he felt was his heavy breathing, the pounding of his heart, and the burning sensation in his leg. Then his senses shut down.

FIVE

"JI!" Fletcher yelled as he saw the guard cut into his ally's leg.

Everything happened in the blink of an eye. Ji fell and the demon grabbed him, swinging his sword back, ready to lop off his head. Fletcher could either stab the demon in the back or block his attack to save Ji. With no time to think, he acted purely on instinct.

The sound of metal hitting metal rang throughout the room as Fletcher's blade met the demon's. The two of them stood still, the human and demon staring at each other, neither moving an inch.

"You could have killed me. Instead, you chose to save this human. Why?"

"I don't expect a demon to understand!" Fletcher snapped, shoving the guard's blade and spinning. As he moved, he brought his blade up, slicing into the demon's bicep.

Simultaneously, the demon pressed his sword into Fletcher's back and pulled the weapon toward himself. Fletcher clenched his jaw, trying to stay conscious as his vision went dark and pain shot through his body.

In one fluid motion, Fletcher pulled his sword free and drove it into the demon's lower stomach, right above his left hip. Instead of pulling it out, Fletcher let go and dodged a blow aimed at his neck.

Missing his attack, the demon tried to knee Fletcher in the face. Fletcher blocked with his arms, crossing them into an X. Fletcher rushed forward, scaling the eight-foot-tall demon like a wall, putting his foot on the blade he had driven into his gut and pushing off. The demon let out a cry of pain, dropping his weapon and grabbing Fletcher. But it was too late; Fletcher was already where he wanted to be.

He drove his thumb into the demon's left eye so deep that he felt his skull. The demon screamed again but held on, squeezing Fletcher even tighter, trying to break his ribs. Fletcher's chest hurt and the air was forced out of his lungs. His face turned blue, and he began to feel himself slipping into unconsciousness. Refusing to give up, he twisted his head and bit the demon's nose. He heard a loud snap as he fractured the bone. Releasing Fletcher, the demon brought his hands to his face and cried out in pain. Blood poured from the wound, gushing past his fingers and puddling at his feet.

"You had me worried at first. But at the end of the day, you lost." Fletcher pulled his sword out of the demon and brought it down toward his head.

The demon turned his body before the weapon made contact, and instead of cutting into his skull, it lodged in his shoulder.

"Shit," Fletcher muttered before he was punched in the chest.

He gasped for breath as he was thrown to the floor by the force of the blow. The back of his head hit the gravel, causing his vision to blur. Blinking and opening his eyes, he saw the demon falling toward him.

Fletcher barely had time to roll away before the demon landed where he had been. Getting on his hands and knees,

Fletcher slowly stood and wiped the sweat and blood from his eyes. He was feeling the pain and exhaustion now. His breathing had grown frantic, and his limbs had become heavy as fatigue crept up on him.

"I'm impressed, human. I'm a rank-five guard and have bested many of my kind. For a human, you—"

"SHUT UP! THAT DOESN'T MATTER! MY ONLY PURPOSE IS GETTING OUT OF HERE AND FREEING MY SPECIES! IF I DON'T WIN, IF I DON'T KILL YOU, THEN MY LIFE WAS MEANINGLESS!"

Fletcher ran at the demon, slowing down slightly and squatting like he was about to jump at him. But instead, he picked up his pace at the last second and slid between the demon's legs. Quickly standing, he turned around and grabbed the demon in a chokehold.

"Foolish slave, you think that will work?" the demon asked. Jumping up, he leaned back, slamming Fletcher into the ground.

Fletcher groaned and spat out a mouthful of blood. He knew it wouldn't be easy to escape, but he didn't expect to be hurt this badly.

Just a little more, he thought as he felt the demon's strength ebb away.

The demon rolled over and stood back up, getting ready to slam Fletcher again. But Fletcher brought his foot down behind the demon's knee, jamming it into the popliteal fossa, effectively forcing the demon down. The demon tried to stand back up, but Fletcher stayed firm. After a minute, the guard went limp as he passed out.

Making sure the demon was unconscious, Fletcher yelled in triumph and let go of him. Walking over to his ally, Fletcher tied his shirt tightly around Ji's leg. Unable to carry both him and the swords, Fletcher was forced to drop the weapons. "Damn, Ji, what have you been eating? You need to lose some weight," Fletcher teased as he struggled to lift the full-grown man.

Walking toward the mouth of the tunnel, he paused before he went in and turned to look back at the demon he had left alive. "I wish I had time to kill you, but I'm sure we'll meet again."

SIX

J i woke up with a pounding headache that only became worse when his head slammed into a hard surface.

"Ow!" he cried, opening his eyes.

"Good, you're alive."

"Who hit me? Are we under attack?!"

"No, that was me. I accidentally hit your head against the wall. Sorry, Ji," Fletcher admitted, not telling him that was the third time.

"Asshole," Ji said, now fully awake and realizing he was being carried on Fletcher's back.

"I saved you back there! I could have let that demon kill you! I had a perfect chance to end him, but I decided to save you instead."

"Thanks. I appreciate you saving my life, especially if it could have cost you yours as well."

"Don't mention it," Fletcher said, standing by his choice to save Ji. "What's the point of winning if we sacrifice our own as if they're objects? I'm sure I wouldn't have made it this far without you, even after spending years preparing for this day."

The two were quiet before Ji spoke up. "I hate the tunnels. I was beaten several times for getting lost down here."

"That only happened to me once. After that, I always

traveled with someone else. Abe knew the tunnels—" Fletcher stopped, crying out.

"What's wrong?!"

"I was wounded in the last fight. Do you think you can walk?" Fletcher asked, desperate to get Ji off the cut on his back.

"I'll be fine," Ji said, lowering his leg and putting weight on it. "Maybe not. That's worse than I thought it would be."

"Never mind. Just stay on me."

"Where are you hurt?"

"My back." Fletcher pointed to the cut.

"That's terrible!" Ji said, staring at the wound on Fletcher's muscular back. "And you had me resting my whole weight on top of it."

"Ji, it's—" Fletcher started, but paused when he heard the deep voice of two demons. "Get on my back, or we're both going to die down here!" he whispered in a demanding tone.

Ji didn't argue and got on his back, trying his best not to move. Fletcher slowly walked down the tunnel, and both he and Ji listened to the demons, trying to make sure they didn't run into them, knowing that if they did, their chance of success would be practically nonexistent.

After a stressful eight minutes, they could no longer hear the guards, and the two of them were down the hall from the military post.

"We're close. It's down here and then through a door on the left," Fletcher said, picking up the pace.

"Will there be any guards there?"

"No. There will be four to six in the armory, but we don't need to go in there, even though I would love to grab better weapons."

"So we get to the garage, and then what?"

"We camp in the back of the patrol car," Fletcher said, stopping at a turn and peering down the hall. Seeing that it was clear, he moved on, closer to the door. "We stay hidden and out of sight until the patrol goes out to scout the borders."

"How do we know that they'll leave soon? What if we have to stay there for days? I don't want to be stuck with you in a cramped space for that long."

"They leave daily. I could see it from the forge, and I found out from Abe that they head over to the kingdom's borders. Why they go out so often, or what they're looking for, I'm not sure. But I know they leave, and getting past the city's walls is all that matters."

"I trust you. The worst that happens is we die...right?" Ji asked, trying not to think about all the ways they could be punished.

Making his way up the stairs, Fletcher squatted, trying to make himself appear smaller and draw less attention. The post wasn't fully lit up since it was night, but it was still bright enough to see someone walking around.

Pausing and listening closely, Fletcher and Ji heard banter coming from their left. "It sounds like there are a lot of guards or soldiers in there," Ji whispered, not wanting to run into either at the moment.

"You spit in my ear!" Fletcher complained, with a look of disgust.

"Sorry," Ji whispered, this time farther away.

Fletcher made his way toward the garage, sneaking across the floor and stopping at the door. Twisting the handle, he opened it softly and went inside.

As soon as Fletcher opened the door, they were met with loud voices, laughter, and glasses being slammed onto a metal surface. Peering in the direction of the noise, they saw over a dozen demons. There were nine soldiers, all rank four-six, and seven guards: two rank one, four rank two-three, and one rank four-six.

"Just our luck, they're having a party the night we try and escape!" Fletcher angrily whispered, closing the door behind him.

"Relax and keep going. Once we're inside the car, we'll be in the clear."

Fletcher grunted and headed toward the other side of the room, away from the demons. He slowly made his way past the red military trucks until he reached the patrol car. "I'm going to put you down. Will you be alright?"

"Yeah," Ji said, putting his right leg on the ground. He bit his tongue as his wound flared in pain, but kept himself from screaming and blowing their cover.

Fletcher got up and opened the trunk of the car. He grabbed a med kit to bandage them both while they waited, then took out the emergency blanket and unfolded it. "Get in, and I'll cover us with this."

Ji managed to climb in with help from Fletcher, who joined him right after. Closing the trunk, Fletcher opened the blanket and draped it over them.

"How long do we have to wait?" Ji asked in a hushed tone.

"I don't know. Just be patient. In the meantime, bandage up your leg and any other areas you need. But make sure to leave some for me."

"It would really suck if we ended up starving to death in here."

"That's not helping, Ji! Worry about taking care of your leg!"

SEVEN

After four hours, the doors to the car opened, and three demons stepped inside. As the engine roared to life, one of the garage doors began to open.

"Where's that lazy-ass, Kazagal?!" asked the guard in the back seat.

"Didn't you hear? His nose was bitten off by a damn slave who stabbed him," the demon in the driver's seat said, starting to drive off.

That was me, Fletcher thought.

"When I found out, I couldn't stop laughing! That asshole was always going on about how tough he was, and then he gets his ass beaten by a slave!" the demon in the passenger seat said. "All I can say is it made my day, that's for sure."

The car stopped, and they heard a window roll down.

"Stupid piece of shit! When are they going to fix this?!" the guard in the driver's seat said. "I put in a request to have this scanner fixed more than twenty times, and I know I'm not the only one!"

"They won't fix it until it completely breaks."

"I don't get why it's so hard to fix this damn thing. Just send one of the slaves to take care of it; we have plenty of them."

Fletcher balled his fist after hearing that. He wanted to

jump out and kill the demon, but he knew it wasn't time yet, and if he sprang into action prematurely, he would only end up getting both him and Ji killed.

Soon... I'll kill them soon.

It was another hour before Fletcher and Ji felt safe enough to make their move.

With no words exchanged between them, they nodded to each other and started the fight.

Ji threw the blanket off of them, and Fletcher instantly moved, grabbing the demon in the back seat and snapping his neck. Due to his inexperience, Fletcher failed to kill him and was punched in the face. Hearing the commotion, the driver glanced in the rearview mirror and slammed on the brakes. The car came to a jarring halt, jolting everyone forward. Slamming against the back seats, Ji quickly clambered over them. He grabbed the shortsword from the demon Fletcher failed to kill and stabbed him in the chest, going underneath his ribcage for less resistance. The demon convulsed before blood poured out of his mouth, and he stopped moving entirely.

Before the two of them could do anything else, the trunk opened. Fletcher was grabbed by one of the demons and thrown out of the car.

"It's slaves!"

The other demon went to kick Fletcher, but he rolled away. Quickly getting up, he backed off and raised his guard. Both demons drew their swords and locked onto him, advancing at the same time.

Fletcher stepped back, avoiding one attack, but was grazed by the other. The blade sliced open his shirt and cut into his chest. Luckily, the gauze Fletcher had used to bandage the cut on his back was thick enough to absorb most of the blow. Nonetheless, the wound was still bad enough that Fletcher cried out in agony. Trying to ignore the pain, he scurried back.

The demon was shocked that Fletcher was still standing. Taking a step toward him, the guard paused when he heard a scream. Facing toward the noise, he saw Ji stabbing his ally in the throat.

Turning his attention to Ji, the demon charged at him, but only traversed a few feet before Fletcher swept his legs. Falling down, the guard tried to get back up, but before he could, he felt a sharp blade pierce into his neck.

Ji yelled as he drove his weapon deeper, pushing the sword in until he wasn't able to anymore.

Breathing heavily, Ji pulled the blade out and looked over at Fletcher, who was panting.

"Thanks for the save. I couldn't have done it without you today," Fletcher said, nodding to Ji.

"No problem," Ji said, wiping the blade on his bloodied shirt. "Thanks for taking me with you. I hated it there, and I would have died living my whole life as a slave if it wasn't for you. Seriously, thank you."

"I think we all were in that boat. But that's going to change," Fletcher said, putting a hand on Ji's shoulder. "It's going to change because of us."

"I couldn't agree more! But first, I think we should take care of our injuries."

"Did you save any gauze so I can wrap my chest?"

"Hold on, you're the one who used the med kit last!"

"If I bleed out, it's your fault," Fletcher razzed, ripping strips of cloth from the demons' shirts and wrapping them around his chest. "That will have to do. I want to get out of here, so let's grab what we need and leave."

The two of them grabbed every weapon the guards had and

a few more strips of cloth. After searching them for anything else that might be useful and finding nothing, they got in the car.

"How do you drive?" Fletcher asked, turning to Ji in the passenger seat.

"Are you sure you don't want me to drive?"

"I would love for you to drive, but how are you going to do that with an injured leg? I'm surprised you even walked in the fight we just had."

"When it's life or death, pain doesn't matter," Ji said, leaning over and pointing to the gas pedal. "That's the gas. You only need to press on it slightly. The one next to it is the brake." Ji pointed to the brake, then moved to the steering wheel. "This is the wheel. You move it back and forth like so, and you can spin it a few rotations."

"Wait, why? Shouldn't it be ninety degrees to completely turn?" Fletcher asked, already not liking this.

"That's just how it is. Now start driving, and if you crash, I'll take over."

"Thanks for the confidence boost." Fletcher started driving, surprising both himself and Ji when he stayed on the road. "This driving thing isn't so bad. Why did you always complain about your job?"

"First of all, my complaining was justified, and second, it wasn't driving the cars that I hated, it was working on them. There's a big difference."

Looking out the window at the night sky, Ji asked, "Where are we headed?"

"The ruined human capital: Admont."

"Why? Also, do you know where you're going?"

"There's a few reasons. The first is that we need somewhere to heal. Both you and I are hurt, and a few weeks or even months are crucial to our success in conquering the first city. The second is so I can forge weapons and try to make armor. Although I'm not sure how the latter will go. The third is that I'm hoping to gather intel from there. Lastly, we need to train, and no one goes there, so it will be perfect."

"Those are some valid points," Ji said, impressed with how well thought-out Fletcher's strategy was.

"You sound like you doubted me."

"To be honest, I expected you to say, 'I'll drive straight to the demon capital and declare war on them.'"

"Now that you mention it, I might change my plans," Fletcher joked with a light smile on his face.

"I don't know who would be more shocked, the demons or me."

"Imagine their faces if we stood outside the gate to Alzuledon in this state," Fletcher said, laughing. "Just two beat-up humans waging war on one of the largest and most powerful cities in Affer."

Ji cracked up at that, feeling great now that he could live as he wanted to. "Being free feels incredible."

"And it's only going to get better from here on out."

"You never answered my second question, though," Ji said, changing the subject, as he still wanted a response.

"Which one?"

"I asked if you knew where you were going."

"I know. I was paying attention to which way the car turned. If I'm correct, we should eventually end up at the entrance to the Forest of the Dammed, better known as Yoxtoll Forest. We just take this road until we see a dirt path on the right."

"When will we get there?"

"I can't be one hundred percent sure, but I would say twelve to thirteen hours."

"Then I'm going to sleep," Ji said, leaning back in the seat and closing his eyes. "Wake me up if you need me."

"Let's hope I won't."

EIGHT

Over half a day later, Ji woke up. Blinded by the sun, he shielded his eyes with his hand until he adjusted to the light. "Where are we?" he asked, peering out the window, then over to Fletcher.

"We're near one of the entrances to the Yoxtoll Forest."

"I'm hungry. Do we have anything to eat?" Ji asked, even though he assumed they didn't.

"I found oat bars in the glove box. I think they're expired, but we can't be picky."

Ji opened the glove box and peered inside. Sure enough, there were a handful of bars. Grabbing one, he opened it and took a bite. "It's dry."

"Stop complaining and be grateful we have something to eat for the time being."

"I am!" Ji said, swallowing before he continued. "I didn't expect to be eating full meals right away. But I do wish we had a few of those triple-chocolate cookies. I think that's the only thing I'm going to miss."

"Get those cookies out of your head! It's not worth being a slave for that!" Fletcher said, lightly punching Ji in the arm.

"What can I say? I have a sweet tooth."

Before the two could jest any more with each other,

Fletcher stopped the car and gazed out the front windshield. "Wow... This isn't what I expected."

Ji rolled down his window and stuck his head out, getting a better look at the Yoxtoll Forest. He opened his mouth but found he didn't have anything to say. Instead, he just admired the breathtaking forest.

"I've heard about this place before, but words don't do it justice," Ji said, pulling his head back inside the car.

"That's for sure," Fletcher said, starting to move again. Turning right, he drove into the forest and was blown away even more. "I never knew the world was this stunning."

The forest was inhabited by massive trees that stretched upward for over two hundred feet, and the distinction didn't end there. These trees had no bark and were a pale white color, many of them glistening, almost as if they were wet. On top of that, the bottoms of the trees were very unique. Instead of a normal stump that went into the ground, the trees had hundreds, or even thousands, of small and large roots holding them up. The roots ranged from only four feet tall to over a dozen feet.

Light blue vines hung from the countless branches of the forest, each one covered in dozens of small bulbs that glowed a dim yellow. Completing the scene, soft, fuzzy green leaves formed a canopy overhead and blanketed the forest floor.

"Even though it's darker in here because of how dense the forest top is, I still wish we could see this at night," Ji said, staring at the yellow bulbs.

"We will. It's going to take a day to get through here and back onto the main road."

"This makes me wonder how the human capital looks," Ji said, remembering all the stories he'd heard about Admont.

"I would like to say it rivals here, but even as a comparison that feels wrong to say."

As Fletcher drove, they caught a glimpse of the animals that resided in the forest. Even they were vastly different from normal ones.

"Is that a deer?" Fletcher asked, slowing the car and staring out the window.

"I think. What else could it be?"

The creature had soft white fur and light-gray antlers that had an alluring glow to them, which was visible even now, and its bright blue eyes pierced through the trees, staring right at the two.

"If we don't get food soon, we'll have to kill something," Ji said, turning his attention away from the animal and toward Fletcher.

"Hunting isn't in my wheelhouse."

"And you think it's in mine?!"

"Absolutely. I have full faith in you."

Ji pointed to his leg. "I'm unable to hunt at the moment. But I'll be there to watch you struggle."

"Thanks, I don't know what I would do if you weren't."

"I'll help the best I can, but hunting shouldn't be too hard. We were able to kill multiple demon guards, and those guys are way stronger than some wild animals."

"He's over there!" Ji yelled, pointing at the wounded deer.

"I have him!" Fletcher threw a dagger at the animal, but hit a tree instead.

"You missed!"

"I don't see you trying to kill him!" Fletcher shouted as he looped back in a circle.

"My leg is hurt, and I told you I'm not a hunter!"

"And I'm not a dagger thrower!"

"That's not even a thing!"

"Then that's why I missed!" Fletcher said, still running after the animal. "Toss your sword to me!"

"This sounds like a bad idea," Ji muttered, grabbing his sword and waiting. When Fletcher was close enough, Ji shouted and threw the weapon.

Fletcher slowed down and caught the sword. Speeding up, he closed in on the deer and aimed at its head.

"I got him!" Fletcher cheered, walking over to the dead animal.

"Well done. I didn't expect you to hit him," Ji said, limping over to Fletcher.

"I was aiming for the head," Fletcher said in a monotone voice, looking at the weapon lodged in the deer's ribcage.

"At least you hit him."

Fletcher carried the animal back to the car and dropped it on the ground.

"So... Now what?" Fletcher asked.

"We cook it," Ji said, raising his eyebrows at the other man.

"I know that, smart aleck! I mean how?"

"I don't know?" Ji said, shrugging. "I wasn't a cook or a butcher."

"Great. I should have brought Tristan with me instead of you," Fletcher bantered. "He was the best butcher in Titanan."

"But he couldn't drive a car."

"You make a fair point. I take it back, I'm glad you're here with me. I just wish you knew how to dress an animal."

The two were able to gut the deer enough to feed both of them for the night. Although they didn't do a good job, they managed to satisfy their hunger. Once they had finished their meal, Ji and Fletcher decided they both needed to rest and agreed to take turns sleeping while the other continued to drive, or in Ji's case, keep watch.

"Wake me up if you need me. Or if you get too tired to stay awake," Fletcher said, lying across the back seats of the car.

"I'll be fine, just rest up," Ji said, sitting in the passenger seat. "I only wish I could drive right now."

"Don't worry about it. There's no rush to get to Admont. Just keep your eyes open and make sure we don't get attacked by demons or the dammed."

"Will do," Ji said, trying to get comfortable. "Also, thanks again for taking me with you. I would have died as a slave if it wasn't for you."

"You do realize we're going to free everyone someday?"

"I didn't mean it like that. I meant it more in the sense of..." Ji stopped, trying to think of how to put it. "If it weren't for you, our species would have been enslaved forever."

Fletcher let out a small chuckle and closed his eyes. "We haven't freed our species yet, Ji. But don't worry, we will."

Nine

Fletcher woke up and opened his eyes. Right away, he saw it was dark out and felt a gnawing hunger. "What time is it?" he asked, sitting up.

"It's time for me to go to bed and you to start driving." Ji turned around and answered Fletcher. "It's ten past twenty-one hundred hours."

"I slept longer than I thought I would. We need to get moving again. I'll drive, and you can have the back seats if you want them," Fletcher said, getting out of the car and hopping in the driver's seat.

Ji got out of the car as well, walking for a minute to get his blood flowing again before he jumped in the back and lay across the seats.

"How's your leg feeling?" Fletcher asked as he grabbed an oat bar from the glove box and began eating it.

"It's okay. It still hurts and is slightly swollen, but it's not infected, which is good. But I could use new bandages." Ji looked at the red gauze wrapped around his leg that was once bright white.

"I could use new gauze, too," Fletcher said, putting the car in drive. "Worst-case scenario, we use the blanket in the trunk. We also need needle and thread to close our wounds, and soap and water to properly clean them. But we'll tackle those needs when we arrive in Admont. For now, get some rest; we have quite a ways to go."

Ji closed his eyes. He wasn't as tired as yesterday, but he still easily fell asleep.

Seven hours later, Ji woke up and stretched, feeling stiff from being curled up in the tight space for so long. He groaned as he sat up and cracked his back. "Sleeping on the floor is more comfortable than these seats."

"For being free, you sure complain a lot," Fletcher said, looking in the rearview mirror.

"I was expecting to be treated like a king the moment we became free," Ji joked.

Fletcher tossed an oat bar back to Ji. "Is that kingly enough for you?"

"Careful, if you keep that up, the power might go to my head."

"Well, that's the last one, so you don't have to worry about that, Your Majesty," Fletcher quipped.

"Thanks," Ji said, pocketing it for later. "Do you want to take a break? I can try to drive for a little."

"I want to hunt first, then we can swap positions, and if you feel up to it, you can drive," Fletcher said, slowing down and parking the car. "Are you ready for more hunting?"

"No, I'd rather go back to sleep, and I hate sleeping back here."

"Make sure to grab a dagger or a sword," Fletcher said, getting out of the car and grabbing one of each for himself.

Ji grumbled but grabbed a dagger and exited the vehicle. "Maybe this time, don't rush straight at the animals."

"In my defense, I thought I could outrun them," Fletcher said with a shrug. "Now I know I can't, so stop whining and help me fetch us breakfast."

TEN

Ten days after they escaped, Fletcher and Ji could finally see Admont in the distance. The castle towered above them, its imposing presence still felt hundreds of years after its demise.

"What a city this must have been," Fletcher muttered as they got closer.

"And to think, this could've been where we grew up."

"Our lives would be so different if the Great War had never happened."

Ji heard both anger and melancholy in Fletcher's voice and felt the same way. As they neared the city, Ji felt a fire rising in him. It wasn't a fire of hatred or rage, but one that filled a piece of him that he didn't know was missing.

Arriving at the main gate, Fletcher saw it had been blown open and drove through. Entering the capital, he slowed the car down, careful to avoid the rubble.

What was once a lively city had turned into a desolate wasteland. The limestone walls had been breached in many spots and were cracked throughout. The buildings weren't better, and some had been fully destroyed. Thousands of weapons littered the streets, and skeletons were piled up all over the city. Rats scurried across the brick paths, and ravens perched upon the rooftops, eyeing the red car as Fletcher and Ji slowly drove past.

"Should we walk from here?" Fletcher asked, not waiting for an answer and stopping the car.

"I don't think we can get much farther," Ji said, popping open the door.

Fletcher got out of the car, pocketing the keycard that started it and closing the door.

"I'm not sure what I expected, but I figured Admont would be in worse shape," Ji said, glancing around.

"I know what you mean. It's worn and ruined, but it still doesn't seem like it was abandoned over four hundred years ago."

"It's as if this place became taboo." Ji moved past the rusted weapons and armor and took a peek inside one of the buildings. "I don't even think the city was pillaged."

"In a way, it is taboo," Fletcher said, walking ahead. "I wonder what condition the castle is in?"

Ji caught up and looked at the gray brick structure in the center of the city. "From here, it appears to be in good shape."

"I hope I'm able to forge weapons here, and that we'll have somewhere to train too," Fletcher said, eager to finally practice with a sword.

"If you want to spar with me, I'll give myself a few handicaps."

"So you have an excuse when you lose?" Fletcher asked, glancing over at his friend.

"I didn't expect you to think of a comeback."

"When you're as smart as me, you can always think of a comeback."

The two arrived at the innermost circle of the capital. This one was the most intact and was home to massive, high-end mansions. Similar to the rest of the city, corpses were littered everywhere, and rodents and birds ran rampant through the streets.

Mother Nature had taken over the vast majority of the city, but here is where she appeared to make her home. Enormous trees were scattered everywhere, bursting from the ground in spaces they shouldn't be, pushing aside the brick paths, sticking out of windows, and even merging with one house. A thick coat of vines covered the walls of every building, and stagnant pools of water were everywhere.

"This area of the capital is oddly stunning."

"It is. I've never seen nature look so...peaceful," Fletcher said, trying to find the right word.

Nearing the castle, they walked down an expansive area of grass over two hundred feet in length and thirty feet wide, with a water fountain at the end. The fountain was made of marble and had intricate detail ingrained into every square inch, representing the skill of a person long dead.

Heading past the fountain, Fletcher and Ji made their way down a cracking brick path to the castle's double doors that were made from ilbar, the strongest metal on Affer. Despite the doors' strength, they were still heavily damaged, and it was clear they had been pried open. Fletcher wasn't sure what was strong enough to rip the doors open, but he knew it wasn't human.

Stepping inside the castle, Ji and Fletcher immediately stopped and stared at each other.

"That's not right."

"I want to disagree with you, but I know you're right," Fletcher said, examining the lit candle hanging on the wall to their left.

"I thought we would get a break from fighting," Ji said, drawing his sword.

"If we run into any enemies, this would be a perfect time to use those sword skills you were bragging about," Fletcher said, taking out his weapon.

"Are you scared?"

"Not at all. But I don't want to see you get hurt."

"Aw, you're not going to protect me," Ji jested, giving Fletcher a slight shove with his shoulder.

Fletcher returned the gesture. "I already saved your life this month, so you're all out of protection."

They entered the circular throne room, which looked like a scene out of a painting. A golden throne sat at the end with a smaller silver one to its right. Both had elaborate patterns etched into the metal. But while the silver one was grand, the other one was truly made for a king. It had thick padding on the seat, arms, and back. The material appeared to be high-end leather, but over time, it had become dry and cracked, with multiple tears throughout. There was a hole in the corner of the seat, where Fletcher guessed a family of mice or rats once lived. Attached to the back of the throne was a large circle made of an ammolite gemstone. Inside the gemstone was another circle, this one made out of petrified wood. The inner circle portrayed each species symbol cast out of silver, whereas the outer circle was left untouched.

The rest of the room was just as extravagant as the throne, with nine chandeliers hanging from the ceiling. They were teardrop-shaped and made entirely of pure quartz, except for the thin white wire holding them together and the silver chain connecting them to the ceiling. However, only one of them was intact, while the others ranged from decent to unrecognizable.

The floor was made entirely of red diamond granite, with a gold crosshatch pattern etched into it.

Both the right and left walls were open to a hallway on the second level, with degrading limestone balustrades lining the open section. A mural was painted on the wall behind the throne. Sadly, the piece of art was almost lost to the hands of time, and the only recognizable part was a man wearing a crown slaying a three-winged angel.

A white fur rug ran from the entrance to the throne; it was discolored, torn, and smeared with blood. Unsurprisingly, most of the blood that was spilled in the throne room was from humans and possibly elves, with only a single spot of golden angel blood in the middle of the room. But to Fletcher and Ji's shock, there wasn't a single corpse in there.

"This place is majestic."

"That's for sure," Fletcher said, staring at the man in the mural.

"Is something wrong?"

"I was wondering if this was the last king of mankind."

"How would they know who the last would be? Unless they updated it for every leader," Ji said, not paying the painting much mind.

"You're right. It doesn't matter who it is or what the painting was. This was long before our time," Fletcher said, making his way to the throne and sitting on it. "Look, Ji, I'm the king!"

Ji started clapping and gave Fletcher a mock bow. "Congratulations on becoming king, Your Majesty. Not even a month ago, you were a slave, and now you are the king of the greatest species alive."

"If my clothes weren't stained with blood and dirt, I would be the spitting image of a king," Fletcher said with a smirk before getting off the chair.

Finding nothing of value, the two decided to move on. As they headed out of the throne room, Ji stopped in his tracks as the dull edge of a blade touched his throat.

"Don't move," a woman said, putting a slight amount of pressure on the blade, drawing a thin bead of blood from his neck.

"Or what, you'll kill him? Go ahead," Fletcher said, staring at the woman.

"FLETCHER!"

"Relax, she won't kill you. She doesn't have it in her."

"I'll kill him, and you if I must."

"Really? Then go ahead, kill me," Fletcher said, dropping his sword, taking a step back, and spreading his arms out wide. "It won't get any easier than this."

The three of them stood still before the woman lowered her sword and lunged at Fletcher. Stunned that she took action, Fletcher's eyes went wide. Moving past the shock, he ducked, dodged her hit, and tackled her to the ground. Her sword slipped from her hands as she hit the floor, and Fletcher stood, kicking the weapon away.

"See, Ji, what did I say?" Fletcher said, turning to face his friend.

"You were wrong!"

The woman let out a moan, sat up, and rubbed the back of her head. "I thought you said you weren't going to attack?"

"I never said that. I just told you to kill me as I unarmed myself," Fletcher said, picking up his sword.

"You deceived me."

"No, you assumed I would let you kill me, although I have to admit, I didn't think you would attack," Fletcher said, looking at the dark-haired woman. "Who are you?"

"If you want a name, I don't have one. The angels' slaves were never given names. We were only referred to by numbers."

"Well, we need to call you something. My friend Ji here is great at picking out names," Fletcher said, slapping him on the back.

"You asshole, I've never named anyone. Why should I name her?"

"Do you want to give her a name or not?"

"I'll think of one. Just give me a moment."

"In the meantime, I have some questions for you," Fletcher said, staring the woman down. "I'll let you pick where we talk."

"How generous of you," the woman said sarcastically, but walked out of the room nonetheless. "Follow me."

Ji and Fletcher followed her to her "bedroom," where she had a makeshift mattress made of torn and dirty cloth. Examining the woman, Fletcher noticed how slender she was. She wore a thin, tattered fabric that appeared to be a bed sheet stitched together. It covered most of her body but stopped above her knees, and didn't cover her arms at all, revealing the many scars that marred her limbs. Her legs and arms were small and looked fragile, like Fletcher could snap her bones with little effort. Her face wasn't better: gaunt, with bags under her eyes, and her long black hair was splitting at the ends, drained of color.

"Make yourself at home," the woman said, sitting on her bed.

Fletcher remained standing and crossed his arms over his chest. "How did you get here?"

"My mother helped me escape enslavement from the angels. She snuck me on a ship leaving Plitin at the cost of her life. I jumped ship half a mile from Swun and swam to shore. From there, I walked here, since it's the only place I could be 'free.'"

"How do you gather food?"

"Traps."

"You must not be good at it."

"Fletcher!"

"He's right. I barely gather enough to stay alive, and I can't remember the last time I felt full."

"How old are you?" Fletcher asked, figuring she was about twenty to thirty.

"Nineteen... I believe," the woman said. "I think I escaped when I was eight, and it's been eleven years since then."

"Didn't you count the winters?" Fletcher asked.

"There's no winter in Plitin, and the temperature stays the same year-round."

Fletcher and Ji turned to each other. Neither of them knew much about the angels, so if she was lying, they wouldn't know.

Fletcher wanted to push her for more information, but he could tell she didn't want to talk about her past, and he didn't want to lose a potential ally.

"We won't pry, and we won't harm you either, but only if you join us."

The woman looked at Fletcher, confused, until he continued. "Ji and I are trying to free our species from enslavement, and we need as much help as we can get. Plus, you know considerably more about the angels than the two of us."

"So you want my help?" the woman asked.

"Yes. Will you help us or not?"

"I assume you plan on going to war then?"

"There's no other way to free our kin," Fletcher said, clenching his fist. "And even if there was, I want to do more than liberate mankind; I want to slaughter those who kept us in chains."

"The angels, too?"

"Why would I spare them?"

The woman jeered, "You must have never met one. Angels are the strongest species for a reason, and their king..." She paused and shuddered. "You won't be able to kill him."

"I guess I didn't make myself clear," Fletcher said, stepping closer to her and bending down so their faces were at the same level. "I'm going to free every last human on this planet, and anyone who stands in my way will be cut down. I don't care if they're an angel, a king, or both."

The woman stared at Fletcher's eyes and saw that he was dead serious. "Because there's a chance of bringing down the angel kingdom, I'll help you."

Fletcher grinned as he backed away from the woman and turned to Ji. "See that, Ji! I've expanded our forces by fifty percent in a matter of minutes!"

"If you keep that up, we'll be unstoppable," Ji said.

The three stared at each other before the woman asked, "Do you have a strategy?"

Shoving a pile of papers covered in cobwebs off the table, Fletcher set down a map of Affer. "The weakest species, besides us, are the elves. Even better, their kingdom is on a peninsula far from any other species. Our initial target is here," Fletcher said, pointing to the elven city, IItu. "This is the smallest and weakest city in the whole world, making it a good starting point. But first, we need to prepare, so we won't be attacking there anytime soon. Any questions?"

The room was silent until Ji slammed his fist on the table and exclaimed, "Crystal!"

"What?" Fletcher asked, worried his friend had taken more damage to the head than he thought.

"As a name for her. I figured Crystal sounded nice."

"What do you think?" Fletcher asked the woman.

"Fine with me. Anything's better than having no name," Crystal said.

Fletcher waited for Crystal or Ji to ask something, but when they didn't, he moved on. "Since neither of you have any questions and Crystal joined us, I'm going hunting. Do you want to come, Ji?" Fletcher asked, already heading out.

"You're not going to catch anything without me," Ji said, but stopped when he felt a tug on his shirt.

"Thank you for the name. It's the kindest thing anyone's ever done for me," Crystal said, genuine gratitude in her eyes.

"Don't mention it," Ji said, going out the door before pausing and turning back. "And thanks for not killing me earlier. I just became free, so I don't want to die yet."

ELEVEN

BANG... BANG... BANG... The heavy blows of metal hammering on metal rang throughout the castle workshop as Fletcher forged his second weapon as a free man. Sweat poured from his brow and rained onto the stone floor, forming a small puddle at his feet.

It had been twelve days since Fletcher and Ji arrived at the castle, and they had already made progress. On the second day, they began setting traps to catch wildlife. There were plenty of small animals roaming outside the city, but they didn't yield much. The larger ones, like bison and elk, provided significantly more meat, but were considerably harder to kill and dress. Ji was getting better at butchering, so Fletcher let him do most of the work while he put his efforts into making the traps. The only thing they needed now was a fridge or freezer. But when Admont fell, electricity, refrigeration, cars, and other modern-day luxuries didn't exist. This meant they had to constantly kill animals for food until they set up a system to make jerky.

"Hey, do you want to spar?" Ji asked Fletcher, poking his head into the castle forge.

"Give me five to ten minutes," Fletcher said, holding up the grip he was working on.

"Is this your first weapon as a free man?" Ji asked, walking farther into the room.

"No, this is my second. I've already made a sword for myself, and this one is for you. I want you to try it and let me know what you think of it."

"I'm sure I'll be happy with anything you make."

"I'm not talking about the quality. I'm talking about the type of sword and how it feels."

"Considering I've only used a sword once before, I don't think I'll like how it feels no matter what," Ji said, watching Fletcher work before he sat in a rugged leather chair. "I hope we can succeed in freeing our kin. Living as I please instead of serving the demons makes me realize how much was taken from us."

"We will succeed. We're going to free every last human on Affer, and I'm going to restore this kingdom."

"Are you going to appoint yourself as king?" Ji asked, figuring he should.

"Of course, when we succeed in freeing our kind, it will be because of me. You've already helped me, and I'll have more along the way, but I was the spark that caused the fire. So it's only right for me to become king. I'll give you a high-ranking position, but if you're competent, I'll appoint you as my right-hand."

"I don't care about power; I just want to be happy and free."

"Same here," Fletcher muttered, inspecting the grip and finally feeling happy with it. "Perfect, I'll assemble the weapon, and you can test it out."

"You mean I can kick your ass with it?"

"Let's see you back those words up when we're fighting."

Ji's seax sword collided with Fletcher's longsword. The otherwise peaceful courtyard rang with the sounds of the two men sparring.

"Put more power into your blows, Ji."

"I'm trying to, but my leg still hurts, and I don't want to injure you by accident."

"Don't worry about me. Just don't aim for the head or neck," Fletcher said, swinging at him.

Ji parried and countered, missing Fletcher's chest by less than an inch.

"That's more like it," Fletcher said, stepping forward and ramming his shoulder into Ji.

Stumbling back from the hit, Ji tried to keep his balance but ended up falling back. As he fell, Fletcher swung at him again, this time coming from the left. Ji twisted his body slightly and stopped the attack with the flat of his blade as he hit the ground. Shoving the weapon away, Ji looped his ankle around Fletcher's right foot and pulled it toward him, throwing him off balance and knocking him down.

As Fletcher tried to catch himself, he dropped his sword but used his arms to cushion his fall. Rolling onto his back, he saw Ji standing and holding both weapons.

"I think this is my win."

"We're not done yet!" Fletcher said, jumping up.

"This isn't going to end well for you," Ji said with a sigh. "Just admit you lost this round."

"A warrior never gives up! The only way he'll lose is by dying."

Ji shook his head but pushed forth nonetheless. Knowing it would be challenging to fight with two weapons, he shoved the seax sword back in its sheath and held the longsword in his right hand.

"You're using that wrong; it's a two-handed weapon."

"Who cares? You can't win this anyway, whether I use one, two, or no hands."

"The last one doesn't even make sense! If you're going to

talk shit, at least make it logical," Fletcher said, giving Ji a disapproving look.

"Do I get points for trying?"

"For trying at what?! You should have stopped at two hands! Now quit messing around and attack me!"

Ji didn't need to be told again and swung Fletcher's sword at him. Ducking underneath it, Fletcher tackled Ji. Unfortunately for him, Ji braced himself and stayed upright.

Before Fletcher was able to retreat, Ji slammed the pommel into his back, right above his cut. Losing his grip, Fletcher slumped to the ground and felt the blade press against his throat.

"Is this my win now?"

"Yes, I admit you have bested me. Just don't hit so close to my wound next time," Fletcher said as Ji removed the blade from his neck.

"Sorry!"

"Don't worry about it, you did great," Fletcher said, standing. "You're exceptional when you don't hold back."

"I'm not trying to, but I've never sparred before," Ji said, handing Fletcher his sword.

Fletcher reached out and grabbed his weapon. "Neither have I. I trained to fight, and I've used the weapons I forged to make sure they meet standards. But besides that, we have the same amount of fighting experience."

"Alright, let's go again," Ji said, drawing his sword.

Fletcher raised his weapon, waiting for Ji to make the first move.

Ji swung at Fletcher's torso, only for his attack to be blocked. Fletcher instantly countered, jabbing his blade at the other man's chest. Ji narrowly dodged the attack, the blade catching the fabric of his shirt and marring a thin layer of skin underneath. Fletcher didn't give Ji a chance to catch himself, though, and slashed at his legs, making contact with his right calf.

Ji screamed as the metal of Fletcher's sword wounded him.

"Sorry, Ji!" Fletcher said, putting his weapon down. "I didn't mean to swing so hard."

"I know you can't make armor without help from a more experienced blacksmith, but do you think you can make some sort of protection?" Ji asked, sitting on the flagstone floor.

"I'll do my best," Fletcher said, grabbing a med kit they had brought with them. "For now, let's bandage and clean this so we can go for a few more rounds."

"You want to keep fighting?"

"Yeah. Why, do you want to call it quits already?"

"No. I'm just getting started," Ji said with a smirk. "I told you I would kick your ass, and I'm already one for one. I want to rack up these wins while I have the chance."

"So you're not counting this match as my win?" Fletcher asked as he grabbed a clean cloth and soaked it in a bucket of soapy water they had prepared beforehand.

"Of course not, you injured me!"

"You're acting like I chopped your leg off," Fletcher said, cleaning the shallow cut.

Fully cleaning the wound, Fletcher wrapped it and stood, offering Ji a hand up. "Ready?"

"Bring it on," Ji said, raising his sword. "I can go all day."

TWELVE

After the two of them were done sparring for the day, Ji made his way over to the bathing room in the castle to wash up before he headed off to bed.

Stripping down, Ji grabbed a towel and made his way inside the large space, but quickly turned back when he spotted Crystal already in the bath. He didn't even take three steps before she called out, "Leaving already, Ji?"

"Um, yeah... I didn't know you were in here, sorry," Ji said, covering himself with the towel.

"Who cares. All of the angels' slaves were forced to share everything, including bathrooms to wash up in, so I'm used to nudity and being seen naked."

Ji looked back at Crystal, who was resting her arms on the marble tile that surrounded the in-ground tub.

"Are you just going to stand there, or are you going to join me?" Crystal asked.

"It feels wrong to join you."

"Suit yourself," Crystal said, turning her back to Ji and making her way to the center of the pond-sized bath.

With her back to him, Ji could see that it was covered with scars. "How did you get those scars? If you don't mind me asking."

"Which ones?"

"The ones on your back," Ji said, curious about the others but deciding it was better if he didn't pry too much.

"They're from being whipped."

"I'm sorry."

"Don't take pity on me. I hate that," Crystal said in an annoyed tone.

Ji walked over to the edge of the bath and sat, keeping the towel wrapped around his waist and trying not to stare at Crystal. He dipped his legs in the tub and let out a slight grunt of pain as the fresh cut on his calf touched the cold water.

"What happened?" Crystal asked, noticing Ji's leg.

"Sparring with Fletcher," Ji said as he watched the water become tainted red with his blood.

"That man is dangerous."

"He is, but that's the leader we need."

"Not if he ends up burning Affer to the ground, because I know he would."

"You sound afraid of him."

"I am. He's dangerous, rash, and has nothing to lose but his whole life's purpose. That is a very deadly combination," Crystal said, her golden amber eyes staring at Ji before she dipped her hair in the water, washing out the shampoo.

Ji didn't know how to respond, so he stayed quiet before changing the subject. "Do you feel free?"

"That's a stupid question, Ji. We're struggling to survive, while the other species have virtually everything they need to live comfortably and then some," Crystal said, getting out of the bath. "I'm done. It's all yours."

"You don't have to go!" Ji said, standing.

"It's fine," Crystal said, making her way out the door before turning back. "Just because you aren't a slave doesn't mean you're free."

Once she was gone, Ji let out a sigh and gazed up at the domed ceiling. "That didn't go so well."

THIRTEEN

Fletcher set down a small pile of papers on the dining hall table and spread them out. "From the information I got about IItu, it looks like the best plan of attack would be to go through here." He pointed to a map of the sewer system. "Since the city is so small, the security is minimal, and the sewer system has no protection whatsoever. Additionally, they only have two hundred thirty guards and no military."

"So it's going to be three humans versus more than two hundred elves?" Ji asked, not liking those numbers.

"At the start, it will be. However, if we can get to the human quarters and free everyone, we can flip the odds in our favor."

"By how much?" Crystal asked. "The majority of them won't be able to fight, so it will only help if there are two to three hundred slaves."

"Let me do you one better," Fletcher said, grabbing a sheet of paper. "According to this, there are over five hundred humans in the city."

"Wait, but aren't those papers from here in the castle?"

"Yeah, and?"

"Do you know how old those documents are?! They can't be right," Ji said in frustration.

"Relax, I'm messing with you," Fletcher calmly said. "Of

course I realize they would be way out of date. Plus, it wouldn't make sense for the cities to have a slave population back then."

"So where did you get them from?" Crystal asked, wondering if Fletcher was pulling this info out of his ass.

"I traded for them."

"Now I have even more questions," Ji said. "Please explain to us how you acquired these papers, Fletcher."

"Remember last month when I was gone for six days, and then I returned and left later that week for four more days?" Fletcher asked, continuing when Ji and Crystal nodded in response. "I was out trading for information. I scavenged the city and filled a few small boxes with valuables. Then I loaded them into the car, and headed back to the main road and down south. I stopped at the dirt path leading to the Yoxtoll Forest and waited. It took time, but eventually I came across a traveling merchant who didn't mind that I wouldn't get out of the car or show my face. I asked him for all the info on IItu that he could provide me, and he agreed."

"I think he scammed you," Ji said, not liking how this was sounding. "Why would he have the exact papers you needed on him?"

"He didn't, let me finish my story," Fletcher said, resuming where he had left off. "He didn't have anything on him, so he went back to his home city of Cartin—"

"HE'S AN ELF!" Ji shouted.

"So what? I was only talking to the elves. Why would I ask for information on an elven city from anyone but an elf?!"

"Why would he give you incriminating data on the kingdom he lives in?! Who would sell out their own species?"

"He wasn't selling them out, Ji, so stop interrupting me and let me finish my story! Now, where was I...? He went back to Cartin, and we agreed to meet up in the same spot in one week."

"So you don't know if the information he provided you is correct or not?"

"What's with the attitude, Ji?!"

"I think it was a good idea," Crystal said, crossing her arms over her chest and looking between Ji and Fletcher.

"See, why can't you be more like Crystal?"

"What?! Why am I the bad guy?!"

"Moving back to the whole point of this meeting: the plan to conquer IItu," Fletcher said, tired of wasting time. "We'll enter the city through the sewer system. But the night before we do, I want to sneak in and disable the alarms. That way, the ward, which is where the guards spend most of their day, won't flood out into the streets and kill us immediately."

"When will we attack?" Ji asked, taking the map of the sewer system and viewing it.

"October first, in the morning."

"Why not at night?" Ji asked.

"Because everything is going to be locked up during the night, and in the morning, everything is open, but the city won't be alive quite yet."

"That makes sense."

"I would hope so, I spent years thinking of it," Fletcher said. "Make sure you're ready for the battle, because October is less than two months away."

"Are you going to make armor?" Ji asked.

"I made us leather armor. What more do you want?"

"I don't know, maybe a set made of metal. Also, the gauntlets are too tight."

"I'll make you a shield and add a metal plate to the breastplate."

"Wait, I thought you were a blacksmith?" Crystal asked.

"I am—"

"He just sucks at making armor," Ji finished for Fletcher.

"That's not true. I can make great armor. I just have trouble getting the proportions right."

"So you can only make armor for decoration," Crystal stated, causing Ji to burst out laughing.

"This meeting is done! I'm going to go train," Fletcher said, leaving the papers on the table and heading out the door. "If you two intend to survive, you might want to do the same!"

FOURTEEN

Tor woke up that chilly October morning thinking it would be another normal day. Getting out of bed, he headed over to the brickyard. Loading a cart, he prepared to take a thousand bricks across the city, where they were constructing the new human quarters. The previous building had been converted into the new ward, and the old ward was temporarily housing the slaves.

Tor would have to take over two dozen trips to deliver all the bricks. Not that he wasn't used to it, because he had been doing most, if not all, of the heavy labor for IItu for twenty-three years.

Ever since he was a kid, Tor had been bigger than everyone else his age. Now, as a fully grown adult, age thirty-six, he stood at six feet eight inches and weighed two hundred fifty-three pounds of raw muscle. With his large size and immense strength, he had been put to work as a laborer from the beginning. He hated it, but after so many years, he became accustomed to the demanding work and put on considerable muscle, becoming the strongest slave in the elven kingdom.

Looking over at the entrance to the brickyard, Tor noticed Potin, one of the elves who oversaw the slaves, coming over to him.

"Tor, hurry it up! The workers are almost out of bricks, and we can't have them standing around waiting on you!"

Tor let out a frustrated grunt but kept going. He might have been the strongest in IItu, but he was still a slave, and currently he had to get a heavy cart full of bricks across the city.

With the cart full, Tor grabbed the handles and started marching down the street.

"Tor, sometimes I feel that you humans aren't grateful to us. Sure, you're slaves, but we give you shelter, food, clothes, and all your necessities. On top of that, we treat you the best out of every species. You know that, right?" Potin said, stopping to lecture Tor.

"No, I'm grateful, sir," Tor lied, wanting to smash the elf's face with one of the bricks in the cart.

"As you should be," Potin said, walking ahead.

Tor kept marching toward the build site, now in view but still another twenty minutes away at his current pace.

"You see that, Tor? That's where we need to be! At an average pace, that's seven minutes away, at the most."

"I'll try to make it in ten."

"Let's try for eight! That's a full extra minute I'm giving you, which is more than generous."

Generous, my ass, Tor thought, but kept walking.

Farther down the street, he heard shouting. Turning to his left, Tor tried to see what was going on. "Is that something we should be worried about?" he asked, stopping and facing Potin.

"I'm sure it's nothing, let's keep moving."

Before Tor could respond, several elves ran past them, splattered in blood.

"RUN! WE'RE BEING ATTACKED!" one of them screamed as they sped past.

"We need to help!" Tor said, dropping the cart and standing straight.

"Are you nuts?! That's not our job; that's what the guards are for! I'm getting out of here! If you want to die, then so be it!" Potin said, turning the other way and running off.

Tor shook his head and walked in the direction of the chaos.

FIFTEEN

letcher stabbed an elf in the chest and pulled the sword out of his dying body, moving on to his next target without hesitation.

Ji, Fletcher, and Crystal snuck into IItu through the sewers and exited right into the town square, where they immediately started killing any guards in sight. They infiltrated the city last night and quickly cut the alarm's power. Unfortunately, they didn't have a chance to scout the place, as the night patrol nearly spotted them.

Heading back through the sewers, they returned to the car and camped out there until it was time to begin the ambush. Going over everything once more, they agreed Fletcher would stay and draw attention to the main square while Ji and Crystal made their way to the largest building in the city, which housed the slaves. Fletcher also instructed Ji and Crystal not to kill the civilians and only target the guards and anyone else who attacked them.

"Fletcher, I think we need to readjust the strategy!" Ji shouted as they were swarmed by more guards than expected. "There are too many elves here!"

"Stick to the plan! I'll hold the city square down; go with Crystal, and free our kin!" Fletcher ordered as he beheaded an elf.

Ji let out a frustrated grunt. He didn't want to leave Fletcher to fight alone, but he knew they needed help. "Fine, but you better not die!" he said, cutting down another elf and sneaking away with Crystal.

"YOU ELVES ARE WEAK!" Fletcher yelled, drawing more guards over to him. "I EXPECTED TO BE A TOUCH AWAY FROM DEATH, BUT NONE OF YOU HAVE EVEN WOUNDED ME! I SEE WHY THE ELVES ARE THE WEAKEST SPECIES ON AFFER!" Fletcher parried an attack and killed his fifth elf. Another three guards entered the city square, bringing the total to seventeen elves. Even though he was greatly outnumbered, Fletcher wasn't worried, as the elves were weaker than he expected them to be.

Sprinting forward, Fletcher dodged a strike and jabbed the elf in the ribs. He blocked a shortsword from another and kicked the guard in the stomach, stabbing him in the neck as he fell. Ducking under a swing, Fletcher pulled his sword free and sliced his enemy in half.

The battle had barely started, but the city center was already covered in blood, corpses, and guts.

With more elves dropping, the remaining ones became hesitant to act. Five of them circled Fletcher, waiting for him to move. Feinting a jab, Fletcher stepped back and spun around, driving his longsword through an elf's sternum. Pulling his blade out, he blocked two swords simultaneously and shoved them back. Before he was able to kill either, another elf charged at him from the side. Timing the attack, Fletcher waited and dodged, moving in and stabbing the elf in the skull. Heading toward the last three, he spotted an opening and stabbed one in the neck. The elf closest to him ran away, while the other sped toward him. Fletcher swung at the elf's sword so hard he knocked it out of his hands. Stabbing the guard in the chest, Fletcher saw the fear in his eyes fade as he died.

Taking in his surroundings, Fletcher noticed that three guards had run away, and only six remained. He smirked as he moved closer to them, but almost slipped.

I need to be mindful of the ground, Fletcher thought, glancing down at the puddles of blood. But it was too late; that small slip-up gave the elves the confidence to attack. He ducked under the right arm of a guard who overswung and moved behind him. Pivoting, Fletcher drove his blade through the elf's leather armor and spine, ending at his heart.

Having killed numerous elves, Fletcher felt unstoppable, but that changed in a matter of seconds.

Just then, an arrow flew past Fletcher, missing him by little more than an inch. Looking to his left, he saw an elf with an arrow nocked in his bow aimed right at him. Fletcher tried to use the remaining elves as a shield, getting in front of one to block the way, but the archer was merciless and determined to kill him at all costs. He shot the arrow at Fletcher, the metal tip going straight through an elf and into Fletcher's chest.

SIXTEEN

"Nice shot!" Ji exclaimed to Crystal, who had saved his life for the third time that day.

"What would you do without me?"

"I'd rather not think about that."

The two of them made their way toward the human quarters. Since it was such a vital part of the operation, the three of them had gone over which building it was multiple times.

With the entrance in sight, Ji heard footsteps running toward them. Turning around, he saw two elves approaching Crystal from behind. Springing into action, Ji shot past her and drove his sword into the elf on the right.

Pulling the blade out of his body, Ji dodged a jab aimed at his chest. Before he could counter, an arrow shot through the side of the elf's throat, adding another corpse to the city streets.

"Thanks," Ji and Crystal both said at the same time.

"Why are you thanking me? You saved me first," Crystal said as she moved to pull the arrow out of the elf she had shot.

"You helped me out there as well. Let's call it even."

"Nope, we're three to one." Crystal shoved the arrow in her quiver and continued toward the human quarters again.

"Does the winner get a prize?" Ji asked, matching his pace to Crystal's.

"Being alive."

"Wouldn't that be for the loser, since they're the one getting saved more?"

Crystal looked at Ji and raised an eyebrow. "Alright, wise guy."

"I was being genuine!"

Arriving at the oak doors of the building, Ji and Crystal pushed them open and entered an empty room. Ji walked to the middle, where it was open to two stories above, and looked up.

"Is anyone here?! We're going to free you!" Ji shouted, his voice heading upstairs and echoing through the halls.

"That wasn't a good idea," Crystal said, nocking an arrow in her bow.

"Why?" Ji asked, but soon got his answer as elves appeared over the railings.

"It's humans!" one of them yelled before he was shot in the face by Crystal.

"There are two sets of stairs in the front. Help me move this to cover the one on the left," Crystal calmly said, pushing a heavy wooden cabinet.

"Sorry, I didn't know they had guards in here," Ji said, helping her move the piece of furniture.

"You thought they would leave the slaves unattended, without a single elf keeping watch on them?"

"I did. The demons didn't keep their eyes on us when we were in our 'home.'"

Before the two of them could exchange any more words, they heard footsteps a level above them.

"I'll push this the rest of the way, get ready to attack," Ji said.

Crystal nodded and stepped back, standing at the end of the hallway that led to the entryway, and taking aim. Ji let out a grunt as he finished pushing the heavy cabinet in front of the staircase. Backing off, he drew his sword and shield as the first group of elves arrived at the bottom of the stairs. The ones on the right charged straight at Ji, while the ones on the left were caught up on the cabinet, slowing to vault over it. By the time the elves reached Ji, Crystal had already taken out two of them and was aiming at another.

Ji parried a swing with his shield and drove his blade forward into the belly of the elf. He pulled the sword out and rammed into the guard with his shoulder, knocking him down. Acting quickly, Ji raised his weapon and barely blocked a strike. Twisting his body, he brought his sword back and slammed his shield into the elf's jaw. He felt bone crack as his metal shield made contact, and before the elf had a chance to recover, Ji decapitated him.

I have to admit, Fletcher's really good at making swords, Ji thought, surprised by how easily he was cutting through the elves.

Crystal shot another guard in the head, leaving four remaining. "I only have two arrows left, so you have to take care of half of them, Ji!"

"This will give me a chance to save you and make us even," Ji said, taking a few steps back.

"Shut up and focus on the enemy!" Crystal said, keeping a steady aim, waiting for the right moment to attack.

Ji brought his sword up, steadied the weapon, and waited for the elves to move.

The whole room stood still, no one moving an inch, waiting for someone else to act. The blood coating Ji's sword started to run down the blade, seeping between his fingers and dripping onto the floor below.

All of a sudden, Ji rushed forward, slashing his sword and making contact with one of the elves' weapons. Crystal let her first arrow fly after Ji had moved, and it lodged in the ribcage of the elf on Ji's right. As soon as he heard the arrow land, Ji diverted his attention from the elf he had locked swords with and took a step to his right. Swinging his sword as he moved, he cut the elf's stomach, slicing through his leather armor. The elf fell, and his guts spilled out onto the ground.

Ji spun around and resumed his clash with the previous elf, using the flat of his weapon to block an incoming attack. The elf drove forward, using his weight to push Ji and slam him into the wall. The two of them shoved against each other as they both tried to attain dominance.

Ji let go of his shield, grabbing the elf by the shoulder and flipping their positions. Inching his blade closer to his enemy, Ji heard a whooshing sound behind him. Ducking on instinct, Ji dodged the strike, and the blow that was meant for him killed the guard he was just fighting.

Springing backward, Ji collided with the elf behind him. Twisting around, Ji slashed his blade across the guard's throat.

Glancing up, he saw that Crystal had shot the last guard.

"You did well," Crystal said, grabbing the arrows she could reuse.

"You weren't so bad yourself," Ji said, standing.

"Now let's see if there are any humans in this building or if Fletcher was sold erroneous papers."

"Err, *what* paper?"

"Wrong, inaccurate, false, take your pick."

"So you do think Fletcher was scammed?!"

"I never said that."

"You teamed up with him against me during that meeting when he first told us his plan," Ji said, making his way down a hall on the first floor.

"That's not true," Crystal said right behind him, with an arrow in her bow ready to fire. "Just focus on staying alive. We don't know how many elves are in here or how deadly they are."

SEVENTEEN

Fletcher felt the head of the arrow fly into his chest. His vision went dark, and his breathing stopped as the air was forced out of his lungs. He closed his eyes, inhaling deeply, and put his hand over his wound. Calming down, he realized the damage wasn't bad. He was bleeding, but the metal on his leather breastplate and the elf's body had considerably slowed the arrow.

Opening his eyes, Fletcher's head shot up as he heard a loud snap followed by a scream. He saw the archer who had shot him was bent over a man's knee, and it was evident his spine was broken. The large man stood and tossed the elf's limp body aside, staring at Fletcher as he did so.

Purely on instinct, Fletcher raised his sword, clashing with another. Getting his head back in the fight, Fletcher took in his surroundings, seeing another elf rushing at him from his right. He moved his sword at the last second and stabbed the guard in the stomach, then quickly went back to the elf he had been fighting. He straightened out his weapon and blocked another attack, forming a plus sign with the elf's sword. They pushed against each other, waiting for one to lose his grip or back down, but neither did, so Fletcher took a risk. He released the pressure he had been applying to his sword and took a step back.

The elf was thrown off guard by the sudden withdrawal of Fletcher's weapon and tumbled forward. He regained his balance, but in the process left himself open. With a chance to strike, Fletcher stepped forward and stabbed the elf in the ribs, adding another kill to his ever-growing list and moving on to his next target.

Fletcher locked swords with another guard, rotating his weapon around and punching the elf in the face. The elf stumbled back, blood dripping from his nose, but still swung his weapon. Fletcher moved to parry the blow, but failed and was hit. He clenched his jaw as the elf's blade sliced into his left trap. Warm blood flowed out of the wound, and he felt it run down his torso.

Fletcher shoved the blade up and out of his body with the guard of his sword, leaving the elf open. Taking advantage, Fletcher cut off the guard's right arm. The elf screamed as blood gushed from the wound. But Fletcher wasn't done. He rammed into the elf with his shoulder and knocked him down. Getting on top of the guard, Fletcher rammed the pommel of his sword into his face repeatedly. It wasn't long until the elf's skull was shattered and Fletcher's hands were coated in blood. Brain matter covered the hilt of his sword, and the elf was left completely unrecognizable.

"I think he's dead," a deep voice sounded in Fletcher's ear.

He paused and glanced up to see the giant man from before. Lowering his gaze, Fletcher noticed that the town square was empty.

"I do what I must to win," Fletcher said, standing.

"That was more than winning; it was savage. You tore him apart like a starving pack of wolves."

Fletcher let out a crooked grin. "A starving pack of wolves would do whatever it takes to stay alive, regardless of how brutal they must act. I intend to do more than stay alive.

I'm going to free us humans, and I'll do whatever it takes to achieve my goal."

"You're going to free us?" the man asked. "All of us?"

"Every last one."

"That's...that's impossible."

"If you believe it's impossible, then it is. But I believe anything can be done," Fletcher said, wiping the blood off his face and peering at the human quarters.

"You're ambitious," the man said. "By the way, I'm Tor. Tor Rendin."

"Fletcher Rush. I sent my allies to free our kin. If you want to help, grab a weapon and come with me."

"That's the ward, where the guards stay, not the humans," Tor said, pointing at the building.

"What?! Damn it. Ji was right."

"I don't know who Ji is, but the building was recently switched. We humans are now cramped into the previous ward."

Fletcher faced Tor and chuckled. "Take that, Ji, I was right! Although that means he and Crystal are going up against countless guards. Hopefully, they leave when they realize that." Fletcher waved it off, figuring they would be alright. "Tor, show me where all of our kin are. We have a city to liberate!"

EIGHTEEN

"How many elves are in here?!" Ji asked, wiping the sweat from his brow.

"Tired already?" Crystal asked, bending down to grab an arrow embedded in an elf's neck.

"You can't talk! I'm doing most of the work!"

"Is that so? Then why don't you handle the rest of the guards by yourself?"

"Do you promise to bury me after I'm killed?"

"Only for you," Crystal teased, a small smile grazing her face.

"I'm touched," Ji said, heading down the hallway toward the stairs. "We've cleared out this floor, meaning we have two left. Let's hope we find our kin on one of those."

"You might have been right about those documents Fletcher bought."

"If I was, he owes me an armor set."

The two of them made their way up the stairs and stood still once they reached the landing, listening for any signs of life, whether it be elves or humans. When they only heard a few creaks of the wooden floorboards, they exchanged a glance and moved down the hallway to their right. They made it halfway down the hall when they heard a pair of footsteps sprinting toward them, followed by a screaming elf.

Turning around, Crystal let her arrow fly, headed directly for his heart, but the elf knocked it away with his shield and kept running at them. Ji moved closer to the elf and raised his sword, getting ready to attack the guard charging at him. When he was in striking distance, Ji swung his sword and made contact with his left ribs. Ji expected the blade to slice into the elf, piercing his lungs and killing him off with ease, but the two sets of chainmail the guard was wearing underneath his clothes stopped him. As Ji pulled his sword away, the elf raised his weapon and swung at his head.

Without hesitation, Ji moved his left arm to protect his head, and felt a sharp pain as the elf's blade slashed into him, cutting his triceps and forearm.

"Pesky scum," the elf growled at Ji.

Ji looped his left arm around the sword and tilted the left side of his body downward, twisting the elf's arm and giving himself a chance to attack. Flipping his seax sword, Ji drove the blade into the elf's thigh, shoving it in an inch before letting go of the guard's sword and backing off. As soon as he stepped back and out of the way, Crystal shot another arrow, this time hitting her mark. The sharp metal flew right through the elf's throat, spurting out blood as his corpse hit the ground.

"We need to take care of that wound," Crystal said, putting her bow down and looking at his arm, which was dripping blood.

"I've had worse," Ji said, setting his sword and shield down and taking off the armor on his arm. "But something to stop the bleeding would be great."

"Sit down, I have a roll of gauze in my quiver."

Ji sat and let Crystal bandage his wounds. Neither cut on his arm was deep, but he was still in pain. "I think we should wait for backup."

"From who? It's only Fletcher and us."

"You're right," Ji said with a sigh. "I underestimated how difficult taking on two hundred thirty elves would be. Maybe this isn't possible."

"Then why are you here?" Crystal asked, tying off the gauze. "You're scared of dying, and that's why you're weak." Crystal stood and offered Ji a hand.

He stared up at her and grabbed her hand. "I do fear death," he said, standing. "And I'm not as strong as you or Fletcher, but I'm not weak."

"Then prove it to me. We have two levels left, so fight like you're not afraid."

Ji watched Crystal head down the hall before he grabbed his sword. He glanced down at his shield lying on the floor, before looking back at Crystal and deciding to continue without it.

The two cleared the level they were on with no signs of any other humans. Feeling disappointed, they made their way to the last floor. At this point, both of them were tired, and Ji's arm was hurting more by the minute.

"Let's finish this quickly and efficiently," Crystal said. "I have three arrows left, and they're at the end of their life."

"There's only one room here," Ji said, surveying the small landing. Eyeing the lone door, he walked over to it, opened it, and froze in his tracks.

"Why'd you—" Crystal paused as she peered over his shoulder. "Oh."

Inside was a total of fourteen elves. Four of them were playing cards, one was reading a book in the corner, and two of them were sharpening their weapons. Another three were eating, and the other four were conversing. But they all turned their heads as the door opened.

The room stood still before everyone sprang into action. The elves drew their weapons and charged while Ji and Crystal scrambled out and shut the door. They both had the same idea and stood on either side of the entrance, Ji ready with his sword, and Crystal with an arrow nocked in her bow.

The door burst open and Ji lunged forward, swinging his sword at the nearest elf, killing him with ease. Stepping back, Ji made sure he was out of the elves' range.

Having lost one of their allies already, the elves proceeded with more caution. The next elf slowly walked out of the door, his sword raised, before he was shot in the head by Crystal. The elves stopped after that and waited for someone else to act.

"You go next," one of the elves said, pointing at his kin.

"Me? Why don't you go?!" the elf said, taking a step away from the door.

"I have an idea," another elf said, coming over and standing in front of the door, before looking straight at Ji and throwing his sword at him. "CHARGE!"

Ji managed to dodge the sword, but in that brief second, the elves gained an advantage and were already pouring out of the room. Crystal killed off one more before she switched over to her shortsword, while Ji became engaged in a one-versus-three battle.

The guard who had thrown his sword hurled a right hook at Ji, connecting with his jaw. His teeth bashed into each other, and his brain rammed into the walls of his skull, causing a light wave of dizziness to wash over him. But that wasn't enough to stop him. Right now, he was filled with adrenaline and was determined to win.

Ji screamed out, swinging his sword and cutting the throat

of the unarmed guard. Turning to the other two, he blocked both weapons simultaneously. They pushed down on Ji, forcing him to brace himself to stay upright.

In the blink of an eye, Ji grabbed a dagger from his belt and cut both of the elves' wrists. Only one of them screamed, but they both dropped their weapons, giving Ji a chance to strike. With his dagger, Ji stabbed the elf closest to him in the neck and swung his sword at the second elf's head. The blade pierced his skull and embedded in his brain.

Pulling his weapon out, Ji glanced over at Crystal, who had killed two elves and was fighting one-on-one. Knowing she would be fine, he put his dagger in his belt and walked inside the room. The remaining six elves stood still, and Ji could tell they were afraid. If he felt better, he would grin, but his arm was burning in pain, his head was pounding, and he felt like passing out. Nonetheless, Ji raised his sword.

"How dare you kill my kin, you filthy scum!" one of the elves yelled and charged at Ji.

The guard swung his longsword and collided with Ji's weapon, a loud clang resonating throughout the room as the blades connected.

"I don't know where you humans came from, but you'll both end up dying here!" the elf said, his face inches from Ji's.

Ji kicked the guard in the groin, causing him to keel over in pain. Stepping back, Ji defended himself against two approaching elves, one on either side of him. He blocked numerous attacks and stayed defensive. Even so, the elves still landed multiple hits.

Ji thought he could turn the tables in his favor, as one guard missed. But before Ji made his move, the biggest elf in the room tackled him, lifting him off the ground and slamming him onto a table. Ji spit out a mouthful of blood as he snapped the wooden table in half.

Looking up, Ji stared at the large elf standing above him. He felt afraid and knew this might be where he died, but more than fear, he felt a burning desire to fight and live another day.

As the guard brought his sword down at Ji's head, Ji blocked the swing. He gripped his seax sword in both hands, holding the flat of his blade in his left hand. Ji used all his strength against the elf, but he was clearly weaker, and he watched the guard's blade slowly inching closer to his face. Then the force completely vanished, and Ji saw an arrow sticking in the elf's skull.

"Five left," Crystal said, shooting another elf in the neck. "Make it four."

"Thanks for finally joining me," Ji said, standing.

Crystal drew her shortsword again and charged into battle. She ducked under one blow and stabbed the elf under his chin, going through the roof of his mouth. Pulling her blade back, she moved over to Ji and beheaded the elf he was fighting.

"Two left!" Ji said, eyeing the remaining elves.

"You take the left, I'll take the right," Crystal said, glancing at him briefly and nodding.

Ji nodded back before he shot to the left, Crystal right behind him. The elf locked swords with Ji, but wasn't prepared for Crystal. Taking advantage of the opening, she stabbed the guard between his ribs, missing the bone and piercing his heart. Crystal pulled out her sword and blocked an incoming attack from the last guard, fending him off until Ji swung his sword at the elf's head.

As Ji pulled his blade out, he wobbled before losing his balance and falling.

"JI!" Crystal shouted, dropping her weapon and grabbing him before he fell.

Breathing heavily and closing his eyes, Ji softly said, "I told you I wasn't weak," before he passed out.

NINETEEN

"When I bought those papers from that elf, I wasn't sure if they were legit. Honestly, if only one fact had been right, that would have been fine. As long as that one fact was the slave population, and I see now that it was correct," Fletcher said, observing the hundreds of humans currently pillaging the armory.

"IItu's been under renovation for the last twenty-four years, which is why there's so many humans here," Tor said, picking up the weapon Fletcher had recommended he use and giving it a feel.

"This should be plenty to take over the city. Since I haven't seen Ji and Crystal, I want to send forty men to the ward. Then I'll have sixty take care of any guards left on the streets, while the rest of us head over to city hall to conquer it and kill the overseer."

"Taking control of the ward isn't going to be easy. Are you sure that's all you want to send?"

"Yes. The only thing that matters is taking city hall and killing the overseer. If we do that, it doesn't matter how many guards are left. They'll all surrender when they see we've killed their leader. I just want to make sure Ji and Crystal aren't in there anymore," Fletcher said, before he addressed his new allies. "Listen up! We're about to attack city hall! It's crucial that we take it and kill the overseer! If we fail here, our kin will never be free! The fate of mankind rests on our shoulders, so fight until you die or we have won! This battle will determine the future of Affer for thousands of years to come! So join me in the first step toward freedom!"

The room exploded in cheers as the humans screamed and raised their weapons above them, following Fletcher into battle.

"Sir, there's a large array of humans headed our way!" one of the elves who guarded the city hall frantically said as he burst into the overseer's office.

"Then kill them! It's insulting that you incompetent fools even let them cause this much damage. Where are the guards from the ward? What, are they dead?!" the overseer, Adven, said.

"I'm not sure where they are, sir."

"What do you know?!" Adven snapped, slamming his fist on his desk.

"I know that we are under siege, sir."

Adven face-palmed at that before raising his head and glaring at the elf. "Do you think you're funny?"

"No, sir!"

"I've had enough of these scum," Adven said, standing and walking out of his office. He stopped atop the landing that overlooked the foyer, yelling at the guards below him, "I want everyone in the building in this room, ready to attack! We are going to wash the streets with the blood of humans today, and put them back in their rightful place as slaves!"

The elves glanced up at the overseer before they went to work gathering their kin and preparing to fight the humans.

Fletcher, along with Tor and one hundred seven other humans, stood outside city hall, a grand structure made of travertine, bronze, and oak.

"I hate to admit it, but the elves know how to build," Fletcher said. "The demons built everything out of knightnium and it looked terrible." He made a disgusted face at the thought of Titanan.

"We constructed this building. As I said, the city's been undergoing renovation and we're the ones who do the work," Tor said.

"Then we humans know how to build," Fletcher said, surprised that his kind had constructed this. "But that's not important now. What matters is going inside that building and killing every last elf in there."

"It's not going to be easy," one of the humans said.

"We wouldn't be here if it were," Fletcher responded, facing his allies. "But remember what I said earlier: this battle will decide the future of far more than us! If we conquer Iltu, it will only be a matter of time until the whole elven kingdom is ours, and from there the others will fall into place! SO FIGHT! FIGHT FOR YOURSELF, FIGHT FOR THE SAKE OF OUR FUTURE, FIGHT TO AVENGE OUR ANCESTORS WHO WERE WRONGFULLY KILLED, AND FIGHT FOR FREEDOM!"

Fletcher rushed toward city hall with the group of humans behind him. Instead of bursting through the main door, he veered to the right and jumped through the window. As the glass shattered, every elf in the room turned their head toward him.

"SLAUGHTER THEM!" Fletcher shouted as his allies burst through the doors and windows. None of them hesitated, and everyone charged at the elves.

The guards aimed their bows at the horde, but it didn't matter because the humans were already upon them. Arrows flew, hitting eight people and killing two. But the elves weren't able to fire anymore and were forced to draw their weapons.

"Attack them, you cowards!" Adven screamed at the elves from the second level as he hid behind his two personal guards.

Fletcher sliced an elf in half, his guts unraveling from his torso as they weren't confined to his body any longer. Twisting to his right, he locked swords with another elf, but didn't have a chance to counter as Tor crushed the elf's skull.

"You were right; I love this thing!" Tor shouted over the sounds of battle and held up his greathammer.

"I was a blacksmith! I either learned to pick out good weapons for the demons or they beat me! With your size and brute—" Fletcher stopped talking and recoiled as a dagger flew past his throat. The blade grazed his skin and left a shallow cut along the left side. Letting out a grunt, Fletcher turned his attention to where the weapon had come from, attacking an elf who was grabbing another dagger from his belt. "Bullseye!" he yelled as he stuck his sword in the elf's chest.

That sounded better in my head, he thought.

TWENTY

"Sir Adven, I think we should evacuate. We have lost over half our guards and have barely killed any humans," the overseer's right-hand, Firnock, said.

"How pathetic," Adven muttered in disgust, pulling out his transmitter and frantically sending out a message for help. "We'll head to Ronann and return with an army so massive that the slaves will be begging for mercy before the battle starts!" Adven removed his eyes from the fight and headed down one of the halls to a secondary staircase.

Arriving at the back exit, he opened the door and was met by screaming elves.

"RUN! THEY'RE MONSTERS, THOSE SLAVES!" one of the elves cried, pushing the overseer aside and bolting indoors.

The rest of the elves followed him into the building, seeking safety, which didn't exist there. Adven turned toward the elves who had dashed past him with a look of disdain. "Rude. Don't they know who I am? I'll make sure to punish them when I return."

"Are you sure about that?!" a man asked, pointing a sword at Adven, who turned back around and was met with a group of humans standing in front of him.

"Let's—" Adven said, but was silenced by the human pressing the blade into his neck.

"Go back inside before I stab you," the man said as he stepped forward. "Even though I want to kill you, I don't have that right. That honor goes to our leader."

Adven wanted to yell at the human that he was their leader, but he bit his tongue and walked back toward the foyer, the sword now pressed against his back. *If I knew this was going to happen, I would have ordered every slave to be executed as soon as I woke up.*

The wooden door to the office was kicked open, and splinters flew everywhere as it split in half and came off its hinges.

The room was empty except for a scared elf hiding underneath a desk. He hoped the humans wouldn't find him, but as a pair of footsteps got closer, he started sweating profusely. Then a hand was placed on top of the desk, and a figure leaned down and looked the elf right in the eyes.

"Tor!" the elf exclaimed, letting out a sigh of relief as he calmed down. "I'm so glad you're here! The humans would have killed me if they found me first."

"Nothing's changed, Potin. You're still going to be killed by a human today," Tor said, setting his hammer down, grabbing the elf, and dragging him out from under the table.

"Wait, Tor, we're friends! I—" Potin yelled before Tor slammed his face into the desk so hard he snapped the thing in two.

"Friends?" Tor said, walking to the window and throwing him through it. "Go be friends with your dead kin."

Potin screamed, his voice fading until Tor heard a loud thump. "I wanted to do that for so long," he said with a grin, picking up his hammer and leaving the room.

TWENTY-ONE

"What do we have here?! The mighty leader of IItu was found running off like a coward! Why am I not surprised?" Fletcher said, pointing his sword at the last enemy elf.

"Don't kill me; we can work out a deal! I have power, just don't kill me! Please, please!" Adven cried, begging for mercy as he frantically thought of what to say. "IItu might be small, but trust me, I have power—a lot of power! Killing me is a mistake. As I said, we can work out a deal."

"You want to make a deal?" Fletcher asked, raising an eyebrow.

"Yes! Whatever it is, I'll do it!" Adven said, hope filling his eyes.

"Here's my deal," Fletcher said, squatting down and getting close to the elf. "Undo the hurt you wrought upon my kind. Bring back the humans you've killed. Give my species the life they deserve to live and treat us as your equals instead of looking down on us as though we're nothing more than trash. Then I'll spare your life."

"What...? I can't do that. It's not possible... I can't... I can't go back in time and change something that isn't even my fault! This is why you humans—" Adven shouted before Fletcher drove his blade into the elf's heart.

The overseer let out a gasp, and his eyes widened as the life left them. Pulling out the blade, Fletcher stood, grabbed his sword in both hands, and decapitated the elf.

Cheers erupted throughout the room. The city of IItu was officially theirs, and the humans were free. Bending down to pick up Adven's head, Fletcher took it and marched up the stairwell. He walked to the center of the landing that overlooked the foyer and hoisted it high. "THIS IS WHAT HAPPENS WHEN YOU ENSLAVE OUR KIND!" he yelled, tossing the head into the crowd. "TODAY THE HUMANS OF IITU ARE FREE, AND THIS MARKS THE START OF THE REBELLION! FROM THIS DAY FORTH, THE REST OF AFFER WILL KNOW THAT WE AREN'T THEIR SLAVES! AS TIME PASSES, WE WILL GROW IN POWER, AND THE WORLD'S EYES SHALL FALL UPON US IN FEAR! THEY WILL RUE THE DAY THEY BETRAYED AND SLAUGHTERED US HUMANS, UNTIL WE ONCE AGAIN RULE AS THE STRONGEST!" He raised his fist, causing more cheers to erupt from the crowd. "IF YOU WANT TO SEE OUR MIGHT RETURN, THEN JOIN ME! TOGETHER WE CAN RISE BACK TO THE TOP AND REBUILD ADMONT BEYOND ITS FORMER GLORY! IF YOU ARE WILLING TO LAY DOWN YOUR LIFE SO WE CAN ATTAIN VICTORY, JOIN ME! JOIN ME ON THE QUEST FOR FREEDOM!"

The crowd cheered again. The shouts of the humans echoed through the streets, filling the city with hope as the first of many steps had finally been taken.

TWENTY-TWO

"Lord Varos, I have important news," the demon-king's servant said, walking into the throne room.

"What is it, Jar?" the king asked, peering down at the demon from atop his throne.

"The city of IItu has been overthrown."

"IItu, that small, worthless city? Why would I care about that?" the king asked, grabbing a cigar, cutting off the cap, and toasting the foot.

"Because the ones who conquered the city were...humans."

"Humans?!"

"Yes, My Lord."

"Humans are nothing more than slaves," Varos said, putting the cigar in his mouth. "They'll remember that soon enough."

Jar bowed and left the room, leaving Varos alone.

Despite my hatred for slaves, I want their power to grow, Varos thought as he let out a puff of smoke. "The stronger they become, the weaker they'll feel if they make it to my kingdom."

"That goes to show you why the elves are at the bottom of the food chain. Those pathetic creatures can't even defend themselves against slaves," Xancore, king of the angels, said.

"Don't be so harsh on them, darling. They are lesser beings," the queen, Zyly, said.

"Elves only accomplished one thing, and that ended up being the downfall of their kingdom. But being overthrown by humans, that's a new low for them."

"Don't forget, humans were once the strongest species on Affer, and at the height of their power, the elves were only the third strongest."

Xancore roared in laughter. "I'll never forget what they were capable of before they fell. But those humans are gone. Now they are weak. Centuries of enslavement have broken them both mentally and physically, and the fire inside them has lain dormant for so long it's impossible to reignite."

"I wouldn't overlook them. All it takes is one spark to burn a forest," Zyly said.

"Let them rise in power. I eradicated tens of thousands of them during the Great War, and I'll do it again if I have to."

Zain, the right-hand of the hybrid king, entered the throne room and bowed to the king. "Your majesty, a message has been sent from the overseer of Iltu asking for help. He stated that the humans have overthrown them, and he is headed to Ronann. It also appears that this message was sent on the wrong channel, as neither the overseer nor the elven queen is answering anyone."

"What?!" Lord Melro yelled, standing from "his" throne. "For decades, we've been breeding extra humans to sell, and those tools go and start an uprising?! This ruins our plans!"

"Silence, Melro," Yinny said in a placid tone.

"How are you not overcome with rage?! We have worked on this for the last thirty-five years, and those tools are about to ruin everything!"

"You're more ignorant than I thought. This will aid us, and the timing couldn't be better. We'll continue selling slaves, and hopefully within a few months the elven kingdom will be ruled by humans."

"You're rooting for the tools?!" Melro shouted in rage.

"That's the best possible outcome for us. Both the elves and humans are weak, so let them kill each other."

"And if the elves win?!"

"Then they'll be weaker, which benefits us, and if the humans win, we'll wait for them to come here and kill every last one."

Melro clenched his fists and glared at Yinny. "You're risking years of work—"

"I must be mistaken, but it sounds as if you're angry with me?"

Melro felt his heart sink as Yinny turned toward him. He shrank back as Yinny walked over to him and pulled on the silver chain, clasping his cape, bringing him down to the same height. Only a few inches away from Yinny, Melro was able to see the dozens of scars on his face and, worst of all, the twisted look of insanity and bloodlust that tainted his eyes.

"No, My King, I could never be mad at you."

Yinny grinned before he let go of Melro. "I know. You're too much of a coward for that."

Melro let out a sigh of relief and sat back down in "his" throne. He was still enraged with Yinny, but fear had overtaken him. He had felt it hundreds of times before, and in every instance, the source of the emotion was Yinny, with one exception.

Valadine read the message on his transmitter and turned to his right-hand, Kage, who was the only other one in the room.

"Why must we fight? We've had peace since the Great War, can't it stay like that?"

"Peace has never been an option! It's an illusion," Kage said, glaring at the king. "And if you refuse to strengthen our army as you have for the last four decades, this kingdom will fall."

"We are not at war with anyone. They have no reason to attack us, and we have no reason to attack them."

"That doesn't matter! Another kingdom will not let us be simply because we are peaceful! Both the demons and hybrids have eyed us for years, waiting for an excuse to strike, and now we have to worry about the humans, too!"

"Kage, you must be traumatized by your past life—"

"And you must be a coward because of yours!" Kage said, leaving the throne room and heading to his office.

The dammed were those who were judged as neither good nor bad by the divine council and given a second chance at life. This life would determine their eternal future. They lived exactly one hundred years after they Awoke from the Graveyard of the Dammed, unless they were killed. For that reason, many of the dammed preferred to stay peaceful, like the king. Even the slaves in their kingdom were treated well, working only five hours a day and being assigned jobs at age fifteen.

The day Kage Awoke and walked from the graveyard to the capital, Wingo, he was disappointed. They were the third strongest species on Affer, but he couldn't see it. All he saw was a kingdom in decline. He had watched the number of guards and soldiers fall each year, and to make matters worse, less than half of them knew how to fight. He had done his best to trick the other kingdoms into thinking they were strong, but that changed today.

"Sir."

Kage looked over to see his right-hand, Whitfield, standing in the doorway. "Come in, and close the door behind you."

Whitfield nodded and did as Kage asked, before sitting across from him.

"I have been a dammed for twenty-eight years, even though I died centuries ago. I always wondered why the divine council Awoke me at this time, but now I understand. Our kind is weak. We have a king who is overcome by fear, and people who are unprepared for war." Kage paused and clenched his fist. "I will no longer sit idle. Strengthen, Ugondt, Flinden, Narain, and Huslond. I want our army to triple in power over the next eighteen months."

"I'll see to it right away," Whitfield said, standing and bowing. "What about here?"

"Don't worry, I'll take care of Wingo." Kage waited for his right-hand to leave before he stood and walked out to his balcony. He stared up from the pit the palace sat in. The white sunhem trees of Yoxtoll Forest towered above him, with the many houses built in them in worse shape than the palace. Frowning at the sight, his eyes clouded with rage. "I died a king in my first life...and I will die a king in this one."

"Mother!" Princess Allica said, bursting into the throne room. "Why won't you attack the humans?!"

Queen Rinn looked down at her daughter from her throne. "Why would I engage in a battle with mere slaves? They've never posed a threat to us, and they never will."

"Do you hear yourself, mother?!" Allica said, her voice rising.

"Watch your tone with me."

"The humans have taken over one of our cities, and if we do nothing about it, they will grow in power until they take control of another."

"You're giving those scum too much credit; they have nothing. Despite my efforts, IItu has always been a city of no value. The humans can use everything there, but within a matter of weeks, they'll be begging for help."

Allica glared at her mother. "If you believe that, then you must be a fool. Even if you are right, the rest of Affer will set its eyes on us. They already view us as soft, but if we do nothing, the elven kingdom will be overthrown, either by humans or another species." Turning away from the queen, Allica stormed out of the throne room.

"Lock her in her bedroom for the rest of the week," Rinn said, looking at one of her bodyguards, who nodded and left. Becoming quiet, the queen thought about what her daughter had said before facing her right-hand. "Light, take your team and pay the humans a visit."

TWENTY-THREE

hy does my arm hurt? Ji thought as he woke up, slowly opening his eyes to a dim room.

"Feeling better?" Crystal asked, putting her book down as Ji slowly sat up.

"What happened?" Ji glanced at his bandaged arm.

"You and I took care of the ward, and you were wounded in the process."

"Ward?"

"Fletcher explained it in Admont. It's where the guards spend most of their day. They train there, maintain and clean their weapons, armor, even live there, and that was the building you and I wiped clean yesterday."

"Wait... You're telling me that we took out the guard stronghold all by ourselves?!"

"All five floors, for a total of sixty-two guards killed."

Ji sat back in bed with a smile on his face. "I can't believe we captured IItu." He turned to Crystal. "What happened with Fletcher?"

"He found where the slaves were staying and freed them. After that, he raided the armory, armed anyone willing to fight, and stormed city hall. A few dozen men came to the ward shortly after you passed out and brought you to a doctor, who stitched your arm. While the city hall was being overthrown, I helped kill the guards on the streets."

"Fletcher owes you and me for sending us to the wrong building."

"In his defense, the ward was recently changed, so the papers he bought were correct."

The two became quiet after that until Ji looked around the empty room and asked, "Was no one else injured in the battle?"

"We lost eleven men, and twenty-three were injured."

"Why is no one else in here?"

"Because you've been unconscious for over a day, and everyone else has already left. Fletcher was the last to leave. He came to see you this morning."

"How badly was he hurt?"

"Worse than you, but nothing that could keep him here. A cut on his left trap was the worst, and his ribs were bruised, but none of them were broken."

"I want to get out of here," Ji said, throwing the covers off him and standing. "I'm hungry."

"The doctor should check on you before you leave," Crystal said. "After that, I'll show you where you can get something to eat."

Ji nodded and sat back down. "Thanks for waiting until I woke up and for saving my life."

"Which time?" Crystal asked with a smirk.

TWENTY-FOUR

"This is quality armor! I could've used this when we were attacking the city," Fletcher said, looking at the shiny steel armor set. He ran his hand along the gauntlet up to the pauldron.

"Didn't you say you were a blacksmith?" the forger of the armor asked.

"I did, but I wasn't good at crafting armor. I could never get the proportions right. I tried, but after beating me so many times and still failing, the demons put me strictly on weapons, something I'm very good at, by the way," Fletcher said, letting go of the armor. "But I'm not here for weapons."

"I take it you want me to craft as much armor as I can?" the blacksmith asked.

"Exactly! You catch on fast. Forge what you can; it doesn't have to be perfect. Whatever you need, let me know and I'll provide it to the best of my abilities," Fletcher said before he departed, heading into the streets of IItu.

"What's next?" Tor asked, matching Fletcher's stride.

"Let's see... I've freed all the humans and given them somewhere to rest. I took away every weapon from the elves and worked out an agreement to coexist with them. I have a group of humans cleaning the city, washing the streets, and burying the corpses. I have weapons and armor being forged as we speak. We passed out every transmitter the city had and put everyone on channel seven hundred twenty-six. The hospital is fully staffed, and everyone who was injured has been cared for. I'll need to assign people to different posts, but that can wait until tomorrow. Right now, I want to start assembling a strong team of allies, and that will be it for today," Fletcher said as he walked down the street, going nowhere in particular.

"I know some strong humans," Tor said, stopping and putting his hands in his pockets.

Fletcher stopped as well and looked back at him. "Introduce me to them."

An hour later, the ward's training room was filled with over two dozen people.

Fletcher examined them before he started speaking. "I need a team that is great at fighting and willing to charge into battle no matter what. We've captured one city out of seven, and that's only in the elven kingdom. If we are to succeed, I need a strong group standing by my side. Tor informed me that all of you are strong individuals, so I'm expecting to be impressed by a few of you. I'm going to pair you up randomly and have you spar to gauge your skills."

"Sir, none of us have any fighting experience," one of the men in the crowd said.

"I understand that. I'm not expecting perfection or seeking an unbeatable soldier. What I'm looking for is someone with grit who is willing to stand back up when they get knocked down. If you want to fight for your freedom, then grab a weapon, and I'll start pairing you together."

The room stood still before the group made their way to the table Fletcher had set up. It was covered with weapons, mostly swords, but there were a few battleaxes and a couple of spears. The clatter of metal being picked up and put back down filled the training room as the men tested out different options.

After a few minutes, they had decided on a weapon and lined up, waiting for Fletcher.

"The pairings are going to be random. I'll do a couple of bouts and see how capable everyone is," Fletcher said, walking down the line. "Also, try not to hurt or kill your partner."

Fletcher matched everyone up and watched them fight, keeping an eye on each person until he narrowed his gaze down to three people that he was impressed with. "Who are they?" he asked Tor, pointing to them.

"The first one is Ethan Aswell. He was a builder but helped me as a laborer more than anyone else, so I know he's strong. Next is Ryan. He was a sculptor, and is Ethan's older brother. He's weaker than me but has a stronger grip and is far smarter. Lastly, the one on the right is Archer Tavee. He's a jack of all trades, master of none, so he was always being moved around, working different jobs."

"I have an eye for this," Fletcher praised himself.

"Well, they do stand out."

"I'm impressed with the three of them," Fletcher said, turning away from the group and pointing at Tor. "However, I'm curious what you can do."

"Me?" Tor asked as he faced Fletcher.

"Why are you surprised I asked? You look extremely strong, killed two elves in the town square with your bare hands, and dominated when we attacked the city hall."

"I did, but I didn't think anything of it, and I've only fought once until yesterday."

"That means you have potential. How much is up to you," Fletcher said, heading down to the main area. "If you're up for it, I would love to spar with you."

"But you're hurt," Tor said, moving to catch up.

"My wounds aren't that bad. Now, do you want to fight, or was I wrong about you?"

TWENTY-FIVE

"It's been forever since I've had a real meal," Ji said, taking a bite of pasta.

"What was wrong with what we ate in Admont?" Crystal asked.

"The meat was always tough, and we had it every day." Ji held up a spoonful of pasta. "I love meat, but I missed this."

Finishing his meal, Ji stood and grabbed a cookie before heading outside with Crystal. "Where are we going?"

"To see Fletcher. I'm sure he'll want to know you're up, and I heard he and Tor are scouting people to fight by our side."

"Who's Tor?"

"He's a tall, strong human. Supposedly, he saved Fletcher in the town square after he was shot, and—"

"Fletcher was shot?!" Ji blurted, stopping in his tracks.

"I forgot, you don't know about that. When I told you his ribs were bruised, that's why."

"He was shot in the chest?!"

"The wound wasn't deep. His armor protected him, and the arrow passed through an elf before it hit him."

Ji sighed. "I was worried that I didn't have metal armor, but it turns out that Fletcher needed it more."

The two fell silent until they arrived at the ward. Making

their way into the building, they heard the sounds of sparring getting louder as they neared the training room.

Once they stepped inside, they saw that everyone there was surrounding one fight. Lightly pushing a few people aside, Ji and Crystal were able to see who was sparring, and they couldn't help but stare in awe.

"I thought you said Fletcher was shot in the ribs?" Ji said, facing Crystal.

"He was. Either it wasn't as bad as it looked, or your friend is superhuman."

Ji and Crystal watched Fletcher and Tor spar. Tor was wielding a greathammer that Fletcher was constantly dodging and even blocking. They weren't sure when the two started fighting, but it had been long enough for Tor to be sweating and running out of breath.

"Come on, Tor, don't tell me you're tired already?!" Fletcher said.

"We've been sparring for over half an hour!"

"It's only been twelve minutes, Tor."

"Shut up, Archer!" Tor said, wiping the sweat from his forehead.

"A battle would last far longer than this, Tor."

"I'm exhausted and sore from yesterday. In peak condition, I could go for hours," Tor exaggerated, shoving Fletcher back.

Fletcher moved in for the finishing blow, evading a swing from Tor and pressing his blade against his throat.

"That's my win," Fletcher said, removing his sword and sheathing it.

Tor slumped to the ground, panting. "I'm glad we're on the same side."

"Me too," Fletcher said, slapping the man on the back. "You fought well." Turning back to the others, he dismissed them for the night. "Good work today. I saw potential in three of you, whom I'll talk to later. For now, get some rest, and I hope to see everyone back here tomorrow morning."

As the room cleared, Fletcher noticed Ji and Crystal. "I didn't see you two. How long have you been here?"

"Enough to see Tor lose," Crystal said.

"Hey!"

"How are you feeling?" Fletcher asked Ji.

"Definitely not my best. I've had a headache since I woke up, and my whole body is sore, but you were also hurt, and you're already training."

Fletcher just shrugged. "Don't worry about me. My wounds aren't too bad, but I know you passed out, so make sure you recover, and when you feel up to it, I could use your help training the recruits."

"I'll help you wherever I can."

"Thanks, Ji. Currently, the most important thing is to build our army, and the more people helping with that the better off we'll be."

"That isn't enough. I'm sure Lilthral has already heard that we've overthrown IItu. What are you going to do if an army arrives at our front door?" Crystal asked Fletcher.

"First of all, it's more than Lilthral that knows we've taken over. I grabbed Adven's transmitter, and he sent out a plea for help right before I killed him. He sent it on the private channel that all the overseers, kings, and queens are on. So everyone who holds a position of power on Affer knows we attacked this city, and the fact that Adven never responded proves we've won," Fletcher said, looking at Ji, Crystal, and Tor. "Second, I've already taken care of numerous tasks, and I'll take even more precautions tomorrow. There's only so much I can do, and training as many people as possible is going to be our most effective asset."

"Why didn't you respond with his transmitter?" Ji asked.

"Because I didn't think of that," Fletcher admitted.

"Our lives are in your hands; you better not lead us to our deaths," Crystal said, glaring at Fletcher.

"Death is a part of freedom. Blood will be spilled whether we fight this war or stand down and stay as slaves. I'm trying to put humans back at the top where we belong. It's all I've ever thought about...freedom and victory. My only purpose in life is to rectify the wrongs of this world, and I'll do whatever it takes to do that," Fletcher said, curling his hands into fists as he spoke.

"That's what I'm worried about. You don't care how many people you have to drag into the grave to fulfill your dream," Crystal said, turning around and leaving the room.

Ji watched Crystal leave before he said, "I'm going to catch up with her. I'll see you tomorrow."

Tor waited until Ji and Crystal were out of sight before he started chuckling. "He likes her, doesn't he?"

"More than a worm loves dirt. But I don't think he realizes that yet."

"He'll figure it out," Tor said, standing. "I'm heading to bed. See you later."

"Night," Fletcher replied, standing in the empty room for a minute before drawing his sword and training by himself for the next two hours.

Fletcher grunted as he collapsed onto his bed. He had taken temporary residence in Adven's home, and it was the nicest place he had ever stayed. The mansion had plenty of expensive furniture, paintings, and even sculptures adorning every room. He would be having the time of his life if he weren't in such pain.

I shouldn't have trained today, Fletcher thought.

He lay on the bed for several minutes before standing, taking off his shirt, throwing it on the floor, and staring at himself in the mirror. The left side of his torso was swollen and black and blue. It looked worse than it felt, but it still hurt badly.

Removing the bandage that covered the wound on his ribs, he realized he had torn it open. "Great," he mumbled, throwing the bandage away and grabbing a roll of gauze, a dagger, and a needle and thread. Lastly, he fetched a clean cloth and soaked it in soapy water.

Sitting, Fletcher cut the remaining thread, careful not to hurt himself. Once that was done, he cleaned his wound and got to work closing it again. He cried out in pain as he dug the needle into his flesh, but kept going.

Several minutes later, Fletcher finished and bandaged the wound with gauze. Standing, he headed into the bathroom and washed his hands, watching the water turn red. "My hands are stained with my blood now, but I like it better when they're stained with the blood of my enemies."

TWENTY-SIX

"Humans, grab your leader! The one who has overthrown IItu and slaughtered our kin! Tell him we are from Lilthral, sent by the queen, and if he does not talk with us, then we shall view this as an act of war!" an elf yelled up to the front gates.

"What should we do?" one of the guards asked.

"Go grab Fletcher. He's the leader. He has to handle this," the other guard said.

"Who requests a meeting at four in the morning? It's too early for this," the guard complained, but headed off to grab Fletcher.

"Sir...sir, wake up!"

Fletcher grumbled, slowly opening his eyes. "What...?"

"Sorry for waking you, sir. It's still early, but we have a situation at the main gate."

"Are we under siege?!" Fletcher asked, opening his eyes and sitting up.

"No, sir, it's nothing like that. But there is a group of elves that state they are from Lilthral, and they wish to speak with you."

"Wonderful," Fletcher said sarcastically, grabbing a pair of clothes and glancing at the clock. "Who wants to negotiate at four in the morning?"

"That's what I said!"

Walking out of the mansion, Fletcher made his way toward the main gate.

Reaching it, he walked up the stairs and peered down at the seven elves standing outside the city walls. "State your purpose."

"We are here on behalf of Queen Rinn Radamon, who wishes to discuss a peace treaty," the elf who appeared to be in charge said.

"I'll let you in, and we can talk in the city hall. But if you're seeking peace, you're not going to find that here."

"Scum. We should kill these worthless slaves instead of wasting our time with them," the elf grumbled and turned to his cohort. "Be on your guard. I'm not sure if the humans will try something."

The gates opened, and the elves walked into the city, leaving their car outside.

The leader of the group walked up to Fletcher and stopped a few feet away. Neither bothered to feign pleasantries to the other.

"I am Light Litchtree, right-hand of the queen."

"Fletcher Rush, leader of the rebellion."

Light glared at Fletcher before he headed off in the direction of the city hall, walking right past him.

"You two stay at your post. I'll be fine," Fletcher told the guards stationed at the front gate, before he went to catch up with the elf.

"If we wanted to kill you, it wouldn't matter if you had a hundred men fighting next to you."

"Tell that to the corpses of your kin that we buried."

Light gave Fletcher a death stare, touching the grip of his sword before calming down. "If it weren't for Lady Rinn, I would have killed you and every last human in this city. Be grateful the queen is kinder than I am."

"Your queen sounds benevolent; I look forward to meeting her someday."

"You'll be dead long before you ever set foot in Lilthral."

"You underestimate me and my army," Fletcher said, his voice laced with confidence. "We humans will reclaim our freedom and take back our rightful spot as the most powerful species on Affer."

"Not only are you delusional, but you're an idiot."

"We'll see if you think that after I conquer your kingdom."

A few minutes later, they arrived at city hall and went up to the second story. Having already walked through the building, Fletcher knew the layout and where he wanted to talk.

He pushed open an oak door and turned on the lights before sitting in one of the soft white leather chairs. In Fletcher's opinion, this was the nicest room in IItu. A grand hand-carved wooden table sat in the center with a small skylight above it that cast a soft glow into the room.

"What has the mighty right-hand of the queen come to talk about?" Fletcher asked when Light had taken his seat at the other end of the table.

"Queen Rinn has given you and your people an offer. If you stand down, promising not to attack any of our other cities, and abide by our rules, we will let you integrate into our society."

"Not that it makes a difference, but what about the other humans? Will they remain slaves?"

"Of course! Why would we free them? Consider yourself lucky to be given this offer." Light scoffed at Fletcher.

"I expected that to be the case, but as I said, it doesn't make a difference in my decision. I refuse your offer, not only because I don't trust you, but because your kind and every other species needs to pay for the wrongs you committed against my people," Fletcher said, standing and putting his hands on the table, leaning slightly forward. "If you think I'm going to stand down and be suppressed by you simply because you have more power, then you're sorely mistaken. I won't stop until I'm dead or I've won, and if that means going to war with you, well, I'm already prepared for that."

"You're in over your head. But so be it. If you want war, war you shall receive," Light said, standing and walking over to Fletcher. "But understand that every human we kill...their lives are on you."

"I get the feeling you don't like me, Mr. right-hand. But don't worry, save that hatred, because we will meet again, and when we do, we'll be fighting to the death," Fletcher said with a sly smirk.

Light punched Fletcher in the chest, causing him to keel over and his wound to reopen.

Fletcher groaned, already feeling the bandages under his shirt getting wet with blood. "I'll get you back for that."

Light punched Fletcher in the face, knocking him to the floor. He pulled out his dagger and was about to stab Fletcher, but he froze. Remembering the order from the queen, he sheathed the weapon and stood.

"You're not going to kill him?!" one of the elves asked.

"The queen ordered us not to kill anyone, Ingrid. Let Ronann take care of these scum," Light said, leaving the room.

Ingrid glared at Light as he left. Bending down, he grabbed Fletcher by his collar. "Humans have been slaves for the last four hundred seventy-three years for a reason. You might have captured IItu, but when Ronann arrives, you'll understand just how weak and helpless you are."

Ingrid let go of Fletcher and stood. Raising his head, Fletcher saw a boot flying at his face. Then he blacked out.

TWENTY-SEVEN

Fletcher's eyes shot open, and he immediately remembered what had happened. He jumped out of bed, and a jolt of pain struck him.

"Careful! You don't want to tear your wound open again," Ji said.

"That doesn't matter!" Fletcher said, walking out of the room.

"Fletcher, where are you going? You need to stay in bed."

"I don't have time for that! The city next to us is going to send their army here, and if we don't act now, they're going to kill all of us!"

"Slow down! What happened?! I heard a few elves came here, sent by the queen, and they talked to you. But what happened after that?" Ji asked, sprinting to catch up.

"I'll tell you later. Right now, I need every able-bodied person preparing for battle this instant. I want holes dug in front of the city, filled with barrels of gunpowder and any other explosives we have, then wired to a controller. Pour IItu's oil reserves at each gate. Barricade the ward as best as we can. Position archers at any high vantage point in the city, and gather every weapon and armor piece we have."

"Fletcher, slow down a sec—"

"JI, THIS IS DO OR DIE!" Fletcher yelled, stopping and

looking him in the eyes. "If you want to leave, you can. You can go back to Admont with Crystal and live an easy life. I wouldn't blame you if you did. But if you stick with me, I need you by my side to help prepare this city for an attack!"

"I've already told you, I'm sticking by your side till the end," Ji said, putting his hands on Fletcher's shoulders. "Now, what do you need me to do?"

TWENTY-EIGHT

"Sir, do you have any more barrels?!" Ethan asked, covered in dirt.

"We have a dozen left. That's all. Once you finish, head over to the ward. We haven't touched that yet, and it plays a critical role in our defense," Fletcher said, pointing to the last pile of barrels.

"Will do, sir," Ethan said, grabbing a barrel and rolling it off to one of the holes his team had dug.

"How are the two side gates coming, Ji?" Fletcher asked as he saw his friend heading his way.

"We barricaded both and poured all the crude oil at the entrances. We're just waiting for Ethan's team to finish before we do the same to the main gate," Ji said, wiping his face and smearing oil on it.

"Good. They're almost done. Give them a few hours, and the gate is all yours. The last thing we need to do is take care of the ward," Fletcher said, casting his view toward the building in the distance.

"We can help you with that until Ethan's done."

"Perfect. Help me move these cannonballs." Fletcher grabbed two himself and started walking toward the ward.

Ji grabbed one and fell into step next to Fletcher. "How much time do you think we have left?"

"Less than half a day. It's obvious they waited until they spoke with the queen before telling Ronann to attack. Based on the time it took Lilthral to travel here, I would say Ronann was informed this morning and should arrive by twenty-one hundred hours today."

"I hope we can finish by then."

"As long as we have the bombs and oil set up, we can continue to work on the ward even if they arrive and we're not done."

"How big is their army?" Ji asked as they stepped inside the ward. "Do you know?"

"I didn't have time to check into it, but Tor told me it's between twenty-five hundred and three thousand. Either way, we're severely outnumbered, which is why we'll be relying heavily on traps and holding up in the ward. My only concern is that they won't send the whole army."

"Why is that bad?"

"Because when the military doesn't return, it will be clear that they lost, and once the elves realize how strong we are, they'll throw everything they have at us." Fletcher put his cannonballs down. "But it's not much better if they send everyone."

"The odds are still better than when the three of us attacked here," Ji said, setting his cannonball down.

"Exactly," Fletcher said, walking out of the ward. "Every battle can be won, and I believe we'll win this one, too."

Twenty-Nine

"I told you, mother—"

"Enough, Allica! I already admitted you were right."

"I'm three hundred two years old, yet you still don't trust me."

"I do trust you. If I didn't, I wouldn't have sent Light to the city," the queen said, turning toward her right-hand. "Take care of the human scum. Send all of Ronann's army to massacre every human in IItu."

"I'll take care of it immediately," Light said, straight-faced as he departed the room.

As Light left, Allica resumed her conversation with her mother. "Every other word that comes out of your mouth is a lie. I'm surprised you haven't killed me yet."

"Allica! I love you. I would never kill you."

"Didn't you love my father?" Allica asked, knowing that Rinn never did. "And you had him executed without any hesitation."

Light sat at his desk and grabbed his transmitter from his pocket. Leaning back in his chair and putting his feet on his desk, he started to write.

You have the go-ahead to attack IItu. Light sent the message from his private channel connecting him to Ronann's military. It was only a few minutes later when he received a reply.

How many soldiers do you want me to send?

All of them. It's the queen's order.

Do we have to take prisoners?

No. But if you're willing, capture their leader: Fletcher. He has medium-length black hair, light skin, and light gray eyes.

I'll capture him and have him tortured until he's begging for death.

Light laughed hysterically as he thought of the arrogant human being beaten and tortured. "Let's see how you act when all your kin are lying dead around you."

The sound of heavy footsteps resonated throughout Ronann's military post as the commander, Yasin Reid, made his way to the main area. The large elf stopped in the center of the room.

"LISTEN UP! IITU HAS BEEN CAPTURED, AND WE HAVE BEEN ORDERED TO TAKE IT BACK! THE HUMAN SCUM HAVE KILLED OUR KIN AND ARE HIDING THERE LIKE COWARDS! OUR JOB IS TO SLAUGHTER EVERY LAST ONE OF THEM!" the commander shouted, getting cheers from the group of soldiers.

"Kill the humans! Kill the humans!" the elves chanted.

"GET READY! We head out in two hours!"

THIRTY

"They should be here soon," Fletcher muttered.

They'd managed to finish all the preparations Fletcher had planned, and now he was standing on the city wall by the main gate next to Ji.

"I'm astonished we completed everything," Ji said, glancing across the field in front of them.

"Me too," Fletcher admitted. "Now it comes down to how we fight."

"We either win, or we die," Ji said, shuddering after he said it out loud.

"Or they capture, enslave, and torture us."

"Not helping."

"Just fight like your life depends on it, because it does."

"What if they don't come?" Ji asked.

"Trust me, they'll come. I might not have confirmation, but based on what that elf said and his temper, I would bet my life on them attacking."

The two didn't say anything after that; instead, they simply kept watch. The light breeze swayed the leaves and small branches of the many trees that dotted their vision. It had grown dark and was difficult to see, but Fletcher and Ji still spotted the dirt kicking up from the convoy of vehicles headed toward them.

"You were correct," Ji said, drawing his sword.

"I don't know what we would do if I was wrong," Fletcher said, taking the remote control from his pocket and getting ready to use it.

The vehicles got closer, and the two saw numerous trucks approach, stretching out as far as they could see, each of them packed with bloodthirsty elves.

"Hey, Ji, no matter the outcome of the battle, I just want to say thanks. I wouldn't be here today without your help," Fletcher said, looking at his friend.

"Don't get sappy on me," Ji said, giving Fletcher a light shove. "But seriously, I feel the same... Thanks, Fletcher."

The lead truck was now close enough that they could see a metal ram mounted on its front.

"Shit, I think they're going to ram into the gate," Fletcher said, turning to the inside of the city where his soldiers were waiting. "Get ready for the first truck!"

Fletcher faced the approaching army right before the vehicle slammed into the main gate. Wood shattered, sending splinters flying in every direction and shaking the quartzite wall.

"Damn—" Fletcher said, getting thrown to the ground by the impact. He got up and checked the city. Elves were already jumping out of the vehicle, drawing their weapons and advancing.

"I'll help hold them off!" Ji shouted, rushing down the stairs.

Fletcher moved his attention back toward the convoy that was fast approaching.

"Wait..." Fletcher softly mumbled to himself, his finger resting on the trigger to the makeshift bombs.

The sound of the engines grew louder as the trucks neared the city, none of them slowing down in the slightest.

Just a bit longer...

"The cost of freedom is blood of the victors, but tonight it will be the elves who pay that price," Fletcher said before he pressed the button, causing the bombs to go off.

The ground ripped apart as the explosives detonated, making contact with the trucks milliseconds later and blowing them to shreds.

A fire immediately engulfed the front lawn as explosions mixed with gasoline in the vehicles' fuel tanks. Over two dozen trucks were destroyed, another five had caught on fire, and the pathway had been completely demolished. The vehicles that weren't affected by the blast slammed on the brakes, causing five trucks to crash into each other.

Turning away from the front yard, Fletcher checked the north and south gates. Sure enough, both were already under attack. "Ji, go hold down the north gate!"

"I'm on it!" Ji shouted, killing the elf he was fighting and running off.

"Tor, I need you on the south gate!" Fletcher ordered as he ran down the stairs.

"Heading there!"

Fletcher drew his sword and stabbed an elf in the back. Moving to another soldier, he decapitated him, leaving four elves left, which were quickly taken care of.

"A NEW WAVE OF ELVES IS APPROACHING, AND THEY WON'T STOP UNTIL SOMEONE WINS! WE NEED TO HOLD OUR GROUND UNTIL OUR LAST BREATH! IF WE FAIL HERE, THE FUTURE OF HUMANITY IS ETERNAL ENSLAVEMENT!" Fletcher yelled, igniting the troops to fight with all they had.

The smoke was dying down outside, and the bright lights from the trucks beamed into the city, growing brighter as they got closer.

"Get ready to light the oil!" Fletcher called up to the archer stationed in the closest guard tower.

A few seconds later, the first truck drove in, going full speed before it slammed into a building.

Fletcher shook his head. "Elves aren't the brightest." In other circumstances, he would have laughed, but at the moment, he couldn't afford that luxury. "Take care of the elves in that truck!" He turned back to the entrance to see that the oil had been lit and a few elves were already burning inside one of the trucks.

"PUT IT OUT!" an elf screamed, bolting out of the city.

Fletcher stood in front of his men, waiting for the first attackers to come. He didn't have to wait long; a horde of elves rushed through the flames and charged right at him and the others. Multiple arrows shot past him and into the enemy, killing one before the humans and elves clashed.

Blood was instantly spilled as the battle began. All the while, the fire was still blazing, and a mini barrage of arrows was constantly being fired.

Fletcher got into a fight with two elves. He dodged one strike and parried the other, countering by stabbing him in the eye. The soldier dropped his weapon, screaming in pain as he disappeared behind his allies. Locking blades with the other elf, Fletcher shoved him, creating the opening he needed. Jabbing his weapon forward, Fletcher stabbed the elf right below his belly button. The elf groaned in pain but gripped the blade of Fletcher's weapon, preventing him from pulling it out and attacking.

"That was a mistake," Fletcher said, putting one hand on the elf's shoulder and driving his sword through his body.

The elf cried out in pain, and Fletcher pulled his blade free. Moving on to another soldier, he parried a blow but didn't see an axe thrown at him from the other side. Fletcher felt his right hip flare in pain and glanced down to see the axe sticking in his body. Luckily, he was wearing metal armor, so the wound wasn't too bad, but it still hurt to put weight on it.

Grabbing the dagger from his belt, Fletcher stabbed the soldier he was fighting in the head. Stepping back, he put his dagger back in its sheath and pulled the axe out of his body. Running his hand over the wound, he determined he would be fine until the battle ended.

Charging back to the front line, Fletcher pierced an elf in the heart, then ducked under a swing and kicked the soldier with so much force he almost lost his balance. The soldier crashed into his allies before Fletcher brought his sword down on his head.

The battle was going better than Fletcher expected, but after half an hour, he knew they had to retreat. The fire had died out, and the elves were pouring into the city faster than ever. At the same time, his men were slowing down and were perishing by the minute. "FALL BACK TO THE WARD!" he shouted, killing one more elf before he turned to the archer stationed on one of the towers. "LIGHT THE SIGNALS!"

The man nodded, igniting an arrow and sending it straight into a stack of wood and hay in another tower positioned near the south gate. Once that was lit, he did the same to the north gate, letting both groups know to retreat.

Fletcher and the group at the main gate rushed to the ward, and the elves took advantage of their retreating state, starting to shoot at them. He heard cries of pain as several of his men were shot and wounded or even killed, but he was unable to do anything about it.

Rounding a corner, Fletcher glanced at the ward looming over them, only a few hundred feet away. He also saw a horde of people up ahead racing toward the building and knew it must be Ji and Tor's group. As he got closer to his team, he noticed hundreds of soldiers chasing both of them.

We need to catch up with them; otherwise, we're going to be blocked out by the elves who are chasing them.

"Hurry up!" Fletcher yelled, disregarding the pain in his right hip and picking up the pace. He watched Tor bolt into the ward and Ji stop by the building's doors. Shortly after, Fletcher ran into the ward and stood by the door across from Ji.

He looked back to see a few dozen humans still needed to get inside. Waiting on their allies, Fletcher and Ji shut the doors and locked them.

"Light the cannons!" Fletcher ordered, sprinting down the hall and standing behind them.

Right before the cannons went off, the elves burst through the doors, charging down the hall and immediately pausing.

"GO BACK! GO—"

BOOM BOOM BOOM BOOM!

The four cannons went off and tore through the elves. Blood spattered the hallway, and limbs and guts covered the floor. Smoke filled the foyer, and everyone's ears were ringing from the blast.

"Get to the second level!" Fletcher shouted.

The staircase on the left was completely blocked by furniture, while the one on the right was untouched and occupied by archers.

"Wait, don't fire yet," Fletcher said, standing next to the archers.

"Now!" he commanded as the elves appeared in their vision. "Swap out!" The humans in front stepped back, making room for the next set of archers behind them. They raised their bows and fired a second volley into the crowd of elves.

"Swap out!" Fletcher yelled again before turning his head toward the sound of shattering glass. An elf was climbing in through the broken window, quickly followed by another. "Ji, man the stairs!"

Fletcher ran toward the invading elves, decapitating one and engaging with another. He took care of the enemy and hurried to the window, bashing his shoulder into an elf who was climbing in. Looking out, he saw an elf climbing up a ladder.

"That's how you're getting in. Well, not anymore!" Fletcher said, kicking the ladder and sending it falling onto the elves below.

"Don't just stand there! Grab more ladders and get back in there!" a deep voice boomed out amidst the army of elves.

"Fletcher, we have a problem at the stairs!" Ji yelled.

Fletcher turned to Ji and saw that the elves had pushed up the staircase with a wall of shields protecting them.

"Great... At this rate, we're going to get cornered on the top floor. We need to buy more time here."

"I can hold the window with Ji and a few others, if you can handle the stairs," Crystal said, nocking another arrow in her bow.

"That works for me, but I'm taking the good ones. You can have all the rest," Fletcher said. "TOR, ETHAN, RYAN, ARCHER, HELP ME DEFEND THE STAIRS!"

"I thought you'd never ask for help!" Tor grinned, rushing at the stairs and tackling the front row of elves.

"I'm not that stubborn!" Fletcher said, falling into the fight next to Tor and stabbing an elf in the face.

Tor swung his hammer, slamming into an elf's rib cage and sending him through the wall into another room. "Sometimes it feels like you are."

"I'd rather be too stubborn than weak."

"Fair enough. But I wouldn't consider asking for help as weak."

"Is now the best time to be conversing?!" Archer said, blocking a strike aimed at Fletcher.

"Thanks," Fletcher said, impaling the elf in the chest. He dodged an attack coming at him, ramming the pommel of his sword against the elf's sternum. The soldier's breastplate caved in, and he stumbled back, falling against two others behind him and giving Fletcher enough of an opening to kill him.

"That's forty!" Tor shouted, killing another.

"Are you seriously counting how many elves you've killed?" Archer questioned.

"You aren't?!" Fletcher and Tor asked at the same time.

"I'm at eighteen," Ryan said.

"Twenty-one," Ethan commented.

"I have the lead! I'm at forty-seven," Fletcher said, taking a step back as he engaged in a fight with two elves.

"Am I the only normal one here?" Archer muttered to himself.

Despite their best efforts, the humans were unable to stand their ground, and the elves took over the second, third, and fourth floors. With nowhere left to run, Fletcher rallied his men and changed their method of attack. He started by blocking off the stairs, using the corpses; the elves were still able to get up, but they were vastly slowed down. Next, he moved the archers to the windows. Since the ladders were unable to reach the fifth floor, and there were plenty of elves standing outside the ward, he took advantage of their vulnerability. Lastly, he switched who was fighting on the front line every ten minutes, giving his troops a much-needed rest. With those changes, the battle turned in their favor. But Yasin Reid wasn't one to give up.

"What is wrong with all of you?! We have them severely outnumbered and out-skilled!" Commander Yasin yelled. The elf had been the leader of Ronann's military for five hundred thirty years and had fought countless battles. Before the Great War, when battle was common, he had led a successful raid on Swun, Grifol, and Muwn. He also helped capture Contilice and Endarcite with the angels. But his first attack as the commander of Ronann was regarded as his greatest feat. Cartin was once the second most powerful city in the hybrid kingdom, and Yasin led the charge to conquer it, along with his former right-hand, Vincent Cent, and the prior king, Harthorn Radamon. The hybrids attempted to take it back five times, but were always unsuccessful, and after the Great War, Cartin remained an elven city. Back then, Ronann was feared and respected, but now, he felt ashamed of his army. "This should have been finished three hours ago, and with no losses on our part! Yet, my kin lay dead everywhere I look!"

"The humans are far stronger than we thought they would be. Not to mention, they have put in place a variety of traps. The bombs at the beginning of the fight, and the fires set by the gates, took out over a thousand soldiers," Yasin's right-hand, Harlow, said. "But we have them trapped on the top floor, so our victory is guaranteed."

"You have no right to talk about victory! Every one of you has brought embarrassment upon the great city of Ronann! I'm taking care of the rest of this myself."

THIRTY-ONE

"Watch it, Ji," Fletcher said, bumping into the other man.

"You ran into me!"

"If that were true, I would have knocked you over."

"You're not that strong," Ji said, stabbing an elf in the head. "And I'm not that weak."

"You've put on muscle. However—" Fletcher started, but was cut off by a crude metal club smacking into his torso, sending him flying through a wall.

"Fletcher!" Ji shouted, glancing over to where the club had flown from. He saw a giant elf, who wasn't as tall as Tor but was clearly heavier and towered over the rest of them. The elf had a rugged appearance that made it easy to tell he had been through many fights and had killed a great number of people. There was a long scar running from the center of his forehead down his nose, stopping just above his lip. He had long mahogany hair, a thick untamed red beard, and faded amber eyes.

"GIVE ME YOUR BEST, SCUM!" Commander Yasin yelled, drawing a claymore from behind his back and sprinting straight at Ji.

Ji panicked before springing into action. He blocked the

sword but wasn't prepared for the elf to swing at him with his fist, which struck his face.

Ji grunted as his head rolled back and his brain collided with the inside of his skull.

By the time he came back to his senses, the claymore was already swinging toward him. He didn't have a chance to act; fortunately for him, he didn't have to, as Fletcher blocked the weapon.

Locking swords with the elf, Fletcher glanced back at Ji and gave him a nod, which he returned. Ji raised his seax sword above his head and brought it down, aiming for the elf's skull.

"You'll have to do better than that if you want to kill me!" Yasin said.

Fletcher and Ji gazed up in amazement, their eyes going wide when they saw the blade of Ji's sword in the elf's hand. It was at that moment that the two of them realized just how little they knew about the world and the unknown strength of their enemies.

The commander let go of Ji's sword and kicked him in the stomach, making another hole in the wall. Ji groaned, sitting up only to be hit by Fletcher flying right at him.

"Sorry about that," Fletcher said, getting up and offering Ji a hand. "We need to be strategic about this. If we don't work together, we're going to die."

"You take the left, and I'll take the right. To throw him off more, go for the legs, and I'll attack his head."

"That works. We don't have time to create a plan anyway," Fletcher said as the big elf forced his way through the hole and into the room.

The three of them looked at each other for a minute, waiting to see who would act first. Then Fletcher jumped forward and swung his weapon at the elf's legs. Yasin smiled and slammed his sword into the ground, splintering the wood underneath him. Fletcher's sword hit the claymore, losing all momentum and sending the vibrations of the blow into his arms. Ji was directly behind Fletcher and followed up with an attack of his own. Feinting a swing and jabbing at his sternum, Ji landed a direct hit on the commander and dented his dark green metal armor. Yasin wasn't fazed and completely ignored the strike. Stepping on Fletcher's weapon, Yasin pulled his claymore out of the floor and swung at Ji. The blade tore through Ji's breastplate and left a cut across his chest.

Ji felt blood flowing out of the wound and running down his torso. He tried to fight through the pain, but was unable to, and dropped to his knees.

Fletcher glanced over at his friend before grabbing the dagger from his belt. Dropping down, he slid the blade under the folds of the elf's armor, stabbing him in the knee.

Yasin shouted, shifting his weight and ramming the pommel of his claymore into Fletcher's forehead.

Fletcher felt his head throbbing as the metal of his helmet was pressing into his skull. Moving back, he took off his helmet and wiped the blood dripping into his eyes.

"Of course you had to stab the weak one!" Yasin said angrily. He reached down to pull the dagger out, but was stopped by Fletcher, who swung at his neck.

Yasin blocked him and countered by knocking the sword out of his hands. Before he was able to kill Fletcher, the elven commander collapsed to his knee, screaming in pain as Ji kicked the dagger still lodged in his leg. All of them heard his kneecap pop and saw the blood gushing from the wound.

Fletcher picked up his sword, about to deliver the finishing blow, but was stopped. Yasin kicked off the ground with his left leg and tackled Fletcher, landing on top of him. The commander slammed his fist into Fletcher's face, and each time

Fletcher thought he was going to pass out. His vision blurred, blood ran from his nose, and he was lightheaded. Letting go of his sword, Fletcher tried to protect himself with his arms. He was hit four more times before the punches ceased and he felt blood pouring onto him. Dropping his arms and taking deep breaths, Fletcher saw Ji's sword sticking out of the elf's throat.

"This elf was strong," Ji said, pulling out his sword and lying down on the floor.

Fletcher groaned as Yasin's dead body fell on him. Pushing him off, he rubbed the spot where he was hit and already felt a bump on his head. "Hey, Ji..."

"Yeah?"

"Remember, the elves are the weakest species besides us."

"Fuck off."

THIRTY-TWO

"Have I said how much I love this hammer?!" Tor exclaimed, crushing an elf's skull.

"Three times today!" Ethan said with a sigh.

Tor wielded his weapon like a madman, swinging his hammer in every direction and even scaring his allies, seeming to forget they were there.

"Watch it, Tor!" Ryan shouted as the hammer flew past him.

"My bad," Tor said, a tinge of guilt laced through his voice.

He blocked an attack with the shaft of his hammer and took a step back before he swept the elf's legs with his weapon. Bringing it back around and above his head, he brought the hammer down on the soldier's face. His skull was annihilated, sending blood and brains flying in every direction, splattering Tor from head to toe.

At this point, the elves' numbers were dwindling, and the ones who were still alive were becoming hesitant to move forward and fight the humans.

"We've almost won," Crystal said, moving away from the window and aiding the soldiers at the stairs.

"How do you know?" Tor asked.

"Because there aren't any more elves outside, at least none that are alive."

Tor grumbled, "I'm not going to get a hundred kills."

"That doesn't matter!" Crystal snapped. "It's impressive that we're even winning." She shot an arrow between an elf's eyes and reached back into her quiver only to find that she was out. Checking the barrels they had filled with arrows before the battle, she noticed they were all empty too. "Wonderful," she said, casting her bow off to the side and drawing her shortsword.

She fell into the fight next to Ethan and behind Tor, who stood at the front with Archer.

"Duck!" Tor shouted at Archer, who did so without hesitation and felt a gust of wind pass over his head. Tor's hammer flew past Archer and right into an enemy soldier, knocking him and two elves behind him to the ground.

Archer stood back up and blocked a jab headed for Tor. Facing the elf, Tor slammed his hammer into his skull, completely shattering it. Turning to Archer, Tor gave him a nod of thanks. Before anyone made another move, they all froze at the sound of a commanding voice.

"LAY DOWN YOUR WEAPONS AND SURRENDER! OTHERWISE YOU'LL END UP DEAD! YOUR LEADER HAS BEEN KILLED, AND YOUR FORCES HAVE BEEN GREATLY DIMINISHED!" Fletcher yelled from behind everyone, holding up the commander's head in his left hand. "You can't win, so don't needlessly throw away your lives!"

The elves glanced at each other, pondering whether they should continue the fight or lay down their arms, while the humans waited to see if their enemies would surrender.

It wasn't long until the soldiers began dropping their weapons and raising their hands above their heads.

Fletcher smirked as the clang of metal being dropped resonated throughout the building.

"Take their weapons and lock them in the human quarters," Fletcher commanded, before surveying the damage that had been wrought by the battle. Corpses of both humans and elves littered the city, growing worse toward the ward. Blood had seeped into the cracks of the bricks that made up the walkways and streets. The ward itself appeared like a sacrifice to Rhytdar, the god of death, with a pile of dead bodies, guts, and bodily fluids covering nearly every square of the building. Topping it off was the horrid stench of death that had taken over the ward.

Having seen enough, Fletcher turned away and watched his men rounding up the elves. Glancing at the aftermath once more, he began executing his next plan. Walking over to the room where they killed the commander, he dug through his armor and pulled out a transmitter. Flipping through the channels, he found a private one to Ronann's overseer and head of security.

Walking back into the hallway, he saw that the floor was empty now, except for Ji, who was sitting and taking off his armor.

"Ji, take care of your wounds and get some rest. We're attacking Ronann soon."

Ji assumed he was joking, but when he looked up at him, he could tell he wasn't. "You don't intend on attacking them tomorrow... Right?"

"No. That's way too soon."

Ji let out a sigh of relief.

"I meant in two days, three at most."

The head of Ronann's security, Vincent Cent, heard his transmitter beep and turned away from the painting he was working on to check the device. He saw a message from Commander Yasin's transmitter. *We have slaughtered the human scum and will rest here for the night. Then we will help our kin clean IItu before heading back home the next morning.*

"That took longer than I expected. The lack of battle has made him incompetent," Vincent muttered to himself, putting the device down and going back to painting.

Vincent was the third most powerful elf in Ronann, the first being Dean Horn, the overseer of the city. He only took orders from Light and the queen; even the princess couldn't command the elf. He was someone Vincent admired and respected, which was very rare for him.

The second most powerful was someone Vincent never saw eye to eye with but whom he did respect. That was Commander Yasin. Vincent had fought alongside the elf for many battles, but Yasin was far more barbaric and bloodthirsty than he was. However, Vincent admitted, Yasin was the leader they needed at the forefront of the army.

Then there was Vincent himself, the elf in charge of keeping the city, its citizens, its workers, the slaves, and the overseer safe. He showed greater promise than any other elf when he was Yasin's right-hand, but his heart was never in fighting. He only joined the military because his father forced him. But after the Great War, he stepped down from his position to start a family.

Vincent let out a sigh and put his paintbrush down. Pouring a glass of red wine, he walked out of his office and onto the balcony attached to it. Taking a sip, he gazed out at the night sky above him, letting the moon's light wash over him. He stayed like that for a while before he looked back at the painting of his late wife, Lylee. She was the only thing he ever painted, and it had been that way since she was killed. Her death was also the reason he asked Dean to be the head of security. He thought strengthening the city and protecting his people would fill that hole in him that Lylee's absence had left, but he quickly realized a part of him would be missing until the day he died.

THIRTY-FOUR

"There they are! Open the gate!" the lookout at the main entrance shouted as he saw Ronann's military convoy approaching in the distance.

The bronze gate slowly opened, and the first car passed through, followed by the others. They piled into the town one after the other until all nineteen vehicles were inside.

They must have suffered heavy losses, the lookout thought, counting the small number of vehicles that returned. But it quickly became apparent that something wasn't right. Seventeen trucks stopped at the slave quarters, while the other two drove past the military post. He wondered what was happening, but his curiosity instantly turned into concern as the lead truck rammed into the ward.

"Fletcher, are you sure this is a good idea?!" Tor asked as they sped toward the ward.

"It's not a good idea, but I never said it was."

"FLETCHER—" Tor screamed right before they made impact.

Travertine bricks went flying, glass shattered, and the front doors of the building flew off their hinges as the car crashed.

"You're going to get us killed!"

"Time to take over Ronann!" Fletcher exclaimed, getting out of the truck and drawing his sword.

"How does he have so much energy? I'm still exhausted from the first battle," Tor said, reluctantly getting out of the vehicle.

"At least this one should be easier," Ethan said, joining Fletcher and Tor. He stepped in a puddle of blood as he exited the truck and noticed Fletcher had killed two elves when he drove into the building.

"I know you're tired," Fletcher said to the fifty men he was fighting alongside. "We suffered heavy losses defending against Ronann's military, and I understand this war might seem hopeless. But we already proved everyone wrong! We overthrew Iltu and defeated Ronann's army with only one hundred eighty men! No other species on Affer could pull off what we have!" Fletcher paused and looked behind him at the elven guards running down the stairs before he faced his allies. "Let this day mark the fall of Ronann!"

Vincent was in his office when the whole building shook. Papers fell from his desk, and books and trinkets tumbled off his shelves. The clean, organized room instantly turned into a mess.

"What the...?" Vincent softly said, eyeing the disarray his office was in before walking out onto his balcony and glancing around the city.

He was trying to see if anything was happening outside, but since his office was at the back of the building, he couldn't see that they were under attack. Before he inquired further about the cause, the doors to the room burst open, and a guard ran in.

"SIR!" the elf said, giving Vincent a salute, which he returned. "We have a problem. It seems the humans defeated our forces at IItu and have infiltrated our city by using our military vehicles."

"What?!" Vincent shouted, shock overtaking him as he came back inside. "That... That can't be! We had them drastically outnumbered! Not to mention Commander Yasin, the greatest commander we elves have seen in our lifetime, was the one leading the attack! Yet, you're telling me that the humans not only managed to win, but are here killing my kin as we speak?!"

"Yes, sir."

Vincent sat at his desk and put his head in his hands. *I failed to protect my city. I thought being the head of security would make me feel better, but it hasn't, and Ronann will fall because of me.* The elf didn't move for several minutes before he looked up and saw that he was alone.

Vincent let out a sigh and leaned back in his chair. He had no intention of aiding in the battle, but as he stared blankly at the wall, his eyes wandered until they stopped on the painting of his wife. Standing, he walked over to the wood-and-glass cabinet that housed his dark green armor. "I won't let the humans take anyone else from me."

Fletcher stabbed an elf in the stomach, then parried a strike from another. They were facing fewer elves than last time, but they were in worse shape.

Before the battle against Ronann, they had two hundred soldiers, but after, only seventy-three remained. Even with Ronann's military out of the way, they were still fighting against six hundred guards. Fletcher knew they couldn't win with the small number of soldiers they had, which is why he sent Ji, Crystal, Ryan, Archer, and sixteen men to the humans' quarters. He was trusting them to free their kin, arm them, and join him in the ward before they suffered heavy losses. Although Fletcher soon realized this was a mistake as they were overwhelmed by guards.

"Fletcher, this was a bad idea!" Tor said, fighting back-to-back with him.

"There's nothing we can do about it now, so continue to fight! Once the others get here, we'll have the advantage."

"If we're alive—"

"This is it?!" Vincent yelled, standing at the top of the stairs and glaring at the humans invading the ward. "You scum have the gall to attack us with so few men!" The elf pushed aside his guards and cut down three soldiers before Fletcher locked blades with him.

"I take it you're the head of security," Fletcher said, faking a frown. "I was disappointed when you never responded to my message."

"You killed an elf, stole his transmitter, pretended to be him, and you're gloating about it!" Vincent said, swinging his sword at Fletcher. "You're depraved."

"If you think that's bad, you should see what I did to your kin," Fletcher said, dodging the slash and countering. He made contact with Vincent's breastplate and cut through his armor, leaving a shallow cut on his torso.

"I've never met a human who was so high-and-mighty."

"To be a great leader, one must be arrogant. The weight of thousands, even tens of thousands of lives, rests on your shoulders, and if you head into battle with the slightest bit of doubt, then you have already lost."

"You're the most insane human I've ever met."

"And that's exactly why I'm going to change Affer forever," Fletcher said, knocking Vincent's sword out of his hands.

Vincent ducked under the next attack and tackled Fletcher to the ground. He rammed his elbow into Fletcher's face and kicked the weapon out of his hand. Both of them had a dagger in their belt, but neither of them reached for it, and it turned into a fist-fight after that.

Fletcher punched Vincent in the throat, and the elf backed off, wheezing for air. Standing, Fletcher hit the elf in the face. Vincent's head snapped back before he countered with a punch. The blow landed, and Vincent repeated the move, but Fletcher caught his fist. Pulling Vincent toward him, Fletcher threw the elf off balance and grabbed him in a chokehold. Fletcher shoved his head down and held him in a tight grasp, but Vincent elbowed him in the liver, and Fletcher's grip loosened enough for the elf to escape.

Spinning around, Vincent copied Fletcher's original attack and punched the man in the neck. Fletcher coughed and tasted blood in his mouth. Dodging the next punch, he grabbed Vincent's wrist and pulled him toward him again. However, this time, he held onto him and gripped his shoulder. Pushing him down, Fletcher bent Vincent's arm back until he heard a loud pop, and the elf screamed out. Letting go of Vincent, Fletcher grabbed the back of his head and slammed it into the floor.

Vincent's head hurt, and he couldn't see straight, but he still stood. Turning around, he was immediately uppercut by Fletcher and fell to the floor again. He gasped in pain as Fletcher shoved his knee into his chest and ripped off his helmet.

"I thought you would be a better fighter," Fletcher said, pulling the dagger from his belt and pressing it against the elf's neck.

"I haven't fought since the Great War, and if you're comparing me to Yasin, he was always better."

Fletcher gripped the dagger tighter, and he became enraged. "You fought in the war that was the downfall of my people?" He removed the blade from Vincent's throat and put it back in its sheath. "I was going to end your life quickly, but knowing you killed my ancestors, I'm going to drag this out until you're begging for death to take you."

Fletcher brought his fist back and repeatedly punched Vincent in the face, only stopping when the elf's head was nothing but pulp.

THIRTY-FIVE

"With all due respect, sir, I think it would be wise to notify the queen that we are being attacked. At the very least, you should head to the safe room."

"There is no need for any of that, Miller. At the end of the day, everything that happens is Khanho's will. He will lead us in the right direction. He always has and always will," Dean Horn calmly stated, peering out his office window at the ward.

"But, sir—"

"Miller, do not fret. Trust Khanho."

"Yes, sir," Miller said, bowing and leaving. As soon as he was in the hallway, he kicked the wall and let out a silent scream. *I want to rip my hair out every time he talks about that false god!*

Taking a deep breath, Miller calmed down and decided to go to the ward and join the fight himself. Making his way down the hall, he headed toward his room in the city hall to grab his armor.

"Fletcher would have done this from the start," Crystal said.

"I don't want to accidentally kill my kin by driving into the building," Ji said, looking at Crystal. "And I'm only doing it now because I have no other choice."

Ji got into the truck and sped toward the human quarters. Hitting the doors, he lurched forward and slammed on the brakes. His heart was racing from the impact, but he slowly backed up and let out a sigh of relief as he didn't see any bodies or blood near the crash.

Stopping the vehicle, Ji got out and walked toward the gaping hole in the building. He stood in the entrance and was met with over a thousand scared eyes.

"Don't just stand there," Crystal said, joining Ji on his left. "Tell them why we're here and rally them behind us."

"I don't know how," Ji admitted, realizing how easy Fletcher made it seem.

"The rest of our group is buying us time and fighting with their lives on the line. If you don't convince the slaves here to help us, we're going to die."

Ji faced Crystal before he turned back to the humans. "I'm sure all of you are confused and scared, but you shouldn't be. We're here to free you, but you have to fight with us..." Ji paused. He knew his speech wasn't sparking a fire in anyone as Fletcher's always did. But Fletcher chose him to take care of this, and he wasn't going to let him down. "Affer has kept us enslaved for nearly five centuries, but that ends with our generation! My leader is a man who never quits! Because of him, we have conquered IItu, defeated Ronann's military, and we're going to conquer this city today! But we need your help! Fight by our side, and I can promise you a future with purpose! I was a slave, the same as every single one of you, and I would have lived a meaningless life if I hadn't risked everything to escape! So I ask you, will you fight with me for a better tomorrow?!"

THIRTY-SIX

"**I**f we don't receive help soon, we're dead!" Tor said.

They had been fighting for over ten minutes, and many of the humans had lost hope. Fletcher even saw a few drop their weapon in defeat and he couldn't blame them; he had drastically miscalculated this plan. Fletcher figured since Ji and Crystal had taken care of the ward in IItu that fifty-three of them could hold out until backup arrived. But the city's alarm went off before the fight had even begun, which meant they were outnumbered from the beginning. Fletcher also underestimated how exhausted his team was and the time it would take for Ji to arrive with reinforcements.

"Stay by me," Fletcher told Tor. "We're the two best soldiers here. If we stick together, we can survive longer."

"I don't have much left in me, but I'll fight until I can't anymore."

The two of them fought together, looking out for each other and staying defensive. They killed several elves, but their priority was staying alive.

As they found their footing and began working well together, Miller burst through the crowd and tried to tackle Fletcher. Bracing himself, Fletcher stayed upright and kneed him in the face. Miller let go of him and backed off before he attacked again, locking swords with Fletcher.

"I can't believe I was worried about my father," Miller said. "There are so few of you, he could handle this by himself."

Fletcher removed his weapon from Miller's and swung at his chest. The elf twisted his body, deflected the hit, and countered with a jab to Fletcher's face. Fletcher parried the blade, then moved forward and rammed his shoulder into Miller, knocking him to the floor. While Miller was down, Fletcher dodged an attack from another elf and stabbed him in the stomach.

Standing back up, Miller and Fletcher exchanged multiple blows, all of which were blocked. Fletcher was clearly the better fighter, but given how exhausted he was and the numerous wounds he had sustained, they were evenly matched.

Miller slashed at Fletcher's right shoulder. He pierced through the armor but didn't put enough force into the swing, and barely cut Fletcher.

"Every time I go up against you elves, I understand why you're the weakest," Fletcher mocked.

Letting out a frustrated grunt, Miller started attacking faster. Fletcher evaded all the strikes and grinned as he realized that the elf fought carelessly when he was angry.

"You fight worse than a child. Who trained you: your father?"

"Don't talk about my father!" Miller said, gripping his sword tighter and swinging faster. "He's the greatest warrior in Ronann, and you could never hope to match him!"

"Being a skilled warrior in a city where no one knows how to fight isn't something to brag about."

"Don't act like you know anything about combat! You're merely a slave!" Miller yelled, overcome with rage. He rapidly swung his sword, missing each attempt and growing more aggravated with every miss.

Fletcher waited for an opening before he made his move, ramming his pommel into the elf's head. Miller's body went limp, and he dropped his weapon before he slumped to the ground.

Before Fletcher could kill Miller, he was attacked and driven away from the unconscious elf. Forgetting about him, Fletcher moved closer to Tor again. They went back-to-back, but neither of them had it in them to keep going, and the guards continued to come.

"I can't go on anymore, Fletch," Tor said, his breathing heavy and the grip on his hammer slipping.

"I can't either," Fletcher said. "But if I die, I'll die like a warrior. Will you fight alongside me for one more minute with everything you have left?"

Tor turned back toward Fletcher and smirked. "What kind of fighter would I be if I died without giving it my all?"

THIRTY-SEVEN

"That's all the weapons and armor," Crystal told Ji.

Ji glanced at the empty trucks. "Then it's time to attack." Climbing onto one of the vehicles, he addressed his new allies. "Everyone who has a weapon, follow me to the ward! We have the advantage in numbers but fall short when it comes to skill, so stick together and kill the elves by teaming up against them!" Jumping off the truck, Ji started heading toward the ward, the humans following behind him.

"You did well," Crystal said, falling into step next to Ji.

"Fletcher would have done better."

"But you're not Fletcher. He's a better leader than you, but that doesn't matter. If everyone was good at the same thing, what would the point of life be? If we all acted, thought, walked, and looked the same, is that really a world you would want to live in?"

"No—"

"Exactly! So don't try to be the leader Fletcher Rush is; be the leader that Ji Vulcrhon is."

Ji stayed silent and pondered what she said.

"And a word of advice, speak louder next time," Crystal said, staring at Ji. "It helps more than you think."

Ji opened his mouth to say something, but stopped when they heard screaming. Getting closer to the ward, he froze in his tracks. He didn't expect to walk into a fight where they were winning, but he was horrified to find the foyer packed with elves.

Drawing his sword, Ji faced his soldiers. "THE YEARS OF ENSLAVEMENT, AND THE LIFE THAT WAS STOLEN FROM US, THAT ENDS HERE! WE WILL CHOKE AFFER WITH THE VERY CHAINS THEY PUT US IN, AND LEAVE EVERY KINGDOM BEGGING FOR MERCY! SHOW ME TODAY THE WRATH THAT LIES WITHIN YOU!"

THIRTY-EIGHT

Tor yelled and crushed an elf's ribcage. Swinging his hammer, he hit another guard, crushing his hip, before Fletcher stabbed him in the neck. Pulling the blade out, Fletcher swung around and stabbed a guard in the heart. He blocked an attack and was about to counter when the mass of elves shifted, and the cry of battle rang in his ears.

Fletcher and Tor looked at each other and smiled.

"Seems like we'll make it out to fight another day," Fletcher said.

"I need a *long* break before I fight again!"

As the elves started losing, they ran away, but there was nowhere to escape, and the humans were taking out years of hate and bloodlust on them. They marched down every hall and searched each room, making sure they found and killed all the elves.

When the foyer was empty, Tor dropped his hammer and lay on the floor, unable to fight even if he had to.

Fletcher glanced at the weapon he had grabbed off a fallen elf after Vincent had kicked his away. Tossing the elven shortsword to the side, Fletcher sat. He stared at Tor, who seemed on the verge of death, but was certain he looked no better himself. His armor had been damaged beyond repair, blood covered him from head to toe, dozens of wounds littered his body, and every inch of him hurt.

Neither Tor nor Fletcher said a word and simply listened to the sounds of battle settling. Footsteps replaced the clang and screaming of the fight, and as the battle concluded, the humans returned to the foyer.

"Tell me you and Tor aren't the only ones who survived," Ji said, stopping on the stairs and staring at Fletcher.

"I wish I could."

The room became dead silent until Ryan yelled, "You're lying! You have to be! WHERE IS MY BROTHER?!"

"He's...gone... He—" Fletcher was cut off by Ryan grasping the collar of his breastplate.

"YOU LED HIM TO HIS DEATH! YOUR INCOMPETENCE—"

Fletcher grabbed Ryan's arm and twisted it behind his back. Gripping his hair, Fletcher shoved Ryan to the ground and pinned him with his knee. Leaning down, he whispered in his ear. "I'm sorry. And I know that doesn't change anything. I made a mistake, and others paid the price. You're right to be angry with me, and I understand if you hate me. Ethan was brave and fought valiantly. He knew his life was on the line, but he still stood by me from the beginning. That doesn't change the fact that his life ended too early, but he died fighting for a future he believed in...for a future where no human will ever have to suffer as we have."

Fletcher let go of Ryan and stood. He offered him a hand, which Ryan swatted away.

"I can't forgive you, but I'll stand by your side until we have won or one of us dies... Because if I don't, then Ethan's death would have been in vain," Ryan said before he walked away.

Fletcher watched him leave the ward. Turning around, he faced the thousands of humans waiting for him to act. "I am

Fletcher Rush, the leader of the rebellion and the man who will free every human on Affer! But I can't do it alone! I need soldiers who are willing to die for a brighter future! These men who fought with me today were some of the bravest I've ever met, and I wonder...are you courageous enough to fight with your life on the line?! Will you march into battle when we're outnumbered and victory seems impossible?! Look inside yourself and admit who you are! Are you a coward who would rather die as a slave, or are you a warrior who will fight for your freedom?!"

Even though Fletcher felt terrible, the cheers that shattered his eardrums reminded him why he started this quest.

THIRTY-NINE

Dean Horn sat at his desk, reviewing a trade deal with the Hybrids' capital, Arkanon, when he began to hear shouting downstairs. It was quickly followed by the sounds of battle, becoming louder over time. Most people would have either joined the fight or run away, but Dean did neither.

The overseer of Ronann was an old elf who was seven hundred twenty-nine years old and had lost his mind centuries ago. He had long, disheveled gray hair, a lengthy dense beard, and glassy black eyes. At one point, Dean served as King Harthorn's right-hand, but after he was captured during the Great War, everything changed for him. Dean had been imprisoned for months, and he wasn't freed until Admont fell. During that battle, King Harthorn was killed, and Dean wanted nothing to do with war ever again. When Rinn ascended the throne, she told Dean he could be her right-hand, but Dean declined. Instead, he asked to be appointed as the overseer of Ronann, where he lived a peaceful life...until now.

The noise outside his office grew louder until his door was kicked down.

Dean looked up and yelled, "HUMANS, THE DOOR WAS OPEN!"

"Are you the leader of this city?" Fletcher asked.

"Me?" Dean asked, glancing behind him.

"Yes, you. There's no one else here!" Fletcher said, raising his eyebrow in confusion.

"In that case, yes. I am Dean Horn, the overseer of this city."

"That's all I needed to know," Fletcher said, walking toward the elf.

"Wait!" Ji said, stopping Fletcher. "I don't see a reason to kill him."

"I wasn't going to. He poses no threat, and I'm sure he has a ton of valuable information in that head of his."

"Nothing is as valuable as Khanho!" the elf shouted, causing Fletcher and Ji to pause.

"What?" they both said simultaneously.

"WHO!" the elf yelled. Walking over to the wall on his right, he gestured up to a painting. "Khanho is the god of faith. He provides great protection to me and this city."

Fletcher and Ji faced each other and started laughing. "I hate to break it to you, but your city's just been overthrown."

"No, on the contrary; this is the will of Khanho."

"Sure, whatever you say," Fletcher said, his laughter dying down. "Ji, hand me the cuffs."

Ji grabbed the cuffs they had taken from the ward off his belt and handed them to Fletcher. Dean was surprisingly obedient and brought his hands up to be locked together.

"Turn around; otherwise you'll have too much mobility," Fletcher instructed.

"Okay, but I have to tell you... I'm naked under this robe."

Fletcher paused, completely confused by this elf and questioning if he was the real overseer. "Are you actually the leader of this city?"

"That's me!"

"How did you earn that position?!"

"Because it was the will of Khanho!"

"I'm glad I don't have to deal with you for long," Fletcher said, putting the cuffs on him and letting Ji drag him along. "The city hall is ours now. I'll deliver a victory speech and then order everyone to round up any elves who aren't dead and put them in prison. After that, we need to make sure none of the elves have weapons, and then we can rest for the night."

Fletcher and Ji arrived in the empty foyer and walked out the door. As they made their way outside, they heard cheering. The last light of day lit up the crowd. Seeing so many of his kin, Fletcher couldn't help but grin.

"I think these are all the humans in Ronann," Ji said, a smile of his own grazing his face.

"I've never seen so many humans in one spot," Fletcher said before he stepped forward and raised his fist. "WE HAVE WON! BUT THIS IS ONLY THE BEGINNING! THE ELVES, DAMMED, HYBRIDS, DEMONS, AND ANGELS, BETRAYED OUR KIND LONG AGO AND NOW THEY WILL PAY! TODAY MARKS A MASSIVE VICTORY FOR US HUMANS, FOR WE HAVE TAKEN OVER RONANN, THE SECOND STRONGEST CITY IN THE ELVEN KINGDOM! HOWEVER, DO NOT TAKE OUR VICTORY OR ANY FUTURE VICTORIES FOR GRANTED! THE ONLY WAY WE CAN WALK FREE IS DUE TO THE SACRIFICES OF OUR KIN! THE BRAVE PEOPLE WHO FIGHT, WILLING TO GIVE THEIR LIVES FOR THE SAKE OF MANKIND, FOR THE SAKE OF OUR FREEDOM! WITHOUT THEM, WE WOULD HAVE NOTHING! WITHOUT EVERY ONE OF YOU WILLING TO FIGHT, TO KILL, TO DIE, WE WOULD NOT BE HERE! I ASK YOU TODAY, NOT AS YOUR LEADER BUT AS YOUR KIN,

AS YOUR COMRADE, WILL YOU JOIN ME AND STAND BY MY SIDE TO FREE OUR SPECIES?!"

As soon as Fletcher stopped talking, the crowd erupted, and the sound of their victory filled the streets all the way to the city's walls.

FORTY

iller woke up with a pounding headache and a throbbing forehead. Slowly opening his eyes, he was met with darkness. Once his vision adjusted, he could make out a stone ceiling above him. Getting up, he looked around to find himself in a cell, and not just any, but Ronann's very own prison.

"What happened?" Miller groaned. "Why am I imprisoned in my own city?"

He rubbed his forehead and felt a large bump. He instantly removed his hand, partly out of shock, and partly because of the pain.

Miller was trying to trace back what had happened, why he was here, and how he had gotten that bump on his head. But before he was able to recall anything, his thoughts were interrupted by a loud voice coming from the cell across from him.

"MILLER!"

Miller jumped and turned toward the voice, and saw none other than the overseer himself. "Dean?"

"That's me!" Dean said, pressing his face against the bars of his cell.

"What happened, and why are we both here?"

"We were attacked by HUMANS! And they took over our city."

"What? But, but how?! Humans are nothing more than filthy slaves! How did they manage to conquer us, the great city of Ronann?!" Miller said, becoming angry. "We're the second strongest city in the elven kingdom."

"Not anymore!" Dean shouted and burst into laughter.

"You coot, this isn't a laughing matter! You're the overseer; shouldn't you be doing something? Better yet, you should have listened to what I told you!" Miller yelled, walking over to the bars of his cell and gripping them so tightly that his knuckles turned white.

"Do something? Like what? I'm in prison."

"What incompetence," Miller muttered in disgust, waving Dean off and sitting on the hay bed. "I don't know how you ever became the overseer of any city, let alone Ronann."

"It was simply—"

"Let me guess: the will of Khanho-whatever. I've heard you praise that false god too many times."

"I wouldn't expect a naysayer to understand. But trust me, everything falls into place exactly as it should."

The two fell silent, the stillness broken by the scurry of rats and the occasional scream of other prisoners.

Now that he knew what had happened, Miller's memory started to come back to him. But he was having trouble remembering anything once he entered the ward. After several minutes, he jumped up and exclaimed, "I remember what happened! Before I found my father, I ended up fighting a human, and he knocked me out."

"Human? Where?!" Dean shouted, jumping up and scanning the hall.

"Not here! Anyway, forget that. Where is my father?"

"Why would I know where he is?"

"You're useless, you coot!" Miller growled in frustration.

His mind started down a dark path as he wondered if his

father was still alive. As much as he tried to think positively, he couldn't. If they had taken over the city, there was a good chance he was dead. The only thing that gave him hope was the fact that Dean was alive, but that wasn't very reassuring, as he wasn't threatening at all. Miller glanced over at the elf and saw him picking his nose.

He's far from intimidating, Miller thought, turning away from Dean and inspecting the cell.

"I need to get out of here," he spoke under his breath.

"What? Were you talking to me, Miller?!"

"No, you coot!"

The old elf kept talking, but Miller ignored him and continued to search for a way to escape. He had made plenty of visits to the prison, but had never paid it much mind, much less tried to find any weak points. Although now he wished he had, since escaping seemed near impossible.

Every cell in Ronann was constructed exceptionally well, and even the thought of someone escaping was something the elves would snicker at. Not to say it had never happened, but Miller could count the number of times someone had escaped from an elven prison in his lifetime on one hand, and he was three hundred forty-nine.

"Miller!" Dean whispered, leaning against the bars. "I need to tell you something."

Miller stopped thinking and looked at the elf, hope sparking in him as he expected Dean to tell him something important. He walked over to the bars of his own cell and whispered, "I'm listening."

"I don't have my medicine."

Miller stood there staring blankly at the elf, almost one hundred percent sure he had heard him wrong. "Huh?"

"I said, 'I don't have my medicine!'" the elf shouted. "How am I supposed to survive?!"

"That's all you have to say!? Are you kidding me?!" Miller yelled, turning away and lying on the cell's hay bed.

"Miller... I might be dead by morning!" Dean whispered. "You're my right-hand, I'm relying on you for help!"

I definitely need to get out of here.

FORTY-ONE

Fletcher sat in the black leather chair in the overseer's office that he had claimed as his own. They had taken over the city three days ago, but Fletcher felt like he hadn't done anything in that time, even though they put the guards in prison, stripped the elves of their weapons, and moved the civilians into their own area.

"We've had some rest, now it's time to get to work. I want to abandon IItu. It's going to be harder to maintain both cities, and it's useless since it's been damaged beyond repair. I want everyone, both elves and humans, to be taken from there and moved here," Fletcher said to Ji and Crystal, who sat on the other side of his desk.

"I'll take care of that," Crystal said.

"Next, I want to rebuild the ward and turn the east wing into a blacksmith."

"Where will we train then?" Ji asked.

"The military post. I've already been there, and the place is huge, not to mention it has two training rooms; one outside and one indoors," Fletcher said, leaning forward and picking up a piece of paper. "We need more weapons and armor for our next attack, and this deal is going to add to that demand."

Ji and Crystal moved closer and took the paper from Fletcher, their eyes widening as they read it.

"This is great!" Ji exclaimed.

"It is. Even better, we have enough currency in IItu that we won't have to touch Ronann's reserves," Fletcher said, leaning back in his chair.

The paper in question was a trade offer from Arkanon that asked for four gold bars in exchange for six hundred fifty slaves.

"But is this a good deal?" Crystal asked, eyeing the price.

"To be honest, I have no idea. At any rate, even if we're getting ripped off, it's worth it. We don't need that much money. We'll need some to survive here for an extended period, but gaining over six hundred allies is too good of an opportunity to pass up."

"You don't know what shape any of them will be in or how many of them will be willing to fight," Ji said.

"That's true, but we only have fourteen hundred soldiers. It's nothing to sneer at, but in terms of war, we're still very weak, and we'll have to rely on outsmarting our enemy as we have," Fletcher said, standing and taking a silver transmitter from his pocket. "With everything else out of the way, I wanted to discuss this."

Fletcher opened the message exchange log from five days ago and showed it to them.

Lady Rinn, the city of IItu has been taken back from the HUMANS! Yasin and the rest of the military have killed every human there. I will update you if any further information arises.

Excellent job, Dean; give Yasin my gratitude. Now that IItu is back in our control, where it rightfully belongs, repairs need to take place and new leadership needs to come in. I'll contact you if I need assistance with the city.

"This is good. They aren't touching IItu right away, and they don't know we've taken over Ronann, which buys us time," Ji said.

"It's good, but I'm going to make it great," Fletcher said, putting the transmitter on the desk. "I'm going to tell the queen that we, the city of Ronann, will fully accept the responsibility of bringing IItu to its former glory."

"You surprise me with how smart you are sometimes," Crystal said.

"Thanks... I think?"

Lady Rinn, after debating for many hours, I have decided that Ronann should be the one to restore IItu. Under my leadership, I will not just reinstate the city, but I will enhance it far beyond what it ever was or ever could be. Do I have your approval, My Queen?

Rinn looked at the screen on her transmitter and let a small, elegant smile paint her face.

I was hoping you would volunteer, though you kept me waiting longer than I would have liked; that's irrelevant. I am willing to send over resources, money, and slaves. Let me know what you need, and I'll have Light handle it.

Fletcher felt his newly acquired transmitter vibrate, and he pulled it out of his pocket.

"That was fast," he muttered to himself, reading the message. "You said exactly what I wanted you to, Rinn."

I believe IItu had five hundred forty slaves when it was overthrown. Because I want to make it better than it was, if you could spare nine hundred slaves, it would be greatly appreciated. As for money, that isn't an issue. That said, can you waive the city's fees and taxes for half a year to offset the cost? Lastly, regarding resources, I will take anything you are willing to send my way.

P.S. Please cancel all of our trade deals for the next six months.

"I might be the smartest person on Affer," Fletcher said, reading over his message before he sent it.

A short while later, the queen replied that she would fulfill his request, and Light would leave for Ronann on the fourteenth with resources and slaves.

If he's coming—if any elves are coming—I'll have to take serious precautions. After all, if I kill even one of them, our cover will be blown. It's time to prepare the city, Fletcher thought.

"Have you lost your mind?" Ji said, walking next to Fletcher. "Do you really think we can fool the elves into believing they still have control of Ronann?"

"If I didn't, I wouldn't have sent that message to the queen."

"And how do you intend on pulling this off?"

"First things first. This plan has a few steps, and they all have to go right for this to work," Fletcher said. "But it's possible to pull this off even with the odds stacked against us."

"I take it back when I called you smart," Crystal said.

"You could have kept that to yourself."

"Why didn't you just tell the queen you would take care of repairing the city? If you didn't ask for more humans and resources, we'd be fine."

"I couldn't care less about the resources. The only thing I care about in this deal is the humans. Any opportunity I have to gain more allies is one I'll take, no matter how challenging it is," Fletcher said, opening the doors to the city hall's meeting room.

Everyone inside stood and acknowledged Fletcher's presence, waiting for what their leader had to say.

Fletcher walked to the head of the table and remained standing as he started talking. "The queen is sending over a group of elves in two days, meaning we only have four full days to work. Before they arrive, we need the city to look exactly the same as it was before we overthrew it. First, I want a team working on all repairs to the city that need to be done. We caused significant damage during the attack, and all of it needs to be remedied. Next, I need to find out who was positioned where and when, who was at which guard tower, who was manning the gate, who was the security detail for the overseer, if he had any, and everything else. Then, I want people dressed up to appear like them. The streets are another part; Ronann is the largest city besides the capital, and there are bound to be elves walking around. So I want everyone else disguised as the elves who lived here. Any questions about these orders?"

"What are you going to do about the overseer and the commander?" Tor asked.

"Leave those both to me," Fletcher said. "Anything else?"

The room was quiet before Fletcher dismissed the meeting.

"We're done here. Everyone, get to work! We don't have much time, and there's a lot to do!"

The sound of a metal door being pushed open filled the silence of the prison. Soon after, footsteps were heard, growing louder until they stopped.

"Dean," Fletcher said, standing in front of the elf's cell. "I need a favor from you."

"It's a human! We're under attack!" Dean yelled, his eyes shooting wide open.

Fletcher opened the cell and grabbed the elf by his shirt, speaking in a low, threatening tone. "I'm not in the mood for fooling around. The elves are coming, and I need you to act like you're still in charge of this city."

Dean stayed quiet before a smirk crept onto his face. "And why would I help you?"

"I'm glad you asked."

FORTY-TWO

Light gazed out the vehicle's window, the platinum-gray quartzite walls of Ronann looming ahead. He didn't visit the city very often, but it still held fond memories for him. It was where he was born and raised, and where he joined the military. From the day he became a soldier, he stood out, and after ten years, he was regarded as the best warrior in the elven kingdom. Even though he was only a soldier at the time, he was a vital part of the front line, fighting next to Yasin, Vincent, Dean, and the king.

King Harthorn constantly praised him, which is why Rinn appointed him as her right-hand after Dean refused. It was his dream to become the first right-hand of the king or queen who wasn't born to nobility. But he felt that he didn't earn the position, because he was the second choice.

"How things change," Light muttered to himself as the bronze gate became fully visible.

The assembly of vehicles sped through the gate, headed straight to city hall, and stopped in front of the building.

Light got out of the car, his driver shutting the door for him. He started to walk up the steps and saw that Dean was waiting at the top.

"Mr. Right-hand!" Dean shouted, giving a slight bow to the elf. "Khanho welcomes you."

"Dean... I see you're still as deranged as ever," Light said, greeting the overseer.

"Someone's got to be!" Dean said, turning and walking inside. "Why don't we discuss matters in my office?"

The two headed to the second floor and walked into the overseer's office. Light sat in a distinguished posture across from Dean while the older elf leaned back in his chair and placed his feet on the desk.

"What did you want to discuss?"

Dean stayed silent before he looked Light in the eyes and said, "I remember, five hundred twenty-six years ago, when we attacked Cartin. You had only been a soldier for ten years, but you were already the best. Harthorn was confident in his army, and he wanted to expand the kingdom, which is why we moved to conquer Cartin. That battle was the first time I heard Yasin praise someone, and that was you."

Light's expression changed, shifting from shock to joy before his neutral demeanor returned. "He never showed me any sort of admiration."

"He might not have to you, but he did to me," Dean said, removing his legs from the table and standing. He walked over to a cabinet and opened one of the drawers, grabbing a bottle of red wine and pouring himself a glass. "Do you want any?"

"I don't drink; you know that."

"I do, but people change, and when I was the right-hand, nothing took away the stress better than getting drunk," Dean said, taking his glass and sitting back down. "Where were we... ? I was also impressed with you. You quickly rose through the ranks until you were fighting on the front line."

"What's your point to this? Did you merely want to talk so you could reminisce?"

"No, of course not. I wanted you to know Yasin held you in high regard, but that wasn't why I invited you here." Dean stopped talking to take a drink. Finishing off the glass, he slammed the empty cup on the desk. "That's better! On to my main point: IItu shouldn't have happened. We had great success taking it back, but we lost a considerable number of soldiers."

"That wasn't my fault. I wanted to kill the humans when I first went there. It was the queen's orders to leave them."

"I wasn't blaming you or the queen. Even if you moved in right away, IItu would have suffered casualties since the humans killed all the guards."

"They didn't take prisoners?!" Light asked, clenching his fist.

"Didn't you go there? You should know that," Dean said, getting up to refill his glass.

"I...I did, you're right. I didn't observe the city at all," Light said, now angry with himself for being so careless.

"You couldn't have done anything even if you knew. The only way this wouldn't have happened is if we weren't weak."

"We can't become stronger. He'll—" Light started to say, but was interrupted by Dean, who leaned down and whispered in his ear.

"We either strengthen our kingdom and risk angering *him*, or we will be overthrown."

Dean backed off and sat, taking a sip of wine before resting the cup on his desk.

"We wiped out the slaves who rebelled. There is no need to worry about another uprising," Light said.

"What about the rest of Affer? This is the weakest we have ever been. I would bet at least one kingdom has its eyes on us."

"What am I supposed to do?"

"Fortify the capital, increase the number of guards there, and never leave the city with more than half the army."

"I'll consider it," Light said, even though he had made up

his mind. "I wish you were always like this. You're a far better leader, and you remind me of how you were when we met."

"You're not the same Light Litchtree as when we met, either," Dean said, before he jumped out of his seat. "Now, time for the fun!"

They left the city hall and walked out onto the busy streets. The city was buzzing with "elves" walking around, going about their day. Seeing it alive, full of the life of its residents, took Light back to before he had joined the military and to the days of his youth. Reaching the ward, they went inside and down to the subbasement.

"I've never been here," Light said as Dean pushed open a metal door, revealing a dimly lit corridor.

"Consider yourself fortunate."

A scream sounded up ahead, causing Light to question where Dean was taking him, but he didn't say anything and kept following him.

As the two of them walked farther, the screaming grew louder until they stopped behind the door from which it was coming.

"I think you'll like what's in here," Dean said, opening the door and going inside.

Light was right behind him, leaving the door open and letting his eyes adjust to the darker space. When they finally did, a sneer appeared on his face. "You're right, Dean, this is a pleasant surprise."

Fletcher was tied to a metal pole in the center of the room. His shirt was ripped, and what remained was drenched in blood. Large cuts littered his body, his torso was black and blue, and the rope around his wrists was so tight it had torn his skin.

"Who do we have here," Light mocked, grabbing Fletcher's hair and forcing the man to look at him. "Didn't you say the next time we saw each other, one of us would die? It seems that someone is you."

"This... Isn't...the end... Not...not yet," Fletcher grumbled, blood dribbling from his mouth.

Light laughed, letting go of Fletcher. "If that's what you want to think, then go ahead, but it appears that you're leaning against death's door. Even so, I have to give it to you, you have confidence, but that only gets you so far. You don't have what it takes to free your kind. You couldn't even liberate your kin from us."

"Don't...act like...you know...me. I, I swear...I'll...kill you."

"You, kill me? You couldn't do that if I were severely injured and you were in peak condition. Just admit it to yourself," Light said, leaning in and speaking softly, "you're worthless. You never had a chance at winning."

Fletcher glanced down and spit out a mouthful of blood before he locked eyes with Light again. "What does an elf know about victory?"

Light punched Fletcher in the face before turning to the figure in the corner of the room. "Good work, Yasin. I knew I could count on you."

"The humans put up more of a fight than I expected, but it wasn't anything I couldn't handle," Tor said, disguised as Yasin.

"You sound different. Are you okay?"

"My neck was cut," Tor said, pointing at the gauze wrapped around his throat.

"I'm glad you're alive."

"The human scum could never kill me, and if I were killed, dying in battle is the greatest honor for a warrior."

"Indeed it is," Light said, thinking of the countless times he had evaded death. "I heard you suffered a good deal of losses taking back IItu. Please give my condolences to the families of those who have fallen."

"I will," Tor said, giving a slight bow. "I'm sure they will greatly appreciate your sympathy."

"I'll let you get back to work," Light said, glancing at the tray of bloody tools next to Tor. He turned to Fletcher once more, letting out a chuckle before he left the room.

"Are you ready, sir?" Light's driver asked, opening the car door.

"Yes, let's leave," Light said. He glanced up at the guard towers, observing the "elves" on duty before he got in the vehicle.

The driver closed the door behind Light and took his own seat.

With the city behind them, Light couldn't help but think about what Dean had said: that the massacre of IItu happened because they were weak. He was right, but Light knew they couldn't become stronger unless they wanted to incur his wrath.

"This is all the humans' fault. They have caused this kingdom more hurt than any species."

FORTY-THREE

"He's gone," Dean said as he entered the torture chamber again.

Fletcher groaned as he was untied from the pole and set free. He fell to his knees and wiped the blood from his mouth.

"Sorry, Fletch—"

"Don't apologize. I told you to do this. It was the only way it would be believable," Fletcher said, standing with help from Tor. "You did an outstanding job playing Yasin; even I was fooled."

"But he noticed the voice was different."

"Of course he did. From the information I gathered, they fought together on the front line for decades. That's why we wrapped the gauze around your neck."

"I didn't think you humans would pull it off," Dean said. "Now fulfill your promise. I've been feeling withdrawal for too long."

"Here you go," Fletcher said, reaching into his pocket and handing Dean a small white plastic bag. "A guard will bring you another batch of the same size every week, just as we agreed."

The elf smirked and held up the bag. "Good doing business with you. If you ever need more help, you know where to find me." Dean left the room, willingly heading back to his cell.

"Are you sure it's okay to let him roam free?" Tor asked, removing the fake bandage from his neck.

"If he wanted to betray us, he easily could have when Light was here," Fletcher said. "Plus, he's not going to wander. I offered him freedom as part of the deal, but he refused, saying he didn't care and was fine staying in the cell as long as I gave him that."

"And what exactly was that?"

"In the bag? It was cocaine."

Miller heard the prison door open, and a sliver of light illuminated the hall before vanishing. The sound of bare feet hitting the cold stone floor filled the room, slowly getting louder until they stopped. Miller glanced up from his bed and saw Dean standing in front of his cell.

"Miller, I'm back!" Dean greeted the younger elf before walking into his cell and shutting the iron-barred door behind him.

"Why...why are you here?! WHAT DID THE HUMAN OFFER YOU THAT WAS WORTH BETRAYING YOUR KIN FOR?!" Miller yelled at Dean, getting up and grabbing the bars of his cell.

"This," Dean said, holding up the small white bag Fletcher had given him.

Miller instantly knew what it was, and a new wave of rage washed over him. "ARE YOU KIDDING ME?! YOU WORKED WITH THE ENEMY FOR COCAINE?! YOU BETRAYED US FOR FUCKING DRUGS?!"

"I wouldn't expect you to understand," Dean said, pouring a line on his forearm.

"Understand what?! That you're a druggie?! You could

have escaped, you could have told the elves what was going on, but you didn't, did you?!" Miller said, his knuckles turning white as he gripped the iron bars even tighter.

"Did I sell out my supplier? Is that what you're asking?"

"Your... YOUR SUPPLIER? THAT'S OUR ENEMY!" Miller screamed, slamming his fist against the bars.

"That feels incredible!" Dean exclaimed as he snorted the drug. "It's been forever since I've had this. I was worried I would die without it."

"You could have saved us! Yet you sold us out for nothing! Every elf that dies now is because of you! Their deaths could have been prevented if you were a good leader!" Miller glared at Dean.

"I don't care about being the overseer anymore. I stopped caring decades ago."

"You disgust me," Miller sneered, turning away from Dean and going to bed.

FORTY-FOUR

Fletcher stumbled out of the ward and was met by a crowd of humans waiting for him outside. "Well done, everyone!" he said, causing the crowd to erupt in cheers. "Without your hard work, we would have been caught. Now that we don't have to rush to prepare anything, we can have a grand feast tonight."

"Fletcher!" Ji said, pushing past the throng and grabbing his friend by the shoulders. "You look terrible."

"Thanks. I may have overdone it."

"You should—" Ji started to say before Fletcher's body went limp and he passed out. "Fletcher! Fletcher!"

"I got him," Tor said, grabbing the man and carrying him under his right arm. "Everyone move!"

The crowd parted, making way for Tor and Ji, who sprinted toward the hospital.

"Stupid Fletcher," Ji muttered as they ran. "You better not die."

THUNK!

Another arrow hit the target right next to three others in the blue circle.

At least my aim is consistent, Crystal thought, nocking another arrow in her bow.

She had been training all day and had shot over two hundred arrows already. Her aim had been steadily improving, but she only hit the bullseye twice. At close range, she was able to hit her mark every time; countless hours of training at Admont's castle perfected that. But anything over one hundred fifty feet was proving to be difficult.

Crystal grumbled as she hit the blue circle again. She nocked another arrow but paused as Ji entered the room.

"Fletcher's out of the hospital. The doctors told him to rest for a few more days, but he's already acting like his normal self," Ji said, walking over to her and looking at the target. "That's impressive."

"It's decent, but in battle this won't suffice." Crystal let the arrow fly; this one landed in the red circle. "If it doesn't land within the yellow nine times out of ten, it will cost lives in battle."

"That's true, but you haven't been training that long."

"Time isn't exactly on our side."

Ji thought about what to say before he completely changed the subject. "Why don't you join us for dinner? The cooks have prepared a feast to celebrate our victory."

"Just save me a plate of food."

"Come on, Crystal, you've been training all day for the past five days," Ji said, putting his hand on her bow and lowering it. "How about this: if you come, I'll spar with you in the morning."

"You're fine with getting your ass kicked?"

"I meant with swords. You know that, right?"

"Yes," Crystal said, setting her bow down.

"And you realize I main a sword while you main a bow?"

"I know, and your point?"

"I'm not sure if I should be insulted by how confident you sound."

"I think we should let the outcome of our spar decide that," Crystal said. "But for now, you mentioned a feast."

"Tor, for the last time, I'll grab my own food," Fletcher said to his friend.

"But I feel bad—"

"Tor, I also said, multiple times, 'It's not your fault.' I told you to cut and beat me to make it as though I was being tortured," Fletcher said, putting a heavy steak on his plate.

"But you passed out, so you should take it easy."

"The doctors already replenished most of the blood I lost, and I was in the hospital for five and a half days. I feel much better, and I'm just grabbing dinner. I'm not doing anything strenuous, fighting, or sparring."

"Not yet."

"I'm surprised you don't enjoy working out. You were remarkable when we sparred. I know you quickly ran out of stamina since you're so big, but if you trained more often, you wouldn't have that problem..." Fletcher paused and eyed his friend. "Wait, you've never trained before, have you?"

"You said you'd grab your own food, so I'll leave you be," Tor said, walking away.

Fletcher shook his head. "He's an exceptional fighter, but he would be unstoppable if he put in greater effort."

"I can't help but agree with you on that," Crystal said, appearing next to Fletcher and filling her plate. Glancing up at his arms, she noticed they were wrapped in bandages. "You went too far. That elf would have been tricked with significantly less, and you unnecessarily put your life on the line."

"I put my life on the line the day I escaped slavery. If I die, then at least I died working toward my dream."

"That's not what I want to hear from my leader."

"This is war, I'm not going to sit back simply because I'm in charge."

"You're worth a great deal more to us alive than dead," Crystal said before walking away.

Fletcher finished filling his plate and looked around the military post's dining room. Even though the space was massive and had sixty tables, each capable of seating thirty people, there was still nowhere to sit, and many were standing to eat. Fletcher himself was prepared to eat while standing, but before he had taken a bite of his food, someone put a hand on his shoulder.

"Fletcher, we saved a spot for you."

Fletcher turned around to see Archer behind him. "Are you sure? That doesn't feel right."

"I think everyone here would gladly give up their seat for you," Archer said, heading off.

Fletcher decided to follow him. Arriving at the table, he was surprised to see Ji, Crystal, Ryan, and Tor were already there.

"Why am I the last one here?" Fletcher asked, setting his plate down. "I was literally talking with you two a second ago." He pointed to Tor and Crystal.

"You could ask anyone here, and they would give you their spot," Crystal said.

"I said the same thing."

Fletcher sat next to Tor and Archer. "What's your excuse, Tor?"

"I figured you knew. Sorry."

"Relax, I'm just giving you a hard time," Fletcher said, finally digging into his food. Eating half his steak and diminishing his hunger, he continued talking. "After taking over Ronann, I realized our strategies need to be thoroughly thought out. I overlooked multiple factors of the attack, and it cost us. Additionally, the army needs to be reconstructed. You five are part of my team, which I'm naming the Vanguard, and I have a right-hand, but I need a lead commander. We gained fourteen hundred soldiers from conquering Ronann, over three hundred from Lilthral, and the ones from Arkanon should come tomorrow, which should put us around nineteen hundred soldiers. I can manage everyone now, but we're growing fast, and the longer it takes for orders to be fulfilled, the more lives it will cost."

"Do you think anyone here is worthy of being the lead commander?" Ji asked, taking a bite of his baked potato.

"I do. I might be wrong, as I haven't met him, but I heard there was a human in Ronann's prison that we freed. I don't know why he was there, but supposedly, many of the elves feared him even after he was locked away. I'm going to spread the word tonight that we're holding recruitment tomorrow. There are still many positions that need to be filled, on and off the battlefield."

"Who's your right-hand?" Tor asked, even though he was sure he knew the answer.

"Ji."

"For real?!" Ji said in surprise and looked at his friend.

"I told you if you were worthy, I would make you my right-hand, and you're definitely competent and skilled enough that you deserve the spot," Fletcher said, grateful to have Ji by his side. "In all of my plans to escape, I never imagined doing it beside someone else. But I'm glad things didn't go as expected."

FORTY-FIVE

"Ji, wake up!"

Ji felt himself being shaken and blinked as he opened his eyes. Sitting up, he was face-to-face with Crystal, who was still holding onto him.

"Get up, Ji," Crystal said, letting go of him. "It's time to train."

Ji grumbled and glanced at the clock on the wall. "It's zero six hundred hours."

"You said you would spar with me. So get up and get ready. I'll wait for you outside."

"I said I would spar with you, but not at six in the morning. You realize you can sleep in?"

"I'll see you outside," Crystal said, leaving his room and closing the door.

"Crazy woman," Ji muttered, getting out of bed. He got dressed, donned his armor, grabbed his sword, and opened the door.

Walking into the hall, he shut the door and looked at Crystal, who raised an eyebrow and said, "Crazy woman?"

"It's a compliment," Ji said timidly with a shrug.

Crystal let out a laugh and started walking down the hall. "You worry too much."

Ji sprinted to catch up with her, slowing his stride when he did. The two walked in silence until they reached the foyer and opened the front doors of the city hall.

"It's so warm here," Ji said.

"It's thirty degrees."

"No wonder it feels like summer."

"You think this feels like summer?" Crystal asked, shocked that Ji wasn't freezing.

"The hottest Titanan got every year was thirty-five degrees, and twenty-five was the average. So this feels nice. Are you cold?"

"Yes."

"But you lived in Admont for years without heat."

"I grew up in Plitin, and I was never fond of living in Admont, especially in the winter. I started fires to keep warm, and only went outside when I had to."

The two remained silent until Crystal turned toward the outdoor training field, and Ji kept heading toward the military post.

"You want to train outside?" Ji asked. "But you're cold."

"It doesn't matter if I'm cold. In a battle, you don't get to choose where you fight."

Ji shrugged and followed her. He was going to say they had fought more times inside than out, but he didn't, and fell into step beside her.

Approaching the outdoor field, they thought they saw movement. But it wasn't until they were closer that they could confirm someone was already there.

"Five hundred seventy-six...five hundred seventy-seven...five hundred seventy-eight..." Fletcher counted as he swung his sword from above his head down in front of him. He had been up since five, repeating the same movement he was currently performing.

"You're up early!"

Fletcher stopped mid-swing and looked over to see Ji and Crystal walking onto the field.

"I could say the same to you," Fletcher said, going back to swinging his sword.

"What happened to taking a few days off?" Ji called out to his friend, who ignored him. Turning away from Fletcher, Ji faced Crystal. "Should we spar now?"

"I'm ready," Crystal said, walking over to an empty part of the field and drawing her weapon. "Give me your best."

"I think you'll be stunned by how good I am with a sword."

"I've seen you fight. Unless you've been holding back, I don't think I'll be surprised."

"Or maybe, you'll see me grow as we spar," Ji said, drawing his sword and pointing it at Crystal.

"Now *that* would surprise me."

"Watch me."

The two of them circled each other before Ji lunged forward, striking at Crystal's side. She stepped back, evading the attack and jabbing her shortsword at Ji's ribs. Ji knocked Crystal's blade away with his own and countered.

The two went back and forth, both trying to gain the edge over the other. Ji was confident going into the fight, but he quickly realized that Crystal trained with more than a bow. She made mistakes and left herself open more than once, but despite that, he was unable to land a single hit.

Ji ducked under a blow and closed the distance between them. He jabbed at her stomach, but she dodged and rammed her elbow into his head. Neither of them was wearing a helmet, and Ji felt a thin bead of blood run down the back of his head. Spinning around, Ji blocked a jab flying at his chest, then rose to his full height, catching Crystal's blade with his guard and shoving her back. While she found her balance, Ji made his move. Instead of swinging his sword at her, as he had been, he altered his approach and rammed his shoulder into her. Crystal was knocked down, but held on to her weapon and rolled back, springing to her feet.

Ji frowned at how easily his attack was nullified, but he changed his mood as he learned why he wasn't winning. Ji was much stronger than Crystal, but he was also bigger and wasn't as light on his feet. While he had been striking with enough force to cut through muscle and fat, Crystal was only swinging her sword enough to cut skin.

Changing his style, Ji advanced toward Crystal and waited for her to make the first move. When she did, he barely swung his sword and was quickly able to counter. Crystal clearly wasn't expecting Ji to act so fast, and his blade missed her breastplate by less than an inch. Pulling his sword back, Ji moved forward and swept her legs out from under her.

Crystal fell to the ground and felt Ji's blade press against her neck. "You fought better than I expected," she said, pushing his weapon away from her.

"Not me," Fletcher said, having seen most of the fight. "You main a sword, Ji; you should have won that easier. However, Crystal, I'm impressed with you. I know you're great with a bow and arrow, but your skills with a blade are impressive."

"I won, though! And you don't have a right to talk, out of the ninety sparring sessions we had in Admont, I walked away as the victor sixty-two times," Ji said, putting his sword back in its scabbard.

"That's talent versus hard work."

"Is that really something you should be proud of?"

"Of course, why would I want to achieve something because I was born with a knack for it?"

"Wait, you're hard work, and I'm talent?"

Fletcher raised an eyebrow. "In what twisted world is it the opposite? I've been training for years, yet you were still better than me when we started sparring."

"But you didn't train with a sword. So technically, we started at the same time."

"You proved my point!"

"But you've already surpassed me!"

"I also put in over a thousand hours with a weapon since becoming free!"

"And I..." Ji paused. "Haven't put that much in."

"Exactly!"

"But I've still practiced for hundreds of hours."

"And that's why you're the second-best in my army. You worked diligently and have tremendous aptitude," Fletcher said, drawing his sword. "But the gap between us isn't even comparable anymore, and I'm going to prove it."

"Now?" Ji asked, knowing Fletcher wanted to duel. "I was just sparring."

"And I was just training. Your point?"

"Fine, give me a second," Ji said, sitting to recover.

"Take as much time as you need, and if you're still afraid, you can team up with Crystal."

"I'll take you up on that offer," Crystal said.

"You're not helping," Ji told her. "Fletcher's ego is big enough; if he wins against both of us, his head might explode."

"If? You mean when?"

"Alright, you're on. We'll fight you together."

"Tell me when you're ready," Fletcher said, setting his sword down and sitting on the ground. "I forgot to tell you both, if you need your sword sharpened, let me know. I sharpened mine once before I lost it."

"I don't use mine often, and I've kept an eye on it," Crystal said.

"What about you, Ji?"

"I'm not sure. I forgot it needs sharpening. But I shouldn't have, I noticed it hasn't been cutting the same."

"Let me see," Fletcher said, reaching out to grab the handle.

Ji handed it to him, and Fletcher's face immediately contorted into one of dissatisfaction. "Ji, as a blacksmith, this hurts my soul to see," he said, looking at the dulled and chipped blade. "I'll forge you an identical weapon later. For now, grab a spare."

Ji nodded, running over to the wooden racks sheltered from the elements in a small room on the side of the field.

"I'm baffled that you managed to kill anyone with this," Fletcher said, holding up Ji's seax sword.

"Is it really that bad?"

"Horrible! It's a butter knife at this point!"

"I'll take better care of my weapons next time."

"For your sake, I hope you do. It would be pathetic if you died in battle because you couldn't deliver the finishing blow from a dull blade," Fletcher said, standing and tossing Ji's sword away. "Are you two ready?"

"I'm set," Crystal said, turning to her teammate. "Ji?"

"Prepared as I'll ever be," Ji said, standing next to Crystal and across from Fletcher.

The three of them got into a fighting stance, waiting for Fletcher to start. He attacked Ji first, bringing his sword down from above his head. Ji parried the strike and countered, which Fletcher dodged. Blocking an attack from Crystal, Fletcher moved toward Ji's right side, which was open from missing his hit. Fletcher rammed his elbow into Ji's breast-plate, knocking the air out of his lungs and pushing him back. He regained his balance, but Fletcher was already on top of him, swinging his sword at him and parrying an attack from Crystal with his left gauntlet. Ji barely managed to defend himself from Fletcher, who instantly backed off. Moving closer to Crystal, Fletcher dodged and rammed his pommel into her hip. Crystal stumbled back but deflected Fletcher's next strike and stayed on defense until Ji attacked Fletcher from behind.

Hearing Ji swing his sword, Fletcher spun around and blocked his weapon. He had an opening to counter, but didn't take it and moved back to Crystal.

Ji and Crystal worked extremely well together and always made sure one of them was behind Fletcher. He was able to keep up and defend against every attack, but he knew he couldn't slip up. He observed them for any weak points but was unable to find any he could exploit.

Fletcher blocked Ji's sword and quickly moved back before Crystal could act. However, she was closer than he expected, and Fletcher was forced to defend himself. Ji moved, intending to end the fight, but Fletcher shoved Crystal and ducked under Ji's hit, tripping him in the process. Kicking Ji as he stumbled, Fletcher knocked his friend down and rushed at Crystal. He already knew she didn't put much weight into her swings from watching her spar with Ji, so he put all his strength into his attack and knocked her sword from her hands.

"Dead," Fletcher said, touching her neck with the flat of his sword and turning back to Ji. His right-hand had gotten up, and Fletcher could tell he was winded. Nowhere near his limit, Fletcher sprinted at Ji and sent countless attacks his way. Ji blocked all of them, but he was slowing down until Fletcher caught his blade and shoved it into the dirt. Swinging his sword, Fletcher stopped the weapon an inch from Ji's face. "And you're dead too."

"I know you've gotten better, but I still thought Crystal and I would win," Ji said, pulling his sword free.

"You two did exceptionally. Fighting on both sides of me was genius, and if you didn't run out of stamina, I wouldn't have been able to separate you two, which was your only advantage."

"I should start training more," Ji muttered to himself.

"We can begin now," Fletcher said, spinning his sword and pointing it at Ji and Crystal. "Ready for another round?"

FORTY-SIX

"Are you Leon Bristofold?"

Leon turned around to see a man with medium-length black hair and light gray eyes looking up at him. "The one and only."

"I'm Fletcher Rush, leader of the rebellion," Fletcher introduced himself, raising his hand. "I've heard you're rather formidable."

Leon shook Fletcher's hand, squeezing it with all his strength. "How come you're the leader?"

"It's because I don't take orders from people who are weaker than me," Fletcher said, crushing Leon's hand.

After they let go, Leon's hand still hurt, as if it had been put in a vise. "So you're saying that if I beat you in a fight, I'll be the new leader?"

Fletcher chuckled. "If you can best me, then this is all yours, and you can do whatever you want with it." He raised his arms and gestured to the city and his army. "But if you lose, then you'll submit and serve me."

"I was going to beat you and take your spot regardless!" Leon said, slamming his fist into his palm. "I'll accept, but only if I get to pick the fight."

"Meaning?"

"I want to spar for real," Leon said, raising his fist. "No weapons, no armor, just me versus you, anything goes."

"If that's what you want," Fletcher said, undoing his belt, causing it to fall to the ground along with his sword and dagger. Next, he discarded his armor and set it aside. "I'm ready whenever you are."

Leon instantly acted, lunging forward and throwing a right hook. Fletcher stepped back and threw a punch of his own at Leon's ribs. His fist made contact and slammed into Leon, directly under his liver.

Getting hit was something Leon was used to. His whole life, he had gotten into fights, and when he was younger, he fought with other humans all the time. He was beaten so often that his mind grew numb to it, but with each fight, he improved. Eventually, he started winning, and he grew stronger, putting on thick muscle from working as a builder.

By the time he was a full-fledged adult, he was unbeatable, even when he was outnumbered. Then, the elves began to fear him and treat him cruelly. They moved him from IItu to Ronann and placed him under the watch of four elves who would beat and harass him, but that ignited a flame in him, a pure hatred that grew and spread until he couldn't contain it anymore. One day, he snapped, letting his wrath out against the elves, killing the four who watched over him and three armed guards with his bare hands. After that, they locked him in prison, bringing him out twice a year to beat him in front of the other slaves. That was the only reason they kept him alive: to be used as a symbol of what would happen when you went against them.

Once the city was overtaken, Leon was freed and left to do as he pleased. He thought he would start beating the elves and even the humans if he must, but he didn't. That lust for fighting was gone. Maybe because it had been so many years since he had been in a fight and his body had weakened, or because he had been beaten so many times, but he didn't feel like himself anymore.

Nevertheless, everyone who knew Leon stayed away from him since they were afraid. He wasn't sure what he wanted to do with his life now that he was truly free. But when he heard they were holding recruitment, he felt that bloodlust rise in him again.

That fire was back, burning inside him. His mind felt clear, and he wanted to fight again, to become the man he once was. So he decided to head to the military post where they were recruiting, beat the leader within an inch of his life, and take his position.

At least, that's what was supposed to happen, but it wasn't going as Leon expected.

Leon grunted as he was socked in the jaw.

"I heard you were someone whom many feared," Fletcher said. "But I can't understand why."

"I'll show you why!" Leon yelled. "I AM THE MAN WHO STRUCK TERROR INTO THE ELVEN GUARDS! I tore out their hearts with my bare hands! I broke their bones, shattered spines, peeled the skin off their bodies, and choked an elf with his kin's intestines! I will make sure you remember my name as you lie broken at my feet!"

Leon punched Fletcher in the gut, and he keeled over. Grabbing the back of Fletcher's head, Leon kneed him in the face. Fletcher blocked Leon's attack with his palms, but he was still hit due to the force.

"You finally drew blood!" Fletcher said, breaking free from Leon's grasp and wiping the blood from his nose. "But you haven't lived up to my expectations!"

Leon charged forward and swung at Fletcher, who dodged and shoved him. As Leon tried to reclaim his footing,

Fletcher threw a weak right hook, causing the man to instinctively block it, which left him open on his right side. Fletcher threw a strong left hook, hitting Leon's cheek and knocking him down.

"That's the ninth time I knocked you down. Why do you keep standing back up?" Fletcher asked as he watched Leon spit out blood and get back on his feet.

"Only a coward would stay down! As long as I'm still breathing, I'll stand back up! It doesn't matter if I'm outnumbered, outskilled, or if every bone in my body is broken! I was born to fight, and I will die doing so!"

"I like you. You have the mind of a great warrior. Unfortunately, you're up against someone who has the mind of a great leader."

Leon moved forward, ducking under an attack from Fletcher and throwing a punch at his jaw. The hit landed, and Leon expected Fletcher to fall, changing the fight in his favor. But Fletcher turned his head with the blow, negating most of the damage.

Twisting back, Fletcher slammed his fist into Leon's stomach. The punch was powerful, and Leon felt as if he was going to throw up. Before he could come back to his senses, Fletcher punched him again, this time in the face, which knocked him flat on his back. "Stay down," Fletcher said, standing on Leon's chest and digging his boot into his neck.

"I told you—"

"Then you will die a pointless death! You have talent and skill, but most importantly, your pertinacious. That can't be taught!"

"What do you want?"

"Join me. I see you crave blood, but you don't know where to look, so you take it out on your own kind. Become the head commander of my army, and I will lead you to your enemy, to our enemy," Fletcher said, getting off Leon and offering him a hand up. "Will you choose to die alone, or will you live fighting for a purpose?"

FORTY-SEVEN

"You're late," Light said.

"I'm precisely on time; the rest of you are early," Ingrid said, taking a seat at the table.

"You're my right-hand. You should act more like it," Light said. Moving on, he addressed the rest of the cohort. "Lilthral is the capital of the elven kingdom, and a kingdom's capital should be its strongest city. Yet, that is not the case for us."

"Respectfully, I disagree, sir," Xavier, a long-time member of Light's cohort, said. "Lilthral is far from the strongest city on Affer, but it is the strongest in the elven kingdom."

"It is in military might, but in terms of defense, it isn't."

"If Lilthral isn't our strongest city, only counting defense, then who is?" Ingrid asked.

"Ronann, and Cartin."

"Did you fall down a flight of stairs and hit your head? No one in Affer, much less an elf, thinks Ronann or Cartin is superior to the capital in any way. We have more guards than both cities combined. Our walls are made of lyfume, a rock that our great ancestors spent three hundred years mining to obtain enough. There are seventy archer towers in the city, each strategically placed. As if that wasn't enough, the third level of the city is stacked with elite guards, all of whom would lay down their lives for this kingdom."

"You are exactly like the queen and everyone else. You praise our walls, yet our gates are made of oak wood that is peeling, warped, and older than both of us. We have seventy archer towers, yet only twenty are used. The "elite" guards are a shadow of what they used to be. The lack of war has turned this city weak."

"You blame us for this city's weaknesses, but when have you done anything to change that? I used to admire you because you were born with less than everyone else in the military, yet you bested them all. The nobles hated you because they couldn't match you, and their anger grew as you became better. Despite your hardships, you never gave up and did what no other has ever done: you became the right-hand, even though you were born a commoner. But you changed after the Great War."

Light's eyes went wide as a bad memory came to the forefront of his mind. Clenching his fists, he stared at the table and growled, "This is all his fault." Even though he had spoken softly, the six members of his cohort still heard him, and hatred was laced in every word. But what surprised them wasn't the hate; it was fear.

Before anyone could mention it, Light slammed his fist on the table. "We can't change the past, and there's no use bickering with each other. I called this meeting to devise a way to recruit more guards and strengthen our defenses."

"Give us your orders, sir," Xavier said.

"When the army goes out to attack, I will lead with Ingrid by my side. Xavier, you'll be in charge of Ramos, Laytin, Eldar, and Yune, protecting the palace. For the city, I want to replace the gates. We have two entrances, and it will take months to build one gate, so let's start with the main, considering no one uses the north gate except Yuun. For guards, I want you to spread the word that we're hiring. Raise the pay for everyone, and lower the standard to get hired, but not too much; it doesn't help us if our guards are incompetent."

"I'll get to it immediately, sir," Xavier said.

"It will take time, but this city needs to become stronger no matter the repercussions," Light said, standing. "This meeting is over. If any of you need me, I'll be in my office."

The elves slowly left, leaving the room empty with only Ingrid remaining. The elf stayed in his seat, staring at the spot Light always sat in. Ingrid had known Light since they were children, and it was him who inspired Ingrid to join the military five hundred nine years ago. Light always encouraged him and was arguably the sole reason Ingrid was in the position he was in today. But something happened the night Admont was overthrown. Ingrid always suspected as much, as that spark in his eyes had vanished, and now he could confirm he was right; the fright in Light's voice made it evident.

Light was never considered to be an unrivaled fighter in Affer. He was the best warrior the elves had, but compared to the greatest fighters in other kingdoms, he was a candle against a blazing bonfire. Despite that, Light always stood tall. Even when he met with the bloodthirsty demon king, his eyes showed no signs of fright, and Ingrid was there to see it. For Light to show fear, he must have been thinking about someone or *something* truly terrifying.

FORTY-EIGHT

"Ninety-seven, ninety-eight, ninety-nine…one hundred."
Miller collapsed as he completed his last push-up.
Panting, he rolled over onto his back and gazed at the
ceiling, his breathing steadying after a while.

Once he had fully recovered, he stood and grabbed his shirt off the hay bed, glancing at Dean while doing so. Since the matter with the cocaine, Miller couldn't look at him the same way. He knew Dean had been addicted to the drug for longer than Miller had been alive, and that didn't bother him. He didn't care that the elf was killing himself. What infuriated Miller was the fact that Dean sold out his own kind for a weekly supply of drugs.

Putting his shirt back on, Miller sat on the bed and lay down, closing his eyes. He had never really been an outgoing person, preferring to work, but right now he wished he were in the center of the bustling city.

"I'm bored," he groaned, causing Dean to initiate a conversation with him.

"Miller!" Dean exclaimed, jumping like he had been shocked. "My right-hand, why are you here?!"

Miller sat up and opened his mouth to yell at the old elf, before closing it and calming down. *Losing my temper won't help. Plus, I'm stuck here with him for who knows how long. I should try to hold a civil conversation with him,* he thought before responding. "Of course I'm here, you coot. Did you see me escape?"

"Escape?!" Dean burst out laughing. "If you want to escape, then listen here, Miller..."

Dean stayed silent for a full minute, his mouth hanging open, before Miller prompted him to continue. "You were saying?"

"What was I saying...?!" Dean shouted, pressing his face up against the iron bars. "I forgot."

Miller grunted, gritting his teeth together. "How can you be so apathetic in this situation? We're imprisoned, and our city has been overthrown. While hundreds—THOU-SANDS—of our kin are dead! Yet you sit here and take this as a joke! Do you even care about those who we lost to the human scum?!"

A flicker of remorse crossed Dean's face for such a brief moment that Miller wasn't even sure it was real before he returned to his normal, wasted expression.

"Miller... I understand that you hate the humans because they killed your mother, but we have taken far more from them than they have taken from us."

"You're saying the humans had the right to kill my mother?!" Miller said, feeling his anger rising. "HOW—"

"Don't put words in my mouth, Miller!" Dean yelled with such anger that Miller felt his composure shatter. "The murder of your mother wasn't right or justified in any way! She should still be here with us today, but if you keep that hate inside you, you'll never live a good life."

"I'm living in this cell, so what does it matter anyway?"

"Just keep training. You're in here now, but be patient."

Miller was about to ask him what he meant, but decided against it. Instead, he stayed quiet and started doing sit-ups.

FORTY-NINE

The cold January air nipped Fletcher's skin as he stepped outside. It was late at night, and everyone else had already gone to sleep; the dark windows of the buildings around him were evidence of that. He had already worked out for seven hours that day, but with the plan to attack Lilthral approaching, he was training every spare minute, even if it meant sacrificing his sleep. Conquering the capital was a critical part of taking the elven kingdom, and if they failed here, everything they had done would be for nothing.

He walked over to the field's light switch and flipped it on, illuminating the grounds. His thin leather gloves wrapped around the cold metal grip of a claymore as he hoisted it and walked to the center of the field. He raised the claymore in front of him and took a deep breath. Letting it out, he saw a cloud form in front of his mouth.

"One...two...three..." Fletcher counted as he swung the large sword over and over. Despite what most people thought, the weapon wasn't heavy and barely weighed over five pounds. However, it was heavier than his longsword, and he was still getting used to it, but once he had, Fletcher intended to make this his main weapon.

Time passed, and the sky grew even darker.

"One hundred forty-nine...one hundred fifty," Fletcher

said, finishing his last training session of the day and resting the tip of his sword in the dirt. He leaned against the weapon and touched his forehead to the metal pommel, trying to catch his breath.

He stayed there for over a minute until his breathing wasn't so erratic, and then stood up straight. Putting the claymore away and turning off the lights, Fletcher headed back to the overseer's mansion where he had been staying. The place was massive, so he had offered each member of the Vanguard their own room in the building, but they all refused, leaving him alone.

He opened the doors and walked through, closing them behind him and taking off his boots. Adding his gloves and jacket to the stand next to them, he walked upstairs to his bedroom.

Fletcher groaned as he threw himself on his bed. He wanted to take off his clothes and get under the covers, but he was so tired he fell asleep right as he was.

Fletcher woke up and opened his eyes. Darkness enveloped his vision, leaving him unable to see anything. In an instant, dozens of lights shot to life, blinding him and forcing him to shut his eyes. Slowly opening them again, Fletcher looked around and realized he was lying in the middle of the training field.

"What...what am I doing here?" he mumbled, standing. Taking in his surroundings, Fletcher saw a few inches of snow had fallen. But that's all he could see: the white of the ground and the black of the night. It was as though the world ended wherever the light didn't touch.

"Something feels wrong," he said. "I remember going to

bed. I shouldn't be here…and it's pitch black. I've never seen night appear this dark before."

Fletcher's mind whirled as he walked toward the darkness. But he stopped dead in his tracks as a pair of bright red eyes appeared and fixated on him. The eyes glowed like fire, easily spotted in the shadows that hid their owner's body.

Fletcher opened his mouth to speak, but found he couldn't. Whether from fear or something else, he wasn't sure. But he was certain that whatever was staring at him wasn't human or any other species. He couldn't describe it, but every instinct in his body told him the eyes staring at him belonged to something far sinister.

Before he was able to give it any more thought, the creature moved toward him. Coming out of the shadows, its body was illuminated. The first and most terrifying thing Fletcher noticed was how massive the monster was. He figured it was only slightly bigger than him, as their eyes were almost on the same level, but what Fletcher didn't know was that it was crouching. As it emerged from the shadows, it rose to its full height. Neither the creature nor Fletcher moved. Standing there, Fletcher's eyes wandered over the monster's body. It was twenty feet tall, forty feet long, and over ten feet wide, shoulder to shoulder. Its tail matched its body in length and had a ten-foot blade made of bone at the end. Four massive spikes protruded from the right and left elbows, going up the biceps, with three more on both ankles. The monster had two legs but four arms, though two of its arms were much shorter, as they were merely forearms that attached to the biceps. A thick coat of muscle covered the creature's body. Lastly, was the face. The monster had no lips or cheeks, and its sharp teeth were fully exposed. Its red eyes rested inside an exoskeleton that covered most of its head and ran down its back.

It felt like hours that the two stood still, but it wasn't even ten seconds before the creature charged at Fletcher. He instantly spun around and started sprinting away. Fletcher had no idea what that monster was or where it came from, but one thing was certain: it wanted to kill him.

Fletcher ran as fast as he could, but there was no outrunning the creature and it quickly caught up. The monster howled as it grabbed Fletcher with its right hand, picking him up and turning him toward it.

Fletcher squirmed in the creature's grasp, but it was no use. He screamed in pain as the monster bit him. Teeth dug into Fletcher's body, ripping through his skin and muscles. Blood gushed from his wounds, his bones broke, and his spine snapped. Then it ended.

Fletcher yelled as he shot up in bed. He was breathing heavily and was covered in sweat, as were the sheets underneath him. "What...what the fuck was that?!"

He threw the covers back and opened the curtains, letting sunlight enter the room. He switched on the lights as well, because the dreary January days weren't very bright.

Walking into the bathroom, he turned on the sink and splashed water on his face. The cold shocked him awake, and he scrutinized himself in the mirror. The stubble on his face needed to be shaved; his hair had grown long and messy, and his eyes were bloodshot, with bags under them. It wasn't the first time he looked this bad, but it was the first since he escaped Titanan.

"I need to wash up," he muttered, shutting off the sink and grabbing a clean set of clothes before starting the shower. Stripping down, Fletcher examined his body in the mirror as he let the water warm up.

He had become more muscular since becoming free. Having enough food ensured his training wasn't wasted and that he could fully fuel his muscles' growth. There were also the many scars that had accumulated on his body, and Fletcher knew he was going to get more as the war continued.

Looking away from his reflection, he walked into the shower and let the warmth of the water wash over him.

Fletcher shoved a book back into its spot on the shelf and grabbed another. He had already gone through two dozen trying to find information on the creature he had seen in his nightmare, but he came up empty-handed every time.

"Can I help you?"

Fletcher turned and saw a man slightly shorter than himself with graying hair. "No, I'm just...browsing."

The man eyed him with a look of perplexity, then said, "If you were just browsing, I don't think you would be pulling books off the shelves like that. I've maintained this library for nearly three decades. If you're looking for something, I can find it."

Fletcher hesitated, deciding against asking for help, then changed his mind as he took in the vast number of books on either side of him. "This might sound really stupid, but...I had a dream, well, more like a nightmare, of this...creature. I've never seen anything that resembles it, and it's probably something my mind made up, but I can't shake the feeling that it's real."

"Sorry, I can't help. I think you're insane," the man said, walking away.

Fletcher stood still, completely appalled by his response.

"I'm just messing with you!" he said, stopping and turning back. "You should've seen your face! I'm Don, by the way, and if you want answers, follow me."

Fletcher caught up with the man and fell into stride next to him. "I'm Fletcher."

"I know who you are. I think everyone in this city does."

Don walked into a separate room and behind a desk. Popping open a secret drawer, he pulled out a key, grabbed the painting on the wall behind him, and swung it open. A small safe sat behind it, and Don unlocked it with the key. Opening it, he pulled out a single book and placed it on the desk.

"Have you ever looked at the map of Affer and wondered why there's nothing here?" Don pointed to the upper-right corner of the map hanging on the wall.

"No."

"Foolish young man. You should ask more questions. There's a reason none of the species occupy this region, and that's because of them," Don said, opening the book to the first page.

"That's it!" Fletcher said as he stared at the monster he had seen in his dreams. "That's what I saw. But how is it real? How did I dream of this...this monster, when I've never seen it before in my life?"

"Simple. These creatures are called Jixxes, and they appear in your dreams when you are vulnerable."

"But why?"

"Because they feed off others' souls and bodies. They live deep in the caves of the northeast, and they never travel out of them. So the only way they can feast on their victims is by luring them to their home. They have the ability to enter others' minds, but the farther away you are, the harder it is for them to do that. So they prey on those in a weakened state since they can enter their minds with little to no effort."

"I'm not in a weakened state."

"Is that so? How much sleep have you been getting lately? And how much have you been training? You might think you're fine, but don't forget, you're only human, and even if you weren't, you're still mortal. Your body needs rest, whether you like it or not," Don said, staring at the bags under Fletcher's eyes. "Get some rest before they enter your mind again. The more they do it, the worse it gets."

"If they can enter my mind in a weakened state, why don't they do it now, and why haven't they done it before?"

"Because you're awake. They can only enter your mind when you're asleep, and they don't bother with slaves, since they can't travel to the caves."

"How do they lure you there?"

"As I said, the more they invade your mind, the worse it gets. They extract information from you and use your vulnerabilities against you. They tempt you to head to the caves for solace, enlightenment, power, or to fulfill your desires. Once you enter, they kill and eat you, devouring your soul, and you are forced to wander the void for eternity."

"You seem to know a lot about these creatures. How do you know so much?"

"I can't be certain about any of it, especially the last part, but this is information that has been passed down since before the Great War."

"I'm glad I accepted your help," Fletcher said, closing the book and handing it back to the man. "I could've ended up dead. Thanks for saving me, Don!"

"Fool! Do you think this book is so thick for no reason?" Don said, taking the book and slamming it on the desk. "You could fit everything I told you on one page—"

"I think it would take two."

"That doesn't matter! My point is, there's a great deal more to these creatures than what I told you."

"And that is?"

"You'll have to find that out for yourself," Don said, handing him the worn-out book. "You can have this, just keep it safe. Only a handful of these books exist."

"Are you sure you can't tell me what I need to know?"

"Read the book, and don't skim or skip pages!"

"Alright, I will," Fletcher said, heading out. "Thanks, old man!"

"I'm not old, I'm only forty-three!"

FIFTY

"**B**ullseye!" Dean yelled as he hit Miller in the head with a stale piece of bread.

"What is your problem?!" Miller asked, kicking the bread out of his cell and glaring at the elf.

"What isn't my problem would be a better question."

Miller snickered. "You can say that again."

Dean tilted his head and gave Miller a confused look. "What isn't my—"

"Not literally, you coot!"

"Then how?!"

"Never mind!" Miller turned away from the overseer and started doing push-ups. Dean didn't say anything for over ten minutes and simply watched the younger elf train.

"Miller," Dean said in a calm and serious tone.

Miller stopped mid-push-up and faced Dean, surprised to hear him speak so authentically while high. "Yes?" he answered, afraid he was going to go on a tangent about something stupid.

"I'm not sure how much longer I'm going to be alive."

"What makes you say that?" Miller asked, standing and walking over to the bars of his cell.

"I have a feeling... After seeing so much death over the hundreds of years I've been alive, I've grown to sense its presence," Dean said, taking a moment to remember those he'd lost. "I want to tell you the truth before I can't anymore. You asked if your father was dead, and I told you I didn't know, but I do."

Miller was gripping the bars of his cell.

"I'm sorry to tell you, your father's dead."

Miller wanted to rip apart the person who killed his father and scream until his throat was raw. Instead, he stood there; silent tears of mourning ran down his face, and he loosened his grip on the bars. The moment he woke up in the cell, he figured his father was dead, since the only people who were taken prisoner were those who surrendered and those like him who were knocked out.

"I figured, but I hoped I was wrong."

He let go of the bars and sat on the floor, tears still streaming from his eyes. He didn't bother wiping them away and let them run down his face.

"He was proud of who you became."

"Don't get emotional on me," Miller said, clenching his fist. "I should've been there. If I had gotten there sooner, I could have saved him."

"Are you delusional?! The humans wiped out our whole army and all our guards, yet you think you could have stopped them?! If you fought alongside your father, you would have died as well."

"Then so be it! I'd rather have died fighting next to him than end up here, rotting in a cell!"

"What a foolish elf you are! Do you think your father wanted that?"

"It doesn't matter whether he did or not! I wanted it."

"Stop complaining! You can't change the past. If you want to do something, then escape and take revenge on those who killed your father."

"Escape?! You coot, I've tried to! Do you think I would still be here if I had the means to leave?!"

Dean laughed, laying out a line of cocaine on his forearm and snorting it.

Miller turned away from Dean and lay in his hay bed. He felt utterly drained and hoped sleep would take him, but he was too grief-stricken.

"Miller, did I ever tell you how great drugs are?! Did I?!"

Miller ignored him, but Dean kept talking. Unable to sleep anyway, Miller opened his eyes and gazed at the stone ceiling. Finally, after half an hour, Dean stopped yapping. With the prison quiet, save for the occasional sound from other elves, Miller closed his eyes again. But that didn't last long, as a few minutes later, Dean started speaking again.

"Don't trust the birds, Miller... They're spies!"

Miller had ignored everything else Dean had said, but at this point, he didn't think he was going to stop. Sitting up, he looked at the elf he had worked for for over seventy years. "What are you talking about?!"

"The small flying animals covered in FEATHERS!"

"I know what birds are—"

"They're watching us, Miller!" Dean yelled, raising his arms toward the sky. "They report to the enemy!"

"Whatever you say."

Miller decided he might as well converse with Dean since he was unable to fall asleep. "Why did you start doing drugs?"

"Me?"

"Yes, you. Who else would I be speaking to?!"

"I don't know, that's why I asked!" Dean shouted. "What was the question again?"

Miller sighed. "I asked, 'Why did you start doing drugs?'"

"Good question! I always wanted to tell that story, but no one ever asked. Four hundred seventy-some years ago, when we were fighting against the HUMANS, me and a group of elves infiltrated the capital. It was supposed to be a simple reconnaissance mission, but things quickly went south when our way into the city turned out to be a trap. The humans knew we were coming because the hybrid who got us in doublecrossed us. We entered the city under the guise of humans from Tylic, their third-largest city...or was it the third-smallest? I can't remember. We thought everything was going in our favor when we were able to enter Admont without any trouble, but as soon as the gates closed, we had over a dozen weapons pointed directly at us. Two of my soldiers tried to fight and ended up being killed instantly, while the other three surrendered without hesitation, leaving me as the only one holding a weapon. All of us were taken to their prison and locked away for two weeks until the humans came to visit us again. They promised to set us free if we went back to Lilthral with false information. The other three accepted, taking forged papers to deceive the elves and give the humans an advantage. But I declined, so they threw me back in my cell. This time, I was there for a month, I believe, before I was transferred to the torture chamber. They tied me to a chair and made me another deal. If I sold out the elves and told them everything I knew about the kingdom, they would set me free. However, I refused—"

"YOU DIDN'T SELL US OUT THEN, WITH YOUR LIFE ON THE LINE, BUT YOU DID NOW? AND FOR COCAINE?!" Miller yelled.

"That's because I wasn't old, and I was King Harthorn's right-hand. Furthermore, shut up! Don't you know it's rude to interrupt someone when they're telling a story?!" Dean shouted back. "Now, where was I?"

"You said you refused to give the humans information."

"Yes! They wanted me to sell out the elves, but I didn't.

So they tortured me for three days straight, and only stopped because they were afraid I was going to die. I had been through a lot since I joined the military, but even I was worn out by their torture. To make sure I didn't die, they drugged me. Instantly, I felt amazing! It was as if I had been asleep my whole life and had just woken up," Dean said, pausing and thinking about the memory. "What a feeling that was..." He went quiet after that and stared off into nothing.

"And?" Miller asked, waiting for the elf to continue his story.

"And what? That's it. That's how I became addicted to drugs. I played around, trying different ones until I found cocaine and got hooked, if that's what you wanted to know."

"No, I figured that part out. I want to hear the rest of your story. What happened after that, and more importantly, how did you escape?!" Miller asked, now intrigued about the elf's past.

"Escape from the human kingdom while they were at the height of their power?! That has to be the funniest thing I've ever heard you say!" Dean said, cracking up. "No one got in or out of any of the human cities unless they wanted them to, let alone breaking out from imprisonment."

"But you literally said you walked into the city."

"And I also said we were killed, put in prison, and tortured!" Dean yelled, spit flying out of his mouth. "I was there until Admont fell."

"Ew...keep your voice down. You got your disgusting saliva all over me!"

"In old folklore, they say that's good luck."

"You just made that up!"

"A wise man is quick to lie," Dean said with a smile.

Miller grinned back and stifled a yawn. "I'm going to bed." He turned away from Dean and lay down on his hay bed, but was interrupted by the other elf once more.

"Two things you should know if you happen to get a chance to escape. The bricks on the floor were laid into place, with nothing binding them to each other or the ground."

"What's that supposed to mean?"

"You'll figure it out."

"Fine, and what's the other thing?"

"If—*when* you escape, go to Arkanon and ask for King Yinny Shade. Tell him Dean Horn sent you."

FIFTY-ONE

"In order to have an edge against the capital, we need to remove their army. If we face them head-on, we'll be defeated, so we have to drag them away from Lilthral to conquer the city. Only then will we have a chance of beating them," Fletcher said, glancing around the table at the Vanguard.

"And how are you going to pull that off?" Ji asked.

"By overthrowing Cartin. When we attack, they'll contact the capital, who will realize we weren't defeated. Once we take the city, we'll free and arm our kin, then drive to Lilthral. Meanwhile, the capital will send its army to Cartin, believing we're still there. By the time their forces arrive and discover we left, it will be too late, and we'll be at Lilthral."

"You're doing it again," Crystal said. "You're rushing into battle without thinking your strategy through, and a mistake in this fight will cost us our lives."

Tor looked at Fletcher and shrugged. "I don't see anything wrong with your idea. I trust you."

"See, Tor understands my genius."

"Are you really going to rely on Tor more than me when it comes to intelligence?"

"I can't argue with her on that," Tor admitted. "You two are the brains, I'm just brute strength."

"We know."

"Hey!"

"Why do we need a plan?" Leon asked. "I never made one, and I'm undefeated."

"That's not true, and even if it was, this is war, not a fist-fight," Fletcher said, wondering if making Leon the head commander was the right choice. Knowing no one else was fit for the position, Fletcher determined the next battle would decide Leon's fate, and moved back on topic. "I spent weeks thinking of this scheme," Fletcher said. "I thought over every aspect multiple times to make sure I didn't overlook anything. But if you've found discrepancies, then tell me what they are."

"Starting with the most obvious problem: once we attack Cartin, Lilthral will know and head toward the city. Half of the road they will traverse is the same as ours, and there's no way we can conquer Cartin and travel past the point where we wouldn't run into each other fast enough. Next, there's no guarantee Lilthral will send their army, and if they do, there's a high chance they'll contact the remaining cities for backup. Even if everything goes right up until then, and we arrive at Lilthral, we'll need to overthrow it and defeat their army when they return. That's three battles back-to-back, none of which will be easy."

Fletcher let out a frustrated sigh. "You're right. Even after all the time I spent on this plan, I still couldn't see the oversights I made." He balled his hand into a fist, mad at himself for failing again.

"You're thinking in the right direction. We need to drag Lilthral's army away to win, but we can't bring them to a city we haven't conquered," Crystal said. "If you'll accept my help, we can come up with a flawless strategy."

"I'd be a fool not to," Fletcher said, standing. "Show me what I've been missing out on."

FIFTY-TWO

"Queen Rinn, you have a package and letter from Dean Horn," an elf said, bowing before he addressed the queen.

Light grabbed the metal box from the elf and set it on the floor. Undoing the two latches holding it shut, Light unlocked the case and froze; his hands shaking in shock.

"This... It's impossible," Light whispered, standing and turning to the elf holding the note. "Give me the letter, quick!"

"Yes, sir!"

"Light?" Rinn asked, looking between him and the metal box resting on the floor. "What is in there?"

"You don't want to know, My Queen," Light said, opening the envelope.

"Light, tell me what's inside," the queen rephrased her question into an order.

Light gazed up at Rinn, the note still in his hand, before he replied, "Inside is a severed head... The head of Dean Horn."

"What?!" the queen yelled, standing from her throne with wide eyes. "That's not possible! Ronann would have to fall for Dean to be murdered! You're lying!"

"My Queen, have I ever lied to you?"

"Show me!"

"As you wish," Light said, bending down to the container. He turned it toward her and opened it. "As I told you, it is the head of Dean Horn."

The queen gagged and turned away, shielding her face with her hands. "I believe you. Now put it away!"

Light closed the vessel and stood, reading the message aloud. "Dear Your Majesty, I am Fletcher Rush, the leader of the humans and conqueror of IItu and Ronann. You may have believed that my people and I were defeated by Yasin and his army in IItu, but I can assure you that is not the case. I control Ronann, and I believe the decapitation of its former leader is evidence enough to prove that. You might be wondering how I have tricked you into thinking I was defeated, but that is irrelevant. What matters is why I am revealing myself to you now. This message is a threat to you and a declaration of war. If you surrender, I shall spare you all. But if you don't, your cities will be bathed in blood. The next city to fall will be Sullin, followed by Yuun, then Qrtta, and lastly Cartin. If you still wish to wage war after that, we shall conquer you as well. We humans are your enemy, but we are not monsters. We do not wish to kill needlessly. Surrendering is the best option for everyone. Think about my generous offer, let the white flag fly from your city when you accept. From your favorite human, Fletcher Rush."

By the time Light had finished reading Fletcher's proclamation, Rinn was seething with anger. "Who does that slave think he is?! Acting like he is in a position to negotiate with us! We are heading straight to Ronann to get rid of these scum!"

"Rinn—"

"Silence! Grab the entire army and show those scum no mercy! Kill every man, woman, and child in Ronann!"

"Yes, My Queen," Light said, leaving the throne room.

"And someone get that disgusting head out of my palace!"

Light marched to the military post, completely enraged. He was infuriated with Fletcher, since he was the trigger for this chaos. Even so, the bulk of his anger landed on himself. He was the one who spared Fletcher in IItu, and he was the one who went to Ronann and met with Dean, only to be fooled into thinking the city was still theirs.

Throwing open the doors to the military post, Light felt thousands of eyes turn to face him. He stood still, calming down before he addressed his soldiers. "The human scum have overthrown Ronann! They killed its overseer and are threatening to do the same with every city, unless we surrender! But we will not submit to them! They conquered Ronann and IItu, but they will suffer defeat at our hands! Our fallen kin will be avenged, and the scum will remember their place! All of you prepare to head out! We leave in one hour!"

Light watched hordes of elves scatter into action. He stared motionless as his soldiers darted past him, and time seemed to slow. The queen's orders rang in his head, but Dean's voice was considerably louder, his final conversation with the elf repeating in his mind.

It's my fault all of this happened. Dean is dead, and Ronann failed to reclaim IItu because of my orders... No, that's not right. I wanted to kill the humans from the beginning. It was the queen who ordered me not to. She was the one who gave the order for Ronann to attack IItu. Nothing is my fault. The Radamons have dug us into this hole. Everything I've done has only helped this kingdom. I'm the greatest elven fighter; I should have been rewarded and respected. I should have been Yasin's right-hand—no, I should have been King Harthorn's right-hand, and when Rinn became the queen, she should have begged me to stay in that position. But since I'm a commoner, I was denied those rights. I was looked down on, and the only reason Rinn chose me was because there was no one else. I'm done taking orders.

"STOP!" Light yelled, causing the room to pause. He clenched his fist until his fingernails dug into his palm and blood dripped onto the floor. "THE HUMANS CAN'T BEST US! THEY TOOK RONANN BECAUSE THE CITY GREW WEAK! YASIN LET HIMSELF GO AFTER THE GREAT WAR! DEAN WAS ADDICTED TO DRUGS, AND VINCENT MOPED IN SELF-PITY! IT'S NO WONDER RONANN FELL! BUT WE ARE NOT RONANN! I AM THE GREATEST ELF THIS KINGDOM HAS EVER SEEN! UNDER MY COMMAND, WE CANNOT LOSE!" Light hesitated and glanced at his comrades, all of whom were confused and concerned. "We will leave with half the army, and I expect those of you who stay behind are prepared to fight just as much as those who come with me."

FIFTY-THREE

"What do you see?!" Ji asked Fletcher.

"Nothing yet, but they only took the package two hours ago," Fletcher responded, taking the binoculars away from his eyes and handing them to Ji.

Two days ago, they had conquered Yuun, the second smallest city in the elven kingdom. They attacked it in the middle of the night with Fletcher's team and fifty others. It was a stealthy operation, so they headed straight to the city hall, killing off the overseer and taking his transmitter. With the city unable to call for help and having no military, they picked off the guards until all three hundred fifty were dead.

Once they had control of the city, Fletcher messaged Leon on their private channel, giving him the all clear and telling him to head over with the army. Eighteen hundred fifty men were with Leon, while the humans who weren't fighting had been moved to IItu together with the elves. Forty human soldiers were staying behind in IItu to make sure the elves didn't rebel. Unfortunately, the small city didn't have a prison, so Fletcher was forced to leave the captives in Ronann, along with five guards to keep watch over them. It wasn't perfect, and if Lilthral's army went to either city, they would be unable to defend themselves. However, Fletcher figured IItu was safer than Ronann, since the elves believed they were still in the larger city.

Dropping off the package with Dean's head and the letter was the last step, which Fletcher and Ji took care of early in the morning. Now, they were waiting to make sure the army left, keeping watch on a hill eight miles from the capital. The distance was enough that the city couldn't see them, but with the binoculars they had brought, Ji and Fletcher were able to see the main gate.

"They're leaving!" Ji exclaimed, peering through the binoculars.

"Let me see."

"Here," Ji said, handing them to Fletcher.

Fletcher brought them to his eyes, turning his gaze toward the front gates. Sure enough, they were open, and a massive convoy of military vehicles was pouring out from the city.

"Perfect. By the time our allies get here, the elves will be far enough for us to attack."

"Exactly as planned," Ji said, clapping Fletcher on the back. "We owe Crystal for this one."

"Give me some credit! I came up with the baseline and wrote that masterpiece of a letter. The one that I said would enrage the queen and have her sending Lilthral's army to Ronann by the end of the day."

"You did, but if it weren't for Crystal, we would have gone with your first idea."

"That's true, but..."

"But what?"

"I need to stop overlooking parts of my plans. We might have lost if she hadn't caught my mistakes," Fletcher said, handing the binoculars back to Ji.

"You're the one who started this rebellion, our best fighter, a great leader, and the one who carves the path for us to follow. You can rely on us for help even if you weren't fond of Crystal in the beginning."

"I never had a problem with her. She's the one who didn't get along with me, and for the record, I never wronged her in any way."

"You did point a sword at her when you first met."

"No, I did not. *She's* the one who pointed a sword at you and cut your neck with a dull blade."

"That doesn't sound like her."

"Ji, you're blinded by love."

"What?!" Ji shouted, dropping the binoculars and jumping up. "That's—"

"Ji, the binoculars!" Fletcher yelled as they tumbled down the steep hillside.

The two watched the blanket of snow being disturbed as the binoculars tumbled away.

"Sorry, that's my bad."

"At least we know they left. We can go back to Yuun and wait to attack."

They started back down the hill, going slowly.

"Do you want to talk more about Crystal, lover boy?" Fletcher teased and gave Ji a small shove.

"No."

"Come on, you didn't get to finish your sentence from earlier."

"I was just going to say it's not like that," Ji said, shoving his hands in his pockets. "Plus, we're in the middle of a war right now."

"Who cares that we're at war? We can't change the path behind us, but we can alter the one in front of us. If you never make a change and take that first step, you'll never get to where you want to be," Fletcher said in a serious tone. "It's your life; do as you please. But do you want to look back with regret?"

"No, but I don't think she feels the same way about me."

"Your point?"

"My point is it's embarrassing to get rejected, and we still have to work together."

"Ji, let me give you a piece of advice. If you care for someone and they don't care for you back, if you love someone and they don't love you back, then don't waste your time on them. Never let anyone hurt you. You're better than that. The most important person in your life is you. But don't get that twisted, that doesn't mean you're better than anyone else; it just means to always look out for yourself. You can watch out for others too, but keep your head up, stand tall, and keep marching forward, because if you stop for even a minute, you'll be swallowed up by the world," Fletcher said, pausing and putting a hand on Ji's shoulder. "We only live so long, so you might as well make sure your life is one you look back on with gratitude and honor."

Ji opened his mouth then closed it, thinking carefully about what he wanted to say. "You're right... I know you are. I'm just too scared to take a step forward. But I want to become a stronger person and live the life I desire."

"You've already grown far more than you realize, Ji," Fletcher said, walking down the hill again. "Just don't give up. Never give up, because if you quit, you'll never know what you could have been."

It took seven hours for Fletcher and Ji to reach the gates to Yuun, having traveled by snowmobile. Slowing down as they neared the entrance, they came to a complete stop.

"Open the gate!" Fletcher shouted.

For a minute, nothing happened, and Fletcher was slightly

worried that something was wrong. But eventually, a head poked out of the watchtower, then disappeared, and the gate slowly opened after that.

Once it was high enough, they drove inside, left the vehicles at the entrance, and walked the rest of the way to the ward.

The streets were empty now due to the cold, and walking through the small city was the most peace Fletcher had felt in a while. Flurries drifted down, and a soft yellow glow from the street lamps illuminated Yuun, while a few houses shone a dim glow through their windows.

Making their way up the steps to the ward, Fletcher brushed the snow off his fur jacket before heading inside. Opening the double doors, Fletcher and Ji were hit with the pleasant smell of dinner.

"I'm starving," Ji said, shutting the doors behind him and throwing his jacket on the floor, before running down the hall.

Fletcher shook his head and picked Ji's jacket off the ground. He set it on a coat rack next to him before he took off his own and hung it next to Ji's. Walking down the main hallway, he heard chatter growing louder. Pushing open the doors to the dining hall, he saw his team was already there.

"Let me eat! I haven't had real food all day!" Ji said, holding a plate and trying to get past Tor to the food.

"Wait for Fletcher! The rest of us waited for the two of you."

"Ji's about to start a fight with his own kind over food," Fletcher said, grabbing a cup of water. "It's like I'm back in Titanan."

"That was one time!"

"Ji started a fight over food?!" Crystal asked, dying to hear the story behind that. "What happened?"

"He—"

"Don't tell the story," Ji said, filling his plate and sitting at the table.

"Sorry, Ji, everyone wants to know what happened."

"That's an exaggeration, Crystal's the only one who asked about it."

"I want to know," Tor said, sitting across from Ji.

"See, everyone's curious," Fletcher said, grabbing a plate and filling it with food.

Ji groaned, taking a bite of chicken. "You always cause trouble, Fletcher."

"You're welcome," Fletcher said as he sat at the head of the table. "This was about four years ago, and Ji was having a great day—"

"It was a terrible day."

"And they were making double—"

"Triple."

"Chocolate cookies, which are Ji's favorite. They were rarely served at meals since we were slaves. But they were serving them that day, and by the time Ji had finished working, they were gone, all but one—"

"It was two."

"And as Ji walked over to grab one, another human took both of them before he could. Ji yelled at him—"

"I asked him for one first."

"But he refused and told Ji to screw off. So Ji beat the shit out of him." Fletcher finished his recollection of the story and started laughing, Crystal and Archer joining him.

"Are we talking about the same Ji?" Tor asked.

"Is that an insult?"

"Do you want it to be?"

"If we can get you to kill for those cookies, then we might be onto something," Crystal said, looking at Ji.

"I was having a bad day, and the guy was asking for it. At

least I didn't break his arm, unlike someone here." He eyed Fletcher.

"I'm proud of that!"

"Who's going to tell this story?" Tor asked, glancing between Fletcher and Ji.

"Let Fletcher tell it."

"No, go for it, Ji," Fletcher said, taking a bite of his meal. "I want to hear how you describe it."

Ji sighed before he started talking. "We all know how Fletcher trains often—"

"Twenty to forty hours a week."

"When we were slaves, he trained every day—"

"Five times a week."

"One day, he was training longer than usual. It was past midnight, and he was still working out, doing push-ups in the corner. However, one of the humans wasn't able to sleep because Fletcher was too loud—"

"Which is absurd. I was counting in my head as I always used to do back then."

"He went over to Fletcher and started chewing him out, and I'm sure you can guess the rest."

"That's the best part!" Fletcher said, taking over the story. "I paused my set and told him I could easily put him to sleep. He didn't find it as funny as I did, loser, then he shoved me and told me to go to bed. So I punched him in the face and snapped his right arm in half."

"I wish I had been a slave in Titanan instead of IItu," Tor said in a disappointed tone. "I feel that I missed out."

"We were still slaves at the end of the day. I don't know how it was in IItu, but it was bad in Titanan. It's better than it was a few hundred years ago, but it certainly wasn't fun."

"Sorry. I didn't mean it like that."

"It's fine, I wish you were there too. I wish we could've

lived free from birth, as we should have been able to," Fletcher said, causing the room to go silent, only to be broken by Crystal.

"It can't be worse than the angels." As soon as she finished her sentence, she realized what she had said. Tilting her head down and staring at her plate, she hoped no one asked any questions about her past.

"You were a slave for the angels?" Archer asked. "I didn't know that. I thought you were with Fletcher and Ji from the beginning."

"Same here," Tor said.

"I was a slave for the angels, but my mother helped me escape..." Crystal stopped, trying to find what to say. She could say she didn't want to talk about it, but what if they asked her again later. She could lie, but she had never been good at it, and the truth wasn't something she was ready to admit.

Before Crystal decided on what to say, Ji knocked over the pitcher of water on the table.

"Ji!" Fletcher scolded, getting up and grabbing a towel.

"Sorry," Ji muttered. "I wasn't paying attention."

Fletcher raised an eyebrow at his friend, knowing exactly what he did. He wasn't mad at him, but he did want to hear what Crystal had to say. They knew very little about her past, and even though he was sure she wouldn't betray them, he still wanted to know her story.

"I'll refill this," Crystal said, standing and grabbing the pitcher.

Ryan sighed and stared at his plate of pasta, which was now soaked with water. "Soggy food, just what I wanted for dinner."

FIFTY-FOUR

"One hundred ninety-eight," Fletcher counted, turning the page of the book on the Jixxes. "One hundred ninety-eight, one hundred ninety-nine, and two hundred." He finished doing squats and sat in one of the chairs in his room.

I think I counted an extra rep, Fletcher thought. *But I'd rather do too many than not enough.*

Fletcher set the book down and grabbed a drink of water. Ever since his first encounter with the Jixxes, Fletcher had been taking better care of himself. He'd rather train for hours every day and stay up all night, but he had to admit he felt better after he stopped doing that. Not to say he slept enough or didn't overtrain, but at least the bags under his eyes were gone. He had also cut his hair and shaved his stubble, making his appearance similar to what it was when he escaped Titanan.

Setting his glass of water down, Fletcher picked the book back up, giving it his full attention. He had been reading it when he had spare time, which wasn't often. With the attack on the capital approaching, he had been spending over twelve hours a day preparing for it, which is why he read the book during training. Currently, he was fifty-three pages in and had found out absolutely nothing new about the mysterious creatures.

"This would have been much better if Don just told me everything about these monsters," he muttered to himself, flipping through the numerous pages he had yet to read. "Maybe I can convince the old man to tell me the rest of the information."

He turned another page and was met with an anatomically correct drawing of the creatures. "Why do I have to know this?! I swear he was messing with me; there's literally nothing in here he didn't already tell me about."

Fletcher was about to skip this part and start skimming over the rest of the book when he remembered what Don told him. Staying on the page, Fletcher read the whole thing even though he didn't see a point to it.

Ji opened his eyes and stared up at the ceiling. It was still dark in the barracks, so he figured it was the middle of the night. Sitting up, he glanced over at the clock. Letting out a yawn, he rubbed his eyes and saw it was barely midnight.

Lying back down, Ji closed his eyes and tried falling back to sleep. The minutes passed by, and he was still awake. He turned to his side, hoping that would help. Unfortunately, it didn't, and he became restless. Sitting back up, he checked the clock again and saw he had been awake for half an hour. Deciding to get up, Ji threw the covers off and walked out of the barracks.

Ji walked down the dark, empty hallway into the kitchen. He opened the fridge and pulled out the leftover chicken from dinner. Putting it on a plate and heating it in the microwave, he waited for it to finish, grabbing a fork and knife in the meantime. Once it was warm, he pulled it out and sat at the table, digging in.

As he was eating, he heard something fall on the floor above him. Ji jumped out of his seat and looked up, about to rush upstairs before glancing back at his half-eaten chicken breast.

"That can wait," Ji said, sitting back down and taking another bite.

Finishing his late-night snack, Ji set the plate in the sink and went upstairs. He thought about heading back to the barracks to fetch his sword or ignoring it and going back to sleep, but he decided against both, figuring—or perhaps hoping—that it wasn't anything to be worried about. Reaching the top of the stairs, he heard a thump. Moving toward the noise, Ji stopped in front of the training room door. Grabbing the handle, he opened it and stepped inside.

"Crystal?" Ji said, staring at the woman alone in the dim space.

She turned toward him and set her bow down. "Sorry, did I wake you?"

"No, I woke up and couldn't fall back asleep, so I got up, and then I heard something fall and figured I should check it out."

"I missed a shot and hit the window," Crystal said, pointing at a pile of glass on the floor. "Also, that was several minutes ago. You took your sweet time checking for possible intruders...unarmed as well."

"At least I came," Ji said with a shrug.

"I'm glad you're never on lookout duty."

"In my defense, if I were, I would have come to check out the noise right away."

"Is that so?"

"Of course, I would have come barging in here, sword in hand, and searched every nook and cranny until I found the cause."

"If that's the case, maybe we should move you to lookout duty instead of the front line."

"I'll pass," Ji said, glancing at the target at the end of the room with two arrows sticking out of it, before he turned back to Crystal. "I take it you couldn't sleep."

"Is it that obvious?"

Ji nodded, hesitating before he asked, "I'm guessing it had to do with dinner?"

Crystal turned away before she answered in a quiet voice. "Yeah... I'm sure you and Fletcher want to know about my past. But, I... You won't look at me the same, and I'm scared to admit who I really am."

It was hard to see in the room with only one light on, but Ji could tell she was shaking. He wasn't sure it was the right thing to do, but he wrapped his arms around Crystal, pulling her against him so her back was pressed against his chest. He felt her stop shaking and stiffen at his touch, but she didn't pull away.

"I can't speak for Fletcher, but you don't have to tell me anything you don't want to. We're on the same side, and you've proven your loyalty, so I see no reason why you need to tell us anything," Ji said softly into her ear. "But if you do want to tell us your past, that's fine too."

Crystal stayed silent for a while before she responded. "Thanks...and thanks for dinner."

"You don't have to thank me for anything," Ji said, letting go of her. "I'm going back to bed. You should probably do the same. Will you be able to fall asleep now?"

"Only time will tell," Crystal said, glancing at Ji. "Even if I can't, I'm not hitting my shots anymore, so there's no point staying here."

FIFTY-FIVE

"Stop the convoy here," Leon told the driver.

"Are you sure? We're still five hundred miles from Yuun, and it's important to get there soon."

"What's important is getting there alive," Leon said, putting his hand on the driver's seat and leaning forward. "And in this weather, I can't see anything. Not to mention all the snow and ice on the streets, which is making it harder to drive."

"Where do you want me to park?" the driver asked, slowing down.

"Right here. I'll inform Fletcher now."

The convoy slowed before coming to a halt. Meanwhile, Leon grabbed his transmitter and sent a message to Fletcher about the situation.

Can anything ever go to plan? Fletcher responded a moment later. *Do you think you'll be back on the move by morning?*

I can't say for sure. If we crash, we won't be able to make it at all, and I'm not risking the lives of my men.

I understand, and I would do the same in your position.

The channel was quiet for a minute before Fletcher sent another message. *Lilthral left earlier today, so we weren't going to leave tomorrow anyway. But, if you're not here the morning after tomorrow, we'll have to leave without you.*

Are you sure?

Yes. We only have one shot at this. If we wait, we'll have no chance of taking the capital.

Alright, I'll update you in the morning then.

Leon put his transmitter away and looked around the convoy. "How much food do we have left?"

"Two full bags," one of the soldiers said, holding a leather pouch in each hand.

"That should last us. We'll just have to ration it," Leon said, walking back into the driver's cabin. "What about gas? Can we leave the trucks on and still make it to Yuun?"

"Depends on how long we're here."

"I'm not taking any risks. Turn the truck off; we'll make do without heat. And tell the rest of the convoy to do the same."

"Yes, sir," the driver said, shutting off the vehicle and picking up the radio to relay the order.

Leon moved back to the main cabin and faced his men. "Grab a blanket and huddle up. We're losing heat, and we might be here a while."

The soldiers started to complain.

"Stop whining!" Leon ordered. "We're soldiers! If you can't handle this, how are you going to fight with your life on the line?! This is war, and if you're not ready for it, you should have stayed in IItu with the women and children! I thought all of you were tough and wanted to fight for the freedom of our species?! Was I wrong?!"

"No, sir!" the men shouted.

"Then shut up and prove it! And be ready for battle! We're closer to it than many of you realize."

FIFTY-SIX

The elves had set up camp for the night, and while everyone else had already fallen asleep, Light was still awake. He had been sitting outside his tent, gazing at the night sky, when his peace was interrupted.

"Are you even prepared?"

Light looked over at Ingrid, who had returned from training and was breathing heavily. "What is there to prepare for? This is most likely a trap, and the real target is somewhere else."

"If you believe that, then why are we here, playing right into their hands?"

"We're not. Why do you think I left half the army in Lilthral? If they attack the capital, they will lose. If they are still in Ronann, we will defeat them, and if they capture another city, then we will gather the kingdom's remaining forces and snuff them out once and for all."

Ingrid stared at Light. Even though the two had been childhood friends, Ingrid had never been able to read Light, and it had only gotten worse over the years. But now, he was utterly baffled by the other elf's thinking. "That doesn't make sense. If you truly believe those scum are plotting to take another city, then leaving for Ronann was a mistake. We should be acting strategically and bringing our forces together, not dividing them up and relying on luck."

"When did I speak of luck? You talk as if we are at a disadvantage and have no possibility of victory."

"You're underestimating them and overestimating us. The humans overthrew Ronann and issued a declaration of war against us. If they didn't believe they could defeat us, they wouldn't have acted."

Light frowned at his comrade. Standing, he moved closer to Ingrid. "I lead this army, you follow it. Do not lecture me on how I command my troops."

The red-haired elf turned away and went inside his tent, leaving Ingrid disappointed in the leader he once admired.

FIFTY-SEVEN

Miller's fingers bled as he dug into the hard, densely packed dirt. Not even fifteen minutes after he had been given his first rations, he went to work. There were at least three guards keeping watch over the prison. Luckily for Miller, they were lazy, and instead of bringing the elves three meals a day, they gave them rations to last the week. Furthermore, they hadn't checked up on the cells at all.

Before Dean was taken, Miller figured out what the elf had meant about the floor. After that, he just had to wait for an opportunity, and it turned out to be better than he hoped.

Miller began with a brick butted up against the bars, but moved to the one behind it since that was proving too difficult. After ripping open the skin on the tips of his fingers, he was finally able to pry the stone enough to lift it. When he had gotten the first one out, the ones next to it were easy, and he slowly removed a vast portion of the cell's floor until he could start digging his way out. It had taken him five hours to move all the stones, and he spent another six digging.

Miller stopped working and wiped his forehead, mixing the dirt covering his hands with his sweat and smearing mud across his face. Grabbing his shirt, which he had discarded long ago, he wiped his hands, getting them as clean as possible before grabbing a slice of bread. He was very hungry, but only ate what he needed, given that the rations were barely enough to last four days.

Digging his way out was already proving difficult, but his goal was to finish in three days. If luck continued to shine down on him, the guards wouldn't check on the elves during that time, and he wouldn't have any issues with food.

As he finished his slice of bread, he eyed the rest of the loaf, debating if he should take more. He decided to grab one more slice, then washed it down with a sip of water before getting back to work.

After one more hour of digging, Miller called it a night, wiping off his hands again before he lay down on his hay bed.

He was so tired he thought he would easily fall asleep, but half an hour later, he was still up. Refusing to toss and turn, Miller stayed on his back, hoping sleep would take him soon; after another twenty minutes, it finally did.

Miller groggily opened his eyes and stared at the boring gray stone ceiling. He had woken up to that view more times than he could count, having lost track after two weeks.

Sitting up, he stretched his arms above his head before standing. He looked down at the hole he had started yesterday and grabbed a stick of jerky, eating it and draining his second bottle of water before getting his hands dirty.

Miller knelt and pressed his fingers into the soil again, clawing at the ground and pulling away clumps of dirt.

He continued to dig for two hours until he eventually made enough progress that the stones outside his cell began to sink. Seeing how close he was, Miller dug more ferociously than before as his determination to escape grew.

Thoughts of avenging his parents flooded his mind, and he worked like he was possessed, ignoring the sting in his hands as his fingertips bled and his knuckles scraped raw against the rocks embedded in the dirt.

Miller suppressed a scream as he completely broke one of his fingernails. Removing his left hand from the hole, he brought it close to his face and saw that the nail was completely gone. Blood flowed from the wound, coating his hand.

Ripping off a strand of cloth from his shirt, Miller wrapped it tightly around his finger, trying to clot the wound. Instantly, the dirty white cloth turned a bright red. Even though the bleeding persisted, Miller continued to dig. By the time he finished, he was covered in sweat and had completely ruined his shirt, having torn it to use as bandages.

Sitting against the wall, Miller grabbed a drink of water. He was utterly exhausted, and his hands and back were throbbing in pain. Freedom was right in front of him, but he wanted to rest before he escaped.

Lying down on his hay bed, Miller was unable to stay awake and accidentally fell asleep.

Miller moaned as he woke. Stretching his arms and legs, he rubbed his eyes, feeling confused, before he realized what had happened. "I fell asleep!" he exclaimed, jumping to his feet.

Letting out a sigh, he removed the cloth from his hand and examined his wound. The nail bed injury had stopped bleeding but appeared infected.

Just what I need.

He grabbed the cleanest strip of cloth he could find—even though it wasn't really clean—and poured the last of his water on it. Once soaked, he used it to wash his wound, then rebandaged it. Grinning, Miller crawled through the hole. At long last, after months trapped in the cell, he was free.

"I'M FREE!" Miller yelled, his cry of triumph echoing throughout the prison, causing the other elves to stir.

Several of them peered out of their cells, and when they saw Miller, they begged him to release them.

"Miller, free me!" an elf shouted, pressing his face against the bars and reaching his arms out. "We were always friends. I would help you if the positions were reversed!"

"No you wouldn't," Miller said, looking back his prior allies. "None of you liked me. You were all jealous that I was appointed as the overseer's right-hand. I know for a fact that you were hoping I'd lose everything, that you could step on me and say I'm nothing but trash. Even if my life depended on it, I still wouldn't free any of you." He turned around and walked away, his kin's screams ringing in his ears.

Reaching the exit to the prison, he cautiously opened the door and peered out. Seeing no one on the other side, he slipped through and closed the door behind him.

I need to grab a weapon, Miller thought, quietly making his way down the hall. He froze when he heard voices, but continued when he realized they were upstairs.

Still proceeding carefully, Miller walked into the ward's small armory and beamed as he saw there were three suits of armor and a handful of weapons. All of them were in rough shape, which is why they were left behind, but Miller wasn't picky.

As he left the room, he heard commotion upstairs. He could sneak out of the military post without running into them, properly clean and bandage his wound, grab food for his trip, and leave Ronann with ease. But he wasn't going to.

•   •   •

"Three of us found that pathetic elf who used to kick us as we worked. He begged for mercy, but we beat him until his eyes were swollen shut and blood covered our hands!" one of the guards said, bellowing with laughter.

"Those elves act tough, but when the tables are turned, it's hysterical how weak they are!"

"Speaking of tables turning..."

The five guards stopped talking and looked toward the source of the voice.

"Filthy elf! Where did you come from?!" one of the guards asked, drawing his sword and pointing it at Miller.

"If you did your job, you would know," Miller said, donning his helmet and drawing his own sword.

"I'll show—" a guard started before Miller sprinted forward and stabbed the man in the chest, his blade easily going through his unarmored body.

The other four jumped into action, to no avail. Miller lost to Fletcher, but he was Dean's right-hand for a reason, and the months he spent training in the prison had paid off. The sword in his hand felt foreign yet weightless, and the thick armor protecting his body was heavier than his own, yet he moved faster.

Blocking two swords simultaneously, Miller shoved them back and lunged at the human closer to him. Dodging under an attack, he slit the man's throat, spun around, and decapitated the one on his left. He parried a swing coming at him and countered by ramming his pommel into the man's ribs. The guard dropped to his knees and spat out blood before Miller grabbed his head and snapped his neck.

"You're the last one," Miller said, glaring at the human cowering in the corner.

"I, I surrender!" the man said, throwing his weapon down and putting his hands in the air.

"And I set you free," Miller said. He saw the man's eyes light up in hope, before they were filled with fear as Miller raised his sword. Blood spattered his armor as he lodged the blade into the guard's skull. Pulling the weapon free, he sheathed it and removed his helmet. Surveying the mess he had made, Miller started laughing maniacally.

FIFTY-EIGHT

Fletcher would be lying if he said he wasn't stressed out. The blizzard was still raging, and Leon was hundreds of miles from Yuun. He hoped the weather would clear up and his army could start moving again. But the minutes turned into hours until the day came to an end, and nothing had changed.

Waking up, Fletcher checked the clock and saw it was zero six thirty. He hadn't expected to get any sleep, but he was pleasantly surprised by how well rested he felt. That said, he was still filled with dread. He knew they would be going into an attack that they had no chance of winning, and he was questioning whether he should change their strategy before he checked his transmitter.

Fletcher was overcome with hope and excitement. Leon had messaged him forty minutes ago, letting him know that the storm had cleared four hours earlier and that the drivers had stayed up all night doing their job.

Finally, some good news! We're unable to wait for you, since we can't leave for Lilthral later than eight hundred hours, but I estimate it will take us ten hours to get there. Try to be there by twenty-one hundred; I don't think we can last longer than that.

Fletcher sent the message and got out of bed, opening his curtains to glance outside. The storm hadn't hit them, but the city was still covered in snow. When his transmitter buzzed, he grabbed it from the nightstand.

I promise we'll be there before twenty hundred hours. Good luck.

Likewise.

"This wasn't part of the plan," Fletcher said to himself. He had been hesitant from the beginning about leaving the bulk of the army in Ronann. But the reason they did was in case things went wrong in Yuun. If they were unable to capture the city or the overseer called for help before they reached him, their cover would be blown. In that case, their backup tactic was for Leon and the army to take everyone and retreat to Admont. Granted, if Fletcher knew they'd get stuck, he wouldn't have bothered with it.

"I'm trusting you, Leon," Fletcher muttered to himself. "Don't let me down."

"That doesn't sound like a good idea!" Tor said, freaking out.

"I'm also not sure about this, Fletch. This is a huge fight. Wouldn't it be better to wait for the others?" Ji asked.

"I can't! We need to get to Lilthral before their army reaches Ronann. If I knew where the elves were, when Leon would get here, and how long it would take us to reach the capital, I could make a better decision, but with this weather, it's impossible."

"I agree with Fletcher. We don't have a choice," Crystal said. "Although we dug ourselves into this situation, we can't do anything about it now other than push forward."

"Thank you!" Fletcher said, glad someone understood why they didn't have any other choice.

"I think the rest of us are lost. Why exactly is this our only option?" Archer asked.

"Let me simplify this. The elves' army is headed toward Ronann as we speak, and once they arrive and see that we're not there, they're going to contact Lilthral. At that point, the whole kingdom is going to go into lockdown because they'll know we're planning something, and if that happens, we won't be able to take the city. As for waiting, we can't do that either. If we stay here, we're sitting ducks, waiting for the forty-eight hundred soldiers from Lilthral to attack us, which is a fight we won't be able to win."

"Why not?" Ji asked. "We were able to defend IItu against Ronann, and we were at a huge disadvantage."

"Because they severely underestimated us then," Crystal said. "On top of that, there's a high chance they'll contact the last three cities for aid."

"The only way we can defeat Lilthral's army is by taking their city and freeing our kin."

"That makes more sense now." Archer nodded.

"So are we going to attack at nightfall as we originally intended?" Ji asked.

"Yes, and hopefully the rest of the army arrives shortly after us," Fletcher said, standing. "There's only an hour until we leave, so start loading up the trucks."

Everyone started to disperse after that, except Ji, who went over to Fletcher and whispered, "There are fewer than three hundred of us here, and we're going up against eleven hundred trained elves. Not to mention, they have the advantage of being on defense and knowing the city much better than we do. Do you believe we can hold out until reinforcements arrive?"

Fletcher leaned in close to Ji and spoke in a low voice so no one would overhear. "I do, but we're going to suffer heavy losses."

"I don't want to say it, but if that's what it takes to win, then so be it. I'm willing to sacrifice my life if it gives us a shot at freedom, and I'm sure many of the others are as well."

"The price for freedom is the blood of others, but that doesn't mean I want to see my allies die."

FIFTY-NINE

Allica stripped down, throwing her clothes onto the tile floor as she stepped into the warm shower.

"That feels good," she said as the water washed over her body. "I needed this."

Ever since Dean's head showed up, Mother has been freaking out, and the whole palace has been on high alert, she thought, letting out an annoyed sigh. *This is happening because of Mother's incompetence. If she had acted like a real leader and dealt with the human rebellion in the first place, we wouldn't have these problems.*

"Humans," she growled, touching her ear.

Removing her hand, she stopped thinking about the whole mess and concentrated on washing herself, basking in the calming water for a few minutes. She had just grabbed the bar of soap when the door to the bathroom was thrown open.

"Princess—"

"Why are you here?! Can't you see I'm showering, you idiot?!" Allica scolded Jax, her bodyguard, as she covered her nakedness with her arms.

"I'm sorry, My Lady, but it's urgent—"

"What is so urgent that you walk in on a naked princess?!"

"We are under attack, My Lady," Jax said, facing away from the woman.

Allica's face changed from anger to worry, then back to anger. "Those scum!" she said before calming down. "I don't care at this point, let me finish washing up and put on my clothes."

"I'll wait for you outside," Jax said, facing her briefly to bow before he left, closing the door behind him.

Allica stared blankly at the door before she went back to cleaning herself. Finishing up, she shut off the water and stepped out of the shower and onto the sea-green and orange slate tile of the bathroom floor, forming a puddle of water at her feet while she grabbed the towel hanging on the wall next to her.

Walking over to grab her clothes, Allica donned a gorgeous white nightgown before gazing at herself in the mirror.

She had long silver hair, the same as her mother's, and bright green eyes like her father's. Her figure was slim, and her face was beautiful. In her eyes, she was perfect, except for one part.

She pushed back her hair and looked at her rounded human ears. Allica hated to admit it, but she was half-elf, half-human. Her mother was a pure-blooded elf, but her father was a filthy human, one that her mother married and conceived a child with. Allica didn't care that she was a hybrid, but she held nothing but hatred for all humans, including herself and her father. Granted, that didn't mean she loved her mother. No, she despised Rinn more than anyone. They never got along, but after Rinn ordered her father to be executed, Allica began to hate her, and when she found out the reason he was killed, it only infuriated her further.

A knock on the door brought the princess out of her thoughts and back to reality.

"My Lady, are you done yet?" Jax called from the other side of the door.

"Yes... I'm coming," Allica said, opening the door and facing Jax. "Where are we going?"

"The throne room," Jax said, heading off down the hall. "It's the queen's orders."

"Of course it is," she murmured.

"Pardon?"

"Nothing," Allica grumbled, walking next to Jax. "This is pointless. The humans will be wiped out before they make it into the city. Mother is wasting my time."

"My Lady, they've already made it into the city."

SIXTY

"We're going to die!"

"Trust me, Ji!" Fletcher shouted.

"I do trust you, that's the problem!"

The two were driving a military truck filled with explosives at top speed toward the north gate of Lilthral. The goal was to smash into the gate and invade the city, sending the elves into a panic as they waited for the rest of their army to arrive.

"Shove the stick in!" Fletcher said, moving over so Ji could shove the metal rod against his seat and jam it into the gas pedal.

"Move your foot over!" Ji said, trying to keep the rod from slipping.

"I can't! Just shove it in! My foot isn't in the way!"

"You're full of shit," Ji muttered, finally able to get the stick into place. "Got it!"

"Now tie your end of the rope to the wheel!" Fletcher shouted, reaching out the window and grabbing his side of the rope that was thrown over the top of the truck.

Ji took his end and moved toward the wheel, putting his feet on the passenger seat and leaning over the center console. He looped the rope around the wheel and started tying it into a knot.

"Ji, hurry up!"

"I'm trying, I just started!"

"We're going to crash into the gate—"

"Then you should've moved your foot earlier!"

"Ji—"

"I'm done!" Ji yelled, moving over to the passenger side and jumping out the window while Fletcher did the same on his side.

They both collided into the snow, but Fletcher hit his right shoulder on a patch of ice.

"That hurt," Fletcher groaned, standing and rubbing what he could of his shoulder.

A thunderous boom resonated from the direction of the city, and the night sky was set ablaze in fiery orange. Not even a second later, Fletcher felt the shockwave from the discharge reverberate through his whole body, nearly knocking him down.

"I love explosives!" Fletcher yelled, staring at the massive fiery void where the gate used to be.

"We almost died!"

"And whose fault is that?!"

"Don't look at me, this whole thing was your idea!" Ji pointed at Fletcher and walked over to him.

"You're right about that!" Fletcher said, stepping onto the side of the dirt road next to Ji. "And it worked out great!"

"It could have gone smoother."

Before the two could argue any further, a bright light washed over them, and a truck pulled up beside them.

"Get in!" Tor shouted, leaning out the window.

"About time you got here," Fletcher said, getting in the back where the rest of his team was. "Any longer and they would have boarded the gate back up."

"Don't lecture us; you and Ji hardly got out of the truck in time," Crystal said, glancing back from the front seat into the cabin behind her.

"But you have to admit that was legendary!" Fletcher said, slapping Ji on the back.

Crystal let out a sigh and faced the front again. "Men."

The convoy of vehicles swarmed into the city's north sector, filling the empty square. Before the trucks were fully stopped, the soldiers started jumping out of the back, filling the streets and drawing their weapons. The city was abuzz with yelling and the blaring of deafening sirens, with elves running in and out of buildings, and lights blazing to life.

"WE ARE HOPELESSLY OUTNUMBERED," Fletcher yelled, turning toward his army as Lilthral's guards rushed down the road toward them. "BUT THIS IS NOT A HOPELESS FIGHT! THIS BATTLE WILL DECIDE THE FATE OF FAR MORE THAN US! THIS IS A BATTLE FOR THE SAKE OF OUR KIND'S FUTURE! FOR THE FUTURE OF OUR KIDS AND THEIR KIDS AS WELL! WE MUST HOLD STRONG UNTIL REINFORCEMENTS ARRIVE! WE MUST FIGHT WITH EVERYTHING WE HAVE AND BEYOND! WE FACE DEATH CLEARER THAN WE EVER HAVE BEFORE, BUT IF I DIE TODAY, THEN I AM GLAD I GAVE MY LIFE FOR FREEDOM!"

Fletcher led the charge up the road, sprinting toward the enemy with his army right behind him.

The two foes clashed, swords hitting swords and screams filling the air as members from both sides were instantly killed. Right away, Fletcher realized they were too compact; he barely had room to move, much less swing his claymore.

"We're too cramped!" Tor yelled, unable to attack and forced to stay on defense.

"I have an idea, but it's risky!" Fletcher shouted, killing a guard and moving closer to Tor. "Swing your hammer and move as deep into the crowd as you can, then do a complete spin!"

"Are you trying to get me killed?!"

"Trust me!" Fletcher said, glancing at his ally to confirm they were on the same page.

Tor nodded and did as Fletcher commanded. Despite the limited space, Tor was able to swing his hammer and knock down three elves. Quickly stepping forward, he rammed his shoulder into an elf, knocking him into a guard behind him. Tor felt a blade slip through his armor and cut his lower back. He grunted in pain but persevered. Gripping his hammer, he swung in a circle once, sending over a dozen guards to the ground and killing one of them. Right as he stopped, several elves lunged at him, only to be beheaded by Fletcher.

"Go back-to-back!" Fletcher commanded.

Tor understood Fletcher's idea and turned around, hovering an inch away from his friend. They worked in sync, constantly moving and covering each other. Tor swung his hammer, taking out two to four elves every time, then swapped sides with Fletcher, who attacked the elves that were knocked down or advancing on them, before switching sides again. The elves began to catch on to their tactics, but they couldn't get close enough to counter.

Unfortunately, Fletcher's strategy was short-lived, as an archer aimed at the two. An arrow whizzed by Fletcher's head, missing him by mere inches and planting itself into one of the elves behind him. In the brief second that he was distracted, the sea of elves parted, and a soldier ran through them, ramming into Fletcher with a heavy tower shield.

Fletcher's body slammed into the shield as he was shoved into Tor, knocking both of them down. The elf who had knocked them down raised his shield and was preparing to bring it down on Tor's head when Fletcher kicked him in the crotch. He groaned and lowered his shield, resting it in front of him, while Fletcher jumped to his feet and grabbed Tor's hammer, crushing the soldier's skull with the heavy weapon.

The elf slumped forward, falling on top of his shield. Meanwhile, Tor improvised, since Fletcher was using his weapon. Grabbing a corpse, he attacked the other elves, using it to keep them at bay and even knocking two guards out.

Using the carcass as a weapon didn't last long, as the bones broke and the body became more like a floppy fish than a rigid club. Unable to deal damage with the body anymore, Tor started swinging him around. Holding the elf by his legs, he spun in circles and built momentum before letting go, sending him into the mass of elves and taking four to the ground.

"That's what I call an elven weapon!"

"Tor, catch!"

Tor turned toward Fletcher and saw his hammer coming his way. Grabbing it, he took a step toward his comrade and swung his weapon, taking out another enemy.

Fletcher ducked, moving out of the way of Tor's attack and grabbing the tower shield from the soldier he had just killed. Standing back to his full height, he blocked a hit and went back-to-back with Tor again. "I'm amazed and concerned that you used a dead elf as a weapon!"

"Should I do it again?!"

"No! We have weapons for a reason, Tor!" Fletcher shouted, grabbing his dagger, only for it to be instantly knocked out of his hand. "Maybe you can do that to Light."

"Who?"

"The elf you fooled in—never mind."

The two of them continued to fight, with Fletcher blocking arrows that flew toward them and protecting Tor from incoming attacks.

"Where is my claymore?!"

"If I knew, I would tell you."

Fletcher bashed an elf in the face. "So we'll keep hitting them with blunt objects and hope they get enough brain damage to be rendered useless?!"

"You're the one who lost your weapons!"

"How did I get stuck fighting with you?!"

"You came to me!" Tor yelled, switching sides with Fletcher.

"That was before I knew we were going to get jammed in a mass of endless elves!"

"That's not my fault!"

"I never said it was!"

"It sure sounded like it!" Tor said, shoving an enemy back and breaking another's ribs.

Fletcher parried a longsword with his shield and slammed it into the elf, knocking him down. Ducking under a strike, he swept the guard's legs out from under him, then dodged an arrow from afar before raising his shield to block an axe.

"I need my sword!" Fletcher yelled in frustration. "I can't kill anyone like this!" He defended against an attack, ramming the edge of his shield into the elf's jaw, shattering the bone. The guard slumped to the ground, unconscious, his allies stepping over him as if he were simply another dead body.

As the battle continued, Fletcher and Tor found it increasingly difficult to defend themselves. Their own allies were falling in droves, and the enemy horde had only gotten bigger. Then Fletcher's boot hit something that wasn't the brick street or a body. Looking down, he saw his claymore buried under two corpses.

"My weapon!" Fletcher exclaimed, picking it up and wielding it in his right hand. "We need those archers taken care of so I can use my claymore as it's meant to be!"

"You're telling that to the wrong person!"

"Someone has to kill them! Our allies are diminishing by

the minute, and it's hard enough to fend off the elves surrounding us! I don't need guards shooting at me on top of that!"

Just then, an arrow shot from the closest tower, flying toward an archer and lodging in his throat. Barely ten seconds later, Ji burst through the crowd, stumbling and running into Fletcher.

"Ji—"

"Shut up! Do you know how hard it was to get here?! You two imbeciles charged ahead, leaving everyone else behind, and I had to fight through a whole crowd of elves to get here!" Ji said, turning around and pressing his back against the two.

"That's great, Ji. Tor and I have been fighting off hundreds of elves the whole time," Fletcher said, discarding his tower shield and gripping his claymore with both hands.

"And whose fault is that?!"

Before they could argue any more, Archer and Ryan burst through the crowd.

"Stop arguing! We're in the middle of a battle!" Archer snapped, raising his shield in his left hand and cutting down an elf with the sword in his right.

"We're not arguing!" Fletcher and Ji shouted at the same time.

Archer sighed and joined the huddle, which now contained five of them. Getting into a rhythm, they moved like a well-oiled machine.

Fletcher ducked, narrowly missing the blade of his foe. Taking a step back, Ji intervened, stabbing the elf in his breastplate and going through to his ribcage.

Archer raised his shield, protecting himself, as Ryan charged in, cutting off the guard's arm right below the elbow. Blood gushed out of the stump, splattering on Ryan and Archer.

The elf screamed and stared at his missing arm in horror before Tor crushed his head with his hammer.

"Fletcher, we can't hold out much longer!" Tor yelled, attacking less and defending more.

"Keep fighting until we win or die!" Fletcher shouted, feeling fatigued as well. He knew things seemed bleak. All their allies were dead; the only exception being Crystal, who had secured a spot on top of one of the guard towers and was shooting down the enemy archers.

This is worse than I thought it would be. If reinforcements don't get here soon, we're dead.

SIXTY-ONE

"I can't say I'm surprised," Light said, chuckling as he looked at his transmitter. "I was right." He tossed the device to Ingrid.

Ingrid raised his eyebrows at the other elf before he read the message: *LIGHT, GET BACK HERE! THE HUMANS ARE ATTACKING US!*

Throwing the transmitter aside, Ingrid grabbed Light by the collar. "How is this a laughing matter?! Our capital is—"

Light kicked Ingrid in the stomach and grabbed him by his dirty blond hair. "There are fifteen hundred guards and twenty-four hundred soldiers there, while the humans can't have more than a thousand men."

"So what?!" Ingrid shouted, grabbing Light and slamming him against the door. "We outnumbered them in IItu, and how did that turn out?!"

Light punched his friend in the face and flipped their positions, pinning him against the car. He heard a crack as he did so and glanced down to see that he had stepped on his transmitter. Letting out a frustrated sigh, Light felt himself falling forward as Ingrid opened the door.

The two tumbled out of the moving car and into the snow. Immediately after, the convoy came to a halt, and a few soldiers peered out of the trucks to see why they had stopped.

"You suspected it was a trap, and yet you played right into it!" Ingrid yelled and threw a ball of ice at Light.

Light dodged the ball and glared at Ingrid. "Were you not listening to me the other day?! THIS IS MY PLAN! Are you so ignorant as to think the humans would have attacked the capital while we were still there?! They expected to face off against eleven hundred elven guards, yet they will be met with thirty-nine hundred adversaries! The human scum launched this battle, assuming they had the advantage, but that couldn't be further from the truth." Light turned away from Ingrid and got back in his car.

"Sir—"

"Park the convoy here. We're setting up camp for the night, and in the morning, we'll head back to Lilthral."

SIXTY-TWO

"Queen Rinn, only six humans remain."

"Serves those scum right. Let this be a lesson to the slaves; this is the inevitable outcome if they try to rebel," Rinn said, glancing down at her transmitter and the message she had sent two hours ago when the humans first broke into the city.

Light hasn't responded. Maybe I shouldn't have bothered him; he can't get here in time anyway, Rinn thought, wondering if she had overreacted.

Before she could ponder her orders to Light any longer, her daughter interrupted her thinking. "Can I leave now, Mother? I want to go to bed."

"Not yet. We can't know if they have any tricks up their sleeve until we have completely dealt with all of them."

Allica groaned. "Why would they wait until they've almost been defeated to act?"

"Stop complaining and sleep on the floor if you're that tired."

"The floor? What am I, a peasant? I'll stay awake," Allica said, making a disgusted face.

"Do you want me to fetch something for you to sleep on, Princess?" Jax asked.

"If I am forced to stay here for more than ten minutes, then yes, I would."

"I'll go grab something now," Jax said, making his way out of the room.

"Jax!" Allica tried to call him back, but he had already left. *Smart aleck... At least he's loyal and obedient.*

SIXTY-THREE

Fletcher's arms were sore, and his legs felt heavy. His armor was uncomfortable, and his movements were becoming sluggish. He knew they couldn't keep this up and felt exactly as he had in Ronann, except this time, Fletcher had no idea where his allies were. But he held on to hope.

Leon had promised Fletcher he would be there by twenty hundred hours, and Fletcher trusted him. He didn't know the exact time, but from the moons' positions, he guessed it was past nineteen forty.

In a final, desperate effort, Fletcher rallied the Vanguard. "I CAN TELL YOU'RE EXHAUSTED! BUT STAND TALL UNTIL YOUR LEGS GIVE OUT, AND WIELD YOUR WEAPON UNTIL YOU CAN'T GRIP IT ANYMORE! YOUR LIVES ARE IN MY HANDS, AND I WON'T LET THEM BE TAKEN UNTIL THEY ARE RIPPED AWAY FROM MY DEAD BODY!"

Filled with a last boost of vigor, Ji, Tor, Ryan, and Archer fought with everything they had. All of them had suffered numerous wounds and were utterly drained. Because of that, none of them were fighting at their best and made more mistakes than they usually would. But any opening they left, Fletcher covered.

Fletcher blocked a jab headed for Ji and grunted as

another guard sliced his right thigh. Ji cut down the elf who hurt Fletcher, before he took a shield to the face. Ji stumbled back, getting behind Fletcher, who protected him while he recovered. He tasted blood on his lips as it ran from his nose, and his ears rang, but once he had his bearings back, Ji charged back into battle as if nothing had happened.

Ducking under a swing, Fletcher countered by decapitating his foe. He stayed by Ji, making sure he was fine before he moved over to Tor, who was struggling to defend himself against two soldiers.

Ramming into one of them, Fletcher stabbed the other. Tor killed the elf Fletcher had knocked down by crushing his ribcage with his hammer and going back on the defensive. He stayed beside Fletcher, doing his best to protect his friend since he was too tired to attack.

"Tor, move closer to Ji and cover him!" Fletcher ordered, realizing the large man was barely holding out.

Tor nodded and moved closer to Ji. Fletcher wanted to join Tor on the other side, but it was clear Archer and Ryan needed the help more. Squeezing in between the two, Fletcher gave it everything he had to defend them both. Ryan was a better fighter than Archer, but he had a wound on his right arm that was slowing him down.

Parrying a strike aimed at Archer, Fletcher stabbed the guard in the stomach. Pulling his blade out, he locked weapons with two opponents. Before he had time to act, Fletcher was hit. A shortsword cut through his breastplate and sliced into his ribs. The wound wasn't deep and didn't even reach bone, but it was still three inches long. As the blade was removed, Fletcher felt blood running down his torso.

The elf went in for another hit, but Fletcher pulled his claymore back from the elves he was fighting and stabbed the guard in the throat. Turning back to the other two, he dodged one swing and countered by decapitating him. Blocking the other's blade, Archer finished him off. Giving his ally a nod of thanks, he looked at Ryan and saw a greataxe moving toward his head.

"Ryan!" Fletcher yelled, tackling his ally and taking the hit himself. The greataxe sliced through his armor and cut his upper left back.

Rolling over, Fletcher blocked an attack from the same soldier. He groaned as a dead body underneath him dug into his back, but shoved the huge elf's axe away. Before he could stand back up, Fletcher was kicked in the face, and the elf with the axe stepped on his neck. He held him off again, but was unable to fight back since his enemy was pinning him down.

As Fletcher struggled to keep the axe blade from inching closer to his face, he was kicked by other elves surrounding him. Just as he was starting to lose hope, he was blinded by a bright light and heard a voice he wasn't sure he would hear again.

"YOU DISGUSTING ELVES, I'LL BEAT EVERY LAST ONE OF YOU TO DEATH!"

The crowd of elves saw the speeding truck and scattered, but the heavy elf who was stepping on Fletcher didn't move. Before Fletcher could act, Ryan lunged at the soldier, throwing him off. In a matter of seconds, Fletcher stood, letting go of his weapon and grabbing Ryan by the collar of his breastplate.

Jumping to the side, Fletcher hit the brick street right before the truck sped past them.

The elf's body exploded as he was run over, and the truck slammed to a halt shortly after.

"CHARGE FORTH, CUT DOWN OUR FOES AND BRING WASTE TO THE CITY STREETS! LET OUR VICTORY BE FELT THROUGHOUT ALL OF AFFER AND STRIKE FEAR INTO OUR ENEMIES!" Leon yelled, jumping out from the first truck and raising his sword above his head. "FOR FREEDOM!"

"FOR FREEDOM!" the humans screamed, jumping out of the trucks. They poured out onto the streets of Lilthral, racing at the elves with adrenaline surging in their veins and a ferocity for victory burning in their bones.

Fletcher groaned and took off his helmet. His body ached, and he had a throbbing headache, but looking up, he saw someone offering him a hand.

"You saved my life. I don't know how to show my gratitude, but...thank you," Ryan said.

Fletcher grabbed Ryan's hand and stood. "You don't need to show me gratitude. The fact that you stand beside me in battle is more than I have a right to ask for."

Before Ryan could respond, Ji came over.

"Do you have a death wish?! You took an axe to the back and were almost hit by a truck!" Ji shouted, frowning at how beaten and injured his leader was. "You shouldn't fight anymore, you're—"

"Don't undermine me! I just need to stitch and bandage my wounds, then don a new set of armor," Fletcher said, taking off his gauntlets and tossing them onto the ground.

"Fletch—"

"I'm not backing out of this fight. I would be a weak leader if I did."

"We need you alive! And no one is going to think less of you if you sit the rest of this battle out."

Fletcher chuckled, removing his breastplate and tossing it aside. "I don't care if anyone thinks less of me. I'm here to free my people, not be praised and idolized. Let them hate or love me, I'm going to do what I want regardless."

"Your chest was wounded too?!" Ji shouted, gaping at the cut on the right side of Fletcher's torso.

"Look who it is!" Leon said, making his way over to the three and glancing at Fletcher. "You look like shit."

"Thanks, we were outnumbered. I wonder why?"

"Hey, it was your plan for us to leave later, and I told you I'd be here by twenty hundred hours! Do you think anyone else could have pulled that off?! Because I don't think so!"

"I was right to trust you. If you had arrived any later, we wouldn't have survived," Fletcher said, now completely stripped of armor.

"Speak for yourself. I was doing just fine," Ji said.

"From what I saw, it seemed all of you were about to die," Crystal said, walking over to the four men.

"Good to see you're still alive," Fletcher said, peeling off his blood-and-sweat-soaked shirt. "Can someone stitch me up? I'm bleeding all over the place."

"And whose fault is that?!" Ji asked.

"What am I supposed to do?! I can't reach the wound on my back, and if I leave it open, I'm going to bleed out?"

"Just stop fighting!"

"I would still bleed out!"

Crystal laughed at Ji. "Fletcher, not fighting. That won't happen. You'd have better luck asking him to forge a piece of armor."

"I'd like to see any of you forge something!"

"That was your profession!" Ji snapped.

"You set a car on fire—"

"That was one time!"

"You did what?" Archer asked, panting as he joined the conversation and held up a med kit.

"Nothing, it's not important."

"Finally! Thank you!" Fletcher said, grabbing the kit from Archer. "Who's going to patch me up?"

"I'm not a doctor," Leon said. "But if I were, then who would be the commander?"

Fletcher raised an eyebrow at his friend. "Why couldn't you do both?"

"What kind of doctor kills his patients?"

"We don't have time for this," Crystal said, grabbing the medical kit from Fletcher and heading into the building closest to them. "I'm freezing, so get inside, and I'll take care of your wounds."

Before Fletcher followed Crystal, he faced Ji, Leon, Archer, and Ryan. "Go take the city center, I'll meet you there, and be careful. We're outnumbered."

"But the rest of the army is here," Ji said.

"Yes, but part of Lilthral's army is here as well. The capital's guards only use longswords and normal-sized shields, if they choose to carry one. Yet there are elves here wielding tower shields, greataxes, shortswords, and more, meaning there are soldiers here. But I don't know how many."

"That's more kills for me!" Leon shouted.

"We'll meet you at the city center," Ji said, before taking off with Ryan, Archer, and Leon.

Fletcher turned back to Crystal, walking over to her and sitting on a stool.

"Keep your back straight, and don't move," Crystal said, holding a thread and needle in her hand. She examined the injury, making sure it wasn't too deep, before she dug the needle into Fletcher's body. He made a grunt and clenched his jaw, but didn't move. Crystal knew Fletcher had a high pain threshold, but she was still surprised by how little he reacted.

When she finished stitching the wound, Crystal's hands were soaked in blood. "Where else are you hurt?" she asked, looking for something to wipe her hands, and finding nothing.

"My right ribs and thigh, everything else is either bruised or isn't big enough to worry about."

"Can you go one fight without getting severely hurt?" Crystal asked, moving to Fletcher's side and pinching the flesh together before she started closing it.

"You know me; it's not a battle if I don't get injured."

"Maybe you should try and change that, Mr. Rush."

Crystal finished stitching the cut on Fletcher's chest and moved over to his leg, which wasn't nearly as bad as the other two. Once she was done, Crystal used three rolls of gauze to cover Fletcher's wounds, even a few she had left open.

"That's the best I can do. They'll need to be cleaned and should be closed by a doctor, but this will get you through the battle."

"That's all I need. Thanks," Fletcher said. "Now, let's hope I can find my claymore, again, and we have a spare set of armor that fits me."

SIXTY-FOUR

"We're headed to the city center," Ji told Tor, who was sitting up ahead and breathing heavily. "Do you want to recover longer and meet us when you feel better?"

"No. The wound on my back isn't bleeding, and the others aren't anything serious," Tor said, standing and grabbing his hammer. "I'm out of breath, but I can keep going. Plus, I'm sure the rest of you are going to need me to capture the center."

Leon laughed. "I kicked your ass before; if we need anyone there, it's me."

"First of all, we only fought one time, and second of all, you're six years older than me. You were almost finished going through puberty while I wasn't even double digits yet."

"We can go anytime," Leon said, walking over to Tor.

"You think you can beat me?"

"Don't fight each other now!" Ji said, standing in the middle of the two large men who completely ignored him.

"I know I could," Leon said with a fierceness in his eyes.

"Let's see about that," Tor said, looking down at Leon. "Whoever can kill more elves tonight is the winner."

"That works for me. But you can't count the ones you've already killed."

"Deal," Tor said, giving the older man a firm handshake. "Get ready to lose."

"You shouldn't talk to yourself like that!" Leon said, sprinting down the street, Tor following behind him.

"I'm utterly confused," Ji said, watching his friends. Turning away from them, he faced Ryan and Archer. "Let's go."

The three of them ran down the street, a fair bit behind everyone else at this point.

Battle, blood, and bodies were everywhere. There wasn't a spot where Ji didn't see any of them. As they got farther into the city, the corpses thinned out, replaced with hundreds of elves and humans fighting. Screams filled the air, and the sound of metal clanging and bashing against each other resonated throughout the capital.

Ji wasn't a stranger to war anymore, but this was still more extreme than anything he had ever seen. The amount of death and chaos that surrounded him was on another level. It looked like a nightmare, except he knew it was real.

Arriving at the city center, Ji came to a halt, with Ryan and Archer right behind him. The area was filled with statues, two fountains, a tall willow tree standing in the center, and dozens of damaged and torn fabric-and-wood shops.

Who hosts a market in the middle of winter? Ji thought to himself before charging into battle. He yelled, raising his seax sword and sprinting at a group of elves who outnumbered his allies. He crashed into one of the guards, knocking him down and landing on top of him. Stabbing him in the chest, Ji stood back up, immediately blocking an attack. Before he could counter, Ryan stabbed the elf in the neck. The guard put a hand to his throat as blood seeped past his fingers, then slumped to the ground.

"Die, human scum!"

Ji turned and spotted a tall elf racing toward him. He

pulled his dagger from his belt and threw it at the guard. The elf moved at the last second, and the weapon missed his neck and struck his shoulder instead. Even after getting hit, the elf continued at full speed. Ji raised his sword and purposely swung too early, missing his target by a foot and taking a step back. The guard had already swung his weapon before Ji moved, and was left wide open as his blade sliced through the empty air. Locking eyes with his enemy, the guard watched helplessly as Ji's sword flew toward him. In an instant, he felt the cold metal touch his chest before it snapped his sternum and pierced his heart.

The elf cried out in pain and collapsed as Ji removed his blade. Clutching at his chest, the guard curled into a ball as his life ebbed away.

Finding his next fight, Ji noticed Archer was outnumbered, three to one. He rushed over to help him, slicing behind the knees of the first elf, causing him to topple backward. As he fell, Ji grabbed him by his helmet and slammed his head into the brick street. But he didn't have time to finish him off since he had to engage with the second elf attacking Archer. Trading blows, Ji stabbed the guard in the stomach, slipping underneath his breastplate. His blade had just dug into his opponent's body when the guard from earlier pulled Ji's legs.

Ji slammed into the ground and dropped his weapon. Scrambling to grab his sword, he ended up with a handful of snow as it was kicked away, well out of his reach.

Looking to see who had kicked his weapon, Ji saw the elf he had just stabbed. Moving to stand, Ji wasn't fast enough and was kicked in the ribs, sending him into a wooden table behind him. The table legs broke, causing the top to fall on him. Shoving it off, Ji stood and charged at the guard, dropkicking him into an empty fruit stand. Wooden shelves shattered and broke apart as he slammed into them.

Ji glanced at the other elf, who was still on the ground. Realizing he wasn't able to walk due to Ji's first attack, he ignored him for now and walked over to retrieve his sword. Bending down to grab it, he rolled out of the way as a chair came flying at him. Sprinting back over to his weapon, he was able to grab it this time.

Standing and raising his sword, Ji stayed where he was as the guard rushed at him. Ji dodged and stabbed the same spot he had before, his blade sinking into the elf's abdomen. Pulling his weapon out, he turned to the other elf who had started crawling away. Ji walked over to him and pulled off his helmet. Grabbing him by his hair, he pulled his head back and ran his blade across his neck.

Ji let go of the elf, his face falling into a growing puddle of his own blood. Checking on Archer, Ji saw he was holding his own and moved over to aid Ryan and Leon.

SIXTY-FIVE

Having grabbed another dagger and a new set of armor, Fletcher only had to find his claymore, which was far easier than last time. Picking up his weapon, he gazed at the night sky as snow started falling.

"We shouldn't waste time," Crystal said, heading down the street.

"Afraid our allies are in trouble?" Fletcher asked, moving to catch up with her.

"No, I trust they're fine, but I don't want to miss out on the fight."

"Same here. It won't be easy to win this battle, so I'm needed on the front line more than normal. After all, I have the highest kill count in Affer right now...at least for a human."

"You don't have much competition," Crystal said, not trying to belittle him but merely stating a fact.

"I disagree. Most of our species is enslaved, so they don't have any blood on their hands, but I have a remarkable team that is only getting better." He looked over at Crystal with a fire in his eyes, but also admiration. "As arrogant and cocky as I can be, I always remember I couldn't do this alone."

The two fell into silence after that, the sounds of battle making up for the lack of talking. Soon enough, the city center was visible, and they were met with a torn-up market littered with bodies and guts.

"We were gone for ten minutes, and this is what happens!" Fletcher said, observing the chaotic scene in front of him.

"Be careful, try not to rip open your wounds," Crystal said, already aiming her bow and taking shots.

"Right," Fletcher said, drawing his sword and running toward the sprawling tent at the end of the town square. The tent sat at the base of the stairs leading to the second level of the city and seemed to be a place to eat, since it was filled with dozens of tables and chairs.

Going into battle, Fletcher searched for the rest of his team. It wasn't long until he spotted Tor and Archer. The two of them had set up a barrier of tables around them as they defended against a dozen elves. Fletcher made his way toward them, killing three guards and pushing two more out of his way. He decapitated another elf and jumped over one of the tables they were using as a barrier.

"Don't attack!" Fletcher shouted as Archer and Tor turned their weapons on him.

"Fletcher!" the two of them said at the same time.

"You got here fast!" Tor said, shifting back to the fight.

"I didn't think it was quick," Fletcher said, facing the elves. "It felt like hours."

"Your wounds were bad. For Crystal to patch them up in the time she did is impressive," Archer said.

"I never said it wasn't." Fletcher sliced off an elf's arm. "Where's everyone else?"

"Not sure."

"I was with Ji before I came to help Tor; he left to help Leon and Ryan, who were being overwhelmed," Archer said.

As they started to clear out the batch of elves they were fighting, several more flocked over to them, making it three versus fourteen until an arrow flew into an elf's head, right through his helmet.

Fletcher looked over to see Crystal standing on one of the tables, surveying the center and picking off elves one after another.

"DUCK!"

Fletcher instinctively ducked and narrowly avoided getting decapitated by a pollaxe. He locked weapons with the elf while Archer stabbed him through the slit in his helmet.

The soldier screamed, dropping the pollaxe and backing away.

Archer put his sword back in its scabbard and grabbed the weapon off the ground. "This might be a better weapon in this situation."

He jabbed the end of the pollaxe toward one of the elves, missing him by an inch, but caught him with the blade of the axe as he brought it back. It cut through the metal breastplate and dug into the soldier's back, making him cry out in pain as Archer pulled harder. Giving it one final tug, the axe sliced through the elf's body, ripping out his intestines and leaving a large gap in his stomach.

"I think I made the right decision."

Meanwhile, Tor and Fletcher were dealing with five elves, three of whom were wielding spears and two protecting them with tower shields. Tor slammed his hammer into the shields while Fletcher knocked the spears away. But the shields were too strong for Tor's attacks, which were all rendered useless. Luckily, Crystal noticed the two struggling and sent an arrow their way, hitting one of the elves with a spear.

Taking her time, she nocked another arrow and aimed it at the soldiers with the shields, waiting for a chance to fire. But before she could, a guard ran toward her. Diverting her attention to the attacker, she aimed and shot him in the head.

Moving back toward Fletcher and Tor, she saw they had moved into an even worse position, and she couldn't hit the elves without going through them.

Fletcher swatted one of the spears away and tried to grab the other one, but was too slow and tore the leather on his gauntlet. Trying again, he was able to grab the shaft of the spear, right below the blade.

"Tor, pull!" Fletcher yelled, holding onto the spear and dodging the other one. Tor looked at Fletcher and realized what he was doing. Dropping his hammer, he gripped the spear with both hands and ripped it out of the elf's grasp.

"I got it!" Tor exclaimed, stabbing the unarmed elf in the neck.

Fletcher knocked the other spear away while Tor jabbed his at the elf. He continued to stab the elf, penetrating through his armor and drawing blood each time. Soon, the elf stopped attacking them and dropped his spear, running away and sparing his own life.

Both soldiers holding a shield drew a falchion sword from their belts. Dropping his spear, Tor picked up his hammer again.

"I'll take the one on the right," Fletcher said to Tor, who nodded.

Tor raised his hammer and swung it at the elf's head. The soldier was barely fast enough to lift his shield and block the blow. As Tor's hammer made contact, the elf felt the impact reverberating down his arm.

With his shield still up, the elf was wide open. Kicking him in the stomach, Tor was surprised the soldier stayed upright. The elf brought his shield back down before swinging his blade at Tor, who took a step back, dodging the weapon. This time, he swung from the side but was stopped again. Changing his method of assault, Tor threw a barrage of attacks, not giving the elf a chance to counter at all.

He landed two hits and was waiting to throw the finishing blow when the shaft of his hammer bent.

"Great," Tor muttered, dropping his weapon.

Stepping back, Tor tripped over a chair and tumbled to the ground. Thinking quickly, he kicked the chair at the soldier. It hit the elf just below his knees and made him fall forward. He dropped his sword and shield, but used his hands to cushion his fall. By that time, Tor had already stood back up and kicked him in the head. Swinging again, Tor missed, and the elf grabbed his other leg, bringing the large man down. Tor hit his head, and the elf crawled on top of him, ripping his helmet off and punching Tor in the face. His first blow split Tor's lip, and the second broke his nose.

Tor cried out in pain and raised his arms to cover his face. He was hit two more times before he brought his leg back and used his full strength to throw the elf off him, sending him hurling into a table, splintering it to shards.

Standing, Tor grabbed the sword the elf had dropped, then walked over to him. The elf pushed aside the broken bits of the table and looked up to see his own sword headed for his face.

Blood splattered Tor's armor and the furniture as he cut into the elf's head. He pulled the weapon out and took a moment to catch his breath. Still panting, he glanced at Fletcher, who had already killed his opponent and moved on to another one.

"Doesn't he get tired?" Tor asked, watching his leader slaughter another elf. "He's injured, too!"

SIXTY-SIX

Leon raised his shield and parried a jab, countering by jabbing his sword into the elf's stomach.

"I questioned Fletcher when he told me to use a shield and shortsword," Leon said, slamming his shield into an elf who was attacking Ji. "But he was right! How come more of our allies don't use this combination?!"

"We don't have enough," Ji answered. "It's the same with armor; not all of us have high-end armor. Plus, not everyone knows how to fight with a shield."

"What happened to the ones from the cities we've captured?"

"We're using all those shields, and most of the armor a city has gets destroyed when we conquer it."

"That makes sense," Leon said, using his shield to block an axe.

"At least we have plenty of weapons," Ji said, stabbing an elf in the neck. "Those are the most important."

"Weapons?! I don't need those! I'd rip our enemies apart with my bare hands!"

Ji glanced over at him and raised his eyebrows. "But you're using weapons now."

"That's because I'm not in my prime anymore. I'm forty-two, but back in my twenties, I was beating the shit out of everyone," Leon said with a smile. "Good times! I kicked Tor's ass, too."

"Wait, you two were in different cities. How did you end up in a fight together?"

"I forgot, I didn't tell any of you: I was originally from IItu. I was transferred to Ronann after I started causing too much trouble. After that, it was downhill for me until you guys came."

The two stopped talking and went back to the battle. Ji ducked under a sword and stabbed his attacker in the ribs. He pulled his blade out and blocked two elves. Staying defensive, he waited until he was finally able to counter, jabbing the elf on his left in the throat and ramming his pommel into the other guard's head. Before Ji could kill the elf, Leon decapitated him.

"THIRTY!" he yelled in excitement, immediately moving on to another foe.

I don't care that he stole my kill, but I don't think Tor will feel the same way, Ji thought.

He looked at the thinning group of elves they were battling and figured Leon, Ryan, and the twelve humans aiding them would be fine without him. Turning away, Ji checked the rest of the center and was amazed to see it was mostly cleared. He didn't know how long they had been fighting, but he knew it had been several hours.

The snow had begun to fall harder, and it was accumulating as time passed. It was also much colder than when they arrived at Lilthral. The chill of night, combined with the freezing winter temperatures, made the air bite their skin, numbing their fingers and faces.

Ji could tell many of his allies were freezing, and he didn't blame them. This was the coldest battle they had fought, and it was shaping up to be the longest as well.

CHAPTER 67

Allica had been lying on a velvet sofa for three hours, which Jax had taken from the hall.

"Are the humans still not dead?" Allica moaned, looking up at her mother, who had stayed resting on her throne the whole time, not moving an inch.

"Yes, Allica, be patient," Rinn said. "You should be grateful that you're in here and not fighting to protect the city."

She sighed, rolling over on the sofa and burying her head in one of the soft pillows. *If I could fall asleep, being stuck here wouldn't be so bad. But that won't happen with my mother and three guards watching me. Even if they weren't here, this sofa is far too uncomfortable to sleep on.*

As she lay there, letting her thoughts run wild, she was interrupted by a tap on her shoulder.

"My Lady, do you need anything?" Jax asked, bending down so their eyes were level.

"No."

Jax silently nodded and bowed, standing guard next to her. Allica stared up at the ceiling, wondering what would happen to her if the humans did win. Would they take her prisoner, or would they outright kill her? Or worse, would they torture her? She wasn't sure, and she certainly didn't want to find out.

Allica decided that if the humans broke into the palace, she'd take action. She glanced at her mother and the two elite guards protecting her, trying to think of a way to use them. When nothing came to mind, she turned to Jax, the tall, muscular elf who had been her bodyguard since birth.

When Jax was first assigned to her, he was below average. He wasn't exceptional at fighting, confident, or strong. But over the decades, he had slowly grown into a bodyguard superior to both of her mother's bodyguards combined. He didn't have the skill of Light or Ingrid, but no one else in the city could best him.

Allica huffed, sitting up, crossing her legs, and resting her chin in the palm of her hand. "This has been the most boring night of my life," she whispered to herself. "If only something would happen."

Not a minute later, a loud boom resonated throughout the building, echoing through the halls and shaking the palace. A statue fell to the ground and shattered while dust rained from the ceiling, getting in Allica's hair. She heard yelling outside the throne room and heavy footsteps marching down the hall.

"Wonderful," Allica mumbled as her mother began to freak out. *It's time to come up with a plan to save myself.*

SIXTY-EIGHT

"We've captured here and here," Fletcher said, pointing to a map. "We still need to take the east, the second level, and the palace. There shouldn't be many guards left on this floor, but our kin are here, and I need them freed, so I'm leaving Leon and five hundred men here to take care of that. Ryan will lead seven hundred soldiers to capture the second story, while everyone else and my team handle storming the palace."

"Why am I leading the charge against the second level?" Ryan asked. "Shouldn't your right-hand be doing that?"

"Because I trust you, and I need Ji to help capture the third level," Fletcher said, looking at Ryan before he turned to Leon and handed him the map. "There are two buildings where the humans live; I marked them both. When you're done, meet back up with us." Fletcher turned to Ryan. "That goes for you, too."

"I won't disappoint you," Ryan said, nodding at Fletcher and leading his group to the second floor.

"How many humans are here?" Leon asked, opening the map.

"Fifty-six hundred."

"That's a lot of allies!" Tor said.

"That's the same as gaining five more Leon Bristofolds,"

Leon said, walking over to his soldiers. He paused and turned back to Tor with a cocky grin. "For the record, I'm at forty-six."

"You're a cheater! I saw you stealing kills!"

"Let's go!" Fletcher said, not in the mood for Tor and Leon's bickering.

They marched up the main staircase leading to both floors, and Fletcher was surprised to see dead elves already littering the second level. He stopped to admire his allies' fast work, then continued up the stairs.

Reaching the top, Fletcher met a slew of guards outside the palace and every one of them was decked out. Their armor was matte black, instead of the dark green the elves normally had, with the elven crest—a white owl perched on a branch surrounded by silver leaves—inlaid in bronze on the breastplate. They were all armed with halberds, and Fletcher could tell the craftsmanship was better than his. Both the blades and the shafts were highly decorated, with ornate detail forged into the metal, and an emerald placed in the center of the axe.

"I want one of those," Tor said, eyeing the halberds and glancing at the falchion sword he was using. "I'm definitely grabbing one."

"There are three hundred of us against a hundred of them, so team up in groups and overpower them with numbers! They're stronger than the elves we fought before, and their armor is thicker, so don't underestimate them!" Fletcher shouted, drawing his sword and sprinting forward. "FOR FREEDOM!"

The others yelled, charging into battle, branching off left, right, and center.

The palace guards raised their weapons and moved toward one another, forming their own groups, but that didn't slow Fletcher down. The elves held steady as the humans rushed at them. They expected to impale dozens of humans, but were stunned when Fletcher jumped over their weapons and slammed right into a guard.

Adjusting himself as he made contact, Fletcher landed on the elf's neck. He saw blood fly past the slit in his helmet and heard him gagging.

Fletcher leaned forward, putting more of his weight on the elf's throat before he was thrown off by one of the other guards. Falling, Fletcher moved into a roll, getting up in an instant and raising his claymore in front of him. The wound on his back was throbbing in pain, and his ribs didn't feel much better. Luckily, neither wound had reopened. Steading his arms, Fletcher clashed with a halberd. Pulling his blade away, Fletcher moved in and swung his sword at the elf's hip. He hit his target but didn't do any damage because the armor was so strong. Bringing his sword back, he barely blocked a swing aimed at his head.

Ducking, Fletcher tackled the guard below the waist. The elf's legs buckled, and he fell, but he stopped his fall with his hands and flipped their positions. Grabbing Fletcher by his breastplate collar, the elf pinned both of Fletcher's arms with his knees.

Taking advantage of the fact that Fletcher was trapped, the elf ripped his helmet off and repeatedly punched Fletcher. The rigid metal of the guard's gauntlets dug into Fletcher's skin and bruised his face.

While Fletcher was being punched, he was working on taking off his left gauntlet. Finally getting it off, he quickly raised his hand and shoved his thumb through the elf's visor. Finding his eye, Fletcher dug his finger in. He felt warm blood wash over his hand and his thumb brush against bone.

The elf screamed, no longer punching Fletcher and desperately trying to pry his hand away. He grabbed Fletcher's arm, peeling his finger out of his eye socket. Taking his knee off Fletcher's other arm, he stumbled backward. Tearing off his helmet, the elf threw it aside and put a hand over the wound.

Taking off his other gauntlet, Fletcher sprinted toward the guard. Dodging under a punch, he got close enough to dig into his other eye.

"GET OFF!" the elf screamed as his vision disappeared and pain overwhelmed him.

The elf wrapped his arms around Fletcher, squeezing with all his might. Fletcher grunted, gritting his teeth, as the elf pressed against the cut on his ribs. He already felt blood flowing out, as the wound was reopened. Knowing he wasn't going to last, Fletcher changed his attack, removing his thumb from the elf's eye and shoving it into his cheek. Pressing hard, he ripped through the skin, causing the elf to let out a distorted scream and loosen his grip. Unfortunately for Fletcher, the elf quickly tightened his hold again. Pulling down, Fletcher opened the wound all the way to the elf's lip, leaving a gaping hole in his mouth.

Finally getting the elf to loosen his hold, Fletcher slammed his elbow into the elf's collarbone until it broke. The elf removed his arms from Fletcher and fell face-first into the snow. Retrieving his sword, Fletcher shoved it into the back of his neck, killing him as he pierced his spine.

"That hurts," Fletcher muttered, rubbing his ribs. Looking up, he noticed three elves fighting against Ji.

Before helping his friend, he tried to find Tor. When he did, he grabbed the halberd and hoisted it above his head. "Tor!" he shouted, throwing the weapon like a spear toward him.

The other man glanced at Fletcher and beamed as he saw the halberd headed his way. Dropping his sword, he caught the weapon, turning it over in his hands.

"Now this is more my style," Tor said, attacking a guard from behind.

The thick blade sank through the armor of the guard, cutting into his back and severing his spine. Blood gushed out of the wound and dripped off Tor's weapon as he pulled the blade free.

Hearing a blade whistling toward him, Tor ducked and spun around. Standing, he raised his halberd and swung at the guard's chest. The strike landed, but the elf grabbed the shaft of his weapon and pulled Tor toward him. Losing his balance, Tor stumbled, and the elf slammed his head into his. Tor's helmet caved in and cut his brow open. Blood ran down his face, getting in his eyes and blurring his vision.

Taking a step back, Tor ripped his helmet off and spit in the guard's face. The elf stopped and wiped the blood from his eyes, just before Tor cut off his legs. Falling to the ground, the guard shrieked as Tor lodged his blade in his chest again; this time, collapsing his ribcage and crushing his heart.

Letting go of his weapon, Tor walked over and ripped a strip of cloth from one of the elven flags and wrapped it around his forehead to keep the blood out of his eyes.

Retrieving his halberd from the twitching elf, Tor rejoined the fight, approaching two guards who were teaming up to slaughter his kin. Swinging his halberd at one of them, he missed, as the elf stepped out of the way and countered. Turning his weapon, Tor managed to catch the axe head with the shaft of his halberd. Pulling it toward him, he tried ripping the weapon from the elf's grasp, but the guard managed to hang on and dig his heels into the ground, preventing Tor from pulling him closer.

Tor removed his weapon from its entanglement in the elf's blade and was about to attack when he was forced to defend himself. The other elf had joined the fight and swung at Tor's neck. Barely managing to block it, he felt his heart racing as the blade was less than an inch from his body. Taking a deep breath, Tor shoved the shaft of the elf's halberd and dodged a jab from the other elf, lining up the tip of his weapon before driving it into his stomach. Blood filled his intestines before it erupted from his mouth, covering the inside of his helmet. Taking it off, the guard retched again, getting blood and partly digested food all over Tor.

Ignoring it, Tor moved his focus to his other opponent, but he was too late. He felt the blade cut through his armor and into his left leg. Luckily, he was fast enough to stop it from penetrating further by shoving the shaft of his weapon in front of the axe head. But the wound was still half an inch deep.

Gripping his halberd with one hand, Tor seized his dagger with the other and stabbed the elf in the bicep. The guard's arm went limp, and Tor pulled the weapon out of his leg. Tossing it to the side, he grasped his own in both hands and swung it at the elf's head. The guard's skull was split open, and he slumped to the ground.

Surveying the fallen bodies beneath him, Tor felt sick. The yard, once elegant and stunning, was now a living nightmare, covered in guts, limbs, organs, and bodily fluids. Tor wasn't squeamish, but even this made him queasy.

Before he could gag, he felt a hand on his shoulder and looked over to see Fletcher.

"Good work. Taking out four is impressive."

"Huh?" Tor said before his head cleared up. "I mean, thanks. It was tough, but I pulled through. Although my leg suffered a bad cut."

"We can take care of that now. We're finished out here, and I don't think the guards inside are coming out," Fletcher said, pointing at the palace doors. "They barricaded the entrance, so we'll have to take care of that. In the meantime, someone can help bandage any wounds you have." He started heading off toward Ji, who was waiting by the stairs.

"How do you plan to get into the palace if the doors are blocked?" Tor asked.

Fletcher turned back with a smirk on his face. "My favorite way: explosives!"

Sixty-Nine

"We don't have to use explosives. There are other ways in," Ji said as he and Fletcher loaded the third barrel of gunpowder into the back of a truck.

"There's not. I checked the city maps, and a blueprint of the palace was included in them. The building was made to be the most secure place in the elven kingdom, and they accomplished that by making the walls twice as thick and only having one entry."

"Then we could..." Ji started, but was unable to come up with any other way to get inside.

"Go on," Fletcher urged him.

"Use a battering ram."

"That's a great idea, Ji! Let's pause this battle and build a battering ram!"

"We're going to need one eventually! You can't rely on gunpowder for everything!"

"I plan on building one, but not in the middle of a battle! Do you think the elves will patiently wait for us as we construct a weapon to fight against them?!"

"What are they going to do?!" Ji shouted, helping Fletcher load the seventh barrel into the truck. "Better yet, we can camp outside the palace. If it's the only way in or out, they'll have to leave eventually."

"What could go wrong there?! Let's leave dozens or even hundreds of guards alive, so when their army returns, we'll be fighting elves on two fronts."

"How would they know we're fighting?!"

"Did you not see the five small windows on the third floor of the palace? The ones we can't reach or fit through," Fletcher said as they loaded the tenth barrel of gunpowder. "Trust me, we don't have any other options right now, so get in."

Ji and Fletcher jumped into the vehicle and drove up the stairs. The ride was rough and rocky.

"This sucks," Ji said as his head constantly bumped against the roof of the truck.

"It's better than carrying the barrels up the stairs. They weigh over a hundred pounds each, and I don't think the two of us could get one barrel up all these steps, much less ten."

Reaching the top, Fletcher parked the truck, got out, and opened the back.

"Give us a hand!" Fletcher ordered his men. Two dozen of them turned toward him and helped unload the heavy barrels.

"We're using explosives?" Archer asked, grabbing a barrel with another soldier. "Where do you want us to place these?"

"Put them together at the center of the doors."

"Are you sure that's a good idea?"

"No, but what could go wrong?" Fletcher said with a shrug.

Once all the barrels were in place, Fletcher took a few handfuls of gunpowder and created a trail leading to the end of the stairs. Making sure everyone was behind him, he sparked the powder by dragging a sword on the ground.

The powder ignited, and Fletcher ran down the stairs, which was the best cover they had.

"How's your leg, Tor?" Fletcher asked as he crouched down next to his friend.

"It hurts, and I won't be fighting at my best, but I'll do what I can."

"Sit out if you need to. You've already outperformed in this battle."

"Should it take this long to go off?" Ji asked, peering over the lip of the stairs.

"No. It probably went out from the snow," Fletcher said. "I'll take care of it."

He hadn't taken one step when the gunpowder exploded, shaking the ground and making their ears ring.

"It worked!" Fletcher yelled, staring at the gaping hole where the bronze doors were a few seconds ago.

"What did you say?!" Archer shouted. "It porked?!"

"Worked! It worked!"

Archer still looked confused, so Fletcher gave up and headed toward the palace. A thick coat of smoke covered the entrance, which was impossible to see through. Walking past it, Fletcher reached the foyer, which was packed with guards.

None of them knew Fletcher, but it was clear that he was no ordinary human. He was covered in blood, his face was bruised, his armor was damaged, yet he didn't show an ounce of fear. Instead, he stood tall, a raging inferno blazing in his eyes as he glared at the elves.

"What are you waiting for?!" Fletcher yelled, drawing his sword and pointing it at the elves. "COME KILL ME!"

Before the palace guards could move, the humans charged into the building, screaming and bolting past Fletcher.

Joining the fight, Fletcher swung his sword, beheading a guard. Ji and Archer appeared on either side of him, and the three pushed forward down one of the halls. Astonishingly, the guards here were the worst they had fought all night. But what they lacked in skill, they made up for in number. They cut down one after another, making such a mess of the palace that outside appeared tame. Blood spattered the walls and ceiling, while bodies and organs piled up on the floor.

"Duck!" Fletcher shouted at Archer as he swung his claymore over his head and drove it into an elf's neck.

Protecting his leader, Ji blocked a swing aimed at him. Archer finished the job, stabbing the guard in the ribs. Only a few guards nearby remained, and each was hesitant to engage the trio. Not giving them a chance to retreat, Fletcher cut one of them in half. Dashing forward, he stabbed another and blocked a hit from the last elf, whom Ji finished off.

"Is that all?" Archer asked, wiping the guts off his sword.

"For this hallway. I'm sure there are more throughout the building, and we still have the throne room," Fletcher said, walking ahead and turning right. As soon as he rounded the corner, he bumped into an elf. Four others accompanied him, and Fletcher instantly recognized them as members of Light's cohort. "I haven't seen any of you since IItu. Did you miss me?" Fletcher jested. When they didn't respond, he moved on. "Where's your leader? Did he run away like the coward he is, or did the five of you get left behind?"

"Silence, slave! You think you can fight because you've made it this far, but I'll show you what a skilled elf is capable of!"

Fletcher didn't say anything, then he burst out laughing. "Did you call me a slave? That's rich! I'm free to do as I please, yet here you five stand, headed to kill us at the order of the queen. Did you also bow down and kiss the floor she walks on?"

Xavier clenched his jaw and went for his sword, but he was stopped by Fletcher, who grabbed his wrist. Even using all his strength, Xavier was unable to overpower Fletcher and draw his weapon.

How is he so strong?

"What's wrong? Is your sword stuck?" Fletcher mocked, kicking Xavier away from him.

Now that Fletcher wasn't holding him, the elf unsheathed his blade and lifted it in front of him. "Yune, kill the blond-haired scum—"

"Hey!" Archer interjected.

"Laytin, take care of the other one. Ramos, Eldar, help me teach this arrogant human his place."

"Yes, Xavier!" they shouted, drawing their weapons and preparing for battle.

"Are you really that scared of me?" Fletcher asked, keeping his guard up and charging at Xavier.

Ramos jumped in, swinging at Fletcher, who ducked under the sword and then parried an attack from Eldar. Fletcher hadn't noticed it when they met, but he realized now that they all used longswords.

Xavier raised his weapon and brought it down, aiming for Fletcher's head. He stepped forward and to the side, narrowly dodging the blade. Twisting his sword, Xavier quickly brought it back toward him and swung it around in an arc before heading back for Fletcher. Ramos swung at the same time, aiming for the waist instead of the chest like Xavier was. The two ended up being blocked as Fletcher steadied his sword in front of him, catching both blades. Twisting his body slightly, he pulled his dagger from his belt and blocked Eldar from behind. With all four of them interlocked with each other, Fletcher decided to make the first move and shoved his sword upward, catching both elves' blades on his guard and pushing them out of the way. Spinning around, he slashed at Eldar's right arm with his claymore, cutting it clean off.

The elf screamed as his limb fell to the ground, and pain rocketed through his torso. "My arm!"

Holding on to his dagger, Fletcher ignored Eldar and took a step back, dodging Xavier. However, he didn't get far enough, and he ended up with a deep scratch across his breastplate.

I need to finish this, Fletcher thought, knowing neither he nor his armor could go on much longer.

Moving toward Ramos, Fletcher locked weapons with him and struck him in the head with the butt of his dagger. The hit disfigured his helmet and caused the metal to press into his skull. Ramos felt blood run down the side of his head and the uncomfortable feeling of his helmet digging into him just below his right ear.

Stepping closer to Xavier, Fletcher dodged the elf and rammed into him with his shoulder.

Fletcher clenched his jaw as the wound on his back started flaring up in pain. The cut had been hurting since he got it, but ramming into Xavier sent it over the edge. As the pain spread, he felt the gauze covering his torso become wet with blood. Ignoring the pain, he concentrated on the fight.

Xavier slid back as Fletcher hit him, but found his footing and stayed upright. He swung his sword at Fletcher, who parried the attack. Eldar rushed at Fletcher, trying to tackle him, but failed to knock him down. Keeping his sword intertwined with Xavier's, Fletcher turned and jammed his dagger into Eldar's exposed neck.

Eldar's grip held tight for a few seconds before he let go and slumped to the floor. Simultaneously, Ramos struck from the other side. Fletcher looked over but didn't have time to do anything and was hit. Ramos's blade made contact with his left arm and sheared through the metal sleeve. The cut ran from the top of Fletcher's shoulder to the bottom of his biceps. His arm flared in pain, and he dropped his dagger.

Xavier's blade remained tangled with Fletcher's, so he took one hand off and grabbed his shortsword. Lunging forward, he jabbed at Fletcher's stomach and was stunned when Fletcher grabbed the blade with his left hand.

Blood oozed from Fletcher's fist as he held on tightly to the blade, preventing Xavier from pulling back and attacking again. Fletcher let go of the weapon and removed his sword from Xavier's. Taking several steps back, he gripped his claymore with both hands, putting distance between him and the other two as he steadied his weapon and waited for the right moment to strike.

Xavier sheathed his shortsword and gripped his longsword properly again, moving next to Ramos as they prepared to act.

The three of them waited for someone to move before Fletcher smirked and eased up on his form. "Do I get a prize for killing one of the queen's loyal mutts?"

Xavier flinched but kept his calm and didn't do anything rash.

"Or do I need to kill all of you for that? Not that it matters; I was planning on doing so anyway. It's obvious none of you can best me. You outnumber me three to one, yet you're still losing. But it makes sense why it was so easy to kill your comrades if you lot are the pinnacle of the elven bloodline," Fletcher said, trying to get Xavier or Ramos to slip up by angering them. "I vividly remember the attack on IItu and Ronann. Your kin cried like children as we slaughtered—"

Fletcher hadn't even finished his sentence before Xavier lunged at him, but Ramos grabbed his arm and held him back.

"Don't! Can't you see he's bait—" Ramos's words died in his throat as Fletcher decapitated him.

Ramos's head hit Xavier as it fell to the ground, and blood shot out from his neck. Xavier watched in sheer horror as his long-time friend and comrade died right next to him. His mind was filled with guilt, rage, and grief as Ramos slumped to the floor, joining the fallen elves.

Fletcher immediately moved in to attack Xavier, aiming for his lower torso. The elf blocked the swing and shoved Fletcher, going on the offensive now. Bloodlust flowed through his veins, and he wanted to kill Fletcher more than ever. Throwing countless blows, Xavier swung his sword non-stop. Fletcher wasn't intimidated by the onslaught, and fully concentrated on defense, waiting for the elf to tire.

Xavier landed a few hits on Fletcher, cutting his right arm twice and both of his legs. His relentless flurry of attacks slowly pushed Fletcher back, but exactly as Fletcher predicted, Xavier started to slow down.

A minute later, Fletcher made his move, swinging his claymore so hard that he snapped Xavier's blade and sliced right through his body.

"I was expecting a fight against tough, formidable warriors, but I wasn't impressed with any of you," Fletcher said, looking Xavier in the eyes as they faded to black.

Dropping his sword, Fletcher grunted in pain. Every inch of his body hurt, but his back was agonizing. He had pushed through all night, but with the capital basically taken, he didn't plan on fighting anymore.

Checking up on his allies, Fletcher saw that Ji was winning, but Archer was clearly struggling against his opponent. Grabbing his dagger, Fletcher sprinted to help Archer, but he was too late.

Time seemed to slow down as Fletcher watched Archer lose his arm and the blade slice into his ribcage, right before an arrow flew through the elf's head.

"ARCHER!" Fletcher yelled, grabbing him before he hit the ground and taking off his helmet.

Archer met Fletcher's gaze. Taking a second, he opened his mouth only to close it. Trying again, Archer was able to speak this time. "I'm...glad I...got to...fight...beside...you...Fletch. Thank you...for making me...feel...like... I had...a...purpose."

"Archer, hey! You're not dead yet, stay with me!" Fletcher said as Archer's blood pooled around him, knowing he wasn't going to make it.

Archer opened his mouth and whispered one more thing, but Fletcher wasn't able to hear, so he leaned in closer.

"Long...live...freedom."

Those were the last words Archer spoke before he was gone forever.

Fletcher lifted his head and saw Crystal, Tor, Ryan, and Ji standing in front of him. "He's...he's gone."

They stayed like that for several minutes before Fletcher closed Archer's eyes. Gently laying his friend's body on the ground, Fletcher stood and addressed his team. "We'll mourn our fallen comrades later. Right now, we need to kill the queen and claim this city as ours."

They all exchanged a glance before Fletcher started leading them down the hall.

Arriving at the throne room, Fletcher pushed open the bronze doors. He wasn't sure what he expected to see. Maybe a few dozen elves ready to lay down their lives to protect the queen. Or even an empty room, since the queen could be hiding, or worse, had run off. He was prepared for both of those and many other scenarios, but what he wasn't anticipating was a bloody mess.

The queen lay at the foot of the throne with dozens of holes in her body where she had been stabbed. A large stagnant pool of blood surrounded her, and a young woman holding a dagger was on top of her. The woman was on all fours, and she looked up at them as the door opened.

She was wearing an elegant white nightgown and had shining white hair, both of which were soaked in blood. The dark red blood marred her body, staining her pale skin. In other circumstances, she would have been beautiful, but at this moment, she resembled a starving animal feasting on her prey.

"This isn't what I expected."

SEVENTY

Allica stood and walked over to Jax. The screams outside the throne room had become worse, and she knew it was only a matter of time until the humans reached them. Luckily, she had come up with a plan to survive.

"Follow my lead," Allica whispered, getting close to Jax and putting her hands on his waist. Slowly reaching around, she grabbed his dagger.

Allica could feel Jax stiffen when she pulled the weapon from his belt, and his eyes filled with alarm. "What are you doing?" he whispered.

Allica didn't answer and turned away from him, hiding the dagger in the sleeve of her nightgown. Walking to the foot of the throne, Allica stopped and stared at her mother.

"Is something the matter, Allica?"

"Mother, the humans have invaded our home, and you know as well as I do that we are going to die tonight."

"That isn't true, Allica—"

"You're right, it's not. Because unlike you, I want to survive, and I'm willing to do whatever it takes. What I'm trying to say is: tell Father hi for me."

Allica pulled the dagger from her sleeve and stabbed one of the guards in the neck.

"ALLICA!" Rinn yelled, immediately standing and staring at her daughter in shock and horror.

The other guard reached for his weapon, but Jax was faster and cut off the elf's head before his sword was even drawn.

"Good work, Jax," Allica said, glad he had picked up and followed her lead. "Now it's your turn, Mother."

"Allica, don't do this! Killing me won't save you!" Rinn yelled, fear laced through her voice as she tried to find a way out. "I'VE NEVER DONE ANYTHING TO WRONG YOU, AND I'VE GIVEN YOU EVERYTHING!"

Allica laughed. "Surely you don't believe that? You hid my existence from the other kingdoms and never allowed me out of the palace alone. I was always looked down upon, and the only elves who treated me with respect were Light and Jax. Even though I'm a princess, I have no power and can't issue a single command to anyone other than my bodyguard, an elf you assigned to me because he was the weakest guard you could find. But that backfired on you." She walked toward her mother and yanked her hair, forcing the queen to meet her eyes. "I can go on for hours about the terrible things you've done to me, but I only need one to justify killing you: my father."

"Allica, I had to have him executed! If the elves found out I loved a human, and you were his child, they would have killed both of us!"

"What a pitiful excuse! All the elves knew. Do you think I don't know why you married my father? Because the kingdom was weakened and you were so young, you had trouble keeping the slaves in check. So, you used my father as a bridge to the humans, showing them that the elves could be trusted until you eventually had the humans under control. Once that happened, you no longer needed my father and had him killed."

Rinn stayed silent, baffled that her daughter knew the truth. "How do you know that?"

"How could I not!" Allica yelled, throwing the queen from the platform on which her throne sat. "I'm far smarter than you think, mother."

Rinn started crawling away when her fingers were stepped on. Looking up, she spotted Jax towering over her.

The next thing she knew, she was grabbed from behind and slammed against the floor. Her head hit the ground, and her vision blurred. Once it started to come back, she saw her daughter on top of her.

"Jax, I'll need you in my plans for the future, so grab a dagger from one of the guards and injure yourself, then go and curl up in the corner," Allica said, glancing at her bodyguard.

"Excuse me?"

"You're an elf, and you look like one. I can weasel my way out of this because I resemble a human," Allica said, pushing her hair back and pointing to her ears. "But you can't, so you need to act as though you were wounded. Otherwise, it will be suspicious since there are two dead guards and one who is unscathed."

"I understand, My Lady," Jax said, walking over and grabbing a dagger from one of the dead guards.

"You're not going to—"

"Shut up!" Allica yelled, stabbing her mother in the stomach.

Rinn let out a gasp and a cry of pain that was silenced by a gush of blood coming out of her mouth.

"This is for my father!" Allica screamed and stabbed her mother in the chest.

"For making my life miserable!"

"For taking everything from me!"

"For treating me like a slave!"

Allica stabbed her mother each time, leaving wounds all

over her torso and completely disfiguring her face. The queen was dead long before Allica stopped impaling her, but she didn't care. After the first stab, it became purely personal, as she took out decades of frustration and hatred she had carried toward her mother.

Allica paused as a scream of pure torment filled the room. Facing Jax, she saw he had taken off his left gauntlet and was running the dagger down his arm. Turning back to her mother, she was well beyond recognition, which was exactly what Allica wanted. If the humans saw her mother's face as it normally was, they would easily see the resemblance between the two of them.

The princess didn't move as she stared at her mother, the full realization of what she had done coming to her. She was slightly surprised to find that she didn't feel guilty at all. Allica didn't dream of killing her mother, but it was something she had thought about more than once.

As Jax stopped screaming, a heavy stillness filled the space, broken by his sobs of pain. A tranquil peace overtook Allica as her heart continued to race. Before she knew it, the doors to the room were thrown open, and she looked up to see five humans enter.

The one in the middle was in the worst condition, but Allica assumed he was the leader by the way he held himself. They stared at each other before he spoke. "This isn't what I expected."

Allica rose to her feet and rushed toward the man, grabbing onto his shoulders and forcing herself to cry. "I'm finally saved! I, I, I was here for years, over and over they, they raped and beat me...day after day. I, I thought it would never end..." Allica was full-on sobbing at this point. "If it weren't for you...if it weren't for you, I would have been stuck in this nightmare forever!"

"I know you're scared, but you need to calm down and tell us what happened," Fletcher said, gently grabbing her arms and pulling them off him.

"I... I was the queen's... I'm not sure what I was called, but whenever the queen was angry, she brought me here. Then she beat me...sometimes it lasted minutes, but some days it lasted hours...and I would lose track of time. After that, the guards would take me back to my cell...and, and they...raped me," Allica said, trying not to sneer at how great her story sounded. "When you attacked the city, I was summoned here...as, as a... sacrifice for victory. Luckily for me, that elf," she pointed to Jax, "he convinced the queen to wait until it was necessary. So the queen waited until the palace was breached, and then she ordered me to be sacrificed to Thylphion, the goddess of victory. But...but the same elf who convinced the queen to wait, he...he saved me again. He decapitated one of the guards, and it gave me a chance to grab a dagger from the other one. But, but because I did that...he..." Allica stopped talking as even more tears ran down her face, and she started to choke up. "He was hurt protecting me...and while all that was happening, the queen tried to escape. So I grabbed her, and I stabbed her...again and again... I didn't want to, but I couldn't stop, all the hate and rage I had...I, I..."

"I've heard enough... I think I understand what happened," Fletcher said, looking at the sobbing woman. "You don't have to worry anymore, you're with your kin now."

Allica buried her face in Fletcher's breastplate. She hated being so close to a human, but she needed to hide her smile or her whole story would be for naught.

You foolish humans, I can't wait to take my kingdom back and make you pay with your lives!

SEVENTY-ONE

letcher pushed the woman off him after a minute. "I still have matters to take care of, so Ryan and Tor will take you somewhere where you can rest."

"Thank you! Thank you, I owe you my life!" Allica said, bowing down to him, getting on her knees, and touching her forehead to the ground.

"Rise. There is no need for you to degrade yourself for me," Fletcher said, bending down and offering her a hand up. "I fight to free my kind. I don't fight for power, wealth, or to stand above others."

Allica raised her head and took Fletcher's hand. "Thank you again, and please take care of the elf who saved me. I also owe him my life."

"I already planned on it." Fletcher then turned to Tor and Ryan. "Take her to the human quarters for the time being, and make sure a doctor patches up that elf before he's sent to prison. Then get some rest; both of you exceeded my expectations today."

"Yes, sir!" Tor and Ryan both said, leaving with Allica and Jax.

Fletcher walked over to the queen's disfigured body. "She must've really hated her."

"She deserved it," Crystal said, glaring at the queen in disgust.

"She did. But now I can't help thinking about other cities. How many of our kin are suffering as she did?"

"That's half the reason we fight, so no human has to endure this. Every city in Affer will be conquered, and every human freed. It doesn't matter what our enemies have; no force will withstand our army," Ji said.

"You sounded like me." Fletcher smiled, proud to see Ji developing. He glanced at the queen once more before walking out of the room. As he headed down the halls, he saw countless people, both elves and humans, lying on the floor. Many of them were injured, and even more were dead. Fletcher had never seen so much death, but he knew this was only the beginning.

Making his way to the foyer, he walked out of the front entrance with Crystal and Ji on either side of him and covered his eyes as the sun blinded him. Once his eyes adjusted, he lowered his hand and saw a horde of humans larger than any he had ever seen before. The massive front yard of the palace was so packed that he couldn't even see the ground.

When the crowd noticed Fletcher, they roared in celebration at the sight of their leader.

"Looks like you're quite popular!" Ji said, slapping his friend on the back. "Show them why you're our king."

Fletcher grinned at Ji before he turned to the crowd and wiped the blood from his face. "MY BROTHERS AND SISTERS, MY KIN, MY ALLIES, WE STAND HERE TODAY NOT AS SLAVES, BUT AS HUMANS! FOR OVER FOUR HUNDRED SEVENTY YEARS WE HAVE BEEN OPPRESSED AND TREATED AS TOOLS, BUT THAT ENDS TODAY! FROM THIS DAY FORTH, THE ELVEN CAPITAL IS OURS! BUT WE AREN'T STOPPING HERE! THIS IS ONLY THE BEGINNING! THE OTHER ELVEN CITIES WILL SOON BE IN OUR

HANDS, AND EVERY KINGDOM ON AFFER WILL FOLLOW! THE HYBRIDS, DAMMED, DEMONS, AND ANGELS WILL RUE THE DAY THEY ENSLAVED US! THEY WENT TO WAR WITH OUR ANCESTORS BECAUSE THEY FEARED THEM, AND WE SHALL REMIND THEM WHY! THE POWER AND FORTITUDE OF US HUMANS HAS BEEN FORGOTTEN, BUT THAT WILL RETURN GREATER THAN EVER! THE INDOMITABLE HUMAN SPIRIT WILL BE AT THE CENTER OF THIS WORLD FOR GENERATIONS TO COME! IF YOU WANT TO SEE OUR KINGDOM RESTORED TO POWER, THEN FIGHT ALONGSIDE ME! FIGHT FOR OUR FUTURE, FIGHT FOR OUR RIGHTS, AND FIGHT FOR OUR FREEDOM!" he yelled, raising his fist in the air. "LONG LIVE FREEDOM!" his commanding voice boomed out as he finished his speech.

"LONG LIVE FREEDOM!" the crowd chanted as the bright rays of the morning sun shone down upon them.

SEVENTY-TWO

Fletcher walked into a rectangular room with an oval pine table in the middle. Ji, Crystal, Tor, Ryan, and Leon were already seated.

"I know you're tired, sore, and hurt from our recent victory, but we still have another battle approaching us," Fletcher said, addressing his team as he sat at the head of the table.

"I'm working more now than when I was a slave," Tor grumbled.

"Stop whining, or I'll trade you with the hybrids."

"I'll just wait until you conquer them."

"I changed my mind. I'll trade you with the angels instead."

"I actually love working!" Tor said, quickly changing his tune.

Fletcher grinned and returned to the matter at hand. "Conquering Lilthral was a success, and I'm proud of all of you. But things didn't go as expected. There were more guards than reported, and over two thousand soldiers were here. Our army was late, which cost every one of our allies from Yuun their lives. Fortunately, Leon pulled through and made it in time. In total, we lost eight hundred twenty-seven men. Despite that, we're the strongest we've ever been, with thirty-six hundred soldiers standing beside us. That said, three hundred of them are out of action due to injuries, and another five hundred seventy are wounded and won't be fighting at their best."

"But we'll still have an advantage," Ji said.

"Not exactly. The allies we gained here haven't been trained, and due to a portion of Lilthral's army staying behind, it's hard to tell how many elves we'll be facing. I estimate it will be between two and three thousand," Fletcher said. "As always, we're at a disadvantage, so I came up with an idea."

"Your last plan almost killed us," Crystal said.

"That might be true, but it's in the past, and I've learned from it." Fletcher stood and pointed out the tiny window at the forest in front of the city. "That's... It doesn't have a name—"

"It's called Fiuden Forest," Tor said.

"It's not on any maps, so as far as I'm concerned, it's nameless. The point is, I want to take the battle there. It's overgrown and difficult to see inside from the road. Because of that, it will be easy to split the elves' army by tricking them into thinking we're on both sides of the forest."

"And how do you intend on doing that?"

"That's the part I don't like. The only way is by putting thirty soldiers on one side, spreading them out, and having them run, leading the elves away from us. Regrettably, there's no way for them to survive, and we'll be using them as sacrifices."

"Why don't we stay in the city?" Ji asked, disliking Fletcher's approach.

"As I said, we're not on equal footing. We either risk losing everything or sacrifice thirty people. Trust me, I hate it, I hate every life we lose, but I fight so that our kind never feels the torment we have." Fletcher balled his hands into fists. "If I could single-handedly change Affer, without any of my kin dying, I would, no matter the cost."

The room stayed silent, and Ji stared at his friend. He knew Fletcher meant every word and realized none of the decisions he made were easy. Fletcher never showed weakness; even when they were slaves, Ji never saw the other man crack. But he understood the weight Fletcher carried on his shoulders would break even the toughest of warriors. "I don't like it, but I understand."

Fletcher glanced at Ji, grateful to have him as his friend and right-hand.

"So we're relying on brute force to win?" Leon asked.

"No! Weren't you listening? This is the most strategic plan I could come up with!"

"Beating elves is right up my alley," Leon said, completely ignoring Fletcher. "Back in my prime, I could've taken this whole city by myself."

"This son of a bitch. Then why were you a slave your whole life?!" Tor asked, glancing at the older man.

"Because they had swords and armor. If it was a fair brawl, anything goes, I would have been undefeated!" Leon said, jabbing his fist in front of him to emphasize his point.

"If that's what lets you sleep at night, then keep believing it. Also, you contradicted yourself."

"What happened with that contest you two had?!" Ji asked, assuming it would spark a fight between them, but his curiosity got the best of him.

"I won," Tor confidently said.

"You're full of shit! We've already been over this. I won!" Leon said, glaring at the large man.

"No, you cheated—"

"I didn't! You're just a sore loser!" Leon shouted, jumping up from his seat.

"I saw you steal four kills from our allies, and that's only what I witnessed!"

"A kill is a kill. Who—"

"Enough!" Fletcher sternly commanded. "You two will bicker all day about who killed more elves, but instead of talking, prove it in the upcoming battle!"

Tor and Leon both settled down and became quiet.

"I expect the elven army to arrive in two days. So rest up, and be ready to fight," Fletcher said, dismissing his team.

Tor looked at Leon. "Do you want a rematch?"

"You already know the answer!" Leon said as they left the room.

"I'm going to sleep. I'll see you tomorrow," Ryan said, leaving as well.

"I take it you're not going to do the same?" Ji asked Fletcher.

"Sleep? No, I still have work to do," Fletcher said. "We need to arm and protect the new soldiers, set up human guards for the city, make sure the elves are weaponless and the guards are imprisoned, take inventory of weapons, bury the fallen, evaluate our new allies, and come up with a strategy to conquer the other three elven cities. Everything doesn't have to be done tonight, but I need to make sure we're prepared for the upcoming fight."

"I'll help you."

"You don't have to; I'm sure you're exhausted."

"I am, but I can't let you do all the work."

"If Ji can muster up the will to help, I guess I can too," Crystal said.

"What's that supposed to mean?!"

SEVENTY-THREE

"Stop the convoy here," Light told the driver.

"Right away, sir," the elf said, grabbing the radio to tell the others while he started slowing down.

"Why are we pausing?" Ingrid asked.

"I'm tired of being stuck in this confined space."

Once the car came to a halt, Light opened the door and stepped outside, his bones cracking as he stretched. "I've been stuck in that vehicle for too long!"

"You must be getting old if you're tired from twelve hours of driving."

"You're not much younger than me."

"I'm not, but I didn't order the convoy to stop," Ingrid said, disappointed in Light for complaining when they were riding in a royal vehicle. "We used to sit on wooden seats in the military trucks for seventeen hours when we were young."

"And I hated every minute of it."

"Sir," an elf said, coming over to Light. "Is everything all right?"

"We've driven enough today. Start setting up camp."

"I'll see to it." The elf saluted Light and left.

"You already plan to settle for the night?" Ingrid asked, becoming more frustrated with the elf.

"Why not? It's already seventeen twenty," Light responded.

"I take it you're not in a rush to get back to the capital?"

"Not in the slightest. There's no possibility that the humans won. Not that I can confirm since my transmitter broke. But in the minuscule chance that they did, whether we arrive today or next week is irrelevant."

Ingrid didn't say anything, but he disagreed with Light. If anything, they should rest more tomorrow, the day before they arrived at the capital, in case they had to fight. This was nothing more than a waste of time.

"Sir, should we prepare dinner now as well?" another of the elves asked.

"Why not? I'm hungry, and I'm sure everyone else is, too," Light said, heading over to one of the tents that was being set up and sitting on one of the chairs.

Ingrid's face twisted into one of complete disgust. *He goes from sitting in the car to sitting out here.*

Shaking his head, Ingrid grabbed a spare sword from the trunk of the car before walking away from the group. Walking into the forest, Ingrid stopped when he could no longer see or hear his kin and drew his weapon. Throwing the scabbard to the ground, he raised his sword in front of him. Taking a few practice swings, Ingrid moved closer to a tree. He took a deep breath and started striking it, changing between hitting the left and right sides hundreds of times.

"Is there anything left to eat?" Ingrid asked as he rejoined his team.

"I saved a meal for you, sir. It's beef soup. I left it on the table," an elf said, pointing to the tent they had eaten in.

Ingrid opened his mouth to thank his ally, but he was interrupted.

"Ingrain! Wair yoo going?!"

Ingrid paused and looked back, swearing that was Light's voice, but surprised by the slurred words. Sure enough, when he glanced behind him, he saw it was Light who had spoken.

"Are you drunk?"

"Who, me?!" Light asked, standing. "I had meself a wee bitter bitt, bit, of ale." He held his fingers close together, as if to show what he had drunk.

"I can't believe you. I've never seen you drink anything, much less get drunk."

"Yee know what they sayy, a bottle of ale keeps the war at bay!"

"No one says that, and if anyone did, it wouldn't be us elves," Ingrid said, turning and walking into the tent.

Inside, he saw a bowl sitting on one of the tables, just as the elf told him.

"At least everyone hasn't lost their manners," Ingrid said, sitting and making a mental note to thank the elf later.

SEVENTY-FOUR

Ingrid rolled down the window and stuck his head out, surveying the city of Lilthral. "The humans...they won," he said in utter astonishment.

"How can you tell?" Light asked, refusing to believe Ingrid.

"The palace is damaged. There's a massive hole where the doors used to be."

"That doesn't mean they won."

Ingrid laughed. "When has a town's palace, city hall, or castle been breached but come out victorious?"

"It happened once before."

"And what city was that?"

Light grumbled at his comrade and ignored the question. "Can you close the window? It's freezing in here."

"The answer is Vero, but I'm sure you knew that," Ingrid said, doing as Light asked.

As the window was rolling up, an arrow shot through the open crack and punctured the seat. Ingrid and Light looked out of the car at Fiuden Forest.

"I think that confirms who won." Ingrid pulled back the detachable cushion in the center seat and reached into the trunk to take his sword and helmet. "See you out there!" He donned his helmet and threw open the door, rushing into the forest.

"This is off to a great start," Light mumbled, grabbing his weapon and helmet as well.

It had only been a few seconds, but the elves were already pouring out of the trucks. With no chance to receive orders from Light, the soldiers randomly ran into either side of the forest.

"They're trying to scatter us," Light said to himself, realizing why they brought the battle here. Putting on his helmet and drawing his sword, Light charged into the left side of the forest.

Running into his first enemy, Light quickly beheaded the man and moved on to the next. Fighting two simultaneously, he ducked under an attack and locked swords with the other soldier. Sliding his weapon down the blade and spinning around, he cut off his enemy's legs. Concentrating on the other man, Light parried a blow and countered, stabbing the human in the chest. Turning to the soldier with no legs, Light drove his blade into the back of his neck.

Checking on Ingrid, Light noticed he was outnumbered, three to one, but knew he could handle it, so he didn't bother helping. On his right, Light saw a human sprinting at him with a spear. Waiting for the soldier to get closer, Light dodged and shoved the spear down with his blade. The weapon lodged in the dirt, and the wooden shaft snapped. The human tumbled down, and Light stabbed him in the spine.

Heading farther into the forest, Light cut down every human he ran into, leaving a trail of blood in his wake.

"Not dead yet?!" Light asked as he went back-to-back with his right-hand.

"I could say the same to you," Ingrid said, moving in a

circle. "After seeing you drunk the other night, I figured you'd be dead within minutes."

"I get drunk once in my life, and now you're always going to bring it up!" Light said, blocking a swing coming at him.

"The Light I knew when I was younger, the one I looked up to, would've never allowed himself to weaken his state of mind! Especially not for something as stupid as simple pleasure!"

"That's your fault for admiring me! You set your expectations too high, and no matter what I do, it will never be enough!"

"I never expected you to be unbeatable or perform impossible tasks!" Ingrid said, switching sides with Light and kicking a human in the stomach. "You were more of a brother to me than my real one! I saw you outwork everyone and climb the ranks, even though you were a commoner like me. You fought on the front line next to Yasin, Dean, Vincent, and the mighty King Harthorn, and they all praised you! What happened to that elf?! Where is the mighty Light Litchtree I once knew?!"

"You speak as if I'm dead! Everyone changes; you're just stuck in the past, lingering on nostalgia! Grow up and accept reality!"

Ingrid rammed his pommel into a human's side, crushing a portion of his breastplate. Knowing he wasn't going to get anywhere with this, Ingrid asked him a question he should have long ago. "What happened during the Great War?"

Light didn't respond at first, and Ingrid assumed he wouldn't say anything. Then he said, "I realized that no matter how hard I train, I'll never be the best."

Ingrid was so shocked that he didn't move and was tackled. Shoving the human aside, Ingrid stabbed him in the chest and stood back up. "That's it? You didn't know there were others who were better than you?"

Light chuckled and parried two attacks coming his way.

"Of course not! I never thought of myself as the best fighter in Affer. But he...he was so much stronger. I felt like a drop of water compared to an ocean."

"Who?"

This time, Light didn't answer, and Ingrid decided he was done with his friend.

"Where are you going?!" Light asked as he watched Ingrid walk away.

"I'm done with you."

"What a pain in my ass," Light grumbled, fully focusing on the fight now that he was alone.

A soldier charged at him from behind, swinging a short-sword at his torso. Light easily deflected the weapon and rammed into him, throwing the human off balance. As he stumbled, Light went in to finish him, but had to stop as a blade came flying at his face. He ducked, barely evading the blow. Standing as quickly as he dropped, Light swung his sword at the soldier. The human blocked the first attack but wasn't fast enough to respond to the second.

Turning around, Light lowered his stance, ready to move in any direction as he waited for his opponents to act. One of the humans became impatient and lunged at him. They ended up over-swinging and left themselves vulnerable, which Light took advantage of, stabbing the man between his ribs. The blade pierced his right lung, and he curled up in a ball as his life slipped away.

With only four remaining, Light went on the offensive, feinting a strike at one soldier and ramming his pommel into another. Diverting his attention to the other two, Light dodged one sword and parried the other. Lunging forward, he slammed his shoulder into a human. A jab came at him from his left, and he lightly blocked it, putting just enough strength into stopping the weapon, before he cut off the soldier's arm.

Hearing the whooshing sound of wind coming toward him, Light instinctively ducked just in time for a blade to pass over him. Spinning around, he swept the human's feet out from under him, then kneed him in the face as he fell. Standing, Light looked over at the last human, who was unharmed and shaking in fear. Taking two steps toward him, Light cut his head clean off before slaying the rest.

"How pathetic," Light sneered as he walked away. He hadn't made it twenty feet before he ran into another human. This one was unaccompanied and clad in full metal armor.

"I'm going to make you pay for all the blood you've shed!" the man yelled, hoisting his longsword in front of him.

"You scum have forgotten your place and become arrogant," Light mocked, lowering his arms and leaving himself wide open to show the human he wasn't afraid of him in the slightest. "I don't know how you were able to take over Ronann, much less Lilthral. I've already killed dozens of your kind, and with each life I take, I'm reminded why you're slaves."

The human didn't say anything and rushed forward, feinting a swing before he stepped back, narrowly avoiding injury as Light's blade tore across his metal breastplate. Going on the defensive, the human moved back and waited for Light to strike. Light dashed toward him, getting in close and jabbing his sword toward his heart. The soldier dodged it, moving to the side, but was hit in the face by the elf's fist. The man's head whipped back as he was punched, but he shook it off and went in to counter, ducking and tackling Light. Surprised by the attack, Light lost his balance and was slammed into the ground, with the human landing on top of him.

Throwing him off, Light stood and kicked him in the torso, which the man blocked with his arms. A cloud of snow was thrown in the air as Light kicked him, masking his vision for a brief second, which was enough for the soldier to make a move. He grabbed Light's other leg and pulled it toward him, making him fall backward and hit his head on a tree root that was sticking out of the dirt. Before Light could recover, the human had already gotten up and was swinging his longsword at him. The elf rolled to his right, and the blade slammed down where he had been, embedding itself in the root. Rolling back, Light kicked the human in the head, knocking him down while his weapon remained lodged in the tree.

"Of all the humans I've fought today, you have surpassed every one of them in skill," Light said, pulling the human's sword out and throwing it behind him. "But this is where you die."

"You're just like Fletcher; both of you talk too much," the human said as Light walked closer. Being patient, he waited until the elf was only a foot away and threw a fistful of snow in his face.

Light paused as he was blinded, and wiped the snow from his helmet. He figured the human would run to fetch his weapon, but was shocked when he was tackled again. Hitting the ground, Light felt a heavy rock slam into his helmet. The first attack hurt, but the second one broke his nose, causing blood to spew out and cover his lips and chin. Light lifted his arms to block the third hit, grabbing the man by his forearms and overpowering him. Using his thumbs, Light dug into the soldier's wrists. The sharp metal of his armor sliced through the leather backing of the human's gauntlets. Pressing harder, Light saw blood running down his arms, and the human dropped the rock soon after. Letting go, Light grabbed the man by the collar and threw him to the side.

"You really love to fight dirty, don't you?!" Light yelled, standing and putting his boot on the man's throat. "I expect no less from a slave!" He raised his sword and brought it down toward the man's head, but was stopped by someone else.

Light's blade made contact with another, saving the human's life and causing both of them to face the newcomer.

"I've lost enough comrades these last few days. I'm not losing any more," Fletcher said, looking down at Ryan with a solemn expression. Turning to Light, his eyes filled with bloodlust. "I think it's time you and I fight."

SEVENTY-FIVE

"You're—" Light began to say, but was silenced by Fletcher punching him in the face, throwing him off Ryan and tumbling down once again.

"Head that way. Tor and Ji could use your help," Fletcher told Ryan, giving him a hand up and then pointing behind him.

Ryan nodded at Fletcher. Grabbing his sword, he sped off in the direction his leader pointed, but stopped when Fletcher called him.

"Ryan!" Fletcher said, turning to his friend and saluting him. "You fought well."

"Thank you, sir!" Ryan said, saluting Fletcher back before he hurried to help Tor and Ji.

Facing Light, Fletcher gave the high-ranking elf his full attention. "It looked as though my soldier was going to kill you. For a minute, I was debating if I needed to come over."

Light stood and took off his helmet, blood still running from his nose as he spit out a mouthful of blood. "You overestimate your men. None of you are capable of besting me one-on-one, not even you!"

"Let's see about that," Fletcher said, swinging his sword in his hand and getting ready to strike.

Light grit his teeth and lunged at Fletcher. The two exchanged several blows in quick succession until Fletcher locked the guard of his claymore on Light's blade. Twisting his weapon, he shoved Light's blade away from him and whipped his sword across the elf's breastplate, cutting through the metal. Dodging the next attack, Light slammed his pommel into Fletcher's helmet so hard that it flew off.

Fletcher backed off after that, retreating to safety and blocking a slash from Light as the elf advanced toward him. Fighting more cautiously, Fletcher waited for an opening before countering. Swinging his claymore, he landed a clean hit on Light's right side. The blade went through his armor and broke two ribs.

Light let out a cry of pain and spit in Fletcher's face. He didn't bother wiping it away and pushed toward the elf, knowing he was trying to blind him and create an opening to attack.

Crashing into Light with his right shoulder, Fletcher knocked him down. Wiping the spit from his eyes, he ducked as Light's sword came speeding at his neck. Standing back up, he kicked Light and swung his claymore over his head, bringing it down where the elf stood. Light managed to evade by stepping back, dodging the tip of the blade by mere inches. Before Fletcher could pull his weapon back up, Light stepped on it, twisting it with his boot so the flat part was resting on the bottom of his heel.

Neither of them moved, and they locked eyes. "You're really so delusional that you think you can win?" Light asked with a sneer.

Fletcher let go of his claymore and threw a punch at Light, knocking him in the jaw and landing another. Light dodged the third punch and swung his sword upward. Fletcher moved back but was still wounded, receiving a cut along the right side of his face, spanning from his jaw to his forehead.

With his weapon behind Light, Fletcher grabbed the dagger from his belt and a large rock from the ground. Throwing the rock at Light, he charged at the elf, ducking under a blow and sweeping his feet. But Light didn't fall as Fletcher expected. Instead, he turned the tables on him and swept Fletcher's legs, punching him in the face as he fell.

Fletcher's head pounded, and his vision spun. Unsure of what was going on, he rolled to the side. Getting on his hands and knees, he slowly stood and looked at Light.

"I finally understand how you scum have made it so far," Light said, seeing Fletcher for the formidable leader he was.

"It's my life's purpose to free my people, so that gets me up every time. You're not bad yourself. I see why you were chosen as the right-hand of the queen."

"That was *my* life's purpose."

The two stopped talking and lunged at each other. Fletcher blocked Light with his dagger, but the elf immediately brought his longsword down and sliced through Fletcher's left gauntlet into his hand. He felt the blade rip through his skin, brushing against his bones. Warm blood spewed from his hand, making his fingers sticky and dripping from his gauntlet.

Light removed his sword and swung again at Fletcher, who ducked and flung his dagger at the elf. Light didn't have time to block and tried to dodge. Unable to move fast enough, the weapon made contact and sank into Light's chest, piercing through his breastplate and going into his body.

By the time he pulled the dagger out and tossed it aside, Fletcher had already grabbed his claymore and was swinging it at him. Light parried the incoming weapon with his own and countered, pushing toward Fletcher.

The two went back and forth, each trying to get the advantage, until Light's wounds caught up to him. Evading an attack, Fletcher stepped forward and bashed his pommel into Light's head. Blood immediately started running from the wound, and Light went limp before stumbling back.

Without pause, Fletcher spun around and sliced the right-hand of the queen in half, spattering blood across the snow and trees. His guts spilled out, thrown far away by the force of the blow, and both halves of Light fell to the ground.

Fletcher walked over to him and crouched close to his head. "I told you next time we fought it would be to the death."

"Scum," Light softly spoke, coughing up blood. "Just... be...because...you def...defeated us... The...others...wi...will... massacre you...you... an...and yo...your...army."

"Then I'll see you after death," Fletcher said, standing and glancing down at the dead elf before he walked away.

SEVENTY-SIX

"How's the battle progressing?" Fletcher asked Ji as he walked over.

"We won. Well, we're on the verge of winning," Ji said, taking off his helmet. "The elves who went to the right side of the forest realized it was a decoy. But after seeing so many of their allies' corpses, over half surrendered. Leon and three dozen soldiers are working on tying them up as we speak, and we're killing the last elves who aren't backing down."

"Great. I took care of their leader, so that should help convince most of them to surrender."

"Your idea worked out better than I expected," Ji admitted, observing the battlefield.

"I may have been a slave most of my life, but I've been thinking about the path to freedom ever since I was forced to work. My plans aren't perfect, and neither am I, but I've put myself through hardship so that I'm worthy of the title of leader."

"I wouldn't follow anyone else into war."

"And I wouldn't want anyone else by my side," Fletcher said, putting his hand on Ji's shoulder. "Now, let's finish this battle."

SEVENTY-SEVEN

The frigid air bit at Ingrid's skin, but that was the last thing he was thinking about as his sole priority was staying alive. When he left Light, Ingrid wandered about, killing small groups of humans until he came across a large fight. There were over seventy people engaged in the fray, and his kin were losing. Aiming to turn the tide of battle, Ingrid jumped in.

He instantly brought his sword down on a human's head, slicing through his body and stopping above his stomach. Pulling his blade out, he slashed to his right, cutting off a soldier's arm before stabbing him in the neck. Staying on offense, Ingrid took on two opponents at once.

Dodging one attack, he moved in and blocked another. Pulling his dagger from his belt, he stabbed a human in the chest. The soldier pulled back, retreating behind his allies and taking Ingrid's dagger with him. Annoyed, he turned back to the prior soldier. Exchanging multiple blows, Ingrid killed his opponent and evaded a swing from the human he had stabbed, but the elf behind him was killed in the crossfire. Twisting around, Ingrid brought his sword down on the man's arm. The human's limb fell to the ground, and he let out a howling scream.

Flipping his weapon, Ingrid jabbed behind him, piercing through the worn-out chainmail covering his enemy's body.

Pulling his blade out, Ingrid grabbed his dagger from the second soldier and slit his throat with it.

He peered down at the elf who had died because of him. Ingrid felt guilty, but that was the reality of war.

Another human came running at him, his weapon raised above his head. The man brought his longsword down and missed Ingrid as he stepped to the side. The elf took the opportunity to act while the soldier was open and decapitated him.

As the battle continued, Ingrid noticed more humans coming over to help, whereas his allies were thinning out until he was fighting entirely on his own. He had nabbed a shield from one of his fallen foes and was using that to stay alive.

Ingrid blocked a jab with his shield and went in to deliver a killing blow to the man, but was forced to defend himself from an incoming attack. Taking a step back, Ingrid bashed his shield into a human's helmet. The soldier dropped to the ground and was knocked unconscious. Turning around, he parried two strikes coming at him. Looking to counter, Ingrid stopped as he felt a blade pierce his armor and slice across his back. He grunted in pain, but continued to fight.

His heart rate increased, and Ingrid fought with everything in him. He couldn't remember the last time he was so close to death, where even a minor mistake would cost him his life. But try as he might, Ingrid couldn't win. Wounds accumulated on his body, and his breathing grew heavy as he ran out of stamina.

Just as he thought he was going to die, he was hit in the head with the flat of a blade. Ingrid collapsed, his body landing on his fallen kin.

"Stay down!" a firm voice commanded.

Ingrid didn't listen and tried to get up, only for a heavy boot to step on his chest.

"You're even worse than your master," the same person said.

Letting go of his weapon, Ingrid removed his helmet to get a better look at who was speaking. "Why am I not surprised to see the mighty leader of the human rebellion."

"I could say the same to you," Fletcher said, staring down at the elf, who gave him a confused look.

"What does that mean?"

"I guess that didn't make sense. Also, you wouldn't know. You're the new leader of the elves, technically. Both the queen and Light are dead, and since you're Light's right-hand, that makes you in charge."

"What? No, that's wrong. I—" Ingrid started to say, but stopped. None of the other kingdoms knew about Princess Allica, so there was a high possibility that Fletcher didn't know either.

"You what?" Fletcher asked, raising an eyebrow.

"I'm not a king," Ingrid said, hoping that was a good enough lie.

Fletcher chuckled. "Of course you're not. The elven kingdom is mine and my kin's. But as of now, the military falls on your shoulders, so command your people to stand down. There's no need for more bloodshed. We've won this battle, and if you keep fighting, your kin will die in vain."

Ingrid glared at Fletcher. He knew he wasn't bluffing, but he also knew that this fight wasn't as one-sided as he was making it seem. Granted, he didn't want all of his allies to die. "Fine... I'll command my soldiers to stand down. Just promise you'll leave the citizens alone. They have no part in this war, and shouldn't have to suffer because of it."

Fletcher looked at the elf with a serious face before he dug his boot into Ingrid's neck. "You elves are so hypocritical! What about when my ancestors were killed and enslaved? We've suffered for centuries because of you and the other species, yet now that we have control, you expect mercy?" he said, pressing the tip of his blade into Ingrid's cheek. "I should kill you and let the wolves devour your corpse... But I won't." He removed the claymore and returned it to its scabbard. "I'm not like the rest of you. I'm not going to enslave anyone, regardless of whether they're my enemy or an innocent citizen. Now call off your army, or this forest will run redder than Arrgon Desert."

SEVENTY-EIGHT

Fletcher raised his glass in the air and let his voice echo throughout the dining hall of the palace. "TONIGHT, WE ARE ABLE TO CELEBRATE OUR VICTORY! WE HAVE SHED A GREAT DEAL OF BLOOD AND LOST MANY OF OUR KIN, BUT IT WAS NOT IN VAIN! EVERY DAY WE GET CLOSER TO A LIFE OF FREEDOM FOR OUR KIND! EVER SINCE I WAS PUT TO WORK AS A SLAVE, I WANTED TO ESCAPE AND BECOME FREE! BUT I DIDN'T WANT TO BE ALONE... I WANTED MY WHOLE SPECIES TO BASK IN THE GLORY OF FREEDOM! TO BE ABLE TO LIVE AS WE WERE BORN TO, NOT CONFINED TO OBEYING ORDERS AND STAYING TRAPPED IN A MEANINGLESS EXISTENCE! TODAY, WE HAVE TAKEN THE LARGEST STEP TOWARD THAT DREAM, AND I COULDN'T HAVE DONE IT WITHOUT ALL OF YOU! LET THIS NIGHT BE REMEMBERED AS THE DAY WE CONQUERED LILTHRAL!" He finished speaking, prompting the dining hall to break into loud applause as everyone shouted and raised their glasses.

"You're sounding more like a leader with every victory," Ji said to Fletcher as he sat back down.

"You think?"

"Undoubtedly!"

"I agree with Ji," Crystal said, sitting next to him on his left. "He's known you longer than I have, but I've seen you grow considerably since we met."

"I don't think the others from Titanan would recognize you."

"We'll find out when we free them," Fletcher said, eager to liberate his home city.

"Where are we attacking next?" Tor asked. "Are we going to the demon kingdom?"

"I'm ready to kill those demon bastards!" Leon said, stabbing his knife into the wooden table.

"Both of you, slow down," Fletcher said, trying to calm the two. "We haven't even fully conquered the elves yet. There are still three cities left, and once we take control of those, we're not jumping all the way to the second strongest species on Affer. The plan is to start at the bottom and work up the ladder, gaining more power and allies along the way."

"As long as I get to kill someone, I don't care," Leon said, struggling to take his knife out of the table.

"What city are we starting with?" Ji asked between bites.

"I haven't decided. We need to recover, so I'll have to come up with an idea to buy us time," Fletcher said just as Leon pulled his knife out. "We'll worry about that in a few days. For now, I want to scout more skilled and talented fighters. We could use extra members in the Vanguard, and I want to start gathering commanders, too."

"What?!" Leon yelled, stabbing his knife into the table again. "You're replacing me?!"

"No. You're the head commander, meaning you serve directly under me. But you can't order tens of thousands of soldiers on your own. I need more people to split the load. At the moment, each commander will order a thousand men, give or take, but later I intend on increasing that to ten thousand."

"I'll be the greatest commander in your army!"

"I wouldn't have given you this position if I thought there was someone better," Fletcher said, leaning forward in his chair and taking a bite of steak. "This is so much better than the food in Titanan."

"It wasn't that bad," Ji said, staring at his friend with a look of bewilderment.

"Seriously? You actually enjoyed the food there? I hated it ninety-nine percent of the time. I figured everyone did."

"It wasn't appetizing, but it was better than what we ate in Admont."

"There's something wrong with you," Fletcher said, concerned that Ji thought the food they ate as slaves was better than what they had at the human capital. "Admont was great!"

"We just had meat, and it was all from wild animals! Everything was tough as a rock!"

"Then you should've cooked!"

"It didn't matter how it was cooked; it was a wild animal!"

"Honestly, I liked the food when you two came to the castle," Crystal said, shivering. "What I ate before was far worse."

"See, Ji, why can't you be more appreciative like Crystal?"

"Appreciative for what?! I'm the one who set up most of the traps and butchered the animals! All you did was cook!"

"I was busy making swords and training! If I didn't, we would've died in IItu!" Fletcher said, throwing his hands in the air. "If anything, you should be showing me gratitude!"

"Fine, thanks!"

"Thanks as well! I'm grateful we didn't starve to death."

"Are you two brothers?" Tor asked, glancing between Ji and Fletcher, trying to find any resemblance between them.

"No!" they said at the same time.

SEVENTY-NINE

"It seems that I was right... I thought I saw them loading you out of the truck."

"Good to see you too, Princess," Ingrid said, glancing up from his cell at the half-elf. "I have a vague idea how you managed to stay free and under the humans' radar, but regardless, I have to give you credit."

"When I want something, the price is trivial," Allica said with a look of malice. "And I *really* wanted to survive."

"Do I want to know how you did it?"

"Definitely not," Allica said, leaning in closer. "I'm the queen of the elves now, and I'm going to kill every last one of those human scum. You'll obey me and serve as my right-hand, or you can rot in this cell."

"Listen here, princess, I've never taken orders from you before, and that's not going to change. With Light dead, that makes me the best fighter in the elven kingdom. You need me, not the other way around," Ingrid said, glaring at the princess.

"Try getting out of here without me."

"Try taking back the city without me."

Allica stared at the elf with disdain. She and Ingrid never got along, and it was clear that wasn't going to change. He never physically hurt her, as her mother never allowed that, but she couldn't remember an encounter between them where he didn't belittle her. She had grown used to only receiving kindness from Light and Jax, but now that she was the queen, things would be different.

She was about to open her mouth and yell at Ingrid when she changed her mind. *I have Jax, a hundred guards, and almost a thousand soldiers to take back the city, so I don't need Ingrid. That said, I can use him to gain trust from the other elves. None of them know me very well, or at all, which means they'll follow Ingrid before me. Luckily, I have a strategy to change that.*

"What do you want?"

"I'm glad you've come to your senses," Ingrid said, standing and walking over to the bars. "Bring me a transmitter that has access to Arkanon's royal channel. I have a message for the king."

EIGHTY

"Were you able to find any worthy recruits?" Fletcher asked Ryan, Tor, and Ji, whom he had assigned to assess their new allies.

"A few," Ji said. "No one beat me, but two bested Tor, and one was able to defeat Ryan."

"Really?" Fletcher asked, looking at the two. "That's impressive! Matching either of you isn't easy, much less winning against you. But when did you fight them?"

"That's the thing: all of them were among the last ten people we sparred with," Tor said. "And we were holding back, since we're not in the best condition right now."

"Let's test them and see how good they really are," Fletcher said, walking into the training room of Lilthral's military post.

The space was filled with people sparring, many of whom stopped and stared at Fletcher and the three other members of the Vanguard as they passed by. Observing the recruits, Fletcher was surprised. "This is the best group we've freed. I already see potential in them."

"Does that mean we can attack the other cities soon?" Ji asked.

"Unfortunately, no. We need to recover before we make any moves."

"How do you plan on doing that? This is the capital. I'm sure the other cities come here often."

"They do. I've taken the queen's personal transmitter; she had over a hundred private channels on it. All of them are linked to someone important. Some were from other kingdoms, but most were groups of elves. Skimming over it, I could tell each city stops by at least once a month. Sometimes it's for taxes, other times it's for a meeting, and the overseers also report to the queen about any major decisions and promotions," Fletcher said, walking up the stairs. Reaching the top, he observed his men sparring on the first floor. "Basically, it won't be easy to hide the fact that we've taken control of Lilthral."

"It sounds impossible," Ji said.

"Something's only deemed impossible because no one's ever done it before."

"That's why you're the leader, no one else thinks like that."

"I doubt it," Fletcher said, leaning on the railing and eyeing a few people.

"No, Ji's right, not many people have your kind of mentality," Ryan said, putting his hands in his pockets.

"I'm just doing what I need to," Fletcher said, waving off their praise.

"Regardless of what you say, you're the only one who could lead us to freedom."

Fletcher looked over at Ryan, surprised to hear him say that. "I can't do it alone. I need warriors like you by my side." He was pleased that Ryan was warming up to him, not that he blamed him after Ethan died. Turning back to the fighters, Fletcher pointed at one. "He beat one of you, right?"

Tor followed Fletcher's finger and was astounded to see that his friend was correct. "How did you know?!"

"I can tell. He acts without hesitation and doesn't make

wasteful movements with his weapon. On top of that, he holds his sword correctly and stands upright with confidence."

"I'm impressed you picked up on that so quickly," Ryan said, trying to see it himself.

"I want to test his skills," Fletcher said, heading down the stairs.

"Fletcher, you shouldn't be sparring!" Ji said, following him down. "You're the most wounded here."

Fletcher stopped and faced Ji. "When did I say I was going to fight him? Even though I'm wounded, it would still be vastly unfair to the newcomer."

Ji let out a sigh of relief.

"That's why you're going to fight him."

"You're kidding."

"Not at all."

Fletcher walked over to the recruit and waited for him to finish his match. A minute later, he pressed his blade to his opponent's throat.

"I win," the man said, removing his longsword.

"Bravo," Fletcher said, causing both men to turn toward him. "You performed exceptionally."

"My Lord, it's an honor to meet you, let alone hear your praise," the man said, bowing.

"Fletcher is fine, and you don't have to bow. What is your name?"

"Mason Ryeheart, sir," the man introduced himself, standing straight.

"Well, Mason, I need warriors who can command my army or fight next to me, and seeing your skill set, I think you can fill one of those roles," Fletcher said, pointing next to him at Ji. "I want you to spar my right-hand, and if I'm still impressed, I'll place you in a high position in my army. Are you up for that?"

"Of course," Mason said, a huge smile on his face. "If it helps to free our kind, I'll do anything."

"Good attitude." Fletcher turned to his friend. "All yours, Ji."

Ji nodded. Drawing his sword, he stepped onto the mat and walked over to the opposite side of Mason. By now, the rest of the room was starting to stir, and a circle was forming around the two.

"Give this your all. I want you to fight as if your life is on the line," Ji told his opponent.

Mason nodded in understanding and took a deep breath, getting ready to clash with Ji. The two waited, seeing who would move first, until Ji swung his sword.

Lunging at Mason, Ji aimed for his torso, turning his blade to the side in case Mason didn't block or dodge. Fortunately, Mason evaded Ji's sword. Pulling his weapon back, Ji spun and crouched, swinging at the legs. Mason jumped over the attack and jabbed his sword at Ji's chest.

Ji parried the strike and countered as he rose to his full height. Mason stepped to the side, trying to avoid the blow. However, he wasn't fast enough and was hit on his left hip with the flat of Ji's blade. It didn't hurt much, but it was enough to make him buckle and let his guard down, something Ji took advantage of, shoving his pommel into Mason's gut. He stumbled backward and fell onto the soft mat underneath them. Looking up, Mason saw Ji swinging his weapon at him, and quickly rolled to his left.

Ji's seax sword slashed into the mat right after Mason moved. Standing back up, Mason swung his sword at Ji, twisting his body to put all his strength behind the attack. Ji dropped, letting go of his weapon, and tackled Mason's legs, sending him to the floor.

Mason's sword flew out of his grasp as he landed on the

mats. Standing, he swung his fist at Ji. He missed blow after blow until he finally threw Ji off with a feint, and socked him square in the jaw. Reeling back, Ji dodged three more punches before throwing one of his own. Mason keeled over as Ji's fist collided with his stomach. Striking while he was down, Ji kneed him in the face, but Mason blocked the attack with his hands. Grabbing Ji's other leg, Mason pulled back, bringing him down. Twisting around, Ji cushioned his fall with his left arm as Mason jumped forward and put him in a headlock. It was a good move, but he left his right side open, which Ji took advantage of. Supporting his weight on his left arm, Ji jabbed his right elbow into Mason's liver. He felt the other man loosen his hold on him before he let go and lay on the mat in defeat.

"Good match," Ji said, standing and offering Mason a hand up.

Mason took Ji's hand and rubbed his ribs, where Ji had hit him.

"I think you'll make a great addition to my team," Fletcher said, walking over. "That is, if you'll accept."

"I'd be honored to join, but I lost."

"I didn't expect you to win. I'm a better fighter than Ji, but he's still the second-best in my army. I would be at a loss for words if you beat him."

"I was the best at one point," Ji said. "And I think I'll reclaim that spot someday."

Fletcher let out a chuckle. "I'm too far ahead for you to catch back up."

"It took you over a decade to get here; I've been training for less than a year."

"We've been over this, Ji! Both of us have been fighting for the same amount of time!"

"Yes, because all those years of training and making weapons didn't help you at all!"

"Of course it helped! But it's the countless hours I've put in since I became free that made me the best!"

"You're a blacksmith?" Mason asked Fletcher.

"I was."

"One who couldn't forge armor," Ji added.

"I can forge armor, I just can't get the proportions right."

"That's the easy part," Mason said, looking at Fletcher as if he told him he didn't know the sky was blue. "I understood that when I was sixteen."

"You were a blacksmith?" Fletcher asked, to which Mason nodded. "That explains why you held your sword correctly and stood with confidence. It's good to have another blacksmith in the Vanguard. I'll provide you with more information about our team and the role I expect you to play in it. For now, do as you please."

"Thank you, sir," Mason said, giving a bow before he left to spar with someone else.

When Mason was out of earshot, Fletcher turned to Ji. "I wasn't expecting you to hold back so much."

"If I ended the fight too quickly, we wouldn't have seen what he's capable of."

Fletcher smiled, proud of Ji for realizing that without being told. Facing Tor and Ryan, he said, "Show me the other two who beat you."

EIGHTY-ONE

"Are you sure that will work?" Crystal questioned Fletcher's plan for dealing with the remaining elven cities.

"When have I led us astray?" Fletcher asked, raising an eyebrow.

"I nearly died when we were escaping Titanan," Ji said.

"You almost died in IItu," Tor stated.

"And Ronann," Crystal added. "Lilthral, too."

"Two members of our team are dead," Ryan retorted.

"You practically killed me the first time we sparred!" Leon shouted, jumping from his seat.

"The last part isn't true," Fletcher said, pointing at Leon. "As for the rest... I've made mistakes—Titanan was completely on you, Ji—"

"Not true!"

"But I own up to those mistakes and my shortcomings."

"How many times has Fletcher almost died?" Mason asked, looking around the table.

"Too many to count," Crystal commented.

"You have that right!"

"Is that really something to be proud of?" Ryan asked.

"Damn right it is!" Leon slammed his fist on the table.

"When I was a boy, I would beat EVERYONE! And the closer I came to death, the better it felt!"

Mason gestured to Leon. "Is he okay?"

"Definitely not. He's been in too many fistfights and isn't right in the head because of it." Ji sighed. "Although he's gotten worse since we met."

"I'm perfectly fine. As long as I can't lose a fight, I'm doing great."

"But you have," Tor said. "You lost to the elves, who put you in prison, and you lost to Fletcher."

"Those don't count." Leon crossed his arms over his chest and sat back down.

"Moving back on track," Fletcher sternly said, standing and placing his hands on the table. "The whole point of this meeting is to discuss what we should do with the rest of the elven kingdom. I want to spend two months recovering before we attack again, which is why I intend to tell the remaining cities we've contracted a deadly virus. That will buy us more than enough time. However, Crystal thinks my concept is flawed."

"Because it is. You're claiming a deadly virus sprang out of nowhere and only affected us. On top of that, if it's deadly, wouldn't we want help?" Crystal asked. "Lastly, if you deny help and say we'll be okay without it, then the virus doesn't appear dangerous."

"The elves aren't smart enough to think about that."

"All it takes is one of them to say something, and your whole scheme falls apart. Face it, any strategy that buys us more than a month will have flaws. We conquered Lilthral a week ago. Within another three weeks, our army will be strong enough to take the last cities with minimal casualties."

"Alright, reduce the time to three weeks, then what?"

Crystal stayed quiet, staring blankly at an imperfection in the wooden table.

"Well?" Fletcher pressed her.

"Give me a minute," Crystal said, working out a plan in her head.

After several minutes of silence, she grinned at Fletcher. "I've come up with an idea that gives us the time we need and eliminates every elven soldier without a single loss to us."

"Explosives?" Fletcher joked, raising an eyebrow.

"Not quite. We don't need Ronann anymore, so let's use that to our advantage. Ruin the city and stage it like an attack, then contact Sullin, Cartin, and Qrtta, informing them Ronann has fallen. Tell them you don't know who's behind it, but to gather in Cartin and prepare for war. Two weeks after that, tell them you found papers for a trade deal with Arkanon for six hundred fifty slaves. Dean made the exchange, but after the transaction, Arkanon demanded a higher payment, and when Dean refused, they invaded the city. If anyone questions it, you have the papers, and the rest will be impossible to trace. To wrap it up, we send the elven soldiers to attack the hybrid capital while we stay behind and "protect" the kingdom."

Fletcher smirked. "I love this approach. I messaged the humans in IItu yesterday, telling them to head here, stopping by Ronann first to grab the prisoners. But I'll have them deface the city on top of that. When they return, I'll message Cartin, Sullin, and Qrtta. Excellent work, Crystal. I'm glad I didn't kill you in Admont."

"How sweet," Crystal said.

"Maybe I should spend less time coming up with plans, considering you'll find all their flaws anyway."

"Unless I can't, and then we're left with a lackluster strategy that ends up getting thousands killed."

"You have a point."

"Why don't you two just work together from the start?" Ji asked.

Fletcher and Crystal looked at each other.

"He'd drag me down."

"She gave me a headache when we worked together on Lilthral's plan."

Ji shook his head. *Hopefully, they'll work together someday.*

EIGHTY-TWO

Ingrid glared at Allica, who was standing in front of his cell. "Are you wearing high heels?"

"I don't even get a 'Hello, how are you? Thanks for risking your life to give me the transmitter?'" Allica said, crossing her arms under her chest.

"You do realize high heels aren't stealthy. In fact, they're the exact opposite," Ingrid said, frowning at how ignorant the woman was.

"I snuck into the palace and got my hands on some of my belongings, shoes included."

"How stupid are you?!" Ingrid said, wanting to rip his hair out. "Why would you sneak into the palace?! Are you trying to blow your cover?!"

"You're the stupid one! I needed my transmitter and the password to Arkanon's royal channel! It might sound crazy to you, but I didn't carry my transmitter on me, and because I'm barely on any channels, I had to grab the codes from my mother's room! Since I was already there, I grabbed enough jewelry to make me rich, so I don't have to work for money. The clothes and shoes were a bonus."

"I don't even want to know who you sold that jewelry to. Just give me the transmitter!"

"This is why I liked Light better," Allica said, tossing him the device.

"Well he's dead, so you're stuck with me."

Not for long, Allica thought as she turned away and left him. Walking down the dim hallway, she went deeper into the prison until she reached Jax's cell.

"My Queen," Jax said, glancing up at the hybrid.

"How's your wound?"

"The same. I can't fight yet if that's what you need."

"Not yet. The humans are still here, but when they leave, we'll make our move. In the meantime, I'm going to sneak weapons in here. Will a dagger suffice?"

"My Lady, I would fight with my bare hands if you asked me to."

"That's great, Jax, but that wasn't my question."

"A dagger is fine," Jax said, wondering how she was going to acquire one, but deciding not to ask. Instead, he questioned the half-elf about retaking the city. "If you don't mind me asking, how do you plan to recapture Lilthral?"

Allica looked at Jax with an evil smirk. "Where do I start?"

EIGHTY-THREE

"My Lord, there's a message for you on the city's royal channel. It's from a new device, so we're unsure who it's from."

Yinny stopped his training to glare at the other hybrid. "If you don't know who sent it, why didn't you read it?"

"I only read who it's addressed to."

"I'm going to strangle you," Yinny said, reaching out to take the transmitter. "I've told you I don't care if you read the messages on the royal channel. Half the time they're not important, and if they are, I'll just kill you."

"That's what I'm afraid of, My Lord," the hybrid said, bowing and leaving the room.

Yinny watched his servant leave and shut the door before he read the message.

Hello, Arkanon. Make sure this message reaches your king, Yinny Shade. I am Ingrid Way, the right-hand of Light Litchtree. The humans have overthrown Lilthral, Ronann, IItu, and possibly others. So far, they have killed the queen, the palace guards, and Light. You aren't aware of this, but we have a princess. She has managed to stay out of prison and is working to set us free. I hope we can work together to eradicate the humans, as it is in both our interests. If you are willing, please inform me.

"

Yinny burst out laughing when he finished the message and started writing back. *You elves are pathetic. You think I don't know about your half-elf princess? I know your kingdom better than you. My scout told me you failed to defend your capital and were deceived by mere tools in Ronann. It's only a matter of time until your remaining cities fall to the humans, yet you reach out to me, thinking we can work together? You have nothing that will benefit me. My army is stronger, my wealth is greater, and my kingdom is larger.*

Ever since IItu fell, I knew the tools would win, because elves are the only species on Affer who are inferior to humans!

Yinny sent the message and tossed his transmitter aside. "Let the humans come. I'll grant them the freedom they seek by delivering them to eternal rest."

EIGHTY-FOUR

"What species dares to attack us, the mighty elves?!" Thevren yelled as he read the queen's message. "We must find out and make them pay tenfold! I don't care if it was the strongest species in Affer; they must die for what they have done to my kin!" He slammed his fist on his desk and grabbed the greataxe from atop the fireplace.

"Sir, what are you doing with that?" an elf asked, quickly receiving an answer as the overseer of Cartin split his desk in two with the weapon.

"What?!" Thevren shouted, turning to his assistant.

"It's... Never mind, sir."

Thevren dropped the weapon and looked down at the broken piece of furniture. "Get someone to clean this up...and have them bring me another one!"

"Right away, sir," his personal assistant said, doing as he was told.

"Glendin, get the army ready! We're going to make the Zenton sea turn gold with the blood of the angels!"

"Sir, I hate to bring you down, but we don't know who attacked Ronann, and rushing in, declaring war on the angels is a terrible idea," Glendin said, trying to de-escalate the situation before the elf did anything rash and ended up destroying their kingdom.

"First it was the humans taking over IItu, and now it's the angels slaughtering the great city Ronann! I need to avenge my fallen kin! If I don't, no one will!" Thevren yelled, kicking his broken desk.

"Sir, I'm confused why you think the angels are behind this, but regardless of whether they are or not, we can't beat them. Even if every elf took up arms, we would still lose miserably to the angels' weakest city. Declaring war on them is a death sentence."

Thevren sighed, kicking his desk once more. "I suppose you're right... But that doesn't mean I can't tell the queen to hurry up and find out who our enemy is!" He grabbed his transmitter and started typing away.

"Dear Queen Rinn, you don't know who attacked Ronann, but I have a great suspicion that it was the angels. I will lead the charge, so please hurry and prepare the army so we can rip THOSE FILTHY, TRASH, SCUM ANGELS TO SHREDS AND SHOW THEM WHY YOU DON'T MESS WITH THE ELVES! Please consider my proposition. Yours truly, Thevren!" he read aloud as he typed. "It's perfect, let's send that!"

"Sir, I'm not—"

"Move it, Glendin!"

Turning around, Glendin saw several elves carrying a new desk. "Where are you going with that?"

"Where do you think?!" the head elf replied with more attitude than Glendin thought was necessary.

"But where are you going to put it? The old one is still here."

The elf in front glanced past Glendin at the broken piece of furniture sitting in the middle of the room. "Come on! Who didn't do their job?!"

"It's your job to remove the old desk and bring in the new one."

"Shut up, Glendin! No one asked you!" the elf snapped, putting the desk down and turning toward the rest of the elves. "This is your fault!"

As the elves started fighting, Glendin resumed his conversation with Thevren. "As I was saying, sir, I don't think it's appropriate to send that message."

"What?!" Thevren shouted, his finger digging in his ear. "Don't worry, I sent it. I'm sure the queen will love it."

EIGHTY-FIVE

"I've called this meeting for two reasons. First of all, I want to introduce our new allies," Fletcher said, gesturing toward the two people on his left and one on his right. "This is Mason Ryeheart. He was here at the last meeting, but I wanted to formally introduce him today. He will be on the front line with us as part of the Vanguard."

Mason gave a bow. "I'm honored to fight next to such incredible warriors."

"As for these two, they're going to be commanders. This is Troy Fyfur," Fletcher gestured to the one with auburn hair and then motioned to the black-haired man, "and this is Welden Pictor. They are remarkable fighters and leaders. With some battle experience, they'll all be vital assets to our army," Fletcher said, dismissing the three and having them take a seat at the table. "The second thing I wanted to talk about is a message from Cartin." Fletcher grabbed the queen's transmitter and read aloud what Thevren had written.

As he finished speaking, the room fell into silence until Ji spoke up. "Is anyone in this kingdom normal? I assumed Dean was an exception, but he appears to fit right in."

"What are you going to do?" Ryan asked. "He doesn't seem rational if he's jumping to a conclusion that would cost tens of thousands of lives."

"I'll respond and try to hold them off from attacking," Fletcher said, putting the transmitter on the table in front of him as he thought of how he could do that.

"Good luck," Crystal said.

"You're not going to help come up with a strategy?" Ji asked, looking over at her.

"I did. I helped create the original plan. This issue is more in Fletcher's wheelhouse."

"That's true."

Fletcher grabbed a pen and paper before he started writing. Everyone watched him work until he threw the pen on the table. "I can buy us sixteen more days. Sullin and Qrtta are already on their way to Cartin and will arrive in four days. Six days later, I'll tell them to attack Arkanon. Three days after that, I'll message Cartin that we, Lilthral's army, are coming to Cartin to protect them. It will take us three days to reach the city, and by then, eighty percent of our army should be fit to fight."

"I have no idea what you just said," Tor confessed.

"To simplify, we're going to have an easy victory." Fletcher picked up his transmitter and responded to Thevren.

Dear Thevren, DO NOT MOVE UNTIL I GIVE THE ORDER! I'm uncertain why you suspect the angels are behind the attack, but I highly doubt they are. I have my elves investigating Ronann as we speak, and will have an answer within two weeks. In the meantime, do as I told you, and prepare for war! DO NOT SEND MY SOLDIERS INTO BATTLE WITHOUT MY PERMISSION! I will contact you as soon as I have found out more information. Lastly, you are an overseer, not a commander, and if you leave the city to fight or disobey orders, I will strip you of your position.

"That's the best I can do," Fletcher muttered to himself, sending the message and shoving the transmitter in his pocket. "Let's hope that works in our favor."

Tor let out a yawn. Standing, he stretched his arms above his head and said, "Are we finished for today?"

"Yeah, I didn't have much to discuss. You're free to do as you please."

Everyone left, leaving Fletcher alone. He glanced out the window at the majestic city of Lilthral before turning off the lights and leaving.

Making his way down the stairs and out of the palace, Fletcher exited the building and made his way over to the ward's training room. Heading down to the first level, Fletcher arrived in the city square. Walking slowly, he took his time to take in his surroundings. He spotted children running through the snow, laughing and playing, while adults shoveled the streets and repaired the damage left by the battle.

Arriving at the ward, he stopped once again and gazed at the night sky. Every time he saw it, he paused. It didn't matter how powerful, rich, strong, smart, good, or evil you were; everyone in the world looked at the same sky. It might not have meant anything to most people, but to Fletcher, it had etched itself inside his head. Yet tonight he couldn't help but feel that the sky appeared more beautiful than normal. It was clearer than he ever remembered it being, and the stars blazed brighter than fire, with the three moons completing the picturesque scene.

As he stared up, it hit him harder than ever that he was free and fulfilling his dream.

"All those years of training while the others laughed at me...it was all worth it," Fletcher softly spoke to himself, balling his hand into a fist. "But I'm not done yet... No, I've only just started this journey. I still have a great deal left to go, and I won't stop until I've won."

He tore his gaze away from the night sky and walked up the steps to the ward. Entering the foyer, he was surprised to hear someone already there. Making his way down the hall to the training room, he stepped inside and saw Ji.

"How are you already sweating?!" Fletcher asked, heading toward him.

Ji lowered his sword and faced Fletcher. "I was wondering if you would show up."

"You thought I wasn't going to train today?"

"You have to rest sometimes, especially with how often you get hurt."

"My back and ribs feel better, and my other injuries were minor. Another two months and I'll be fully healed."

"Until you get hurt again," Ji said, tossing Fletcher a longsword. "Do you want to spar?"

"You know the answer to that," Fletcher said, spinning the weapon. "But, before we start, I wanted to tell you earlier, the prisoners and guards we left behind in Ronann were all dead when IItu got there."

"How did that happen? And why didn't you mention it in the meeting?"

"I didn't mention it to the others because they don't need the weight of more death on their shoulders. I'm telling you since you're my right-hand. As for how, one of the elves escaped. He pried up the bricks on the floor and dug out of the cell. I'm assuming the guards were too lax, and the elf was able to work without being checked on. Once he was free, he probably raided the armory and killed the guards, but I'm not sure why he murdered his kin. I also don't know which elf escaped."

"So there's an elf running around who wants to kill us and his own kin. Any other good news?"

Fletcher smirked and raised his sword. "We're one step closer to freeing Titanan and getting our hands on those triple-chocolate cookies."

Ji grinned, striking at Fletcher's chest. His friend dodged and countered, aiming for Ji's legs. He stepped back, evading the blade, then moved forward, locking weapons with Fletcher, who shoved him. Regaining his footing, Ji ducked under a blow and jabbed at Fletcher's stomach. Fletcher turned his body to the side, avoiding the hit and swinging at Ji's neck. Ji brought his sword back and blocked the attack, sliding his blade down Fletcher's until the guard stopped him.

Shoving Fletcher's sword down, Ji rammed his pommel into his sternum. He thought it would give him the edge, but he was disappointed when Fletcher grabbed it with his left hand.

"Good one, Ji," Fletcher said, pulling the weapon out of Ji's hand and throwing it behind him.

Ji was now unarmed, but he wasn't going to quit. Dodging, he turned toward one of the weapon racks. Bolting straight at it, he grabbed a shortsword just in time to block Fletcher.

"The old you would have given up."

"This me doesn't! Seeing you fight against impossible odds has inspired me to become stronger!"

"Good! Because I don't need cowards in my army!" Fletcher said, shoving him into the rack. Ji crashed to the ground, taking the stand with him and scattering weapons in every direction. "I need warriors!"

Ji rolled to the side as Fletcher brought his sword down where he was. Getting up, he cut his left hand on one of the weapons that was lying on the floor.

Fletcher moved closer before he swung at Ji. Parrying, Ji went on the offensive, pushing forward and jabbing at Fletcher's abdomen. Before he was able to make contact, Fletcher already had the tip of his sword pressed to the fabric of Ji's shirt, where his heart was.

"I win," Fletcher said, removing his weapon and glancing down at Ji's blade hovering an inch from his lower stomach. "Although, if this were a real fight, we would've killed each other. You should have attacked slightly higher."

"I was going to, but your arm was in the way."

"If you started low and swung upward, you could have avoided my arm and cut under my ribcage." Fletcher grabbed Ji's blade and demonstrated what he meant.

"I didn't consider that."

"Think about fighting more often; envision yourself doing it. In the heat of battle, it's challenging to make a split-second decision, and it can be the difference between victory and death. But if you've played out a scenario in your head hundreds of times, it will help you. Granted, that only goes so far. You can't predict what your opponents will do, what condition you'll be in, or any other factors of a real fight, but it helps. Add real battle experience and muscle memory, and you'll be one of the best soldiers on any battlefield. It's the best defense and offense you can have, letting your body react and move on its own before you even command it."

"You make it sound like you can't be defeated."

"I wasn't trying to," Fletcher said, bending over to pick up the weapons rack. "Don't get it twisted, anyone can lose at anything. There's no such thing as being untouchable. Any battle could be my last, same as you and everyone else we fight with."

"That's the risk of war," Ji said, setting the shortsword back where it belonged and helping Fletcher pick up the rest. "But the more we train, the better chance we have of staying alive."

"That, and outthinking our enemies," Fletcher said, putting the last weapon back. "Are you ready for a few more rounds?"

"Of course I am. I haven't even warmed up yet!"

EIGHTY-SIX

With so little time to prepare for battle, the humans worked nonstop. They outnumbered Cartin more than six to one, but Fletcher wasn't going to let ego cloud his vision. He learned from the elves that underestimating your foes is a costly mistake. He would've preferred to rest longer, but once Cartin was in their hands, he planned on waiting a month before they attacked the hybrid kingdom. Despite this, he was still happy with how everything was going.

As they left Lilthral, Fletcher couldn't help but grin. Motivation was at an all-time high, they had more armor than ever, the soldiers' skills were improving, and the first kingdom was basically theirs.

Ji walked next to Fletcher, who was standing at the end of the truck's cabin and staring at the rain. "You're in a good mood."

"Why wouldn't I be? This is the first battle where we have the advantage. On top of that, look at our army. We're quickly becoming the humans who were once feared."

"We still have a ways to go."

"With each city, we get closer."

The vehicle was silent, and the only sound was the rain pouring down.

"I hate this weather," Tor groaned.

"It's the middle of April. This is normal."

"Trust me, I know. Working as a laborer, I was always outside, no matter the conditions, and April was my least favorite month because of the rain."

"You're full of shit," Ryan said, laughing. "You complained every month. It was raining or snowing; the sun set too early, too late; it would be too hot or too cold. There was never a month when you weren't whining."

"That's easy for you to say! You worked inside all day."

"Tor's right, working outside sucks," Ji said.

"What are you talking about?!" Fletcher said to his friend. "You never worked outdoors."

"When we couldn't move a car in the garage, I had to fix it outside. Also, you never saw me work, how would you know?!"

"You worked inside as well," Tor said, pointing at Fletcher.

"Why are you attacking me?"

"None of you understand the hardship of being a construction!"

Everyone stopped talking and looked over at Leon. "You mean a constructor?" Fletcher asked.

"That's what I said."

"You're as dumb as the bricks you used to build with," Tor said. "And nowadays, we call them builders."

While the five of them continued arguing, Crystal got up and moved to the front of the truck. Closing the door that separated the cabin, she sat in the passenger seat. "How much longer until we arrive at Cartin?" she asked the driver.

"Three days, Miss."

"That's three days too many."

EIGHTY-SEVEN

"Do you see that?" one of the elves in Cartin's watchtower asked.

"No. Give me the binoculars," the other guard said, taking them and casting his gaze toward the sparse woods. "What is that?"

"I don't know. I can't see anymore."

"Try again." The elf gave the binoculars back to his ally. "You have better vision than me."

The guard took them and peered through the lenses before removing them and exclaiming, "It's the military convoy from Lilthral!" Looking down from the tower, he yelled to the two elves below, "Open the gate!"

"About time they got here," the other guard mumbled. "They told us we might be attacked four days ago!"

"At least nothing happened, and now that the capital's here, they'll protect us."

"Your idea actually worked," Ji said, watching the gate open.

"Of course it did," Fletcher said, joining Ji in the front cabin. Putting his hand on the passenger seat, he turned to the driver. "Head inside and stop in the city square."

"Yes, sir."

When the convoy came to a halt, Fletcher jumped out and drew his claymore. Raising the weapon, he addressed his men. "WE HOLD THE ADVANTAGE IN THIS FIGHT, BUT DO NOT LET UP! SHOW THE ELVES OUR STRENGTH AND DRAIN ANY HOPES OF VICTORY THEY HAVE! BREAK THE CHAINS THAT SHACKLE US AND LET CARTIN FALL!" Fletcher lowered his sword and charged forward. His allies fell into step behind him, and from there the city was quickly overwhelmed. The streets were flooded with humans, and the elves ran as their forces were cut down. Even the ward didn't stand a chance, and the guards were forced to give up or die protecting their city.

With every area taken, only one spot remained: city hall. The guards who had been hiding in there since the battle commenced trembled as the humans closed in.

"Drop your weapons, and we'll spare you!" Fletcher shouted. "You will not be remembered for your bravery if you fight us; you'll only achieve a pointless death! So stand down!"

The elves started dropping their weapons until Thevren entered the room.

"DO NOT SURRENDER!" the overseer yelled, pushing his way past his allies and coming face to face with Fletcher. "You scum think we'll obey you simply because you outnumber us?! We elves are not cowards! You may defeat us, but Lilthral will crush you! I've already sent a message to the queen, and it's merely a matter of time until they arrive."

Fletcher couldn't help but roar out in laughter. "You mean this message?" he asked, pulling out the queen's transmitter and showing it to the overseer. Fletcher saw Thevren's expression turn from confidence to dread.

"Impossible..." Thevren muttered, his voice unsteady. His

hands shook in fear, and he dropped his greataxe before falling to his knees.

"That's it, you're submitting?" Fletcher asked. "What happened to the overseer who was ready to lay down his life attacking the angels? Was that nothing more than an act?"

Thevren clenched his jaw as rage overrode his fright, and he picked his weapon up again. Striking while he was on his knees, the overseer drove his greataxe upward toward Fletcher.

Parrying the strike, Fletcher instinctively countered and beheaded Thevren.

The city hall became silent as the overseer's body slumped to the ground and the elves stared at Fletcher. "He killed our leader!" one of the guards shouted.

The room shifted, and the elves attacked. Those who had laid down their weapons picked them back up and joined the fight. But they stood no chance and were easily killed.

With the city taken, Fletcher turned to his team. "We still need to free our kin and separate the civilian elves, but this was the easiest conquest we've had."

"It would have been effortless if you didn't open your mouth," Ji said.

Fletcher shrugged. "The other species have scorned us for centuries; they deserve a taste of their own medicine."

"This weapon was forged for war," Tor said, picking up Thevren's axe. "I'm taking it."

"You just changed your main weapon, and now you're going to change again?" Crystal asked.

"Why not? This is the first full battle I've used the halberd, so I'm still not accustomed to it yet. Plus, do you see this?" Tor held up the double-headed greataxe made of chromium. Both blades bore the elven symbol, inlaid in bronze, and an intertwining diamond pattern, also in bronze, ran along the shaft. "And it's good to have a few weapons saved up just in case you need another."

"Here we go," Fletcher muttered, finding Thevren's transmitter shoved in his boot. "That's not where I put mine, but to each their own."

"What do you need that one for?" Ji asked. "You have the queen's. Isn't that the only one you need?"

"To prove we've taken over the city," Fletcher said, taking off his helmet and setting it down. "I'm going to send a message to Qrtta and Sullin, the last two elven cities that aren't under our control yet. I'm going to try to make them surrender; I don't see why they wouldn't. We have them vastly outnumbered and have already killed their queen."

"Then we've completely taken over the kingdom."

"If the cities surrender, then yes. After many months and a great deal of loss, we have finally conquered the elves," Fletcher said, shoving Thevren's transmitter into his belt. "From this point on, the battles are going to become tougher. The hybrids are far stronger than the elves, but in return, we'll gain many more allies. So be prepared, because any battle could be our demise. This won't be easy, but by outsmarting our enemies and fighting with everything we have, I feel confident that we can free our kind." Fletcher stood and sheathed his claymore on his back. "Since this war began, every one of you has proven your worth on the battlefield, and I know that will continue."

EIGHTY-EIGHT

Yinny walked out of his castle and looked down at the vast, barren desert surrounding him. From the sixth level of the city, where the castle sat, he was able to get a perfect view of the pitiful elven army in front of him. "I wondered where they were headed when they left Cartin, and I was confused when they entered my kingdom, but now, I'm just perplexed. The elves lost their capital to the humans, and for some reason, they think fighting me is the way to reclaim it?"

"Maybe it's not elves, but humans using their military trucks. After all, they don't have any of their own," Yinny's right-hand, Zain, suggested.

The king shook his head. "The humans know better than to attack our capital, and Chion reported it was elves who left the city."

"What are your orders, My King?"

Yinny smirked. "Butcher them like the worthless beings they are, and leave their bodies to rot."

"Right away," Zain said, bowing and leaving.

It wasn't long after Zain left that the massacre began. It started with a volley of arrows pelting the elves, breaking windshields, popping tires, and bringing their convoy to a halt. While the elves exited their military trucks, two of

Arkanon's gates opened, and over fifteen thousand hybrids marched out.

Arkanon was built against a colossal mountain, so it just needed to protect itself from the front and only required one entrance. But the city was built with three large gates anyway; one to receive incoming trade, one to deliver exports, and one in the middle for everything else. However, when Yinny became king, he converted two of the gates and dedicated them to the army. That meant he had to destroy the prior military post and build two new ones. But he didn't mind. Yinny had grand plans, and he needed a powerful army to achieve them. He had been building his forces for the past sixty-two years and had been breeding more humans than any king before him had. As a result, the hybrid kingdom had the second most slaves in Affer, only topped by the demons.

After all this time, he was finally putting his strategy into action, selling off hundreds of slaves to fund his war and establishing a monumental army. In half a decade, he would be ready to take his first step of many in his plan to conquer Affer, and it began with taking over the dammed and elves. That was the idea; then the humans came along and did half the work for him.

Yinny's sole scout, Chion, had a marmerlif—a bird they used as scouts—keeping watch over Lilthral, Ronann, and Cartin for the last five years. But when IItu fell, he became more interested in the humans. He didn't expect much from them, but the more they won, the more entertained Yinny was. His original concept was scrapped when Lilthral was captured. Now he was waiting for the humans to come to him. There were always four marmerlifs keeping watch over Arrgon Desert, and they spotted anyone who entered the hybrid kingdom. Once the humans came to attack him, Yinny would send Arkanon's army to wipe them out.

"My kingdom will cover all of Affer," Yinny said, tapping his fingers on the sandstone railing of the sixth floor. "And I'll finally have my revenge on everyone."

Eighty-Nine

Your wound finally healed."

Jax peered up at the princess before he glanced at the scar on his arm. "It looks healed, but it still hurts."

"At least you're alive," Allica said, taking a dagger from the folds of her dress. "It's smaller than the one you normally use, but this was all I could acquire."

"How did you get this?" Jax asked, taking the weapon and examining it.

"All you need to know is that the humans can't resist my beauty." Allica flicked her hair back and put her hand on her hip. "I won't be back until we start the attack, so if there's anything you need, this is your last chance."

"I would love my armor and sword, but I understand you can't sneak that in here."

"You won't need those. There are barely any human guards here, and I heard that more are going to leave. Just be patient and keep recovering. Other than Ingrid, you're the elves' best fighter, and I'll need your strength."

"I won't let you down, My Lady," Jax said, standing and giving her a bow.

Allica left Jax and headed to Ingrid. She hadn't seen the elf since handing him her transmitter, and judging by his expression, he had failed. "Did someone not get their way?"

"Shut up, half-breed!"

"I'll take that as a yes," Allica said, grabbing the second dagger she had. "Give me my transmitter back, and I'll give you the dagger."

"A dagger? What am I going to do with that?! Why wouldn't you bring me a sword?!"

"You're a hypocrite! You told me not to come in the prison at all, and now you're asking me to sneak a sword in here! The daggers are hard enough to hide; where am I going to put a sword?"

Ingrid glared at Allica and threw the transmitter to her. "If you wanted to, you'd find a way."

"If you wanted to defeat the humans in Fiuden Forest, you'd have found a way," Allica mocked and tossed the dagger into the cell.

"Don't talk to me about battle! You've never seen the terrors of war, much less know the feeling of being seconds away from dying. You've never even taken another's life."

Allica faced away from Ingrid so he couldn't see the smirk on her face. "I have soldiers for that."

"Then don't lecture me about fighting."

Allica looked at the elf. "Then don't tell me what I can and can't do. I don't like you, and you don't like me, but that doesn't mean we can't work together for a short time."

"There is no working together. Once we retake the city, the army will obey me. The soldiers barely know you, and I've fought beside them for decades. None of them will see you as their leader. Even the civilians know me better than you."

Allica opened her mouth to respond, but stopped as she felt something brush against her foot. Glancing down, she screamed, "RAT!" and ran away.

Ingrid chuckled as the woman rushed off. The rat that scared her scurried into Ingrid's cell before it was stabbed.

Kicking it away, Ingrid cleaned the dagger and hid it under his hay bed. "I thought she was clever and would work with me, but it's clear I was wrong. Restoring the elven kingdom falls to me, and if the princess or her bodyguard gets in my way, I'll have no choice but to kill them."

Ninety

A knock at the door caused Fletcher to peer up from his desk and set his papers down. "I take it everything went well?" he asked Leon, who was standing in the doorway.

"It was too easy, and Tor kept going on about how he wished every city was this simple!"

"We wouldn't be slaves if that were the case," Fletcher said. "Did they give you any trouble?"

"They weren't even armed! It was like we were royalty. The humans were waiting for us, and while they got into the trucks, I took five hundred soldiers and searched the city to make sure they weren't hiding any humans."

"Smart call. Thanks for taking care of that. I would have gone, but I didn't want to step away from Cartin. We have resources pouring in to take to Admont, and I'm trying to prepare for the next step."

"Don't worry about it. It's my job after all."

"I still appreciate it. I'll make sure to thank Ryan, Mason, and Tor later, but for now, you should get some rest. You look tired."

"I am. We didn't stop and set up camp yesterday, which is why we're already back, but it cost us sleep," Leon said, giving Fletcher a quick wave as he left the room.

Fletcher grabbed the queen's transmitter off his desk. "Now that we have officially conquered the elven kingdom and freed all the humans, it's time for the next step." He switched to the private channel with every leader and started writing.

Greetings, kings and queens of Affer. I am Fletcher Rush: the man who has defeated the elves and will do the same to you. I've dedicated my life to freeing my kin and exacting revenge on those who have kept us enslaved. No species on Affer shall escape my wrath, and you will suffer a hundred times what we humans have. So prepare for war. When my army tears down the gates to your cities and slaughters your people, you will feel helpless. You will watch your kingdom fall, just as my ancestors did. And when that time comes, I want you to be the strongest you've ever been. I want you to know that even at the height of your power, you could not defeat my kind.

Cherish the peace you have now, because your grave grows deeper by the day.

He read over it twice and then sent it. *Let's see how that goes,* he thought, putting the device on his desk. Returning to his previous task, Fletcher read over the info they had on Jumin.

Half an hour later, he heard another knock on the open door and glanced up to see Ji.

"Hey," Ji said, coming in and sitting across from Fletcher. "I saw that Leon and the others are back. How did the recovery go?"

"Excellent," Fletcher said, laying his papers down. "Which means we have officially taken over and defeated one species!"

"I had my doubts at times, but we've come far. It feels like a few weeks ago when we were escaping Titanan."

"It's almost been a year. Not too bad considering we started from nothing and nearly died several times."

"Speak for yourself," Ji said, letting out a yawn.

"Why are you tired? It's the middle of the day," Fletcher asked, raising an eyebrow at his friend.

"I didn't get much sleep. I was up until two in the morning with Crystal."

"Were you two…?"

"Huh…? NO! No! We were training!" Ji exclaimed. "I went into the ward at seven and ran into her. Time went by fast, and it was past midnight before either of us knew it. Did you train yesterday?" he asked, trying to change the subject.

"I didn't have time. I've been reading about the hybrid's kingdom and preparing our next step."

"Are we going to launch a surprise attack on one of their cities?"

"That's not going to work. Every kingdom in Affer knows we've taken over the elves."

"How?! Do we have a spy in our ranks?!"

"No, it's because I told them. I sent out what was essentially a declaration of war to all the species," Fletcher said, leaning back in his chair and putting his feet up on the desk.

"Why?!" Ji shouted, his eyes going wide. "Isn't secrecy our greatest card?!"

"It was. Now it's fear. The demons, dammed, and angels would have found out soon, and the hybrids are already aware that we've conquered the elves. You probably haven't seen, but there have been marmerlifs, birds native to Yoxtoll Forest that the hybrids use as scouts, watching both Lilthral and Ronann. There's one here, too, which I'm leaving alive until we leave to attack the hybrids. I don't know why they're stationed in the elven kingdom, but that doesn't matter."

"Don't you think it's because we took over IItu?"

"No. There wouldn't be enough time to travel from Arrgon Desert to Ronann, and there was no one watching over IItu or Yune. We didn't stay in either for long, but if they were spying on us, that wouldn't matter. I might be wrong, but I believe they were spying on the elves."

"Why would they do that?"

"Your guess is as good as mine. But I learned that the hybrids are far smarter than I thought. Their king is Melro Vuldafield, but from the messages on the queen's transmitter, I found out that he is just a figurehead, and the real king is Yinny Shade. On top of that, they have the most slaves of any kingdom, besides the demons. I knew this, but I didn't think much of it. That said, there are papers here showing that Cartin bought slaves from Rinner. It was only a hundred, but it got me thinking, why are the hybrids selling off slaves, as they sold us some in Ronann, too? I searched through the queen's transmitter and found one private channel she was on that included the hybrids and demons. After two hours, I found out that the demons were also buying slaves."

"So the hybrids are broke?"

"Or they're trying to fund something."

"Like a war?" Ji suggested. "The scouts would make sense in that case."

Fletcher slammed his palm on the desk. "I didn't think of that! It all adds up! Well done, Ji!"

"Thanks," Ji said, yawning again.

"Go rest. We're not doing anything important today, and you're not going to get anything done as you are."

"I will." He stood and headed toward the doors. "Oh, Fletcher... Thanks for everything. Not only for taking me with you when we escaped, but for being the leader we need. Without you, we would have died as slaves."

"As I've said many times before, I need all of you as much as you need me. I'm not a one-man army, and without my team, I'm merely a man with dreams too big to achieve. When we end up victorious, it won't be solely because of me. We're reaching the top together, and the human kingdom will become greater than ever."

"And when that day comes, I know you'll rule over us as a benevolent king," Ji said before leaving.

Fletcher sat in silence, watching Ji walk down the hallway until he turned a corner and disappeared out of sight.

Spinning his chair around, Fletcher stood and pushed open the glass doors leading to the balcony. Leaning against the balustrade, he looked out at the city of Cartin and saw humans living as they pleased. Seeing them free made the pain and suffering he endured worth it.

This war still seemed impossible, but he didn't care. He knew the cost of his journey before he started.

A brisk wind hit him, and the sun vanished behind a cloud, almost as if the world itself was ridiculing him. But he wasn't fazed. It didn't matter who or what went against him.

Fletcher glanced around the city before he gazed out at the vast expanse beyond. "Give me your best, Affer, because you don't stand a chance otherwise."

EPILOGUE

Miller stopped and wiped the sweat from his forehead. The truck he had stolen from Ronann broke down seven hundred miles ago and he had spent over three weeks walking. Finally, Arkanon was in sight; the massive city built into the mountainside towered above him. But that wasn't why he stopped. Before him, lay his kin. There had to be over a thousand soldiers lying on the ground, some of them almost fully covered in sand, but all of them dead. He wasn't sure what happened, but it appeared to be a one-sided battle. The city walls were in perfect condition, and not a single hybrid corpse was to be found.

Not giving his fallen kin a second thought, Miller started toward the main city gate. About fifty feet away, one of the hybrids yelled at him. "State your business!"

Miller stared up at the guard tower on the left side of the entrance and saw a hybrid aiming a crossbow at him. "I am Miller, I come from the great city of Ronann, and I request a hearing with your king!"

"You request to see the king?" the guard laughed. "You're delusional, elf! Get out of here before I kill you."

"I am here on behalf of the late Dean Horn, overseer of Ronann, and I will not leave until I speak with King Yinny Shade!" Miller said, standing firmly in the same spot.

"King Yinny? You should have started with that; it would have made things easier."

Miller looked at the large gate in front of him as it opened. As he walked into the hybrid capital, he was instantly surrounded by four guards. "We will escort you to see his majesty. Stay in the middle of us, and keep your hands away from your weapons."

Miller nodded and walked with the guards, matching their pace as they made their way up the city. After ten minutes, they arrived at the front doors to the castle. Two guards pushed them open, and Miller walked inside. The four hybrids who had escorted him left, and another four took their place. This time, they were already waiting for him in the castle foyer.

"You are about to see the king, so you will need to rid yourself of any weapons. Make sure you hand over everything. If you don't, we'll behead you before you ever see his majesty."

"I'd love to see you try," Miller said, but obediently handed over his dagger and sword. "That's everything. Feel free to search me."

The castle guards did just that, patting Miller down and making sure he wasn't lying. Once they confirmed he was unarmed, they escorted him inside.

Another pair of guards pushed open the silver doors to the throne room. As he entered, Miller couldn't help but stare in amazement. The floor was constructed from a single purple agate geode. The walls were made of the same red sandstone as the mountains and had inlays in them every so often. In the inlays were life-size marble statues of past kings and queens. Behind the statues, the wall was made entirely of silver and decorated with a herringbone pattern. The ceiling was arguably the most stunning part. A mural of Arkanon, with the mountain range in the back and their god, Sylos, shining down from above, encompassed every inch. At the end of the long rectangular room sat a single silver throne. Sitting on the throne was Lord Melro, and standing next to him was Yinny.

"Who do we have here?" Melro asked, resting his chin in the palm of his hand and staring Miller down. "I heard Dean Horn told you to come here and ask for me, but give me one reason why I should help you."

Miller eyed Melro. "You're not the king," he said and turned his head to Yinny. "You are."

"What makes you say that?" Yinny asked with a straight face.

"I put it together that he," Miller pointed to Lord Melro, "is just a figurehead. Truthfully, it wasn't hard to figure out, since the guards changed their tone with me when I mentioned you."

"You're smarter than most. Let me ask you, what purpose do you have in coming here?"

"I want to avenge my mother and father. The humans have taken them both from me, and I vow to make them pay with their lives."

"How far are you willing to go?" Yinny asked, walking over to him.

"As far as it takes. I'm willing to do whatever must be done in order to kill those filthy scum," Miller said, getting on his hands and knees. "Please train me to be capable of killing anyone who stands in my way. I swear I'll give you my undying loyalty and fight for you as long as I live!"

Yinny stepped closer to the elf, his grin stretched ear to ear. "Rise."

Miller stood and looked Yinny in the eyes.

"Tell me your name," Yinny commanded.

"Lord Yinny, my name is Miller... Miller Cent."

PRONUNCIATION

CITIES

HUMANS

Admont (Add-mont)

Dysicingore (Die-sick-in-gor)

Forgeflint (Forge-flint)

Tylic (Til-ick)

Octtail (Oct-tail)

Vero (Ver-o)

Contilice (Con-til-lice)

Endarcite (End-dar-cite)

Armormyth (Armor-myth)

ANGELS

Plitin (Pli-tin) Xero (Zero)

Swun (Swun) Kren (Kren)

DEMONS

Alzuledon (Al-zule-don)

Titanan (Tight-tin-on)

Ikkyondfor (Ick-yon-for)

Vorcrumb (Vore-crumb)

Artin (Art-tin)

Gonttermire (Gon-tter-mire)

Zenfirme (Zen-fur-me)

Jarmyth (Jar-myth)

Wradmsoul (Rad-mh-soul)

DAMMED

Wingo (Win-go)

Flinden (Flin-den)

Huslond (Hush-lond)

Ugondt (U-gondt)

Narain (Na-rain)

HYBRIDS

Arkanon (Ark-anon)

Telfin (Tell-fin)

Yuton (You-ton)

Muwn (Mewn)

Grifol (Griff-fol)

Rinner (Riner)

Jumin (Jum-in)

ELVES

Lilthral (Lilth-ral)

Qrtta (Keer-ta)

Yuun (Yune)

Ronann (Roe-non)

Sullin (Sull-in)

IItu (I-two)

Names

CREATURES

Jixxes (Jix-is)

Marmerlif (Mar-mer-liff)

CHARACTERS

Ji (Gee)

Whitfield (Wit-field)

Chion (Chi-on)

Valadine (Val-a-dine)

Allica (Al-a-ca)

Vulcrhon (Vul-cron)

GODS

Rhytdar (Rye-dar)

Khanho (Khan-ho)

Thylphion (Thill-fee-in)

Sylos (Sigh-loes)

PLACES

Yoxtoll Forest (Yox-toll)　　Zenton sea (Zen-tin)
Arrgon Dessert (Ar-gon)　　Fiuden Forest (Fi-u-din)

MATERIALS

Knightnium (Knight-ne-um)　　Lyfume (Lie-fume)

For more information about the world of Conquest,
visit the site below, or scan the QR code.

theconquesttrilogy.com

9 798999 938801